# PEOP

Georgina Hammick ........ ......ort-story collections, *People for ...... and Spoilt*. *People for Lunch* reached no.7 in the *Sunday Times* bestseller list – unprecedented for a collection of short stories – and the title story won *Stand* Magazine's short-story competition. She has contributed to a number of literary journals and story anthologies, and her work has been selected for *Best Short Stories* in 1987, 1988 and 1991. Several of her stories have been broadcast on Radio 3 and Radio 4. She is also the editor of *The Virago Book of Love and Loss* (1992). Her first novel, *The Arizona Game*, is published by Chatto & Windus.

## BY GEORGINA HAMMICK

*People For Lunch*
*Spoilt*
*The Virago Book Of Love And Loss* (Editor)
*The Arizona Game*

Georgina Hammick

# PEOPLE FOR LUNCH
# SPOILT

VINTAGE

Published by Vintage 1996

2 4 6 8 10 9 7 5 3 1

*People for Lunch*
Copyright © Georgina Hammick 1987
*Spoilt*
Copyright © Georgina Hammick 1992

*People for Lunch* was first published in Great Britain by
Methuen London Ltd, 1987
*Spoilt* was first published in Great Britain by
Chatto & Windus Ltd, 1992

Vintage
Random House, 20 Vauxhall Bridge Road,
London SW1V 2SA

Random House Australia (Pty) Limited
20 Alfred Street, Milsons Point, Sydney
New South Wales 2061, Australia

Random House New Zealand Limited
18 Poland Road, Glenfield,
Auckland 10, New Zealand

Random House South Africa (Pty) Limited
PO Box 2263, Rosebank 2121, South Africa

Random House UK Limited Reg. No. 954009

A CIP catalogue record for this book
is available from the British Library

ISBN 0 09 946381 4

Papers used by Random House UK Ltd are natural, recyclable products made from wood grown in sustainable forests. The manufacturing processes conform to the environmental regulations of the country of origin

Printed and bound in Great Britain by
Cox & Wyman, Reading, Berkshire

# ACKNOWLEDGEMENTS

## *People for Lunch*

The title story was a winner of *Stand* Magazine's 1985 Short Story Competition, and appeared in the Winter 1985-6 issue of *Stand*. 'Mad About The Boy' was first published in *Fiction Magazine* and included in *Best of Fiction Magazine* (Dent paperback 1986). 'A Few Problems in the Day Case Unit' was published in the Autumn 1986 number of *Critical Quarterly*. The quotation from 'Return to Sender' is used by permission of Carlin Music Corp. The quotation from 'The Shadow Play' by Noel Coward is used by permission of Methuen London Ltd.

## *Spoilt*

'The American Dream' was first published in *Winter's Tales* (New Series 5). 'Uncle Victor' appeared in *Critical Quarterly* and was subsequently published in *Best Short Stories 1991* (Heinemann). 'High Teas' first appeared in *The Listener* and was subsequently published in *Best Short Stories 1988* (Heinemann) and *The Minerva Book of Short Stories 1990*. 'Habits' was first published in *New Writing*, a British Council-Minerva anthology, 1991-2. The lines from the poem by Gerald Bullett quoted in 'The Wheelchair Tennis Match' are reproduced by permission of the Peters, Fraser & Dunlop Group.

# CONTENTS

## *People for Lunch*

## *Spoilt*

# PEOPLE
# FOR LUNCH

*In Memoriam*

F.M.T. AND A.A.N-S.

# THE TULIP PLATE

'There's a man I often see here,' Nell said, as she walked round the lake with her weekend visitor. 'No matter what time of day I choose – on Saturdays and Sundays, that is – he's nearly always here too.'

'How romantic,' said her visitor, whose name was Margaret and who was interested in men. 'What sort of man? Perhaps he has conceived a passion for you.'

'No,' Nell said, referring to the words romantic and passion. 'I don't know what sort of man. It's his dog I'm interested in – you don't see so many white bull-terriers about these days.'

Margaret said she wouldn't know a bull-terrier if she met one. She had to be honest about it, she'd never liked dogs or trusted them. Presumably, if it was fully white, it must be albino and have pink eyes?

Nell said yes to this and notched up one more thing they didn't have in common. To prove the point she called out 'Hurry up, Dearest!' to her own dog who was busy in the reeds, looking for water rats.

They had to keep moving because of the cold. The lake was a large one for southern England and, with its inlets and varied vegetation, gave the appearance of being natural, when it was man-made. Three quarters of the way round it ran a metalled path-cum-roadway, wide enough for single motor traffic, on the waterside of which creosoted wood stumps, like dwarf telegraph poles, had been set at intervals to deter cars from parking on the bank. They were having to stick to this path and not venture into the woods that bordered its other side because Nell, writing to confirm train times, had omitted to tell Margaret to bring boots.

'I should have told you to bring some boots,' she said, 'so that we could walk in the woods.'

'I don't own any boots,' Margaret said. 'I never walk at home if I can help it – except to go to the shops, of course. But I'm quite enjoying this,' she added, understanding suddenly that her truthfulness, of which ordinarily she was not ashamed, might just occasionally be mistaken for rudeness. 'It reminds me of the Round Pond in Kensington Gardens.'

'North America, more like' – Nell was astounded by such inaccuracy – 'or Canada to be precise. Look.' She stopped, and Margaret stopped, and they both stared beyond a slatted landing stage across the dull water to where nameless waterfowl skied and flapped, and to where, in the far distance, little boats with coloured sails raced in the wind. On the opposite bank a mixed forest, dominated by giant pines or firs, climbed into the sky, and beneath it, right on the shore line, they could just make out a log cabin with a flagpole jutting from its roof. This was the sailing club, Nell explained. 'You see,' she said, 'it's not like England at all. It makes me think – especially when the sky's a really bright blue – of those photographs in the *National Geographic*.' She was pleased with this piece of observation, and used some version of it to the infrequent visitors she brought to the lake, most of whom were in wholehearted agreement.

'So it is! How clever of you!'

'You're absolutely right – we could be on Golden Pond! Did you see that film, by the way?'

Margaret, however, merely shivered and nodded in the direction of the boats and remarked, 'Red sails in the sunset,' in a dry voice.

'Have you had enough?' Nell felt she had to ask. Margaret's clothes were too thin and smart for a cold country walk. But what was she going to do with her if they turned back so soon? Tea would be a bit of a diversion, but after that? They had no friends in common anymore. What would they find to talk about for the rest of the evening?

The night before, the day of Margaret's arrival and first visit for nearly twenty years, they had talked shop. Or rather Margaret – following Nell from sitting room to kitchen, from kitchen to cellar, from fridge to cooker, while breathing down her neck or standing on her toes (and Nell was a claustrophobe) had talked shop, and Nell had interjected the odd 'yes, but,' or 'don't you think – '. But if there is a limit to how long two persons – the one a librarian, the other a bookseller, the former doing most of the talking, the latter most of the listening – can maintain an enthusiastic discourse on stock-control systems and library cuts, Public Lending Right and the Net Book Agreement, they had reached it; if there is a point when analysis of sales and borrowings, a debate on the problem of unreturned books and shoplifting ('They're both theft, mind you, straightforward theft, and should be punished as such,' Margaret had exclaimed, with a jerk of her elbow that had sent a china candlestick flying), becomes less than enthralling, then ditto. Even the topics they were agreed upon – the rudeness of customers, the inefficiency of publishers, the vanity of authors ('They never come into the shop to buy, you know,' Nell said when she could get a word in, 'merely to check that their own dreary books are on the shelf') – had lost their edge by midnight. 'Must hit the hay now, folks,' Margaret had announced in what she thought of as an American accent, 'or I won't have gotten my beauty sleep.'

For Nell, the worst aspect of the evening had been the discovery that Margaret did not drink or smoke. She'd made one small glass of sherry last nearly two hours, drumming the table lightly with manicured fingers each time Nell reached for the whisky bottle or for her cigarettes. On the other hand – and it seemed odd in one so thin and birdlike – she had an enormous appetite for food. Nell had imagined the cottage pie would do at least two meals, but Margaret – 'Do you mind if I do? It seems a pity to waste it' –had helped herself three times until nothing remained but a spoonful of mashed potato. The fruit salad had disappeared likewise. When

Margaret finally put down her spoon, a solitary slice of banana was left swimming in the bowl.

The problem of what to have for supper now beset Nell as they passed two umbrellas, all that could be seen of two fishermen wedged below them on the bank. Perhaps if she were to open a tin of baked beans and another of mushrooms, and fry an onion or two . . .

'I'm game to go a bit further,' Margaret said. She always made the best of things. And she felt no inducement to return to Nell's freezing house and sit, as they had yesterday evening and this morning, in Nell's squalid sitting room in front of Nell's pathetic fire. Also, Nell had threatened her with a tour of the garden. It was incomprehensible to Margaret how gardeners could stand around in cold and mud and enthuse – and expect others to enthuse – over a collection of dead and indistinguishable twigs. 'Do you enjoy cooking?' she asked, to cover the loudness of her shoes and Nell's boots on the tarmac. The digestion of a pub lunch of bread and cheese was not being helped by the memory of last night's grey mince, and what could only have been instant mashed potato.

'Not in the ordinary way,' Nell said. She stopped briefly to pierce a last year's oak leaf with the spike of her walking stick. 'But I like doing it for special occasions.'

Margaret wondered which category her own visit came into. 'I love it,' she said, with an emphasis that made it sound a virtue. 'I enjoy my food, I'm not ashamed to admit. Planning meals, shopping for them, preparing them – surely one of the great pleasures of life.'

Nell yawned and said nothing.

'Is that your man?' Margaret asked, as they stepped to the verge to avoid collision with a young-looking father and two children in red anoraks. The bigger child, his head thrust forward and over the handlebars, made motorbike noises and zig-zagged his tricycle; the smaller one hung over the side of his pushchair and scraped a stick along the tarmac.

'Aggression starts early in the male,' Nell said to no one in

14

particular. 'No, he's always alone – except for his bull-terrier, that is. He's not my man, incidentally.' They climbed down from the bank, but Margaret lingered for a moment in the road, looking over her shoulder and repeating 'Boys will be boys' in an admiring voice.

They walked on in silence. A pale sunshine, that had been struggling all day with the clouds, gave up, and the afternoon grew increasingly dark and wild. It was the end of March and officially spring, but there was no sign yet of green and growing things. Margaret folded her arms and hugged the chest of her Country Casuals coat. She was ready to go back. Not back to Nell's, but back on the train to her own tidy and centrally-heated flat, and the prospect of supper – sole *bonne femme,* perhaps, with croquette potatoes and braised celery hearts.

'That's it – we'll have to turn round now,' Nell said, eyeing Margaret's shoes. A few yards ahead of them the road dwindled into a waterlogged track, winding between alders bent double in the wind. She swung the dog lead round her head and whistled for Dearest who was doing her best to follow a squirrel into a tree.

It was after they'd turned round, with the wind in their backs now instead of their faces, that things began to improve between them.

'Do you remember Miss Benson?' Nell suddenly asked.

'Miss Benson,' Margaret repeated, 'Miss Benson? *Joan* Benson. Oh dear. I never thought to hear that name again.' And she started to laugh.

'She was in love with Elaine Crabtree,' Nell went on, 'when Elaine was hockey captain and head girl.' Nell remembered this because she'd been in love with Elaine Crabtree herself. Elaine had had an oval, freckled face and untidy eyebrows she combed in front of the glass with a pocket comb kept for the purpose. Margaret, who hadn't loved anyone at school apart from Shelley, didn't remember this detail, but she could see Miss Benson and Elaine, in particular the former's thighs as she belted down the pitch, blowing her whistle and shouting, 'Reds, get free! Mark your opponent, Sally!'

'Miss Benson was sacked, you know,' Nell said, 'shortly after we left. I can't remember who told me. She was found on the hockey field in the middle of the night, dead drunk apparently and singing bawdy songs.'

'You're making it up,' Margaret said. But she was pleased with the turn their conversation had taken.

The memory of Miss Benson led them on to other members of staff and other girls, to school buildings and classrooms and dormitories, to the prefects' study and 'Pre's Teas' of cold baked beans and condensed milked sucked from the tin. Prompting and correcting each other, they were able to conjure up the jacaranda trees that bordered the drive, the wood smoke ('That smell,' Nell said, 'I keep it here, at the back of my nose'), curling into the sky from the staff bandas that lay below the games fields in an exclusive cluster out of sight of the main block. They recalled mornings that, because they were six thousand feet above sea level, remained coldly misted until midday, afternoons so wiltingly hot that failure to wear a hat was punished by an order mark or with sunstroke.

'She must be dead now,' Margaret said. She was speaking of the biology mistress, whose luxuriant moustache and habit of throwing chalk at her pupils they had just been dissecting. 'Very probably, they're all dead. It's nearly forty years ago, you realize.'

This terrible truth brought them both to a halt. What have I done with my life? Nell thought, What have I got to show for all these years? On an impulse, she put her arm through Margaret's, regretted it at once, and had to leave it there.

'Quiz time, now,' Margaret said, encouraged by the intimacy Nell's arm betokened. 'What did we sing in that inter-school choral comp we were expected to win and came bottom of?'

'A La-a-ake and a faer-ie boat,' Nell sang, 'and something else. Can't remember what. Oh yes I can – in Hans' old mill his five black cats – '

'Three black cats.'

' – his three black cats watch the bins for the thieving rats –

Jekyll and Jessup, and o-one eye-eyed – help.'

'Jill,' Margaret said.

'Jill. Cats are never Jill though, are they. Supposing they were, someone called Hans would have cats called Gretchen or Gertrud. Why are children made to sing such nonsense? A lake and a fairy boat – I ask you.'

'We are walking beside a lake,' Margaret pointed out, 'and the fairy boats are over there.' But when they scanned the water, the boats were somewhere beyond a promontary and hidden from them by the trees.

A sudden cloudburst of hailstones sent them running down the bank to a rustic bench and the shelter of a yew tree. The yew formed a black tent above their heads, and they sat cosily together watching the hailstones tear the surface of the lake.

'What's that scent you're wearing?' Nell said. It came from Margaret's silk scarf, and the collar of her coat. It was strong, and in some way unsettling: she never wore scent herself.

*Jolie Madame,*' Margaret said. 'How do we stop your dog whining? Does he do it all the time?' Nell picked up Dearest and held her on her knee, where she dug her claws in and trembled and continued to whine. A reek of wet dog displaced the *Jolie Madame.*

'Odeur de wet dog,' Margaret said. She turned her head away. She turned back to Nell. 'You weren't very nice at school,' she confided, poking her in the ribs. 'I hated you at the beginning.'

'*We* thought *you* were too big for your boots,' Nell said, recalling how Margaret, whose father had been a major or colonel in some regiment sent out from England to put down the Mau Mau, had arrived in the middle of a Lent term and gone – at only fifteen – straight into the sixth form. She'd made the rest of them – settlers' daughters like herself, whose parents farmed in remote up-country places, District Commissioners' daughters, daughters of doctors and dentists and government officials in Nairobi – feel that 'colonial' equalled not just naive and unsophisticated, but stupid. Nell couldn't remember now how they'd ever become friends. Perhaps on her own side, it had been a question of finding when you couldn't beat someone, that it might be expedient to join them.

Margaret reminded Nell that she's never owned any boots. She asked if Nell missed Africa in general, and the farm at Hoey's Bridge in particular, and Nell said she did, and more and more as she got older. But she'd never go back, she said, never. They talked about Hoey's Bridge for a while. Margaret remembered playing pingpong in the creamery and how green and cold it was in there compared to outside, and how they'd been caught once by Nell's mother dipping their fingers in the vats. She had a clear picture of Nell's mother, she said, in mens' brown trousers and an aertex shirt and bush hat; in fact she was prepared to swear Nell's mother hadn't worn anything else during the whole of her visit, which must have been three weeks. She remembered being woken every morning by the shamba boys sweeping the tennis court and singing, if you could call it that; and she remembered a tennis party with twin brothers who'd come from Kitale for the weekend, and how rude and cocky they were, especially the smaller one who had ginger hair.

Nell wondered if it was working in a library that made Margaret talk so much. She watched the storm ending. Like a cine film run backwards, the hail was drawn off the lake and back up into the clouds. Afterwards the banks, the bushes and the rough grass at the water's edge were left with a granular coating, like imitation snow.

'Behold, a white dog,' Margaret said when they were back on the roadway. 'It must be your man at last.'

'Yes, that's him.' A long way off, a man and a dog could just be seen heading in their direction. 'Since you're so interested in what you insist on calling *my* man, I dare you,' said Nell, on whom all this chat about school and childhood had had the effect of making her feel frivolous and fifteen, 'to say something when we meet. Engage him in conversation.'

'Whatever for?' said Margaret. But she was intrigued, nevertheless.

'Because,' said Nell, 'because it would be amusing. I'd like to know what his voice is like. I imagine it to be Scots – Edinburgh, not Glasgow.'

Margaret said it would make more sense if Nell spoke to him because she was the one who saw him all the time. But Nell said no. She didn't explain that it was too late to speak to anyone with whom she had not even exchanged nods. He always looked preoccupied and unapproachable, his eyes on the ground or on the lake. Even their dogs avoided each other. She had no grounds for approaching him. But Margaret didn't care who she said Boo to. 'You could say "Good evening",' Nell told her, 'and perhaps something about his dog. You could say "that's a handsome dog – is he a Staffordshire bull-terrier?" – I happen to know that he is, but it's a legitimate question to dog owners. We enjoy compliments and enquiries,' she added pointedly.

'I'm not fond of dogs, as you know,' Margaret said. As she spoke, and as if to confirm her opinion, Dearest defecated hugely and wetly on the grass beside them, afterwards stretching out her back legs and kicking up a shower of slush and mud.

'Talk about the weather then,' Nell said. 'If you do it,' she encouraged, 'if you can keep him talking for at least five minutes, I'll let you have the tulip plate.'

The evening before, Margaret had admired the plate that had contained her cottage pie. It had a pattern of intertwined red and yellow tulips round the rim, and in the centre, once the mince and potato and watery beans had been forked up, she'd discovered a wicker basket with red and yellow tulips springing from it. 'What a very pretty plate!' she'd said. 'Is it part of a set?' Nell, who thought the design feeble and the colours crude, had merely shrugged and smiled.

Nell's offer acted as a spur to Margaret. If the plate were hers – she'd even decided this as Nell took it away and put it in the sink – it would hang on the sitting-room wall. She had just the right spot for it, in a little alcove above the bookcase. And it would go with the curtains which, while neither red nor yellow, had splashes of both in their multicoloured pattern.

'I'll see then,' she said to Nell. 'I won't promise, but I might.' A sense of conspiracy quickened their footsteps. As her quarry came nearer, Margaret tried to size him up, but he kept getting lost behind the trees, or hidden by a curve in the lake, and when he was visible she couldn't see his face because he was looking at the ground. He'd evidently not sheltered from the storm, for as he came into focus she could see that his hair was sopping and flattened to his scalp. The dog was wet through, also: a pink piggy skin showed through his saturated coat. A hideous creature, surely, even by dog lovers' standards: tiny pink eyes, a pink belligerent nose, wet fat slapping as he rolled rather than walked –

It was at this moment, when they were perhaps fifty yards from certain encounter, that a car, going too fast for the place and the weather, overtook them, its tyres sending out a burst of grit and slush. Margaret's camel coat, her twelve denier tights, her tan court shoes, took the worst of it. Cursing, she bent down to examine the damage. Nell seized her by the elbow.

'Don't bother with that now,' she said. 'It'll brush off when it's dry.' But Margaret was no longer in the mood for schoolgirl games. She kept swivelling to see the back of her coat. It was wrecked; from what she could see of it, a major disaster.

'Go on, go on, cowardy custard,' Nell said out of the side of her mouth. But as they came face to face with 'her' man, it was Nell who was the coward. She stepped well clear of the confrontation and made for the trees with Dearest, neck fur up and tail down between her legs, at her heels. Abandoned on the tarmac, Margaret hesitated for a moment, and then went up to the man and stood in front of him so that he was forced to stop and look at her. He had pale blue eyes and a tired face, but it was a much younger face than Margaret had been expecting. Nell had said nothing about his being a young man. He couldn't have been more than thirty, at the most.

'Good afternoon,' she began, and stopped. Out of the corner of her eye she could see Nell, some way ahead and out of earshot, pretending an interest in a larch cone she'd found in the grass. A question about the bull-terrier, at that moment sniffing her shoes and ankles and the hem of her coat, a comment on the freakishness of the storm, half formed themselves, retreated, evaporated altogether. She had nothing to say to this fellow at all. She opened her mouth. 'Tell me, how is Mary?' she heard herself say.

The man looked at her, and it was a look more curious than surprised. He swivelled his head and looked up at the sky, and then back at Margaret. To her alarm, his eyes filled with large, blistery tears.

'Not so good today,' he said in a sad, flat voice. 'It can't be long now, she's very weak.' He blinked, and the tears tipped out of his eyelids and broke on his cheeks. He brushed them away with the back of his hand. 'She sleeps most of the day, when the pain lets her.' He nodded towards the bull-terrier. 'I'm taking a little breather with Tray.'

'I'm so sorry,' Margaret said, appalled. She'd never seen a man cry.

'If only she'd fought more,' the man said, 'if only she'd put up a proper fight – ' his voice tailed off. He clenched his fists and stared out at the lake. 'But you know Mary,' he said, turning back to Margaret with a sad smile, 'she's always been a fatalist. She just accepts things.'

'I'm so sorry,' Margaret said.

'Thank you,' the man said. 'I suppose you work at the Centre,' he added – and it seemed to Margaret to be not a question, but a statement requiring only her confirmation – 'with Janet and the others.'

'Yes,' Margaret nodded, 'yes I do.'

'Janet has been a particular help,' the man said. His emphasis made Margaret feel that she herself had not been. 'She's sitting with Mary now, reading to her, holding her hand.'

'That's good,' Margaret said. 'I'm glad about that.' She stepped backwards and then sideways, to give him a chance to walk on, but he didn't take it.

'Give her my love, please,' she said. She put out a hand and touched his sleeve. It was soaking. 'Goodbye,' she said. 'God bless you.'

'Whom shall I say?' the man called after her. 'Whose love shall I give?'

'Alison's,' Margaret said, over her shoulder, without looking back.

'Alison's,' the man repeated, 'Alison's.' He watched her walk slowly away from him, her shoulders hunched, her head bowed, the posture – at once reverent and self-conscious – of one who has just left the altar rail after receiving Communion.

'Well,' Nell said impatiently, coming out of her ambush, 'you've won the tulip plate, I see. You were hours – I nearly died of cold.'

'It was awful,' Margaret said, more to herself than to Nell. 'I walked into some sort of family tragedy.'

'Must be his wife who's dying,' Nell said when Margaret, haltingly, and omitting the 'Alison' and the 'God bless you' her thirty-year-old atheism was still smarting from, had recounted the conversation. 'Cancer, I should think, from the sound of it.'

All lies, Margaret murmured wonderingly to herself, one lie after another, I told him nothing but lies.

'Or one of his children,' Nell said. 'The Centre could be a day nursery, or a clinic, or a home for handicapped children.' And she was silent, trying to imagine what it would be like to have a child; a healthy child, a sick child, a child you loved and who loved you; a child who died. If it was me dying, she thought suddenly, who would weep? Would anyone?

'I still don't understand,' she began as they reached the car, 'what – ' She was going to say, what made you ask about *Mary*?, but knew that however she phrased it, it would sound like the question that really occupied her, which was: How could something so strange happen to someone as insensitive as Margaret? And why should a man she'd seen countless times on her walks, and who'd never so much as glanced in her direction, choose Margaret, of all people, to tell his troubles to?

She opened the rear door to find her shoes, and then leant against the car while she took off her boots. Margaret got into the passenger seat without saying a word, and did up her seat belt.

Nell didn't like this silent Margaret. Silence was the prerogative of the imaginative. Moreover, this silence had a secret, exclusive feel. 'A cup of tea is what we need, Meg,' she said, switching on the engine. 'It'll cheer you up. I hope.'

But Margaret did not cheer up. (Something momentous had happened, something that would alter her life. She had been chosen, she knew. But for what? For what?) She sat stiffly in her ruined coat, and stared ahead as the windscreen wipers raked and squeaked.

'Just going to see if they've got any tea-cakes, then,' Nell said crossly, pulling up without warning outside the village shop – an action which provoked a swerve, a blast on the horn and a rude gesture from the driver behind.

# A FEW PROBLEMS
IN THE DAY CASE UNIT

My name is Lettice Pomfrey and I am thirty-four years old. I am sitting in the gynaecologist's waiting room waiting to see the gynaecologist. I tell you this now, at the beginning, in case gynaecology is not the subject for you; in case you find some aspects of it distasteful; in case you would rather be somewhere else than in this waiting room on a hot and sunny July afternoon.

I don't want to be here; I've a high failure rate in gynaecologists. The first one I saw was a misogynist and an extortionist, the second a lecher. The third one might have been all right, I can't positively say he wasn't, but we moved house before I had a chance to find out. The fourth one, Mr Gamble, I haven't yet met. He's been recommended by my doctor and by several people I know who variously say he's sympathetic, attractive, dishy. A surgeon's wife I share the school run with told me Mr G. is the envy of his colleagues, who've had to watch him sweep the gynaecological board, not just of the county's childbearers, but of the menopausal. They seek him out, according to her, for hysterectomies, for removal of ovarian cysts and ovaries, and for Hormone Replacement Therapy. This is enough to put me off him, but I'm telling myself to keep an open mind.

The waiting room is in the consulting rooms an ENT man, a paediatrician and Mr Gamble share. They see their private patients here, and their NHS patients at the Infirmary. I'd have been quite happy, not being on BUPA, to see Mr G. at the NHS clinic he holds on Tuesdays, but my doctor explained that because of the consultants' dispute, and as I can't be called an urgent case, it'd mean tagging on to the end of a long waiting list. Impossible to say when I'd get an appointment. It could be years, not months. Centuries even, my doctor said, with one of his occasional flashes of humour. Milleniums.

The waiting room is very smart. Its colour scheme is white and fawn and chocolate brown. The ceiling is white, the walls fawn, the carpet fawn with a chocolate Greek key pattern round the edge. The chairs are white tubular with chocolate wool seats. There are two rubber plants, one either side of the fireplace, standing in white, square jardinières. In front of the plate-glass window is a large table with a glass top, and on this are magazines. They've been arranged like a game of giant clock patience, but in the centre, where the king of hearts or spades should be, is an enormous ashtray, square and glass to match the table. I would like a cigarette at this moment, but don't want to be caught smoking. Also it seems common courtesy to keep my breath sweet for Mr Gamble, even if my mouth is not the part of me he'll be seeing most of.

Apart from the furniture, the waiting room is empty. I walk up and down, try out different chairs and angles, tidy a thumbnail, sniff the magazines. These are new, or recent, issues of glossy monthlies; no stimulating reads here, no *Diver* or *Motorcycling Weekly* or *Aircraft Modeller*; no *Exchange & Mart*. The only mag on this table that could be called specialist is *Horse and Hound*. The number I've got hold of contains a round-up of last year's hunting season, with copious photographs. A Good Day Out With The Whitemore Vale, I read. Colonel Jim Vane-Fitzpatrick, joint master, shows hounds –

Mrs Pomfrey, ready for you now.

The nurse who's come for me is a dark girl, and pretty except for some serious and disconcerting spots (no matter how often you come across them, spotty nurses, like dentists with bad breath and hairdressers with hacked hair, are always somehow shocking). I follow her to a little room where I am weighed, and where my blood pressure is taken. As she pumps me up I squinny to see the reading, but she's too quick for me. That's fine, she says grimly, unwinding the black mackintosh from my arm.

Mrs Pomfrey for you, Mr Gamble, she says, opening a connecting door. Mr Gamble gets up from behind his desk and comes forward and shakes my hand. Then he squeezes my shoulder, a gentle pressure that encourages me to sit down on the chair my side of the desk and facing his chair. When he has returned to his place he leans towards me on his elbows.

Well, Mrs Pomfrey, he says, well now.

Mr Gamble is a good-looking man; he may even be attractive. Somebody told me he's a bit like James Stewart, and he is, about the mouth and chin. His eyes aren't blue though, they're brown. They're kind eyes, and the expression in them of sympathy and concern is intensified by the furrows in his brow. They cannot be a misogynist's eyes. I'm sure. And there's no hint of lechery in them.

Mr G. begins to ask me questions – my date of birth; my husband's date of birth; the dates of birth and sexes of our four children, etc. – the answers to which he jots down with a fountain pen on a sheet of unlined A4. I wonder why he bothers with this: most of the information must be in the letter from my doctor I can see on his desk, or in the file containing my medical notes, ditto. Perhaps he hasn't read the letter or had time to glance through the notes; or perhaps he prefers to do his own spadework in what for him is new ground, in what for me is old ground, dug over many times before.

How old was I, Mr G. wants to know, when I had my first period? Can I give him a brief account of the births of my children? Am I a smoker? Do I have any problems at all with bowels or waterworks?

Mr G. lays his pen on the paper. Would I like to tell him, and I can take my time, about the various methods of birth control I and my husband have tried during the course of our marriage? We started off with my using a cap, I tell him, and Mr G. picks up his pen and writes Diaphragm on the sheet of paper. Then we started a

baby – on purpose, I explain, and then after the baby was born I
went on the pill. Oral C, Mr G. writes down. And how did that
suit? he asks, leaning forward again.

The truth is it made me sick and fat and gave me headaches, and I
tell him this. Mr G. writes, Usual side effects and something else I
can't read. Sounds as though you should have been on a low dose
pill, he says. I was, I assure him, on the lowest dose available at the
time. And after the second baby? After our second baby I tried a
Coil. I.U.D., Mr G. writes. Will I describe for him, if I can, this
Coil? It looked like a firework, I tell him, you know, a squib. Ah,
I *see*, Mr G. says, rubbing his chin, How did that work for you?
Were you happy with it? I hesitate – but what is the point of
mincing words? He's asking me, after all; he wants to know. I got
the curse very badly, I tell him, every ten days. And I had a
dragging, stitching pain, low down. Heavy loss, Mr G. writes,
Discomfort. And after the third baby? Another pill, same side
effects. And after the fourth (which I've already told him was a
mistake, and which he has decided was unplanned)? Another Coil,
a different sort, with the same results only more so. It became
embedded, I explain, and for them to remove it I had to spend a day
in hospital and have a general anaesthetic . . . .

You don't seem to have much luck, do you? Mr G. still sounds
concerned, but at the same time ever so slightly disbelieving, just
the teeniest bit resentful. Has he decided I'm a difficult patient? So,
he says, looking down at his hands, So what's the score at the
moment? What method are you using now?

I must think about this. I can't say French letter to *him*. But the
official words, the words I know I ought to use, stick in the throat.
My husband is taking precautions, I say. Mr Gamble writes down
Sheath, and asks if it's satisfactory for us, me and my husband.

Pictures float into my head; my husband groping in his bedside
drawer, having knocked the lamp over; me lying in the dark with
nothing to do and going off the boil, if I was ever on it; our
children wandering round our bedroom before breakfast while I'm
getting dressed or putting my face on, touching things, picking up

things, opening drawers. What are these, Mum? What are they *for*? Not just pictures. Some man once told me that doing it in a French letter is like sucking a sweet with the wrapper on.

It's not ideal, I say to Mr G.

No, it's not. Mr G. says. It's not much fun for your husband, I can promise you that. Even more important, perhaps, it's not really *safe*. The accident rate is high. Have the two of you ever considered – he pauses, he presses the tips of his fingers together, and then pushes them apart – sterilization? A vasectomy? I tell him we have, but one of us might, you never know, die of a heart attack or get run over by a bus, and the other might then remarry someone who hadn't had children and who wanted some.

Mr G. glances at his watch. Let's re-cap, he says. Which method you've tried was, d'you think, if not entirely satisfactory, then on balance the best for you, the best for both of you? Remembering, of course, that no method – apart from sterilization, and we've ruled that out – is a hundred per cent?

The Coil, I say. Because it has to be the Coil. At least with the Coil you know it's there, and you don't have to remember to swallow anything; or coat something with sperm-killing cream and stick it up yourself. And remember to take it out afterwards (but not too soon, not before the sperm-killers have had a chance to be effective), and wash it and dry it and dust it with talcum powder; and not leave it on the basin when the telephone rings.

Mr Gamble, looking at me, opens a drawer in his desk and places what he finds there on the surface between us. He pushes at it with his forefinger. This is the Copper Coil, he says, triumphantly, like a conjuror at the end of a difficult trick, and I think we should give it a try.

The Copper Coil is very small. It is not shaped like a coil; it is a piece of bent fusewire; half a hairpin; a shorthand character; a rest in music. How could it possibly prevent a baby?

We're not exactly sure, Mr G. admits, still pushing the wire around with his finger, but we know it does. Of course there's bound to be some failure rate, but it's a low one as these things go.

I'd like to try it for at least three months, to give it a chance to settle down, and then if you aren't happy with it, or have problems of any kind, we've still got the low-dose Pill to fall back on. The side effects have been minimized since you last tried it. Failing that, a Diaphragm in conjunction with a sperm-killing gel. Right then – Mr G. leans back in his chair and pushes at the desk as though he's trying to get rid of it – I think we'd better have a little peep at you. If you'd like to pop up on the day bed over there. Just remove your tights and pants and bra, but keep your slip on if you're wearing one.

We get up together. My skirt is sticking to my bottom and to the backs of my knees. Am I supposed to take my bag with me, or leave it on the floor by my chair? I walked to the curtained-off corner where the day bed waits, Mr G. to the cabinet where, presumably, his disposable gloves and his instruments are.

It's dark behind the curtain. I take off my shirt, my skirt, my shoes, my tights, my pants. With difficulty and without removing my petticoat – for although it's a hot day I am wearing one, I knew I should need it – I unhook my bra. I fold all these things on a chair, covering my underclothes with my outer clothes. I clamber onto the day bed, which is high. It has a hard flat pillow and draw sheet, across which has been laid a square of linen the size of a baby's cot sheet. Am I meant to lie on top of this, or under it? I lie under it, or rather arrange it to cover as much of my lower half as it will. My feet are turned out; my heels are resting on a length of cellophane that crackles when I move them.

A light snaps on above me. The curtains rattle back. It's Mr G. who does this. He is just going to examine my breasts, he says, he is sorry if his hands are cold, he's washed them, can I slip my shoulder straps down for him please!

If people can be divided into those who look better, and more themselves, naked, and those who look better, and more themselves, wearing clothes, I must come into the second category. My mammary glands, in particular, don't stand up to scrutiny. They aren't, alas they never were, composed of two firm and perfectly moulded hillocks from which twin rosy budlets spring. They fall, when I lie on my back, flatly away from the breastbone and sag either side of the ribcage like two badly-filled shopping bags. An exaggeration? My bosom is a sad sight; if I allow myself to think about it, I weep; if I glimpse it in the bathroom glass, I turn my back. Were it not that my husband professes, once every five years, to be fond of my bosom, I should have cut my throat long ago.

I stare at the ceiling and tell myself he has seen worse sights than this, while, with the flat of his hands, Mr Gamble goes over the part of me I've just described. Do you do this at home? he asks, as he squeezes, prods and cups. You should, you know, at least once a month, in front of the mirror. That's fine, he says (How does he know it's fine? How, with all these lumps and bumps, could he tell if any of them were unusual?) He pulls the cot sheet up over my top half, so that my lower half is now exposed. He presses the folds of my stomach, he pushes his fingers in hard at the sides, just above the groin. Any tenderness here? Or here? Relax. Let yourself go limp. Now, now I'd like you to roll over onto your side and draw your knees up for me as high as you can.

I roll over on my side to the wall and draw my knees up, just a little. Higher, if you can, Mr G. says. He tucks my petticoat out of the way; he tweaks the cot sheet from my shoulders and removes it altogether. I grip the edge of the mattress. I screw my eyes tight shut– for by doing so I may be able to blot from my imagination the terrible view Mr G. now has of me: the spots on my bottom I tried to disguise with talcum powder before I set out; the corrugated skin in the groove below my coccyx; the –

Try not to tense yourself, Mr G. says, as his gloved hands part me. One of these hands, the left hand, stays on my left *buttock*; the other hand, the right hand, bypasses my (now what would he call it? *Anus*? *The opening of the alimentary canal*?) bum hole; enters somewhere below this. Excavates. Explores. Probes. La la la, I sing to myself, la la la, to shut out the sound (of old men drinking soup, of gumboots being pulled from a bog) that accompanies the withdrawal of this hand. La la la la la.

You may feel this a little, Mr G. says. No, don't tense, let yourself go. La la la la, pom, pom, pom, pom, let yourself go, I sing to myself, as the plunger, or whatever it is, twists in deeper and deeper, to my very core, centre, kernel, essence, nucleus, thesaurus. *Thes*aurus? Or thes*aur*us? Which should it be? If in danger, cross your legs; if you can't be good be careful; if sex is inevitable, relax and enjoy it; if –

All done, all finished, Mr G. says, you can get dressed again now.

I suppose I'll bleed a bit, I say to Mr G. when I am dressed again and back in my chair. (I'm an old hand at this; I seem to remember a bloody aftermath to Coil insertions.)

I see no reason for that, Mr G. says. He looks puzzled. Oh I see – I should have made myself clearer. What you've had was merely a routine smear test, long overdue. If all's in order in that department, you'll get an appointment card from the Infirmary. Until very recently, he confides, I did Coil insertions here, in the Consulting Rooms, but it's safer and more hygienic in Theatre, where everything's to hand. It's better for the patient. More comfortable.

I've never had it done in a hospital before, I say. (I'm not at all sure.) I'm not sure –

There's absolutely nothing to worry about, believe me – Mr G. stretches a pinstriped arm across the desk and pats my hand – Feeling all right now, dear?

We get up. Mr G. walks with me to the door, one arm lightly around my shoulder. There's nothing sinister about this, I'm certain. I'm quite sure this is the way he dismisses all his patients.

*

And now it is evening, our children tucked in their beds, what's left of the fish pie back in the larder. My husband is sitting in an armchair, reading a book. I am sitting in an identical chair, cobbling a seam in a pair of my son's jeans. There was no blue cotton in the sewing box, so I am making do with green.

I went to see the gynae today, I say to my husband.

My husband turns two pages at once of his book, Alan Moorehead's *Gallipoli*. He has read it before, a long time ago, but is looking something up.

What? Oh yes. How did it go? Is he a good egg, d'you think, your Mr Whatsisname?

I don't know. I think he may be. He took a lot of trouble (for it's true; he did take a lot of trouble). His name is Gamble.

Ho ho, my husband says, going back to the index. You'd think he'd change it. He runs his finger down the page. Can't seem to find it, damn, he says.

He's giving me another Coil, I say. I've got to have it done in the Infirmary.

Why's that? What for? my husband asks, his eye still on the index. What does that mean exactly? *In nuce*, mind you, not *verbatim*, says my husband who is a Latin tag man, a man for whom all invoices are, *per se* and *ipso facto*, (if *a priori*) *pro forma*, all payments *ex gratia*, all evidence *prima facie*, all quids *pro quo*.

It's safer and more hygienic in hospital, in Theatre, Mr Gamble says.

That makes sense, my husband murmurs to the index, that makes sense.

I'm not too keen on the idea of Theatre, I say. I'd rather have it done in the Consulting Rooms, or the Clinic, like last time.

Don't then, my husband says. He takes off his spectacles and puts them back on again. You're the customer, I'm paying for this, remember. Do what you want to do. Have it done where you want.

But Mr Gamble doesn't do it in the Consulting Rooms any more. He said –

You told me what he said, and it makes sense to me, my husband says. He clearly has a *causa movens*. Stop worrying, he says, *nil desperandum*.

There is silence for a while. My husband leaves the room and returns with the whisky bottle, which is nearly empty. We must have clobbered it before supper, he says.

I had to have an internal examination today, I tell him.

I'm sure you did, my husband says. He sips his whisky. Poor you, he says, how horrid for you, poor you.

When we were newly married my husband came with me on my first visit to a gynaecologist. I wasn't sure I wanted him as a matter of fact, but he insisted. He was very distressed. I cannot bear the idea of another man touching you, even looking at you, he said as we drew up outside the surgery. I cannot bear it, you are mine – and he thumped the steering wheel in despair. When I came out an hour later I found him hunched in the driving seat, and when I got in beside him he clung to me. My baby, he said, his eyes full of tears, my precious, precious baby. I imagine that my husband, who is a positive, forward-looking man and, Latin tags and military campaigns apart, never one to dwell on the past, has long since forgotten this incident.

I bite off the end of my cotton and take another item from the mending pile at my feet. Emerald green will not do for the rip in Angelica's scarlet party dress, but there's a reel of crimson Sylko in my lap which will have to.

\*

The queue in Reception is very long, and I join the end of it. I'm annoyed by this queue because it wasn't easy getting here on time. I had to organize, which means beg, someone else to do the school run; we had to have breakfast before seven; I had to drive my husband to the station, get back, make sandwiches for two school lunch boxes, put the dustbins out, and then walk the dogs – because who knows how long they're going to be shut up for. All this so I could leave the house by ten to eight, so I could be here by half past.

There's a telephone on the Reception desk. It rings and rings. It rings all the time I'm waiting, all the time I'm inching up the queue. No less than three people to deal with appointments and enquiries, and yet none of them can answer this telephone. None of them so much as looks at it, and it's odd. I know I couldn't work at a desk where a telephone was ringing without doing something about it, without at least taking it off the hook, or shouting at it.

Follow the sign to B2, the Receptionist says when I hand her my card, and she jerks her head to her right. Your telephone is ringing, by the way, I tell her. Card please, she says to the person next in line.

I follow the signs to B2. Left from the desk through swing doors, right at the end of the corridor, up two levels in the lift, more swing doors, B2. A nurse is heading towards me. She's going fast, and when I accost her she has to brake, so that her black shoes squeak on the lino. I tell her my name and what I'm here for, and she turns back the way she's come and points to a door on the right. Go in there, she says, take off your clothes and put on a theatre gown and a dressing-gown, and I'll be back in a jiff.

In the room there's a cupboard, partitioned down the middle: theatre gowns on the left, dressing-gowns on the right. I take off my clothes and put on a theatre gown. It is like a high-necked apron with sleeves, and it fastens at the back with tapes, one of which is missing. I bend my head into the cupboard and sniff the dressing-gowns to see if they've been worn, but they smell of nothing. I put one on. It is voluminous. Its sleeves come down over my hands, its skirts trail over the floor. I hitch it at the waist, and blouse and bag it over the tie-belt. I don't like these clothes, and the nothing smell of them. I want to pee. I want to go home.

I sit on the bed and swing my legs and wait for the nurse. She doesn't come. I've got time to consider what I don't want to consider, the question I meant to ask, and didn't ask, Mr Gamble, the problem I meant to discuss, and didn't discuss, with my husband, namely this: Is it all right to have a Coil? Is it all right to put a foreign body, a *piece of wire* (even if copper wire) in the womb? Does the womb like it? Is it dangerous in any way? To the womb? To me in general? Last time, and the time before, I bled like a, like a *stuck pig*. I was a social embarrassment. I had to leave dinner parties in a hurry. I mean, is it okay to have a Coil? Is the Coil an okay thing to have?

I get off the bed and shuffle to the window. Far below two tiny figures in navy capes are being blown along a concrete walkway. They weave in and out of the buildings, disappear, reappear beside a grove of sapling poplars, vanish into Pathology, a shack like all the other shacks. Angelica's classroom is a shack. She will be in it now – arithmetic, first period after prayers. She didn't want to go to school today. She didn't feel well, she said. She had a headache and a tummy ache, she felt *sick*. She says this, or something like it, every morning. Every morning I want to keep her at home and let her mess up the kitchen table with paintwater and scissors and gummed squares; every morning I send her to school.

I go out into the corridor. There's a cleaner with a hovercraft outside my door. She shows me where the lavatory is, just in time.

I am back on the bed, curled up, reading the mail that came as I was leaving the house. My mail is one postcard, from a friend who's on holiday in Kenya (was on holiday, I should say. I saw her in Tescos yesterday, at the cheese counter. She was busy, I was busy, we pretended not to see each other). The card is addressed to Memsahib Pomfrey. It says Jambo! Habari? We are having a *fantastic* time. See you soonest, Love V & C. I turn it over. The picture side has a hippo with its mouth open, half submerged in a pool, surrounded by smaller hippos.

A man's head appears round the door of my room. I've come to take you to Theatre, he says. Leave your handbag and your clothes in the locker – and your watch if you're wearing one.

Are you a nurse? I ask the man when we are in the lift together, descending to G level. The man has his arms folded across his chest and is staring at the ceiling the way people tend to in lifts. I know I do, because it's the only way to avoid eyeball to eyeball confrontation with strangers. He uncrosses his arms and points to a badge on his overall which says Porter, green letters on white.

At G Level we follow signs to X-Ray and Haematology, but at

the last moment bypass these and make now for Pharmacy, Out-patients Surgical, Gynaecology and Shop. We walk out through plastic swing doors, Emergency Exit 2, and I lift my skirts, costume drama style, onto covered concrete, uncovered concrete, covered concrete, through swing doors, into lino corridor, where we stop. Put on a pair of overshoes, the porter says, and take a seat here.

Against the wall are two chairs and a row of see-through galoshes, all the same size; it doesn't matter which pair I choose. I take a seat in the corridor. On my left are the shut double doors of Theatre 1 and Theatre 2, and opposite to me on the wall is a notice in red: This is a No Smoking Zone. I look from the notice to the doors and back again. Zone. It's an odd word; the longer I stare at it, the odder it is. Zone. *Zone*. What does it mean? Does it mean anything? No. No such number, no such zone. (This time I'm gonna take it myself, and put it right in her hand, and if it comes back the vurry next day, *then* I'll understand the writing on it) –

The doors of Theatre 2 open, a stretcher trolley shoots out, swings round, one person behind it pushing, another in front steering, holding the drip steady. I keep my head down as they trundle past at a trot, but I see because I want to see, because I have to, because I must: a white face, a dead face, surely, chin tipped up, mouth hugely open, a tube in the nose – or was it the mouth? Gone.

How long have I been here? Ten minutes? Twenty? I keep checking, but on my left wrist, printed across unbleached hairs and a mole, is only the ghost of my watch. Where is Mr G.? Why doesn't Mr G. come?

Ready for you in theatre now, dear.

It isn't Mr G., it's a nurse, in green, masked and gowned, who leads me, clopping in my overshoes, out of the darkness of the corridor into the light of Theatre 1.

It is very bright in Theatre. Interval time. The house lights are up and there's a party going on. It's a tea party, I can tell, because the six or seven people wandering about chatting have cups and saucers in their hands. It's surprising really, all this activity and chat and tea drinking, because you tend to think of hospital theatres as sterile, hygienic places, as Mr G. said, places (or areas, or *zones*) you can only enter if you're wearing overshoes.

Someone comes forward and helps me out of my dressing-gown. Someone asks me to take off my overshoes and my shoes. This same person gives me a hand onto the stage. (No, not a stage, a table. An operating table, for operations.) I lie down on my back, feet together, arms by my sides. Lift your tail, please. And at once, when I comply, the theatre gown is rolled back, up over my knees and thighs, and then folded above my waist. My legs are separated into a V. My right leg is carried up and away and placed in a sling and strapped; my left leg is carried up and away and placed in a sling and strapped. I raise my head. The slings are attached to a contraption suspended from the ceiling. It's like a Big Top up there: lights, wires, machinery, all the gear for tightropes and trapeze.

My bottom, my *tail*, is no longer on the table. Somebody slips a pillow underneath me, wedges it into the small of my back.

And that's all. Nothing else happens. I am on my back, with no knickers on, my legs wide apart and in the air – and nothing happens. The tea party is still going on, to be sure, all round me I can hear chatter and laughter and cups being returned to saucers – but I'm not part of it somehow, no one offers me a cup, no one chats to me.

This is not the first time I've been in this position; our second daughter, in no hurry to be born, had to be induced. But that time there were only two people in the Treatment Room – me, and the hospital doctor (Brown? Yes, Brown) who explained nothing, who said nothing, as he strapped up my legs. I remember the pain when he *ruptured the membranes;* I remember thinking it must be blood that gushed out and ran back underneath me and soaked the hospital gown and the sheets; I remember the ward sister in the corridor who, as I staggered out into it, took one look and snapped her fingers: Nurse! That girl needs some pethadine! I can think of all this, and concentrate on the detail and the pain because nothing that happens today, nothing that Mr G. has got up his sleeve, can be as bad as that.

Or can it? At least last time there was an end-product, a baby, Michael, to be born, at least there was someone to look forward to. What Mr G. is going to do (why doesn't he do it?) is prevent a baby being born; and at the same time rob me (when I am tired or cross, or simply not in the mood for love) of the best, the most convincing, the least hurtful, of my nocturnal excuses: D'you think we should, darling, when we know it isn't *safe*?

There's a game I used to play with my brothers, that I daresay everyone plays with their brothers – or sisters – if they have them: the Would You Rather Game. Would you rather be (here describe the worst horror you are capable of inventing) or go to bed with (here name the most repellent specimen, of either sex, known to you all). Would you rather be on your back under a search light with your legs apart and no knickers on in the middle of a tea party, or . . .

All right, Mrs Pomfrey, dear? I'm afraid you will feel this, it will be a bit painful. But if you can relax and just allow yourself to go floppy, it will make it easier for you. It's Mr G.'s voice. It's Mr G.'s face, bending over mine, I recognize his eyes. He has pulled his mask down, below his chin, so that he can speak to me. I can see the bristles on his top lip and the hairs, wonderfully luxuriant hairs, in his nose. Has he been here all the time?

There is less chatter now, no chinking of cups. But no one has left the Theatre; I'm certain of this because if I roll my head to the right I can see the doors, and even if I couldn't see, even if I were blind, I'd feel the draught. Mr G. prepares to insert the Coil. While he does so, he gives a commentary, an *ex tempore* lecture, my husband would say, to the throng at the end of the table because, yes, that is where the tea party is now assembled. They are students, of course they are! And I am the demonstration model. Watch closely, Mr G. says, I'm just going to lubricate the vagina prior to insertion. Can you tell us about the relative safety and efficiency of this Coil? a male voice, eager beaver, enquires. How does this Coil, the copper Coil, compare with other Inter-uterine devices currently available?

All over, Mr G. says at last, all done. Good girl.

My legs are unstrapped, removed from their slings and returned to me. I am helped down from the table. An S2, please, Mr G. says, and someone springs forward with a cellophane packet which, snipped open, contains two sanitary towels, individually and hygienically wrapped. You will have a period now, Mr G. promises, placing one of the sanitary towels between my thighs, but if the loss is unduly heavy don't hesitate to give us a ring. Take two aspirin four-hourly if there's any discomfort.

Dressing-gown on, shoes on, overshoes on. Out of theatre. A six-yard stumble on cardboard legs. Overshoes off. And here is the porter, come to take me back to my clothes.

There are some questions I forgot to ask Mr G. and the tea party in Theatre 1. How do you hold a sanitary towel in place when you haven't been given a belt or a pair of pants? How do you keep up with a porter in a hurry when your legs refuse to function properly, and when you're trying to glue your thighs together so that your ST won't leak or land on the floor? When your dressing-gown was designed for a giant and is intent on tripping you up? When your insides are falling out, when your eyes are blurred and you can't see where you're going, when the pain is so bad you will surely faint, if not actually die?

In the lift, ascending to B2, a trickle – hot, sticky, but which cannot be amniotic fluid, not today – descends the inside of my right thigh, circumnavigates the knee muscle, finds a route down the calf, steers between the ankle and heel, arrives in my shoe, collects there.

Outside my door the porter and I part company. Here we are then, he says, the first words he's spoken since we left the theatre, and he goes. I reach out for the door handle of sanctuary, and then I notice it, a red-black splash on the beige lino at my feet, the size of a coin, a little ragged around the edge. I turn, and look, there are more of them, all down the corridor back the way we've come, dark two-penny pieces, regularly spaced, as far as the eye can see. I've left a trail, like Hansel and Gretel did in the forest! Supposing, just supposing, I wanted to go back to Theatre now, I wouldn't need a porter to show me the way.

*

*Afterword 1: The Letters*

Unposted letter to Mr Gamble.

Dear Mr Gamble,

A week after my experience in the Infirmary I wrote you a letter.

I decided to write to you for two reasons: a) because I felt you should know what it was like to be on the receiving end of your lack of attention, and b) because I thought it incumbent on me, being articulate, to suggest ways of improving your set-up.

I took trouble over my letter. The first two drafts were too emotional (you mustn't be allowed to excuse yourself on the grounds that you were dealing with an hysteric); the third too rude. In the end my letter was polite, neither sarcastic nor acrimonious. I gave you a matter-of-fact account of what happened to me. I said I thought you'd want to know about it, so that the experience couldn't be repeated for anyone else. I suggested a few things (a female nurse to take the patient to and from Theatre; fewer people, if possible, present in Theatre; the provision of a sanitary belt or pants afterwards) to make it less of an ordeal for other women in future. Yours sincerely, etc., etc.

Nineteen days later I got your reply: seven typewritten lines, sincerely regretting 'the problems you encountered in the Day Case Unit', hoping the Coil was 'proving satisfactory' – signed in your absence by your secretary, and enclosing your bill.

Could you please tell me, because it wasn't quite clear, which part of the Infirmary was the Day Case Unit?

*Afterword 2: The Titles*

I had difficulty deciding on a title for this story. I hope I chose the right one (the right one, that is, for the story, and also for you). It cannot be said to mislead, although it may be on the dull side. If you did find it dull, you might be interested to see, in case there's one here you prefer, the other titles I rejected in favour of it. Before I list them, I'd like to tell you my reason for discarding them. It's that, when I typed them out, I saw they could all be construed as containing bitter little ironies; they all seemed to smack of, if not quite feminist, womens' or alternative writing.

I was worried they might, if you're a man, put you off.

Here they are, then, in order of invention, not merit:

1) The Would You Rather Game
2) That's Enough Gynaecology – Ed.
3) *Volenti Non Fit Injuria**
4) How to Make Your Man Happy in Bed.

*Which is what Lettice's husband said, not unsympathetically and among other things, when she told him what happened in Theatre. It seemed quite neat for a while, perhaps the best of the bunch, I nearly settled for it; but not everyone appreciates Latin tags, some people consider them a joke or pretentious, not everyone understands them.

# MAD ABOUT THE BOY

He got her through school which she hated. On Saturdays, and on weekday evenings after prep, they were allowed to play the gramophone. She would take hers, a German machine in a blue-black leather case her father had found in Berlin at the end of the war, into a corner of the gym and set herself up. The inside of the gramophone had an intoxicating smell. Each time she lifted the lid she sniffed hard. Years later, searching a junk shop for something to stand plants on, she came across an old gramophone and opened it up and sniffed and was immediately taken back; she could see that German machine: the catches on the case that released the lid, the heavy head tucked safely to the side, the winder secured by two brackets inside the lid, the sliding compartment for needles, the needles themselves in their shiny tin boxes.

She was nine or ten when the passion started and her collection of his records amounted to less than a dozen. She had stolen them from her mother and her aunts. All, with the exception of 'Don't Let's be Beastly to the Germans', were pre-war and recorded before she was born. Three were twelve-inch and scenes from plays *(Private Lives; Cavalcade; Tonight at 8.30)*. The rest were ten-inch and songs, sung solo by Noel with a piano accompaniment. Sometimes she listened in silence, kneeling close against the gramophone with her head inside the lid so as not to miss a syllable; more often she sang along with him in a clipped tenor as near his own as she could manage. Soon she was spending all her pocket money on records: 'Don't Make Fun of the Festival'; 'There are Bad Times Just Around the Corner'; 'Matelot'. His voice in these seemed rounder – or was it thicker? – which fitted in with his being almost bald now and not as thin as he'd been in the photographs she owned of *Private Lives*.

Noel's popularity was at a low ebb in the early nineteen fifties, a fact she discovered from the gossip columns of the daily newspapers. He seemed to be in trouble with the press for living most of the time in Bermuda or Jamaica and thereby avoiding income tax, and he was having a rough time with the critics for writing plays which, they were all agreed, showed none of his pre-war brilliance. He was not popular at her school, Belmont, but that was because most people had never heard of him, the few that had knowing him only as a vague figure – like Fred Astaire or Jack Buchanan – from their parents' youth. The decline in his fortunes suited her very well and made her feel protective. She alone really appreciated him. She alone understood him and his problems. She alone knew, and sympathized with, the weaknesses of his literary style. These included an over-fondness for adjectives and an inability to resist, in his plays, the witty line even when it was at odds with the character who had to speak it.

By the time she was twelve she knew, she was sure, everything there was to know about him; not just about the plays – date, theatre, cast, length of run were all at her fingertips – but his private life and his character. He was kind and sentimental and generous and hardworking, someone who never put off till the afternoon what he could do in the morning. He did not suffer fools. He was of course clever, but perhaps not in an intellectual way. He was witty and funny. He had no false modesty about his talents. He was not a believer, except in himself, and this was bothering because God might strike him down. She was keen on God and often spent as much as an hour on her knees on the splintery boards of Burne-Jones (the dormitories were named after painters) before getting into bed. She had once heard Colonel Symes, an acquaintance of her father's, refer to Noel as 'that old pansy'. This, so far as she could gather, meant that he preferred men to women in some respects. If he did, it didn't bother her. It was so obvious that he liked women and that he loved them too. He was always loyal about the women he loved. She knew who they were: his mother and G. E. Calthrop (Gladys) and Lorn Loraine and Joyce Carey. And Gertrude Lawrence. She loved Gertie almost as much as she loved Noel and kept a scrap book for each of them into which she pasted newspaper cuttings, theatre programmes and notices.

In the school holidays she haunted the second-hand bookshop in the market town where her mother did most of her shopping. The shop, Burkes, had high ceilings and the bookshelves went right up to them. There were books everywhere, not just on the shelves but in untidy stacks on the floor and in parked trolleys that blocked the aisles. A rickety staircase led to more books upstairs, but she seldom climbed them because the theatre section was on the ground floor. The shop, poorly lit and with alleyways that turned corners and resembled streets, made her think of a town at dusk.

Among her finds at Burkes was a brown book with a battered spine entitled *The Amazing Mr. Noel Coward* by Patrick Braybrooke. The book, in itself disappointing, had been made special by its previous owner who'd stuck photographs and press cuttings on all the available space of the end-papers. There was a caricature of Noel and Gertie taken from *The New Yorker*, a newspaper clip of Noel and Beatrice Lillie dining 'intimately' at a restaurant, and another cutting, so large it had had to be folded over, the caption of which read: 'At Goldenhurst Farm: Gertrude Lawrence, Noel Coward and Jack Wilson his Business Partner'. The photograph showed a tea party on a lawn. Gertie, sitting up very straight, poured out from a silver tea pot while a huge dog, a setter possibly, leaned across the table and licked her nose. Noel lay in a wicker chair, which was old-fashioned and had a wheel at the back. One of his knees was bent up. He held a saucer in his left hand and a cup in his right which partly obscured his face, and he eyed Gertie over the rim. The business partner who sat astride another wicker chair which did not have a wheel, was reading a magazine. Behind him a bag of golf clubs posed against a brick pillar. The domesticity of the scene was thrilling, although Goldenhurst – from the photograph all diamond panes and beams – was not to her taste.

Reading Noel was not easy to do at Belmont, where books brought back by the girls had to be passed as suitable by the headmistress, Miss Church. You put your books on an oak chest outside her drawing-room door and at some time, probably in the middle of the night for no one ever saw them go, they were taken inside. If they passed, they reappeared two days later in the same miraculous fashion, and you were then free to remove them and read them. She'd put *Fallen Angels* and *The Vortex* out once but had not seen them again until the end of term, when they were handed to her with a wan smile. After that she smuggled his plays in and kept them under a packet of sanitary towels in her underclothes drawer. She learned them, in bed and with a torch, after lights out.

Before falling asleep she invented a 'dream' about him. The dream was always the same. On a foggy afternoon she would escape down the drive (pitted tarmac and enclosed by species rhododendrons and ponticums, now glistening unpleasantly in the fog) and walk the two miles to the station and the London train. At Waterloo she'd take a taxi to 17 Gerald Road, the studio flat he lived in when he wasn't in Jamaica or wherever. He came to the door himself, peered down, saw at a glance how fascinating she was under her cloak of shyness, and invited her in for tea. Tea was crumpets in a silver dish, accompanied by light and witty conversation. She made him laugh a lot. After tea he showed her his treasures and his books and pictures (these included two landscapes he'd painted himself) until they were interrupted by actor friends dropping in for cocktails. He was proprietorial about her and introduced her to them with pride, as though he himself had invented her. Occasionally he'd pat her head, which made her blush with pleasure. When his visitors were invited to stay on for supper she stayed too and helped Cole (she knew about Cole from reading *Present Indicative*) serve it. They had cold roast mutton and baked potatoes and onion sauce and salad, followed by apple pie and cheese and biscuits. There was red wine to drink.

Coffee was served in the drawing-room. Noel ('Do stop calling me Mr. Coward, there's a darling') sat down at the grand piano and played a few bars. 'Antonia!' – he beckoned her with a finger – 'Come and sing a duet with me.' They sang 'You Were There' from *Shadow Play*. She owned the record of this, and had sung Gertie's part so often, copying every idiosyncratic note, that she sounded just like her, she thought. Noel seemed to think so too. Eventually the visitors began to drift away, fetching sable wraps – the women – and capes and white silk scarves – the men – from Noel's bedroom. When she said 'I must go now,' he said 'Not in this fog dear, and in any case you've missed the last train.' So she stayed. Dressed in a pair of his pyjamas – they were slub silk and striped in pink and grey – she slept, curled up beside him in his huge double bed under a black satin quilt with scarlet roses on it.

At home she was teased about her passion, but not unkindly. Her mother – 'I was a Coward fan long before you were born' – quite liked him, and her sister Fran, who was eighteen, liked him very much. Fran's teasing often took the form of trying to trip her up on dialogue from the plays. They might be sitting at lunch when Fran would suddenly stare out of the window and point and say: 'That hedge over there is called Cupressus Macrocapa,' to which the only possible reply (there were no hedges of the sort in their garden) was: 'Do you swear it?' Or again, she might be minding her own business in an arm chair with a book, when Fran would materialize at her side and ask: 'Are you engaged for this dance?' The correct answer, which of course she always gave, being: 'I was, but I'll cut it if you promise to love me always and never let anyone or anything come between us, ever.' Her father addressed her, and often in the third person, as Lady Coward, even though Noel at the time was plain Mr. 'Some more roast beef for Lady C.?' – he would turn from the sideboard with his carving knife and his eyebrows raised. Or 'Lady Coward is in a pretty bloody mood today, it seems.' Asked for something for her autograph book, he wrote unkindly on one page: *Nobody loves a fat girl/Nobody gives me a date/The only game I play with the boys/Is sitting and guessing my weight*, and on the facing one, right in the middle: *I am a Nole and I live in a hole*. He drew a picture of the hole, and beside it a signpost on which he printed: *Montego Bay 3 miles*.

One day, feeling fat and bored and sad, she looked Noel up in the A-D volume of the London Telephone Directory, not expecting to find him there. Yet there he was, his name in ordinary print like everyone else's and there was his telephone number: SLOane 2965. For three days she did nothing except chant the number. Say she got through and managed to speak to him? A furious: 'Who are you? What do you want? Go away, please.' Click – the likely outcome – would put paid to her fantasy for ever. So she compromised. The compromise consisted of asking the operator for SLOane 2965 and then sweating with fear while the number was obtained. When it was engaged, which was often, the anti-climax was balanced by a dull relief. Whenever the operator said: It's ringing now, caller,' she felt sick with terror and replaced her receiver as soon as his was lifted. Sitting in her father's chair in the empty drawing-room, she would shake and speculate: Who had lifted the receiver? Was it him? Or Cole? A maid? A friend? A lover? The thrill lay in the knowledge that she had caused a bell to ring in his house and that if he were in he must surely hear it. If only in the minutest way she had affected his life. Because of something she had done he had perhaps called out: 'Answer that, Coley, would you?' or 'Who the hell's that? Tell them I'm not in'. Or, if Coley and maids and cooks and friends and lovers were absent, he himself might have padded – in his dressing-gown? – to the telephone and picked up the receiver with his own hands. The possibilities were endless.

As with a drug, the telephone episodes satisfied for a time and produced highs and lows. Soon a stronger dose was needed. So that when her best friend from school with whom she sometimes stayed in the holidays, dared her to speak to him, she decided to take on the dare. They did it from a telephone box outside the Post Office and Stores in the Suffolk village where Christina lived. There was a good deal of preliminary giggling and pinching – Christina carried on like that much of the time in any case – and scrabbling on the filthy floor of the call box for the pennies they kept dropping. Eventually the operator said: 'You're through now, caller', and after a pause and some clicks, a male voice that was not his said: 'SLOane 2965.' 'Hello', she said. 'Could I speak to Mr. Coward please?' 'He's at the theatre at the moment, I'm afraid'. The voice sounded wary (but it could have been true, she decided afterwards. He was playing King Magnus in *The Apple Cart* that summer). 'Can I take a message?' 'My name is Amanda Prynne,' she spoke very fast, turning her back on Christina who was bent up with laughter and clutching her stomach. 'Isn't that a coincidence?' 'It certainly is,' the voice said politely, disbelievingly. 'I can't wait. I can't, I can't' Christina had started to wail. 'I'm going to do it NOW.' She wasn't sure what to say next to the voice on the telephone. Instead, it spoke to her: 'Mr Coward will be most interested to hear about you. Thank you for calling. Goodbye.' 'Wait!' she shouted, but the line had gone dead. Christina uncrossed her skinny legs and unleased a stream of pee that struck the floor of the box as a waterfall strikes rocks, splashing their bare legs and soaking their sandals. They quarrelled all the way home to the Regency rectory where Christina lived, but by the time they reached the bathroom and were unpeeling their smelly clothes they were giggling again. 'What did he say? What did he say?' Christina aimed a loaded sponge at her and missed. 'Who's this Amanda person, anyway?'

The following day she shut herself in the lavatory, and took up her pen: 'Dear Mr. Coward, As you may have heard, I telephoned you yesterday . . . ' She covered two whole sides. She told him how much she admired him and how she knew everything he'd ever written. She said she hoped he didn't mind her writing to him. She signed herself Amanda Prynne. The letter was written on Christina's mother's headed paper: Bumpstead Hall, nr Haverhill,

Suffolk, which she hoped would impress him. Leaning out of the carriage window as her train pulled out of Audley End station, she asked Christina, as casually as she could, to forward any letters that came for Amanda Prynne.

Silence is ambiguous stuff, she discovered. Almost anything could be read into it. Sometimes he opened her letter, scanned its contents briefly, crumpled it and dropped it in a wastepaper basket. Sometimes (he did this more often) he read her letter carefully and with increasing interest, then sat down at his desk, unscrewed his Parker 51, filled it with Quink and wrote a reply. It was a kind note, quite short, and it ended with an invitation (to tea, but she knew where *that* would lead). When the weeks that went by became months and she could no longer believe in his letter, she allowed herself to think that he didn't want to spoil things by writing, but that he kept hers on his bedside table, tucked inside a favourite book – *Barchester Towers*, perhaps. She knew everything about him. She knew of his addiction to Trollope.

It was about this time that something happened to bring the real world and the fantasy world briefly if electrifyingly closer. Copies of *The Times,* the only newspaper considered suitable reading for the girls at Belmont, were kept in a Jacobean oak cradle in the hall, disproportionately large and imposing for the house which had been built at the turn of the century in baronial style for, rumour had it, a Spanish ambassador who for some reason had never arrived. The floor of the hall was on two levels, the lower level, nearest the front door, being paved with large black and white stone squares and empty except for an enormous J. Arthur Rank gong struck at mealtimes by Brooks the butler whom everybody hated; the higher level oak-boarded and part-covered by an ancient (that was easy to believe: it was almost threadbare) and, so they were always being told, priceless, Persian carpet no one was allowed to tread on. No one, that is, except for Miss Church. The cradle was on the higher level, and beside it was an oak chest you sat on if you wanted to read the paper (it was forbidden to remove *The Times* from the hall). She was seated there one morning at break,kicking her heels against the chest and giving the personal columns on the front page her usual close attention, when a small paragraph winked at her like a neon sign: 'Mr. Noel Coward will be at the Times Bookshop at noon tomorrow (Tuesday) to sign copies of *The Noel Coward Song Book*.'

There was no chance of escaping in fog (it was in any case July) on the London train. She'd spent her pocket money for the term and had nothing for the fare. She did not know where the Times Bookshop was. She tore a page from her rough notebook (it was forbidden to tear pages from your rough notebook) and wrote to Fran who was doing a secretarial course in Bayswater and who lived with three friends in a basement flat off Royal Avenue:

> Darling Fran,
> Noel Coward is signing copies of the N.C. Song Book TOMORROW (Tues.) at the Times Bookshop. Please get one for me in yr lunch hour. I swear I will repay. I'm sorry to be such a nuisance. Please please PLEASE!
> T.O.L.
> Ant.

She gave her letter to the under-matron, Miss Tankland, who shopped in the town on Monday afternoons. Miss Tankland did not like her any more than she, or any other of the girls, liked Miss Tankland, who was spiteful, two-faced, a snob and stupid (she had once said to Camilla Arbuthnot: 'I believe you're quite well connected' and had not perceived the irony in Camilla's reply: 'Yes. The ninth earl died last week'). It was quite on the cards that Tank would lose her letter on purpose.

The next day was a day of suffering. Would Fran get her letter – always supposing Tank had posted it – before she left for Bayswater? If she did get it, would she act on it? She had a feeling she hadn't told Fran what time Noel was supposed to be at the shop.

After tea, which as usual had been buns and compo strawberry jam out of a tin with woodshavings added for pips, she was searching her desk for Geography Today Bk 3 – there was a prep on watersheds that evening – when Alice Hodges from Remove skated over the glassy boards into Vb form room. 'Antonia *Pen*rose – you're wanted in the study'. She sang this with relish and then skated away again.

The study, which was also Miss Church's drawing-room, was furnished with highly-polished Edwardian Sheraton pieces and Persian rugs. There was an ornate break-fronted bookcase full of unappetising books on one side of the fireplace, and the wall opposite to where she now stood, her back to the double doors, was taken up by a mullioned bay window, from which she could see the top of the latticed stone terrace wall and beyond it yellowing lawns sloping down to the tennis courts, on the left, and The Military Building, a leftover from the Army's occupation of the house during the war, on the right. In this dark and draughty shed (its north side was entirely open to the elements) which had a tarmacadam floor that minced your knees if you fell over, they played team games with bean bags when the weather was considered too bad for tennis or lacrosse.

Miss Church faced her from a chintz-covered armchair by the fire. She had a smallish, square head, a beaky nose and highly-coloured cheeks. Her hair, cut like a man's at the back, was thick and wiry and not yet entirely grey, and it stuck out in tufts above her ears. The head sat oddly on a huge unfit body that tended to wobble in an unpleasant way when she walked and was always draped in loose navy or maroon garments, uninfluenced by fashion of any period and peculiar to Miss Church.

She had once seen a photograph of Miss Church as a young woman during the first world war. It was difficult to think of the thin and flat-chested person who held a boat-shaped tennis racquet with what looked like purpose, and who smiled at the camera from under an amusing hat, as having anything to do with the headmistress she knew. Miss Church taught English literature and scripture. She had a habit, when seated before the class, of holding her fountain pen vertically and letting her thumb and index finger slip down it to the nib. She would then about-turn the pen very slowly, tapping on the table as she did so. The action was usually accompanied by some ominously quiet instructions, apparently directed to the book in front of her: 'Jessica. I believe you learned the Gospel according to St Mark, Chapter 4, for preparation. Would you,' a pause, and she would look up at this point with a little smile that was not a smile at all, 'recite verses 10–23 for me please, darling.'

Miss Church did her pen trick now, tapping it on the notebook in her lap. She did this for some moments and then put the pen down on a little table which, when visiting parents were present, sometimes supported minute glasses of dry sherry. She opened the notebook. There was a small yellow envelope between its pages which she handed to Antonia. 'What does this mean, darling?' Miss Church asked her.

She unfolded the telegram – it had already been opened – and read: 'All is performed stop arent I a good sister Fran'.

'Yippee,' she said, and did a little jump. Miss Church looked at her unsmilingly. 'Children are not permitted to receive telegrams here,' she said, 'except on matters of the utmost gravity. I should like some explanation, please.'

She did not fancy telling Miss Church about Noel and his Song Book and what she'd asked Fran to do. It was not Miss Church's business. 'It's a private matter. Nothing to do with school,' she said brightly. 'I see,' said Miss Church, turning a nasty shade of purple. 'I'm afraid you are a rather silly and superficial person, Antonia. I think you like to imagine yourself as different from other people, superior in some way. I have to say I have not found your work to be superior. You tend to run away from anything at all difficult.' There was a pause, during which she felt uncomfortable for a moment, knowing that Miss Church referred to the music exam she'd been supposed to take last term but had refused, at the last minute, to sit because she knew she'd fail.

'It is perhaps your parents' fault that you are spineless and spoonfed,' Miss Church went on, 'but if you can't cure this you will never achieve anything very much.'

Out of the window she could see a group of figures straggling up from the tennis courts. Caroline Timpson, or it might have been Rosemary Bailey – it was hard to tell from this distance – was bouncing a tennis ball on her racquet. Every so often the ball bounced out of the racquet's reach and rolled away over the tussocky lawn, and Caroline – or Rosemary – chased after it. Meanwhile, Miss Church was winding up: 'You will be late for your preparation, Antonia, and must do an extra half hour. Before you return to your classroom, run up to Matron, will you, and tell her I'm sorry to have to bother her – I know how busy she is – but that I had to send you for a clean tunic because your own is so,' she looked briefly at the lentil soup and ink stains on the brown serge bosom, and then turned away, 'soiled'.

She had to wait until December 25th for the Song Book, which Fran said was her Christmas present. She made Fran go endlessly through her experience in the Times Bookshop. There had been a long queue. Noel had sat at a large table, piled with books, signing away. He'd worn a grey pinstripe suit, a pink shirt, a navy blue and white spotted bow-tie. When her turn had come, she'd said: 'Would you sign my book please?' and he'd said: 'It will be a pleasure.' When he'd signed his name, which he did rather fast in blue biro, she said 'Thank you very much' and he'd said: 'Not at all.'

The book when it came was large and important-looking, the paper cover designed, not very well she thought, by G.E. Calthrop. The signature was eccentric and ran diagonally across the title page, fitting neatly between 'The Noel Coward Song Book' in large lettering at the top, and 'London, Michael Joseph' in much smaller print at the bottom. The flourish of the 'd' in Coward sliced through 'with an introduction and annotations by Noel Coward'. On the facing page was a portrait by Clemence Dane of Noel in a yellow jumper. His hair was unflatteringly short. His forehead and ears looked pink and cross, and his pursed mouth was a bright lipstick red.

She ran her fingers over the signature as though it had been in braille. His ballpoint pen had nearly pierced the paper on some strokes; how nearly was obvious when she turned the page over. He had written this with his pen. She copied the signature again and again in her rough notebook and was soon able to execute a perfect forgery and at speed.

It dawned on her gradually that Noel was never going to be interested in the real Antonia Penrose, who at fourteen was not just fat but spotty and greasy-haired and uncomfortably like Mrs. Worthington's daughter. He could only be drawn to the Antonia Penrose she had invented for him, who was thin, attractive (not beautiful: she hadn't thought that necessary) and talented in the same sort of ways that he was. The only chance she had of winning, if not his love, then at least his respect, was by *doing* something. She removed a new exercise book from the form room cupboard and started work on a play. It was to be a musical play, she decided. She called it *Court Circular* and it centred on the social round and marital difficulties, two subjects she knew next to nothing about, of a couple in their thirties whose names were Paul and Theresa Felton.

Getting the dialogue to sound convincing wasn't as easy as she'd anticipated. But she enjoyed writing the songs, or lyrics as she always thought of them (as in 'book and lyrics by so-and-so'), and she composed the tunes and fitted the words to them while walking round and round the lacrosse pitch while supposedly 'off games'. 'Off games' was the expression employed by the school to denote the first three days of the your 'period'. 'Period' was the word Matron used for what your mother called 'the curse'.

Of the songs *Queen of Sheba:*

I think you're the Queen of Sheba,
You know I do
And somehow I sort of feel a
Passion for you.
I don't care if the Atlantic's between us

So long as it's still romantic between us
I think you're a bit of my heaven come true –

had perhaps the best tune, but the smartest lyric was undoubtedly
*When the Moon is Blue:*

When the moon is blue, darling,
I'll be true, darling, to you.
There are quite a few, honey,
Apart from you, honey,
I'm fond of too.
But I'll be faithful sometime,
You may be sure
When I've had my fun time,
Then I'll be your
Baby
When the moon is blue, darling
I'll be true, darling,
To you

The cover of her notebook said: *Court Circular*, A Musical Play
in Three Acts, but she ran out of steam after the first Act and wrote
nothing more. Noel was not to know this, however. She copied
the First Act into a new notebook and wrote him a letter:

Dear Mr Coward,
I thought you might be interested to see the first Act of my new
musical play, *Court Circular* . . .

He would be obliged to reply now, if only to return her
manuscript, and for weeks she believed this, sometimes racing to
the Junior Room – the mail was given out there – at break,
sometimes staying edgily in her form room in the hope that the
prefect in charge of the mail would seek her out: 'Huge envelope
for you, Antonia'. 'Oh thanks,' would be her bored reply as she
took the packet without even glancing at it. It was years before she
realized that he probably received hundreds of unsolicited
manuscripts a week, and that the only ones that had even a hope of

being returned, possibly accompanied by a discouraging note from a member of his staff, were those which had self-addressed and stamped envelopes attached to them.

The silence that greeted *Court Circular* marked the end of her obsession as it had been. She still loved him, and she still wrote to him sometimes, but she never posted the letters. What she did post to him, every year, was a birthday card, drawn and painted by herself. The wording never varied: 'To the Master, With best wishes for a Happy Birthday, from Antonia Penrose.' She always wrote her address on the bottom left hand corner, just in case, but she no longer expected a reply. What was permitted was to picture him at breakfast, slitting the heaped envelopes with a silver paperknife. He hurried through them until he came to hers, exclaimed with pleasure, called everyone round to look, and then stood the card up in a place of honour on the piano.

One December when she was nineteen and teaching English and Art at a girls' preparatory school – a post she had no qualification for and had managed to get because her parents knew one of the governors – she read in the paper that he was ill in bed at the Dorchester Hotel. She read this on the 13th. There were three days to go before the birthday. She took great pains with the card, an ink and wash drawing, rather Cecil Beatonish, of an Edwardian couple walking in a park. The woman held a parasol and a little dog on a lead. Behind the couple, who walked arm in arm, was a suggestion of railings and a park bench. She pasted the picture onto a stiff blue card and wrote inside: 'To the Master. Happy Birthday. I hope you're feeling better'. She was about to sign her name as usual when she hesitated, and wrote *Anthony* Penrose instead.

Two days later she was just setting off for the school when the post arrived. Among a pile of stuff for her parents, there were two other items: a communication for her from Lloyds Bank which she did not open, and a white, square envelope addressed in blue type to Anthony Penrose, esq., The Glebe House, Monkerswell, nr Salisbury. She opened it quickly and took out a greetings card. Its entire front was taken up by a black and white photograph of

Noel. He was sitting cross-legged in a white tubular chair on top of a rock in the middle of the sea. He wore a dark jacket and white trousers and espadrilles and he had a book on his knee. It was impossible to tell what book. He was seated sideways to the camera, his face half towards it with an amused expression that was not quite a smile. She opened the card. At the top, a blue seal, the sort some people stick on Christmas parcels, said: 'Merry Xmas' in fancy silver lettering above two silver holly leaves and berries. Underneath this was a signature: Noel, in red biro. There was nothing else at all.

This card, and how she came by it, became in time her 'Noel Coward story', and she told it through the years at what she judged to be the right time to the right company. It was not a story that improved with embellishment. It depended for its effect – gratifying hilarious, nine times out of ten – on a fast Coward delivery:

Cue (approximate): 'As Noel Coward might say . . . '
A: I can't remember if I ever told you my Noel Coward Story?
Cue: No. Do tell.
A: I was madly in love with him from about the age of eight and used to write to him from school, and ring him up – SLOane 2965 – and always for his birthday I drew him a card and he never replied. And then one year when I was about nineteen I did him a rather Cecil Beatonish card – he was in bed at the Dorchester with 'flu – and I wrote 'To the Master' at the top as usual, and was just about to sign my name 'Antonia Penrose' when I stopped and wrote Anthony Penrose instead. And I got a reply by return of post.

She felt no disloyalty at telling this story, being certain that, if he could hear it, he'd laugh louder and longer than anyone else.

She had been married to James for six years and had had three of her five children when the Great Coward Revival began in the mid-nineteen sixties. She went twice to see him – his last stage appearance – in *Suite In Three Keys*. Separated from him by only the orchestra pit she was shocked to discover how like her own father, who had died the year before, he was, not just in obvious physical ways of height and shape (their ears were almost identical) but in facial expression, in speech – particularly delivery and timing – and in gesture. The way Noel sat in an armchair, for instance, one leg crossed over at the knee, his arms stretched along the chair arms, fingers lightly drumming the ends, was at once familiar, as was the way he held a cigarette, the way he inhaled smoke and released it, the way he nodded his head in emphasis. None of these similarities had been discernible from photographs. He seemed, curiously, to be more like her father – whom she had loved but had never bothered to get to know until it was too late – than her father had been himself.

Sometimes she and the children had Noel Nostalgia Evenings, when she played them all her old scratched 78s. Flora, in particular, was attentive and appreciative. 'I really love Noel,' she said once, but Flora loved lots of things, and most people. James always absented himself from Noel Nostalgia Evenings, either going to bed earlier than usual, or shutting himself in the study with his dictaphone and his in-tray.

She thought about Noel whenever his name was mentioned in the press or on the wireless which was increasingly often. They were not real thoughts, more a feeling of tenderness. It was comforting to know that he was alive somewhere, getting up in the morning, cleaning his teeth, eating, making jokes. Nothing too terrible could happen to a world that contained him. But he was old and, according to reports, often ill. The day could not be far off that she dreaded when she'd turn on the wireless unsuspectingly and hear a newsreader announce: Sir Noel Coward died today at his home in Jamaica (or Switzerland; or wherever he happened to be), and then, after a brief biography, go on to give the cricket scores, as though the world were still the same place.

She was glad that he was being fêted in his old age, though a part of her felt resentful that he was everybody's darling now. There was nothing special or peculiar or different about loving Noel

Coward. Even his critics had stopped being critical and seemed to think that everything he'd ever written was bloody marvellous. This was surely insulting, and a mistake she'd never made, even at ten years old.

When Christina, whom she had not seen for years, telephoned and suggested they go together to see *Cowardy Custard* at the Mermaid, she was tempted to refuse. Only Noel Coward could sing a Noel Coward song. She did not want to see a camp chorus perform dance routines with top hats and canes or hear them wreck his songs by sticking too closely to the melody in places where he would sing seconds or merely speak the lines. But she went because it would be nice to get away from James and the children for once, and she enjoyed herself because it was fun seeing Christina (fat now, hooray, whereas she had remained eight stone five – except during her pregnancies – for the past twenty years). *Cowardy Custard* itself was exactly as she'd thought it would be.

Three weeks later she got back from the afternoon school run to find a note stuck in one of the children's gumboots outside the front door:

> Your telephone's out of order. We've got one spare ticket for *Cowardy Custard* on the 17th, and knowing your passion for N.C. thought of you. Please come if James can spare you. Supper in the Garrick afterwards.

After a little thought – it was very kind of the Evanses to ask her and she didn't want to seem ungrateful – she refused the invitation, explaining that James had already spared her once to see it, and suggesting the ticket should go to someone who hadn't because it was a wonderful . . . (she paused here, because the word 'show' was so disagreeable, but how else could she describe it?). She also said, which was true, that there was a parent-teacher meeting at Flora's school that evening, and that she ought to be there. Flora's maths being what they were.

On the morning of the eighteenth she had washed up the breakfast things, wiped some surfaces, made the beds (Jack's had to be stripped because he'd wet his sheets without telling), collected socks and knickers from the floor of every bedroom and put them in the dirty linen basket, stared out of Flora's bedroom window unseeingly for half an hour, wished she were dead, and was just about to start on the mountain of ironing she'd been avoiding for days because it was all tangled up with laddered tights and matted and odd socks, when the telephone rang. She recognized Jane Evans's voice:

'Antonia – It's Jane here. I can hardly bear to tell you this, but we were sitting in our seats at the Mermaid yesterday just before the curtain went up, when NOEL COWARD walked into our row and sat down in the seat next to yours – I mean the one you'd have been in. He got a standing ovation. The whole theatre clapped and roared for at least ten minutes. He was on his own and seemed very frail and old and his hands shook and he wept throughout the entire performance. It was rather upsetting, really, but wonderful too, of course. You never did meet him, did you? And if you'd been there you'd have sat NEXT TO HIM,' (she shouted this). 'I really can't bear it!'

After Jane had rung off, she sat on her bed and stared at the floor. Tears, for sad Noel and for herself, spilled over and ran, slowly at first and then faster and faster, down her cheeks. They fell onto a join in the carpet that had come unstuck, its edges curled back to reveal the underlay. The carpet, once a subtle shade of blue, was grubby now, and needed not just hoovering but a good going over on hands and knees with a sponge and a bucket of *1001*, something she'd been putting off for months.

# PEOPLE FOR LUNCH

'I must get up,' Mrs Nightingale said, but did not move. During the night she had worked her way down the bed so that her feet were now resting on the brass rail at its end. Two years ago today it had been Edward's feet striking this same brass rail with peculiar force that had woken her. 'I don't feel well,' he'd said, and she'd replied – sleepily? sharply? – she needed to know but could not remember – 'Then you'd better not go to work today.' When he'd gone on, haltingly,to murmur: 'No. I can't,' she'd sat up, wide awake and afraid. For Edward was a workaholic. Nothing prevented him going to the office. She'd leant over him and seen that his face and neck were beaded with sweat. She'd touched his forehead and found it as cold and green as marble. 'I've got a pain,' he said, 'in my chest.' Each word was a single, concentrated effort. 'I can't breathe.' Stumbling to the telephone which lived on Edward's side of the bed, she'd started to panic. How could she explain to the doctor, probably still in bed and asleep, how serious it was with Edward lying beside her listening? It was then that she'd begun to shake, and her teeth to rattle in her jaw like pebbles in a bag. She'd knocked the telephone directory on to the floor and misdialled the number half a dozen times. (It was not true that anxious, panicky people proved themselves level-headed under fire.) 'Be calm, Fanny. Go at it slowly,' Edward had said, lying still, his eyes unfocussed on the ceiling.

A shuddering sigh on Mrs Nightingale's left made her turn her head. Lying close on the adjoining pillow was the face of Bone.

The dog's small body was concealed by the duvet, as was Mrs Nightingale's own. Mrs Nightingale stared at Bone's black nose, at the white whiskers that sprouted from her muzzle and chin, at her short sandy eyelashes. Bone's eyes were shut, but the left ear was open, its flap splayed on the pillow to reveal an intricacy of shiny and waxy pink coils. Mrs Nightingale leant across and blew gently in this ear. Bone opened one eye and shut it again. Mrs Nightingale put her arms round Bone and laid her head against the dog's neck. It smelt faintly of chicken soup. Bone jerked her head away and stretched her legs so that her claws lodged themselves in Mrs Nightingale's stomach. Mrs Nightingale kissed Bone on the muzzle just above the black, shiny lip. Bone opened her jaws wide in a foetid yawn and stretched again and went back to sleep. Mrs Nightingale got out of bed and left Bone, still covered to her neck by the duvet, sleeping peacefully.

Bone was not allowed in beds, only on them, and she reminded the dog of this. 'I don't like dogs,' she added untruthfully. The house was very quiet. Mrs Nightingale walked out bare-footed on to the uncarpeted landing and stood for a moment listening to the inharmonious ticking of the clocks downstairs. There was no sound from her children's bedrooms and their doors were uninvitingly shut. 'I hate being a widow,' she said aloud.

The bathroom door was blocked by a wrinkled dustbin sack full to overflowing with clothes intended for a jumble sale. She dragged it out of the way. From its torn side hung the yellowing arm of a Viyella cricket shirt. From its top protruded a brown Harris tweed skirt. Liza's name was still stitched to the tiny waistband. Had she ever really been that size? Mrs Nightingale had meant, before the move, to unpick the nametape from Liza's old uniform and take it back to the school for resale, but there had never been the time. This black sack was one of many about the house. Before moving she'd labelled them as to contents, but on examination recently they all contained the same things: out-grown clothes, single football boots, curtains originally made for Georgian sash windows that would not fit the small casements here, curtain hooks, picture hooks, bent wire coat hangers.

Lying motionless in the bath Mrs Nightingale saw Edward on the stretcher being carried into the ambulance. He had joked with the ambulance men. She would never forgive him for that. It had been his joking, and the doctor saying on arrival, just before he'd sent her out of the room: 'If you move, Edward, you're a dead man. If you lie still and do exactly what I say, you'll be all right,' that had given her hope. She could see Edward now, calling out from the stretcher to the twins, shivering in their night things on the front door step: 'Be good, monkeys. I'll be back soon.' And she could see herself, wrapped in his dressing gown, bending down to kiss his cold cheek before the ambulance doors closed. She'd wanted to go with him, she'd needed to go with him, but had had to wait for her mother to come and look after the twins.

The bath water was by now tepid and Mrs Nightingale's finger ends were white and shrunk. As she lay there, unable to move, the church bells began a faint tolling through the shut window and at once the image of the ambulance with its frenetic blue light turning out of the drive was replaced by a picture of dead tulips and lilac in the vase beneath the lectern. She'd seen these on Friday when she'd gone to the church to check the Flower Rota List and found her name down for this Sunday. She forced herself out of the bath and pounded down the passage to Liza's room. She shook the mound of bedclothes.

'Liza – did you remember to do the church flowers yesterday?'

Liza was gliding through a dark lake on the back of a sea-serpent. She opened blank blue eyes for a second and then shut them again.

'Did you do the church flowers?'

The eyes opened again, flickered and then closed. Waking was a trial for Liza.

'Liza – '

'No. I didn't. Sorry.'

'You're the absolute end.' Mrs Nightingale was furious. 'You asked what you could do to help and I said – '

'Sorry, Mum.'

'You're not asked to do much. And you're eighteen, not six.'

'Don't flap,' – Liza's voice sounded as though it had been dredged from the bottom of a deep lake – 'the congregation's geriatric. No-one will notice if the flowers are dead.' She yawned. 'You're sopping wet,' she said incuriously to her mother.

'I need your help,' Mrs Nightingale cried. 'Get up at once, now, before you fall asleep again.' She stood for a moment awaiting results, but as there were none, left the room banging the door behind her.

Mrs Nightingale visited the twins' room next. They were fast asleep on their backs. Lily, on the camp bed they took turns for, was snoring.

'Wake up, both of you,' Mrs Nightingale said. She trampled over their discarded clothes. 'Wake up now.' They sat up slowly, looking hurt and puzzled. 'It's late,' Mrs Nightingale said, 'Nine o'clock. They'll be here by half past twelve and there's a lot to do. You must get up. Now.'

'Who'll be here?' Poppy asked.

'Nine o'clock isn't late, it's early,' Lily said. 'It's Sunday.'

'Now,' Mrs Nightingale said and left the room.

When Mrs Nightingale opened Dave's door he was propped on one elbow, reading. His hair, which had been recently cut by a fellow student using blunt nail scissors, stuck out in stiff tufts. Here and there patches of scalp were visible. They'd had a row about the hair when he arrived. Usually Mrs Nightingale cut Dave's hair, and when she did he looked very nice. This present cut, which he'd admitted he wasn't that keen on himself, was an example of the perversity her son was given to and that Mrs Nightingale found exasperating and incomprehensible. He glanced up at her as she came in.

'Hallo, Mamma. How are you, darlin'?'

The question took Mrs Nightingale off-guard. Suddenly, she wanted to tell him. She wanted to say: 'Daddy died two years ago today.' She wanted to collapse on Dave's bed and howl, perhaps all day, perhaps for ever. Instead she stayed in the middle of the room and stared at the row of hats that hung from hooks above Dave's bed and which, together with the accents – foreign, regional – he adopted, formed part of her son's disguise kit.

'If you're awake, why aren't you up?' Mrs Nightingale heard herself say.

'Stay cool,' Dave said. 'I'm just tucking into Elizabeth Bishop.' He waved a paperback in the air that his mother recognised as her own and removed from its shelf without permission.

'How do you rate her? Compared to Lowell . . . ?'

'Get up, please,' Mrs Nightingale said.

'Okay, Marlene. Tuck in.'

Marlene, the second syllable of which was pronounced to rhyme with Jean, was not Mrs Nightingale's name, which was Frances. Marlene, which sometimes became Marlena, second syllable to rhyme with Gina, was the name Dave had bestowed on his mother some years ago when she'd started regularly cutting his hair. 'I'm due for a visit to Marlene's salon,' he'd say, ringing her from Leeds. 'Is the head stylist available?'

Mrs Nightingale moved backwards to Dave's door and fell over the bicycle wheel she'd noted on her way in and taken care to avoid.

'Shit. And your room's in shit, Dave.'

'Cool it.'

'Look, it is in shit and it smells. Do you have to sleep with the window shut? Why are you wearing that tee-shirt in bed?'

'I haven't any pyjamas, that's why,' Dave said reasonably.

'I know if I leave now you'll just go on reading – ' Mrs Nightingale was getting desperate – 'so get out now, while I'm here.'

'I will as soon as you go. I've got nothing on below this tee-shirt, and the sight of my amazing, user-friendly equipment might unsettle you for the day. Tuck in, Marlene.' He yawned, showing a white tongue and all his fillings, and stretched his huge arms above his head.

Mrs Nightingale returned to her bedroom and dressed herself in scruffy, everyday clothes. Then she pulled Bone out of the bed and swept the bottom sheet with her hands. Being white, Bone's hairs did not show up well against the sheet but Mrs Nightingale knew they were there, and sure enough they flew around the room and settled on the floorboards like snowfalkes in a paperweight snowstorm. Mrs Nightingale straightened the duvet and banged the pillows while Bone sat on her haunches, sorrowfully watching. As soon as the lace cover was on Bone leapt back on the bed and made herself comfortable among the cushions. Mrs Nightingale looked at her watch. This time two years ago she had just arrived at the hospital having driven at ninety most of the way. There'd been nowhere to park so she'd parked in one of the doctors' spaces. 'You can't park there,' an old man planting out geraniums by the hospital steps had told her, having watched her manoeuvre. Three floors up, on Harnham Ward, Sister had looked up from her notes and said: 'The specialist has examined your husband and would like to see you now.' Mrs Nightingale suddenly remembered the specialist's nose, aquiline and messily freckled. She'd stared at it as they sat opposite each other, divided by a desk. 'He's on the edge of a precipice,' the specialist had said. 'It was an almost total infarct – that means the supply of blood and oxygen to the heart has been severely reduced. A large part of the heart muscle is already dead. The next forty-eight hours will be crucial. If he survives, and I can give you no assurances, the dead muscle will be replaced in time by scar tissue, which is very tough and can do the same sort of job – '

I hate doctors, Mrs Nightingale thought as she went downstairs. Hate them. She took one look at the kitchen, then shut the door and went into the drawing-room, a room too poky to deserve the title that, from the habit of a lifetime, she had given it. It smelled of soot and damp and cigarettes, and of something indefinable that might have been the previous owners. Mrs Nightingale got down on her knees in front of the fireplace and swept the wood ash and cigarette stubs she found there into a dome. She stuck a firelighter on top of this, but the log baskets, were empty except for two pieces of bark and several families of woodlice, so she got up again and started to punch the sofa cushions into shape. Dave came in while she was doing this. He was still wearing the tee-shirt but to his lower half he'd now added an Indian tablecloth which he'd wrapped twice round himself and tucked in at the waist.

'You left a filthy mess in the kitchen last night,' Mrs Nightingale said, remembering the slag heap of coffee grounds decorated by a rusty Brillo pad on the kitchen table. 'I thought you were going to get dressed.'

'Liza's in the bathroom.' Dave scratched his armpit, then sat down heavily on the sofa cushions and rested his head on his knees.

'Dave, I've just done that sofa. We've got people for lunch – '

'Yup. Sure thing. Sorry. What can I do?' He stayed where he was and Mrs Nightingale stared, mesmerized, at his large yellow feet. The toenails were black and torn. Black wire sprouted from his big toes. The same wire twined his calves, visible beneath the tablecloth. It stopped at the ankles, but continued, Mrs Nightingale knew, beyond his knees to his thighs, where it no longer twined, but curled. It was impossible that this huge male person had ever been inside her body. 'Well, the log baskets are empty, as you see,' Mrs Nightingale said, 'so when you're dressed – '

'Sure, sure.'

'I did ask you, you know,' Mrs Nightingale bravely continued, 'when you arrived, if you'd be responsible for getting the wood in, and you said – '

'Yeah. Yeah. Sure. Yup. Tuck in.' He sat for a moment longer and then got up, hitching the tablecloth which had slipped a little. He looked round the room. 'I like your little house, Marlene.'

'It isn't *my* house.' Mrs Nightingale was hurt by Dave's choice of possessive adjective. 'It's *our* house. It's home.'

'Yup.'

'No chance, I suppose,' she said as he padded to the door, 'of your wearing your contact lenses at lunch?' Dave stopped dead in his tracks and turned sharply. 'What's wrong with my specs?' He whipped them off and examined them myopically, close to his nose. They were bright scarlet with butterfly sides, the sort typists wore in the Fifties. One arm was attached to the frame by a grubby selotape bandage.

'Nothing's wrong with them. It's just that you look nicer without them. You're quite nice looking, so it seems a shame – '

'Oh Christ,' Dave said and then hit his head on the beam above the door. 'Fuck. I hit my head everywhere I go in this fucking house. Cottage. Hen coop. Hovel.'

By the time Mrs Nightingale had finished scrubbing the potatoes they were all down in the kitchen with her. The kitchen was too small for five people comfortably to be in at one time. She had once, when they were all tripping over each other, made this observation and had received a long lecture from Dave on the living conditions of the average farm-labourer and his family in the latter part of the nineteenth century. Her son was nothing if not inconsistent, Mrs Nightingale thought, remembering the hen coop remark.

'Who's finished the Shreddies?' Poppy was on her knees on the brick floor, peering in a cupboard.

'Dave had them last night – don't you remember?' Liza said, sawing at a grapefruit with the bread knife. A pool of cloudy juice and pips spread over the table, soaking an unpaid telephone bill. Mrs Nightingale snatched it up.

'Here, have this' – Liza plonked the grapefruit halves into bowls and handed one of them to Poppy. 'This is better for you. You're too fat for cereal.'

'Speak for yourself, you great spotty oaf. At least I haven't got suppurating zits all over my face – '

'You will soon,' Dave interrupted cheerfully. 'You're into a pubescent exploding-hormone situation. Tuck in.'

'If you had, they might detract from your nose which, by the way,' – Liza glanced at it casually – 'is one big blackhead.'

There was a skirmish. Mrs Nightingale caught the milk bottle as it leapt from the table.

'Cool it, girls.' Dave had seen his mother's face. 'Marlene's trying to get organized. Aren't you Marlene?' He was propped against the Rayburn, dressed now in one of his father's city shirts and scarlet trousers, the bottoms of which were tucked into old school games stockings, one brilliantly striped, the other grey, and shovelling Weetabix into his mouth from a bowl held within an inch of his face. Each time the spoon went in it banged horribly against his teeth. 'Is the Rayburn *meant* to be off?' he asked, mock-innocently, between mouthfuls.

Mrs Nightingale was about to burst into tears.

'What? Out of my way please.' She pushed the red legs to one side, and knelt on the dog bed in front of the stove. Inside an erratic flame flickered. She turned the thermostat as high as it would go.

'Why's the heat gone down?'

'How the fuck should I know? The wind, probably – '

'Don't swear, Mummy,' Poppy said, grabbing a banana from the fruit bowl and stripping it.

'Put that banana back! It's for lunch.'

'We've got rhubarb crumble for lunch. I made it yesterday, remember.' Poppy took a bite out of the banana, folded the skin over the end and replaced it in the fruit bowl on top of a shrivelled orange.

'Look,' Mrs Nightingale said, 'we'll never be ready at this rate. Couldn't you all just – '

'Keep calm, Mamma. Sit down a moment and drink this.' Liza handed her mother a mug of coffee. 'There's nothing to do. Really. They won't be here till one at the earliest. All we've got to do is get the joint in – '

'Are we eating animals? Yuk. Unreal. Animals are people – '

'Shut up, Lily. – Do the spuds and the veg and lay the table and light the fire and pick some flowers – five minutes at the most.'

'The whole house is in chaos,' Mrs Nightingale said, 'it's composed of nothing but tea chests and plastic bags.'

'They're not coming to see the house. They know we've only just moved. They're coming to see *you*.'

'Actually, they're coming to inspect our reduced circumstances,' Dave said in a prissy voice. He picked up a piece of toast and stretched for the marmalade. Mrs Nightingale pushed it out of his reach. 'No, you've had enough.'

'Daddy couldn't bear them,' Lily said, staring into space.

'Couldn't bear who?' Poppy paused at the door.

'The Hendersons, stupid.'

'The Hendersons? Are *they* coming to lunch? Unreal.'

'Where do you think you're going to, Poppy? You haven't cleared up your breakfast things – '

'I'm going to the lav, if you must know. I'm coming back.'

'While you're up there, Fatso, take some of the gunge off your face!' Dave shouted at her.

'Have you got the logs in?' Mrs Nightingale asked Dave, knowing that he hadn't.

'I'm just about to. We shouldn't *need* a fire in May,' he said, resentfully as though his mother were to blame for the weather. 'Right, Marlena.' He rubbed his hands. 'Here we go -o,' he added in the manner of an air hostess about to deposit a snack on the knees of a passenger. He sat down on Poppy's chair and pulled a pair of canvas boots from under the table. A lace snapped as he put them on.

'Are you going to shave before they arrive?' Mrs Nightingale asked, eyeing him.

'Dunno. Oi moigh.' – Dave rubbed his chin so that it rasped – 'an' yere agine oi moigh 'na'. Don't you like me looking manly and virile?' Mrs Nightingale said No, she didn't much. No.

'Mrs Henderson will, though. She's got a yen for me. She'll really tuck in.'

'Oh ha ha,' Liza snorted from the sink.

'Mr Henderson has too. He's always putting his arm round my shoulder. Squeezing me. Kissing – '

'I don't suppose he's that desperate to get herpes. He hasn't seen you since you were about ten – '

'Do something for me, Lil, would you,' Mrs Nightingale said, as Dave minced from the room flexing his biceps. Lily sighed. Did she know what today was? Mrs Nightingale thought perhaps she did. It was impossible to get near Lily at the moment. She resented everything her mother said and did, prefacing her argument with 'Daddy always said' or 'Daddy would have agreed with me that . . . ' She'd been in a sulk since the move because the cottage was thatched i.e. spooky, witchy, bug-infested – and because her father had never been in it. 'Wake up, there,' – Mrs Nightingale waved her hand slowly up and down in front of Lily's face. Lily managed not to blink.

'Go and get Bone off my bed and put her out. She hasn't had a pee yet.' Lily went on sitting there, expressionless. Then all of a sudden she leapt up, scraping back her chair, and ran out of the room.

'Bone, Bone, my darling one, I'm coming.' They could hear her clattering up the stairs, calling 'Bone, beloved angel, Bone – '

'She's mad,' Liza said, stacking plates in the rack. 'All my family's mad. And Dave is completely off the wall.' Mrs Nightingale kissed Liza's spotty face, pink and damp with steam. 'I love you, Lize.' she said.

As Mrs Nightingale rootled in the kitchen drawer looking for enough knives to lay the dining-room table with, Dave's face appeared at the window above the sink. He flattened his nose against the pane and drummed on it with his fingers. 'Open up! Open up!' he shouted. Liza leaned across the taps and biffed the window. It opened in a rush. Dave's face disappeared for a second, and then reappeared half in the window. 'Ladies,' he said with a South London inflexion and in confidential tones, holding up what looked like a piece of string and dangling it from between his fingers and thumb, 'do your hubbies' jock-straps pass the window test? If not – ' he leered and let go of the jock-strap which fell across the sill and draped itself over the hot tap, and then held up a packet of something: 'Try new Weedol! Fast-acting, rainproof and guaranteed to eradicate all biological stains for an entire season. Just one sa*chette*' – he paused to consult the packet – 'treats 160 yards, or – if you ladies prefer a more up-to-date terminology – 135 square metres, of normally soiled jock-straps.' He backed away from the window, creased with laughter, and tripped over a flower pot.

'Pathetic,' Liza said, tugging at the window catch, 'quite pathetic.'

'Logs!' Mrs Nightingale shouted at him, just before the window jerked to, scattering them with raindrops, 'Logs, logs, logs!'

Mrs Nightingale did her best with the dining-room which, not being a room they had so far needed to use, had become a dumping ground. There were ten full tea chests stacked in one corner, her husband's golf clubs in a khaki bag, a clothes horse, innumerable lampshades and a depressed-looking cockatoo under a glass dome. Beneath the window precariously stacked books awaited the bookshelves Dave had promised to put up in the summer holidays. Everything in the room, including a dining-table much too large for it, was deep in dust. Mrs Nightingale looked at her watch. This time two years ago she'd sat beside Edward, who'd lain on his back without pillows, his chest and arms wired to a machine. Attached to the machine was a cardiograph that measured and recorded his heartbeat. The signal had gone all over the place, sometimes shooting to the top of the screen, and the bleeps, at each beat, had been similarly erratic – six, say, in succession followed by a silence which, each time it occurred, she'd felt would never be broken. 'The heroin was delicious,' Ed had murmured in a moment of consciousness, 'it took all the pain away, but they won't let me have any more in case I get hooked.' Why couldn't you have died at once, Mrs Nightingale thought, remembering her agony watching the nurse adjusting the drip, which had kept getting stuck, and checking the leads on Ed's chest which, because he rolled around a lot, were in constant danger of coming loose. This had happened once, when there'd been no nurse in the room. She'd been on the edge of her chair, her eyes alternately on Ed, and on the screen, when suddenly the bleeps had stopped and the signal had flattened into a straight, horizontal line. A red light had come on at the side of the machine and with it a whine like the unobtainable tone when you dial. He's dead, she'd thought. Sister had rushed in at once and checked Ed's pulse and then the leads and after a minute or two the crazy signal was back and the bleeps. 'Try not to worry, dear,' Sister had said. 'Worrying doesn't help.'

Mrs Nightingale forced herself out of her chair and went in search of a duster.

'The joint's in the oven,' Liza said. She had an apron on which bore the message I Hate Cooking, and was standing at the stove stirring a saucepan. 'I'm making onion sauce.' She looked up. 'Are you okay, Ma?' By way of an answer Mrs Nightingale enquired if anyone had seen the silver anywhere. Poppy knew. She and Lily were scraping carrots and glaring at each other across the kitchen table. She got up and helped her mother drag the despatch box from under the sink in the washroom. Back in the dining-room she stood and watched her mother dust the table.

'Mum – can I have a friend to stay – Julia, I mean, in the holidays?'

'Maybe. If we're straighter by then.' Mrs Nightingale didn't like Julia. On the child's last visit Mrs Nightingale had caught her in her clothes cupboard, examining the labels and checking to see how many pairs of Gucci shoes Mrs Nightingale owned, which was none. Mrs Nightingale didn't own a Gucci watch, either, and evidently wasn't worth speaking to: Julia hadn't addressed one word to her in five days. She'd managed a few indirect hits, though, as when at breakfast one morning, having accepted without comment the plate of scrambled eggs Mrs Nightingale had handed her, she'd leaned on one elbow to enquire of Poppy: 'Presumably your mother will be racing at Goodwood next week?' Mrs Nightingale was damned if she'd have Julia to stay again.

'I get bored without a friend,' Poppy moaned on. Mrs Nightingale wasn't having any of that. 'You can't be bored,' she said, 'and you've got Lily.' She unwrapped a yellowing candlestick from a piece of yellowing newspaper. 'Here, take this.'

'We don't get on,' Poppy said. 'We've got nothing in common.' That was rubbish, Mrs Nightingale told her.

'It isn't rubbish. She's so moody. She never speaks – just sits and stares.'

Since the truth of this could not be denied, Mrs Nightingale changed tack:

'As a matter of fact you don't deserve to have a friend to stay.' Poppy put down the spoon she'd been tentatively rubbing with a duster and stared at her mother with her mouth open.

'Your half-term report is the worst yet,' Mrs Nightingale continued, 'and we ought to discuss it. Not now. I don't mean now. Later. This evening, perhaps, when they've gone.'

'Miss Ansell doesn't like me. It's not my fault.'

'It isn't just Miss Ansell,' Mrs Nightingale said, more in sorrow than in anger. 'No one, no one – apart from Miss Whatsername – you know, games mistress – had a good word to say about you. You won't get a single 'O' Level at this rate. Lily, on the other hand – '

'*Don't* compare me with her. She's quite different to me.'

'Different *from* me. Yes. She knows how to work, for one thing. And she reads. You never open a book.'

'I do.'

'The Beano annual. And you're *thirteen*.'

Poppy grinned sheepishly at that. 'Oh, Muzkin,' she said, and sidled up to her mother and put her arms round her waist.

'Muzkin nothing,' Mrs Nightingale said, disentangling herself. For it really was worrying. Poppy never did open a book. If ever she happened by some mischance to pick one up, she'd drop it again as soon as she'd realized her mistake. As a result of this her ignorance went wide and deep. Mrs Nightingale spent sleepless nights discussing the problem with Bone.

Liza's head appeared round the dining-room door.

'Bone's eaten the Brie, I'm afraid,' Liza said, 'so there's only mousetrap for lunch.'

'Where is she? I'll kill her!' Mrs Nightingale cried preparing to do so.

'I've already beaten her,' Liza said. 'It's my business, she's my dog.'

Not when it comes to spending millions of pounds a year on Chum and Butch and Winalot and vet's bills, Mrs Nightingale thought. Not when it comes to clearing up mountains of dog sick and dog shit. Then she's my dog. She followed Liza back to the kitchen. 'Where's Dave?' she asked crossly. 'Where's the wood?'

'He's gone to get some milk and the papers,' Liza said, knowing what her mother's reaction would be.

'*What*?'

'I asked him to go because we're out of milk and you'll want the papers so that the Hendersons can read them after lunch.'

'Has he taken my car?' Mrs Nightingale was beside herself.

'Of course he's taken your car. How else would he go?'

Mrs Nightingale hated Dave taking her car. She hated him taking it because being stuck up a track with rusty bicycles the only means of escape made her feel a prisoner. She hated him taking it because he hadn't asked permission and because she didn't trust him not to drive like a racing driver – i.e. a maniac. It was her car. She hated Dave too because he ought to have remembered what the day was. There was something wrong with him that he hadn't. Something very wrong indeed.

'He has no business to take my car,' she said, 'he'll be gone for hours.'

Liza was taking glasses out of a cupboard. 'Don't be stupid,' she said briskly. 'He'll be back in a minute. He's only gone for the papers, for God's sake. He was *trying* to be helpful.' She held a glass up to the light. 'These glasses are filthy. I'd better wash them.'

'Get up, Lily,' Mrs Nightingale was now in a state of rage and panic. Lily was lying in the dog bed on top of Bone, kissing Bone's ears. 'Get up! Have you made your bed and tidied your room?'

'You can't make a camp bed.' Lily got up reluctantly, her navy jersey angora now covered with dog hairs.

'Answer that, would you, on your way,' Mrs Nightingale snapped as the telephone rang from the drawing-room. Lily returned almost at once.

'It's Granny.She wants to talk to *you*.'

'Fuck,' Mrs Nightingale said. 'Didn't you tell her we've got people for lunch?' Lily shrugged. 'Well,go back and tell her I'm frantic – '

'I'll say,' murmured Liza, putting glasses on a tray. 'These glasses are gross – did you get them from the garage?'

' – and that I'll ring her after tea. Go *on*. Hurry.'

'Granny sounded a bit hurt,' Lily said when she came back, 'She said to tell you she was thinking about you today.'

'What for?' Liza said.

What for, Mrs Nightingale repeated to herself, what for – ? 'What can Dave be doing?' she said, 'He's been gone for hours.' She opened the oven door. The joint seemed to be sizzling satisfactorily.

'Stop flapping,' Liza said.

'Did you put garlic on the joint? And rosemary? I couldn't see any.'

'Of course. Stop flapping.'

'Poppy, you're *soaked*! Couldn't you have worn a mac?' Poppy squelched into the kitchen and dumped a collection of sodden wild flowers on the table.

'*I* was going to do the flowers,' Liza said.

'God, the gratitude you get in this place,' Poppy fingered the limp cluster. 'What are these?'

'Ladies' smocks. *Must* you do that in here?' Liza said as Poppy found an assortment of jugs and lined them up on the table. 'I'm trying to get lunch. You can't put wallflowers in with that lot,' she added in disgust.

'Why can't I?' Poppy wanted to know.

'Because they're orange, stupid.'

'Piss off. I like them. I like the *smell*.'

Mrs Nightingale left her daughters to it and took the tray of glasses into the dining-room. Perhaps Dave *had* had an accident. Perhaps, at this very moment, firemen were fighting to cut his lifeless body from the wreckage. That was all she needed. It was typical of him to put her in this position of anxiety today of all days. 'If he's alive I'll kill him,' she thought aloud, knowing that when – please God – he did walk in she'd feel nothing but relief. As she went back into the kitchen he came in by the other door, accompanied by a smell of deep frying. The Sunday papers and two cartons of long-life milk were crushed against his chest. He uncrossed his arms and unloaded their contents into the watery mess of broken stems and leaves on the kitchen table.

'Hey – mind my flowers,' Poppy said. She sniffed. 'I can smell chips.'

'Whoops. Sorry.' Dave straightened up and caught sight of his mother. 'Hi there, Marlene.' He licked his fingers, slowly and deliberately. 'Finger fuckin' good,' he said when he'd finished. There was a silence, succeeded by a snort of laughter from Liza, succeeded by another silence.

'Dave, could I have a word with you, please – ' Mrs Nightingale spoke through clenched teeth. She jerked her thumb towards the door. 'Outside.'

'Righto, Marlena.' He snatched up the *Observer* and followed his mother into the hall.

'Watch out, Dave,' Poppy sang out after him. 'You're in deep trouble, Boyo.'

'What are you so screwed-up about?' Dave asked when Mrs Nightingale, determined that they shouldn't be overheard, had shut the drawing-room door. Dave plonked himself into the nearest arm chair.

'Get up out of that chair! Put that newspaper down!' Dave got up, very slowly. 'Take that smirk off your face!' Mrs Nightingale shouted. He towered above her, shifting from one foot to the other, while his eyes examined the ceiling with interest. 'I've had you,' Mrs Nightingale went on, her voice shaking. 'I wish you weren't here. You're twenty years old. You're the only so-called man in this house. I should be able to look to you for help and support. You had no business to take my car without asking – '

'Liza said we were out of milk – '

'It's not her car. It's *mine*. And *I*'d asked you to get the wood in. That's *all* I asked you to do. All all *all*!'

'Oh come *on* – '

'I won't come on.' Mrs Nightingale's voice rose. 'You were gone for hours while everyone else was working. Did you really eat chips, by the way?'

'I was hungry, I'm a big boy,' Dave said, perhaps hoping to appeal to that need (he supposed all women had) to mother and protect huge grown men as though they were babies.

'You didn't have breakfast till ten. And it'll be lunchtime any minute. You can't have been hungry.' Dave said nothing. He was bored with this interview and showed it by jiggling his knee 'That finger business wasn't funny,' Mrs Nightingale said. 'It was disgusting. How could you, in front of Lily and Poppy?'

'Lily wasn't in the kitchen, actually,' Dave said. He started to pace about with his head down, a sure sign that he was losing his temper.

'Don't be pedantic with me, Dave.' Dave stopped pacing and swung round and pointed his finger at his mother in a threatening fashion.

'Fuck *you*,' he said. 'You're a complete hypocrite. No one in this house uses filthier language than you. It's "shit this" and "bugger that" all fucking day. We took the words in with your milk – ' There was a pause, during which Mrs Nightingale considered reminding him that the twins, at least, had been bottle-fed, but Dave was quite capable of turning this fact to his advantage, so she said nothing. 'Well, I'm sick of your dramas and panics,' he continued, warming to his theme of self-justification. 'I can't stand the atmosphere in this place. I can't *work* here. I'm going back to Leeds. My tutor didn't want me to take time off to help you, and I've missed two important lectures already.' He made for the door.

'Typical,' Mrs Nightingale said, taking care not to say 'fucking well typical' as she would normally have done. 'You can't take any sort of criticism, ever. You just shout abuse and then walk out – it's too easy. What's more, you haven't been any help to me at all. You haven't lifted a finger – '

'Mum,' – Liza's head appeared round the door as Dave reached it. He took two steps backwards – 'Shouldn't you be putting your face on? It's after twelve.'

'Go away,' Mrs Nightingale said, 'I'm talking to Dave.'

'Sounds like it. Poor Dave.' Liza's head withdrew. The door banged shut.

Mrs Nightingale and her son stood in silence, both waiting for something. Dave stared at the floor and at the front page of the *Observer* which lay at his feet. He pushed at it with the toe of one green canvas boot.

'Sorry I was rude,' he said at last without looking up.

Mrs. Nightingale gave a sigh. Dave was good at apologies – much better than she was – and sometimes indulged in them for days after a particularly bloody row, castigating himself and telling anyone who'd listen what a shit he'd been. The trouble was, the apologies changed nothing, as Mrs Nightingale had learned. They never prevented his being rude and aggressive (and unfair, she thought, *unfair*) next time round. She didn't want his apologies. She wanted him to stop the behaviour that made them necessary. She watched him now get down on his knees and take off his specs and rub them on a dirty red-and-white spotted handkerchief and put them back on his nose. He picked up the *Observer* with his left hand and then struck at it with the fist of his right.

'I'm going to kill Mrs Thatcher,' he said, 'listen to this – ' Oh dear, thought Mrs Nightingale.

Dave and newspapers did not mix. Cruise missiles, violence in inner cities, child abuse, drug abuse, vivisection, famine, rape, murder, abortion, multiple births, divorce rate, pollution, terrorism, persecution of Blacks and homosexuals, sex discrimination, unemployment, pornography, police brutality, rate capping – the stuff that newspapers were made of – were a daily cross he bore alone. 'You can't take the whole burden of the world on your shoulders,' she'd tell him when he rang from a Leeds call box desperate over the destruction of South American rain forests, or the plight of the latest hi-jack victims. 'The world has always been a terrible place,' she'd say, 'we just know more about it now because of the media. Horror used to be more *local*.' Then – since it seemed important to end on a positive note – she'd go on to remind him of ways in which the world had changed for the better, instancing the huge advances made in medicine this century (T.B. and polio virtually wiped out, infant mortality and death in childbirth negligible, etc) and reminding him that there were salmon in the Thames these days, and that people could fall into the river and swallow whole bucketfuls of its waters and not die. 'Try and get a sense of proportion,' she'd say, something she'd never managed herself. She knew that when she lectured Dave it was herself she was trying to comfort. The world was a far nastier place than it'd been when she was a child, even though there'd been a world war going on for some of that time. Far nastier.

Thinking about all this she was spared hearing Mrs Thatcher's latest pronouncement, although it was impossible to miss the passion in Dave's recital of the same. She came to when he stopped in mid-sentence, and put the paper down.

'It's the twenty-third today,' he said, 'Did you realize?'

'I know,' Mrs Nightingale said.

'Oh, Mum, I'm sorry. Why didn't you say?'

Dave, on his knees, began to rock backwards and forwards, his arms folded across his stomach. 'Poor old Dad, poor old Dad,' he said. Then he burst into tears. Mrs Nightingale got down on her knees beside her son. She put her arm round his shoulders which reeked of wet wool and chipped potatoes. She sensed that he did not want her arms round him but did not know how to extricate himself. After several minutes he blew his nose on the red-spotted handkerchief and licked at the tears which were running down his chin.

'I must get the wood in and light the fire.' He disengaged himself and got up. 'Then I'll shave. Sorry, Mum.' He gave her a pale smile. At the door he turned, and said in a sharper tone: 'But I still don't understand why you didn't *say*. And why didn't we go to church this morning – or did you, before we were up?'

'No,' Mrs Nightingale said.

'And why are the fucking Hendersons coming to lunch? You don't like them and Pa couldn't stand them. None of it makes sense.' He shook his head, spraying the room with water like a wet dog.

'Look, Dave,' Mrs Nightingale began. She explained that she hadn't asked the Hendersons, they'd asked themselves. She couldn't put them off for ever. Also she'd thought that having people to lunch might make the day easier in some way. And as for church – well, he didn't like Rite A any more than she did. It always put them into a rage, so there was no point, was there, in going.

'True,' Dave said.

It *was* true, she told him. But what she thought they might do, once they'd got rid of the Hendersons, was drive up to the churchyard and take Poppy's flowers perhaps, and put them on Daddy's grave.

Dave's eyes started to fill again. ' . . . and then go to Evensong in the Cathedral, if there's time. It'll be a proper service with proper singing and anthems and sung responses.'

'Yup. Cool.'

'All right, sweetheart?' Dave nodded and fiddled with his watchstrap, a thin piece of canvas, once red and white striped. 'I suppose you realize,' Mrs Nightingale lied, 'that when I asked you to give me a hand this week, it was just an excuse for wanting you here today. I needed you.' But perhaps it was not a lie, she thought. Perhaps, subconsciously, she had needed him.

'I'm getting the wood now,' Dave said. He peered out of a dismal mullioned window, against which a yew branch flapped in the gale. 'I think the rain's stopping.'

The kitchen when Mrs Nightingale entered it was clean and tidy, everything washed up and put away. Liza was taking off her apron.

'All done,' she said.

She was a wonder, Mrs Nightingale told her, a real star.

'Mum you must get changed, they'll be here – '

Mrs Nightingale stopped in the doorway. 'Lize – do you know what today is?'

'It's the day Daddy died,' Liza said. 'Go on, Mum, I'll come and talk to you when I've done the ice.'

The back door banged as Mrs Nightingale climbed the stairs. She could hear Dave's grunts as he humped the log baskets into the hall. It was a relief to be on her own for five minutes. She needed to be alone with Edward who – she stood on the dark landing and peered at her watch – this time two years ago had been about to leave her. Suddenly, without warning and without saying goodbye. Not even a look. Not even a pressure of the hand. She'd hated him for this, until it had dawned on her that it was inevitable. He'd been hopeless at partings. The number of times she'd driven him to Heathrow and been rewarded not with hugs and the 'I'll miss you, darlings' and 'take care of your precious selves' other people seemed to get, but with a preoccupied peck and then his backview disappearing through the barrier. 'Turn round and wave, you bugger,' she used to will him, but he never did.

'You two ready?' she called, in hopeless competition with Madness, through the twin's bedroom door. Then she opened her own. The room looked as though burglars had visited it. The drawers of both clothes chests had been wrenched out; garments spilled from them onto the floor. A brassière, its strap looped

90

round a wooden drawer knob, trailed greyly to the rug where two leather belts lay like coiled springs. Mrs Nightingale turned her gaze to the dressing table. Here unnumbered treasures drooped from every drawer and orifice. The surface of the table was littered with screws of cotton wool and with unstoppered scent bottles, from which all London, Paris and New York disagreeably breathed. A cylinder of moisturizing lotion lay on its side oozing cucumber extract into the contents of her jewel case which sat, open and empty, on the stool. Three cotton wool buds, their ends clotted with ear wax, had been placed in the china tray which normally housed Mrs Nightingale's lipsticks. Only two lipsticks remained in the tray; the rest, which had been torn apart and abandoned with their tongues protruding, were jumbled up with beads and cotton wool. Mrs Nightingale recognized her daughter Poppy's hand in all this. She opened her mouth wide in anger and despair, but no sound came. Instead, the telephone screamed from the table by her bed. When after the eighth ring no one had answered downstairs, Mrs Nightingale picked up the receiver.

'Mrs Nightingale? Mr Selby-Willis here.'

'Oh hallo, Jerry,' Mrs Nightingale said. (Fuck fuck fuck fuck fuck). 'How are you?'

'How are *you*?' Jerry Selby-Willis asked, in his best bedroom drawl.

'Well if you must know, I'm frantic. I've got people arriving for lunch any minute.'

'One normally does on a Sunday. Grania's just gone off to the station to meet our lot. I can't imagine *you* being frantic about anything – '

'It just goes to show how little – '

'When are you going to have luncheon with me?' Jerry Selby-Willis interrupted her. 'Or dinner?'

'Jerry, I've only *just* moved house – ' Mrs Nightingale began. She had accepted none of his invitations. ' Then you're in need of a nice, relaxing dinner. Tuesday. Have you got your diary there?'

'No. Look, I'm afraid I must go. I haven't got my face on – '

'I'll ring you tomorrow, from the office.'

She must remember to leave the telephone off the hook tomorrow, Mrs Nightingale thought, as she wrenched garments from hangers, tried them on, examined the result in the looking glass, and tore them off again. Or else get the children to answer the telephone and say she was out.

'I've got nothing to wear!' she wailed, as Liza came into the room.

'That looks fine,' Liza said. 'Where's your hairbrush?'

While Liza brushed her mother's hair, Mrs Nightingale perched on the dressing-table stool and searched for her blue beads.

'I can't find my blue beads,' she said, turning out another drawer.

'Poppy's wearing them,' Liza said. 'She said you said she could. Time you dyed your hair, I think, or else made with the *Grecian 2000*,' she said kindly, putting the brush down.

'I think I heard a car,' Mrs Nightingale said, 'do you think you could round everyone up and go down and tell the Hendersons I'm coming. Give them a drink.'

Alone, Mrs Nightingale looked at her watch. It was ten past one. Edward was dead. He'd been dead a full quarter of an hour. At five to one, no doubt when she'd been fending off Jerry Selby-Willis, the signal on the cardiograph had flattened into a straight line for real this time, and the bleeps had ceased. She had not kept vigil; she had not been with him, holding his hand. She sat on the stool, twisting her wedding ring round and round her finger, for comfort. When at last she lifted her head she caught her reflection in the glass and was dismayed to see how pinched and wary and closed her face had become. 'Things have got to get better,' she said aloud. 'I must make them better.' There was a little moisturizer left in the bottle. She squeezed some into her palm and rubbed it into her forehead and cheeks, into the slack skin under her chin, into her crêpey neck. 'I am alive,' she said, 'I am not old. I am a young woman. I could live for another forty years yet.' She fumbled for the blusher, and worked it into her cheeks. 'I am a *person*,' she said threateningly into the glass. 'I am me, Frances.'

There was a thundering on the stairs, followed by Dave, out of breath at the door.

'Hi, folks, it's Lamborghini time,' he hissed. 'The Hendersons are in an arriving situation.' He had not shaved, after all, but on the other hand he was not wearing his red secretary spectacles either. You could not have everything, Mrs Nightingale supposed.

'Hurry up, Marlene,' he said. 'You can't leave us alone with them.' He vanished, and then immediately reappeared. 'You should know that Mrs H. is wearing a salmon two-piece, with turquoise accessories. Tuck in.'

Mrs Nightingale grabbed a lipstick from the table and stretched her mouth into the grimace that, with her, always preceded its application. At the first pressure the lipstick, which had been broken by Poppy earlier and stuck back by her into its case, toppled and fell, grazing Mrs Nightingale's chin as it did so with a long gash of *Wicked Rose*.

# Deathcap

After I'd killed my wife I went downstairs and made myself a cup of tea. My hands shook as I spooned the tea leaves into the pot, and later, when I poured out, a few drops splashed the table-cloth, clean on that morning. But the giddiness had gone, and apart from the slight shaking I've mentioned, I have to say I felt calm – empty as the grey sky outside the window, but calm. 'It's going to be all right,' I told myself as I sat at the kitchen table, dredging the cup with a spoon (my wife had neglected to return the tea strainer to its drawer).

'It's going to be all right,' I repeated, louder this time but with perhaps a shade less conviction – for the future escaped my efforts to confront it, drifting away like the steam from my cup. As I sat there, it was the past, in random images, that began to fill up the emptiness. Here was my wife Angie on our wedding day, assisting me to cut the cake, attired in an old-fashioned navy two-piece that had belonged to her mother. Its buttons were new, purchased by my wife and sewn on by her the day before our nuptials.

'Old, borrowed, blue *and* new,' she'd said to her sister, 'that can't be bad.'

'I hope you're right, Ange, I definitely hope you're right – we all do,' Helen had said, meaning they all knew she was making a mistake.

What they were hoping for was to be able to say *I told you so* in a couple of months' time. For it could hardly work, could it – marriage between a thirty-six-year-old school teacher and a trainee bank clerk, a mere boy of nineteen?

I sat on at the table, holding my cup in both hands, my elbows resting on the table-cloth. I saw us on honeymoon, huddled in a rented cottage near Swansea. It had been so cold we'd had to take the curtains down and pile them on the bed, and no inside toilet meant that by the end of the week we'd been a rash of nettle stings acquired on nocturnal visits to the water closet at the end of the garden. I saw myself leaning over my wife's shoulder, watching her mark the exercise books she brought home every evening to the flat above the electricians we lived in the first three years of our marriage, before I got promotion. She was a tough marker, and I saw her now in the lamplight, scoring through whole paragraphs, underlining mistakes with a red biro, putting SP in the margin, or a question mark. One time, she'd written at the bottom of the page: 'This is nonsense. Come and see me about it after school.' 'Please Miss,' I'd murmured into her hair. 'Please Miss, may I come and see you after school?'

I drained my cup and got up to pour another. Through the open door I could see my wife's luggage, one small suitcase, packed and ready in the hall. On the hall shelf was her ticket to Lyme Regis. Only the day before, my wife, who eight weeks earlier had undergone a hysterectomy from which she'd been slow to recover, had caught the milkman on the front doorstep.

'I'm going away tomorrow,' she told him, 'to the seaside for a fortnight, and my husband will only require one pint every other day.'

From the hallway I'd seen the milkman replace his crate on the step and note the change of order on his pad. 'Looks like we're in for an Indian summer,' he said, slipping his pencil behind his ear. 'Should be nice at the sea.' He lifted his head and sniffed, as though he could detect salt on the breeze. 'Mornin',' he greeted me as I emerged into the sunshine and strode past him on my way to the car. At the gate I swung my briefcase in salute.

'Will you be back for tea?' my wife called out in a faint, post-operative voice.

'Thought she meant me for a moment, guv,' the milkman said,

and then we all laughed – the milkman heading towards me down the path, myself unlocking the car door, and my wife, thin and pale in her dressing-gown, on the front doorstep.

We'd bought her train ticket late that afternoon, on my return from the bank. First I'd driven her to the chemist in the High Street for some necessaries, then we'd walked the short distance to the bookshop, with a view to obtaining some paperback holiday reading. She'd hung on to my arm, and I'd had to slow up a bit. 'Silly, isn't it,' my wife confided, 'but I still feel as though I were made of cotton wool.'

In the shop she didn't seem to know what she wanted, just 'something to get me out of myself, nothing heavy.' The assistant hadn't been any use. He stayed behind the counter and gestured vaguely at the shelves. In the end my wife chose a couple of historical novels, by women authors, and a who-dunnit. 'That'll do,' she said, I read so slowly these days.'

'Half a mo,' I said, suddenly inspired, 'What about *The French Lieutenant's Woman?* Just the ticket as you're off to Lyme Regis.'

'I wasn't that keen on the film,' my wife said.

'Have you a copy of *The French Lieutenant's Woman*?' I asked the assistant who was busy reading. He came to at that, and put down *Exchange & Mart* and got off his stool and came round our side of the counter.

I'm sure we have, sir,' he said, all authority now, ignoring my frown. 'The Le Carrés are over here.'

I ask you! He didn't even have the grace to blush when I pointed out his mistake, nor again when I found the book for him – merely shrugged.

'You win some, you lose some,' he said cheerfully as he rang up the till.

'You'll lose all your customers, matey, that's for sure!' I told him, snatching the parcel and propelling my wife out of the door.

My wife was silent in the car going home. 'We'll go back via the station,' I told her, turning left instead of right out of Fish Street, 'It'll save time and bother if we get your ticket now.'

All this had happened yesterday, less than twenty-four hours ago. Thinking about it, looking for clues and portents, I realized I hadn't drunk my second cup of tea. It had gone cold and scummy and there was a fly struggling on its surface. As I tipped it down the sink, the giddiness returned, and I had to grip the taps for support. It lasted only a moment or two, a swimming, spinning sensation like the vertigo that accompanies a fear of heights, and when it subsided I was left with an urgent need to relieve myself.

Attending to the calls of nature necessitates a trip upstairs to the bathroom, passing the bedroom en route. I hastily undid my laces, removed my shoes, and then crept up the staircase in my socks, levering myself on the bannister rail as I did so. The bedroom door was just ajar. The curtains were drawn across, but even in the dim light I could see the dishevelled bed with the eiderdown half off, trailing to the floor, and a straggle of hair escaping from the pillow. Without making a sound I pulled the door to and then tiptoed along the passage to the bathroom.

Mission accomplished, I was standing before the bathroom window, chasing a sliver of soap round the wash-basin, when a movement in the garden below caught my eye. I parted the curtains and peered down. Unlatching the wicket gate in the hedge that separated our back premises, stepping through it, pausing to examine the state of our runner beans, and now, walking purposefully down our path, armed with a basket, was Pam Mason, our neighbour and a close friend of my wife's. I gave my hands a perfunctory wipe, and then crept back along the passage and down the stairs. I had reached the back door and opened it before Pam had a chance to knock.

'Saw you coming,' I said, but the words did not sound as breezy as I'd intended, and my voice sounded unfamiliar and shrill, like a woman's voice.

'I promised to give Angie these,' Pam said. She held up the basket in which I could see a sheaf of knitting patterns and some balls of peach-coloured wool. I put out my hand to take the basket, but she held on to it.

'Mind if I come in? I'd like to have a word and wish her all the best – is she all packed up?'

I hesitated for a moment, disconcerted by Pam's questions and by her gaze which had fixed itself on my feet.

'She's in the land of Nod at present,' I said, putting a finger to my lips, 'but do enter, by all means. Would you care for a cup of something?'

'Asleep?' Pam looked at her watch. 'At this hour?' She followed me through the utility room to the kitchen, and placed her basket on the formica worktop.

'Have a pew,' I said, moving nimbly to the kettle in my stockinged feet. The phone rang from the hall.

'Better answer that,' Pam said, 'or it'll wake Angie.'

It was my wife's sister on the phone, something I hadn't bargained for. 'She's just popped out, Helen,' I told her, 'for some last minute shopping – shall I get her to buzz you back?'

'Don't trouble her,' my wife's sister said, 'just remind me again the time of her train.'

'3.32,' I said, 'arriving Lyme Regis 6.29.'

Back in the kitchen, I put my shoes on, placing each foot in turn on a chair seat while I tightened the laces.

'I took the liberty of making the coffee while you were on the phone,' Pam said, watching me, 'but I didn't sugar yours.'

'Cheers,' I said. I dropped two sugar lumps in the cup, and then sat down opposite her, at the table.

'What's up with Angie?' Pam said, plucking a piece of fluff from the beige cardigan she always seemed to be wearing whenever I saw her. 'I thought you said she was still in bed?'

'Correct,' I said, 'but Helen would've taken on if I'd told her that. Angie didn't sleep last night,' I explained, 'and I knew she'd never manage the journey without any shuteye, so I advised her to stay put. She took a sleeping tablet at six.'

'You've had a worrying time, Ken, haven't you?' Pam's tone was quite pleasant for once (for I knew she'd never liked me. It showed in hundreds of ways, but mostly it was her tone of voice –

brisk, offhand – whenever she addressed a remark in my direction. And she never would look at my face, always to the left or right of it. I used to mind. I used to say to Angie in the early days: 'Your friend Pam doesn't go a bundle on me,' – but I'd long since given up caring). I shrugged, to indicate Yes, I had had a worrying time, but I could handle it. Pam leaned towards me across the table.

'No, I mean it Ken, you need a holiday after all you've been through. It's a shame you can't go with her.'

I said nothing. Until the operation, my wife and I had never spent a night apart in thirteen years of marriage. I'd wanted to go with her to Lyme, even though it meant a fortnight of Helen, but I'd taken my holiday, all of it and more, when she'd come out of hospital, so that I could look after her.

' . . . she's on the mend now, I'm sure,' Pam was saying, after something I hadn't caught, 'even if she isn't picking up *quite* as fast as Doctor said she would.'

Silly bitch, I thought, you silly, silly bitch. 'She's lost over two stone,' I said flatly, and I remembered the way my wife used to be, well-covered, not to say plump – and energetic, always on the go. Suddenly I saw the bed upstairs, with that untidy hair, my wife's hair, on the pillow. I put my head down quickly and took a swig of coffee.

'You okay, Ken?' Pam said when I looked up. 'Perhaps I shouldn't tell tales out of school, but Angie's really concerned about you, you know. She says you haven't been yourself this last couple of weeks. She's afraid the strain's telling on you, that you may be heading for some sort of, well, how shall I put it, breakdown, or something.'

I've killed my wife, I told Pam silently, I've killed Angie.

'Nothing wrong with me,'I said, 'I'm right as rain.'

Pam pushed herself up from the table. 'Well, I'd best be off now,' she said, 'seeing as Ange is not available. We're going over to Mother's today, even Bob. Makes a change.'

Pam was a golf widow at weekends, I knew, but I wasn't going to say anything supportive. If she and Bob didn't enjoy the close relationship Angie and I had always shared, it was hardly my fault. Or my business. I got up to see her to the door, but in the utility room she stopped and turned round and looked at me, actually looked at me, and her face was bright red.

'I feel I should tell you, Kenneth,' she said, 'that Bob and I reckon you've been a good husband to Ange over this operation. I don't mind admitting I never thought you'd stick with her, and I told Angie as much. Have an affair with him by all means, if you must, I told her, but don't marry him. Okay, so he needs a mother at the moment, and you fit the bill, but soon as he grows up and knows what he's missing, he'll be off, you'll see – '

'I'd never leave her,' I said, swallowing hard, as though the action itself might in some way aid the digestion of Pam's unpalatable home truths. 'She knows I'd never leave her.'

'That's what I'm trying to tell you,' Pam said. 'I was wrong. And all those flowers you bought her – ' she laid her hand on my arm, and her pebble eyes were misty ' – this place looked like a florist's shop when she came out of hospital.'

A florist's shop, I thought, and immediately I saw the girls in Murphy's off the High Street, snipping and tying and stripping stems of their leaves. Only this time the girls' deft fingers were weaving the flowers, white lilies and freesias, into wreaths, and pressing them into crosses shaped from damp moss.

'Cheerio, then,' Pam was saying. 'If there's anything you need while Angie's away, give us a shout. Oh, I'd better have that basket back – ' After I'd fetched it, I stood and watched her until she was halfway down the path.

I came inside, and washed up the tea and coffee cups and tidied the kitchen. I swept the floor and emptied the rubbish bin into a plastic sack and put the sack outside the back door. Then I went through to the living-room. I vacuumed the carpet and emptied the ashtrays and dusted the ornaments and photographs. I blew on the plastic dahlias and crysanths the kids in Angie's class at the Middle School had sent round after the operation. They'd stuck the flowers into a birch log, polished in carpentry by one of the boys, which bore the message *An Autumn Bouquet* in burnt-on lettering round the base. All this time I kept a weather eye on Bob's Sierra, parked in the road. Eventually they came out, and Bob mustered his troops down the path – Pam in front with their two youngest, Jimmy and John, and bringing up the rear Stephen, their skinny fifteen-year-old, shouldering a fishing rod. I was glad my wife couldn't witness this family outing, too good to be true, like a scene from a telly commercial. She'd wanted children, they were part of her decision to marry me, I couldn't kid myself they weren't – and all I'd given her were four miscarriages. 'I'm too old, Kenny,' she'd said after the last one, six years ago, 'I'm just too old. You should've married someone younger.' But I hadn't wanted children – except to please her – and I'd never wanted someone younger, only Angie.

I stood back from the window and watched as Bob swivelled round to check the passenger doors. He wound the window down, pulled on his seat belt, and the car drew away from the kerb and out of view. Even though I'd been waiting for them to go, it wasn't a good feeling when they'd gone, knowing there was no one next door, no human creature beyond the wall that separated their lives from ours. As I stacked the cleaning things in the cupboard under the stairs, I pictured their silent rooms: unmade beds in the poky boxrooms the boys made do with; abandoned toys on the living-room floor; congealing breakfast dishes piled in the sink. In the hall I stood still for a moment, one hand on the bannisters, looking up the dark stair-well listening. There was no sound. I collected my car keys from the ledge, stepped round my wife's small tartan suitcase, and went out through the front door.

I left the Saturday car washers and shoppers and drove away from the centre of town to the wooded residential hills on its outskirts. When I reached the Forestry Commission land bordering the golf course, I backed the car on to the verge, exchanged my shoes for boots, and then began walking up a muddy track overhung with yellowing silver birches. I'd never walked there before without

Angie, and it seemed strange, and lonely, just as I'd known it would be. I tried to concentrate on the problem, the problem of how and where I was going to dispose of her.

The question had come up before, more than once, on this very walk. We'd be strolling along arm in arm, chatting about this and that, when suddenly I'd stop and say: 'If I did away with you, here, now, no one would ever find out.'

'Yes they would,' my wife would argue. 'We passed that man with the Great Danes earlier – he'd remember seeing us. Like as not you'd meet him again on the way back, and he'd wonder where I'd got to. Then, when he'd seen the headlines – '

'I could do it on a day we hadn't met anyone,' I'd insist, parting the rhododendrons to point at the jungle beyond, where gorse, heather, bracken, holly bushes, infant oaks and Christmas trees all struggled to free themselves from the stranglehold of ivy and bramble. 'I'd encourage you to explore that undergrowth – on the pretext of searching for rare orchids or edible fungi – then I'd kill you and bury you there.'

'Tracker dogs,' Angie'd say, unimpressed, 'there are such things as tracker dogs. You'd never get away with it. Anyway, husbands are always the first suspects when wives go missing. Even good husbands.'

On one occasion we'd come across a Deathcap, half-hidden in the bracken. 'Look at that,' I said, decapitating it with my toe. 'Look at those evil white gills. I could slice this and fry it for your breakfast, mixed in with mushrooms. It would seem like an accident.'

'Not if you didn't die too, it wouldn't,' Angie said. 'Anyhow, as you know, I don't eat a cooked breakfast.'

'Supper then,' I went on, relentless. I had a morbid imagination, my wife told me. I should have been a crime writer or an actor, not a bank official.

'Perhaps all this nonsense is a cover-up,' she said, squinting at me through her thick hair. 'Perhaps you really do want to get rid of me.'

'That's it, my dear,' I murmured – and Vincent Price couldn't have played it more sinister – 'it's a double bluff.' I placed my fingers round her neck and squeezed.

'Don't,' my wife said, pulling away from me, 'don't.' She hated her neck being touched.

In the car going home she asked me why I did it, why I kept on doing it. It was just a game, I told her, I'd played it with my brother when we were small, it was only a game.

'No, seriously, Kenny, I want to know. I used to think it was funny, but you do it too often.'

'Okay,' I said, inventing fast to pacify her. 'You know what it's like at the top of a ladder, or on the edge of a cliff, when you're frightened of falling? What you want to do most, so that you can't fall, is jump. Right? Well, under this macho exterior is a little lad who's constantly afraid he'll lose you, that you'll go off with somone else or die – so a part of him wants to kill you first, to prevent it happening. Q.E.D.' I laughed. I was pretty pleased with this solution, trotted out like that, unpremeditated – nonsense of course, yet plausible enough in all truth. But my wife didn't seem to be, and she didn't laugh, as I thought she would.

'I don't know, Ken,' she said as we drew up in front of the house, 'but what I do know is I'm fed up with that game, so could we give it a miss for a bit? It's beginning to give me the creeps.'

Thinking about all this, I found I'd walked further than I'd intended to, and I turned round and started back. I'd met no one, unusual for a Saturday. As I walked, I examined the woodland, hoping for a suitable burial ground to present itself. Burying my wife wasn't going to be easy, it occurred to me. I wouldn't be able to carry, or drag her far, and driving the Cavalier any distance up the track was impossible because of the mud. And supposing I didn't get stuck, there was the problem of tyre marks, no doubt easily identifiable. Husbands were always the first suspects, my wife had said, even good husbands. Would the neighbours, would anyone, testify to my being a good husband? The milkman, maybe, and okay, so Pam seemed to have come round to me at last, but there was a backlog of thirteen years' mistrust she'd be bound to revert to. 'Never liked him,' I heard her say between sobs, 'never trusted him, the bastard.' Then there were all those loose ends I'd given no proper thought to: How was I to get my wife's body out of the house and into the car without being seen? How could I be certain to get her out of the car and into the wood? I saw the courtroom at the local assizes, and myself in the dock staring straight ahead, my knuckles whitening on the rail.

You say you put her on a train, the 3.32 for Lyme Regis?
Yes.
Yet no one remembers seeing either of you at the station, and the ticket collector recalls no one answering your wife's description on the train.
I put her on the train.
How do you account for the fact that the tickets you say you purchased for your wife on the evening of Friday, the twenty third, was never handed in at Lyme Regis?
All I know is, I put her on the train.
And that she never arrived at her sister's house, where she was expected?
I don't know.
Perhaps you would care to explain to the jury why you told your neighbours that your wife had telephoned from her sister's on the evening of the twenty-fourth, to say that she'd arrived safely and was settled in . . . ?

I began to sweat then. It was dark in the wood, the sky overcast, ready to rain, and I walked faster, keeping my head down in order to avoid the brackish puddles in the ruts. I didn't see them until I was almost upon them – two tweedy crones with walking sticks, and an overweight sealyham nosing in the bracken. I kept going, not slackening my pace at all, and they moved to the bank as I approached and leant on their sticks, waiting for me to pass. I knew they were staring at me. As I drew level, one of them said something I couldn't catch.

I sat in the car for a long time, leaning my head on the steering wheel, with my eyes closed. I tried to focus my mind on Angie, on our past and my future, but I couldn't fix on anything. When the rain started, in a cloudburst, pummelling the roof and bonnet, cascading down the windscreen with the force of an automat car wash, I switched on the engine and the wipers, and drove home.

At the front gate I stopped, and stood still in the rain, and stared up at the house and saw it as a stranger might. It looked solid and normal, an ordinary semi like its neighbours – half orange brick, half stained pebbledash; green windows, green down pipes and guttering; a clematis (*Jackmanii*, I'd given Angie for her fortieth) strung over the porch. Yet as I stared, the house faded to a black and white photograph, to smudged newsprint with an arrow and a caption. I clicked the gate shut and walked up the path.

'Some Indian summer,' my wife said. She was dressed in the blue paisley frock I'd bought her to go on holiday, and had her back to me, bent over the stove. The ridges of her spine showed clearly through the thin wool. 'Where'd you get yourself to, Ken?' she said. 'Do you realize what the time is? You did say you'd wake me at one, remember.'

'Angie,' I heard a voice say. It was my voice, or a tape recording of my voice. 'Angie – '

She turned round then. 'What is it, Kenny? What's happened?'

I knew, a part of myself knew, that something had to be said, that explanations were required. But I'd gone too far with it this time. I couldn't get back. Even when she came over to me, it wasn't me who stood there, hands stiffly at his sides, but a dummy, just someone who looked like me.

From a long way off I watched her take the dummy's hands in hers and chafe them. She put her arms round his waist and held him.

'You can tell me, Kenny,' she said, 'you can tell me. You can tell Ange.' And very gently she laid her head against his chest and kept it there, as though listening for a heart beat.

# TALES FROM THE SPARE ROOM

Whenever they are invited to, they play cards with the maids in the maids' sitting-room.

Alice has got the Queen, Barbara says, pointing a finger at Alice who retreats into the sofa clutching her cards close to her face, so that Barbara shan't see them.

Barbara leans across and tweaks a card from Alice's hand. She looks at it and pouts and pulls her bottom lip and then raises her eyes to the ceiling in what seems to be despair; and then she slots the card into her own hand and spreads the cards into a fan. Mollie and Lucy, on the other side of the table, and on chairs, snigger. Hee hee, Barbara's got it now, Lucy says. Hee hee hee.

Fooled yer, Barbara says. She whips two cards from her fan and slaps them face up on the oilcloth, and sure enough she has a pair – two threes, hearts and spades.

Barbara is always fooling them. She is the sharp one of the maids, and as unlike Mollie, her sister and elder by two years, as it's possible to be. Barbara is short, not more than five foot. She has a round, pimply face and small features; her eyes are grey and sly, her no-colour hair is scraped back from her forehead. Because of her sharpness and her grating and sarcastic remarks, her singing voice comes as a surprise. She sings 'Open the door, Richard' (her young man's name is Dick) and 'Give Me Five Minutes More' and 'I Surrender, Dear' very sweetly when she cleans the bathrooms and the stairs.

Mollie is perhaps two inches taller. She hasn't got a young man (which is strange because she is prettier than Barbara), and she hasn't got spots. Her dark hair waves and curls round her oval face; her cheeks are red, her eyes brown. Mollie's eyes fill easily with tears. A sad song, a baby in a pram, a bunch of primroses – and Mollie's eyes brim and she dabs them with a drenched handkerchief.

More embarrassing even than her tears is her habit of hugging and kissing them. Each time they come to stay at Grandmother's house, she is waiting in the hall when they arrive – hands clasped together, lips parted, face pink and radiant in its halo of curls. Oooh, aren't they lovely, aren't they grand, Mollie says in a sort of gasp; and she grabs them in turn and lifts them off the ground and covers their eyes, their cheeks, their mouths, with kisses and tears. She presses their faces to her bosom so they can't breathe; she murmurs Darling, Sweetheart, My Love into their hair. It is terrible, but there is no way of avoiding it.

Even though experience has taught them she is not to be trusted, they prefer Barbara and Barbara's style. She takes no part in the welcome ceremony. If she happens to be in the hall, she stands on her own by the stairs, hand on hip, tapping a black shoe and looking the other way. When she does look at them, her expression is cool; if she does speak, her words are brief and uncomplimentary:

What a great fat thing you are now, Lucy – couldn't get me arms round you if I wanted. Which I don't. Look at Alice, dressed up to kill. Quite the little London lady, aren't we – eh?

Barbara calls them Southern Spivs and Foreigners. She mimics the way they pronounce bath and path. When she's in a bate she says they're toffee-nosed. If either of them unthinkingly begins a sentence 'I really think' or 'Actually, I', Barbara will pounce: Oh I *rarely* think, don't yoou? *A*ctually, my deah – and she blows smoke rings at the ceiling, transferring her cigarette from its normal position (between index finger and thumb) to the one (between index finger and second) film stars and nobs use. When Barbara mocks them, Mollie's eyes fill and she touches her sister's arm: Don't Barb – it's not their fault, poor loves – and then she turns to them and chats about her and Barb's mother who is a widow and lives in a terraced cottage down by the railway line; or she asks about London, where she and Barb have never been. Is it much bigger than Liverpule? What are the shops like, like? Is there a Marshall's? Bigger than the one in Lord Street?

They do not love the maids, but they are fascinated by them, especially Barbara. They do not love their grandmother, whose house this is and has always seemed to be though their grandfather bought it, and though until two years ago he was alive and going daily on the train to his sack business in Bootle. When they think of him they think of his pipes and wiry hair and middle parting, his habit of changing red bedroom slippers for black shoes in the dining-room after breakfast; they remember the way he – sitting at the head of the table beneath his boardroom likeness on the wall – ate that breakfast; chomping so hard they feared he might dislocate his jaw, while grease from his bacon and egg ran in shiny, interesting rivulets down his navy blue chin; blotting his chin with a stiff-as-card napkin, before chomping his toast and marmalade. Grandfather left early and returned late, and in the evenings and at weekends was protected from them by Grandmother (Don't disturb your Grandfather!) so they never saw much of him at all. Grandfather is dead, and they miss him, but they feel he can't have gone far: his check caps and smelly mackintoshes – so long they almost graze the slopped water from the dogs' drinking bowls on the tiled floor – still hang in the porch; his walking sticks and canes and golf clubs still clutter the stick rack.

They do not love their grandmother. There is only one person in her house they love: Edie, who came to look after their own mother when she was a baby and never got away. Edie is housekeeper, cook (since Kate left in a huff), chauffeur (since Thomas left in the war) and slave to Grandmother's whims. And she does everything for them. She washes and irons their clothes, she gets them up and puts them to bed. She takes them on the train to the cinema in Southport and to the theatre in Liverpool. She drives them to the Village and buys them sweets and comics and drawing paper and pencils; she walks them to the shore, and on the endless journey back (between grey asparagus fields and wind-bitten pines), she carries their wet bathing things. She reads to them by the hour, although they are, as Grandmother says, great girls of eight and nearly ten and can read for themselves. When she dozes off, which she always does (her head falls on her chest, her spectacles mist up, she snores), they prod her awake and make her carry on.

Edie is tall and big-boned. She has a high, receding forehead, a big nose, big eyes – very dark brown behind her specs – a big mouth and big teeth. Her hands (the gloves they gave her one Christmas wouldn't pull on at all) and feet are man-sized, her bosom a pillow whose weight of feathers collects just above the waist. Edie wears pale silky blouses with tucks and pleated fronts and little collars, under which she pins a cameo or pearl tie-pin. Even when the weather's boiling, she wears a cardigan – voluminous, and buttoned below the pillow with three buttons. She wears loose skirts of soft wool and elasticated knickers that reach almost to the knee; thick stockings, through which, when she sits down (not often, she's always on the go) they can see the ridge of her support bandages. For Church and for expeditions to Town, Edie wears a hat – felt, with a wide brim and a bow at the side, secured by a hat pin. Surprisingly for an unfrivolous person, she loves hats. Sometimes she says to them: Do you like my new hat, dears? and they stand on tiptoe and examine it from all sides and say, Yes we do, but the new hat is the same as her old one, the same as all her other hats. When Edie wakes them in the morning she wears her old dressing-gown, which is a man's and thick and heavy as a carpet.

Edie never alters – how old is Edie? If they ask, she is ninety-nine next birthday, dear. Has Edie ever been in love? That would be telling, Duck. Edie does everything that servants do, but she is not a servant. She never has a day off. Also, she calls Grandmother Mummy, though she is not Grandmother's daughter, and not young enough to be. Grandmother calls Edie Nurse, a cold starched title that does not suit her, and treats her badly, bullying her at mealtimes and bossing her. Edie never answers back. While Grandmother's blows fall, she sits in silence, staring out through the thick glass of her spectacles and the window, or at her plate. If Lucy asks, Why is Granny so horrible to you? Edie says, Oh I don't know, Duck – she has her problems, I daresay, and changes the subject and gets out the ironing board.

Edie gossips about no one, has no small talk, keeps her thoughts to herself. She talks to the cocker spaniels, she calls them Old Dear, Old Darling, Old Lady while she defleas their coats and untangles their ears with a steel comb. After breakfast she feeds the spaniels with Radio malt kept for that purpose in the nursery on a curtained-off shelf. The malt falls from the spoon on to the first finger of Edie's left hand, she spins the spoon and the malt winds round the finger like a bandage. The dogs have a finger of malt each. With their tongues they pull and tug at the bandage, and the malt enters their mouths in long strings, like rubber bands. This happens every morning, after bedmaking, after going to the lavatory, and it is very interesting to watch.

It is now, just about now, that Grandmother comes to the nursery. She huffs and puffs through the door; she blows out her cheeks; she sits heavily in the rocking chair; she leans back and rocks; she stares around her in disapproval. She has come to order the shopping. Edie makes a list and Grandmother huffs and puffs and blows out her cheeks. Grandmother is ugly and her ugliness is made worse by all the huffing and puffing. Does she know she does it? If she could see herself, would she? She leans back in her chair and crosses and recrosses her legs, examining her ankles, twisting them round. She is proud of her ankles and her calves and her small feet. Her clothes cupboard contains hundreds of pairs of shoes, all from Raynes, all new-looking, all with tissue paper crushed into their toes. Grandmother judges people by their extremities. If asked her opinion of so-and-so, she will answer: Pretty ankles – i.e. Yes – or Ugly calves – i.e. No. It is as well she doesn't judge people by their stomachs. Her own is a barrel that gurgles and heaves as she rocks.

What are the girls going to do today, Nurse? Grandmother asks Edie, puffing and rocking. If she addresses them directly, it's You girls, if indirectly, The girls. Grandmother doesn't like girls. Men (sons-in-law are the exception) are gods, boys heroes, girls nothing and good for nothing. Girls have no brains, no talents, no virtues. Grandmother has two sons and four daughters, four grandsons and six grand-daughters, but you would never guess this from the snapshots of curly-headed heroes she keeps by her bed, or from the studio portraits of uniformed gods that stand on the piano. Grandmother doesn't conceal her prejudice or bother to defend it. Example: Alice and Lucy are good at drawing and painting; they do it all the time, they've won prizes, they fill a drawing book a week. If they take their drawing books to Grandmother for her inspection, she flips the pages without looking or stopping. Handing them back without comment, she then praises the efforts of their cousin Robert who, as everyone knows, can't draw for toffee. (Once, when their drawing books were full, and Edie busy in the kitchen, they went to Grandmother and asked her for threepence each for a new one; and Grandmother said, Why should I pay out good money for your scribbles? and turned on her Raynes high heel.)

Example 2: On one occasion, when Robert – at that time a shaven-headed thug of six – was over for tea, he hit Alice on the head with one of Grandfather's golf clubs he'd taken from the porch. The blow was intentional; it knocked Alice out and produced a large bump on her temple, but it was Robert who cried. While Alice was left for dead (until Edie came, summoned from the fruit cage by Lucy), Grandmother took the bellowing hero on to her lap and kissed and comforted him and fed him liquorice allsorts from a paper bag.

Grandmother must, presumably, have been a girl herself once. So why doesn't she like girls?

When Grandmother asks Edie in that snide way (which implies they are lazy good-for-nothings) what the girls are going to do today, they want to ask: What are *you* going to do today, Granny?

They know what they will be doing. Shopping with Edie, drawing, reading (the bound volumes of *Little Folks* and *The Girls' Own Annual*; the Red, Green and Violet Fairy Books); walking the dogs; quick-stepping to Geraldo and Jack Payne and Roy Fox (on the radiogram in the Big Room); lining up lead soldiers and lead nurses and stretcher bearers; staging a drama in the toy theatre (a model of the Liverpool Playhouse, with working lights and scenery and an orchestra pit): staging a drama in the dolls' house (a model of Grandmother's house, even to the motor cars in the garage and the petrol pump outside it); dressing up – as pirates (clothes and jewels from the dressing up chest on the landing); building card houses and brick houses; playing snakes and ladders and ludo (with Edie); playing Old Maid (with the maids). And in summer the list is longer. In summer they can add riding the cranky bikes that belonged to their aunts when they were young; knocking up on the red tennis court; paddling and bathing in the sea. (Or, if the sea is too far out, which it very often is – a thin smear between the sand and the sky – shrimping in pools on the ribbed sand). They will be plunging their hands for frogs in any one of five lily ponds; jumping off the stone balls that surmount the terrace wall; eating their way through hot houses and vegetable gardens and plum orchards. They know what they will be doing. What will Grandmother be doing?

Grandmother will be sitting and rocking, if not in the nursery upstairs, in the drawing-room downstairs, if not in the drawing-room, in the morning-room, if not in the morning-room, in the summer house. Or, should the day be really hot and sunny, she will be found under the awning of the swing seat on the terrace, swinging and perhaps reading. (And that – apart from loading the bird-table and feeding the red squirrels and the goldfish – is all Grandmother seems to do.) When Grandmother reads, she holds the book like a shield in front of her face and moves her head from side to side and mutters the words aloud. She reads the same books over and over again – *A Little Green World* is the title of one of them. As Edie coaxes the tea trolley over the crazy paving (the maids are off duty till six) and unstacks the brown-spotty tea service cups and plates, Grandmother goes on reading. Alice drags a teak table to the swing seat, Lucy jumps to with a cup of tea and a plate of sandwiches, but Grandmother doesn't say thank you. She stretches a hand for a sandwich without looking up from the page, and goes on muttering. Grandmother is rude.

Grandmother is mad. It must be madness that brings her, in corsets and petticoat, into the spare room where they sleep. (They don't sleep; they lie awake till early light, reading and discussing the madness of Grandmother.) She comes at bedtime, or after lunch when they are resting on their beds. She huffs into the room and leans against the clothes cupboard, or on her elbows over the mahogany foot of the nearest bed. She massages the back of her left hand with the fingertips of her right. Her shoulders are grooved with pink shoulder straps, three or four to each shoulder. Edie comes to the spare room to tuck them up (they lock their arms round her neck; they won't let her go) and draw back their curtains in the morning; to say, Sweet dreams, darlings, or Time to get up, Lucy old duck; Edie comes to take away their dirty clothes or bring them clean ones, to help them make their beds. Grandmother comes for one purpose only: to tell lies about her eldest daughter (their mother) and her daughter's husband (their father). Grandmother tells them their mother is a hussy and irresponsible; that she has abandoned them and gone off to America because she does not love them and can't be bothered to look after them. She says their father is a fortune hunter who married their mother for her money; that he is idle; that he is dull; that he is too clever by half; that there is bad blood in his family; and that she could tell them a thing or two . . . .

If they lie still and shut their eyes and ears and say nothing, she eventually goes away, banging the door behind her. But she is always back. They count to twenty and watch the doorknob and it turns, and there she is again, in the doorway, huffing. And another thing – she begins, and goes on and on and on. She may leave and return half-a-dozen times to tell more and worse lies about their parents; or she may stand huffing but without speaking, just inside the door, one hand on the doorknob. If one of them (Lucy is the braver) sits up and shouts, How dare you say such wicked lies about our parents? How dare you? Why do you do it? Why? Grandmother closes her puffy eyes and smiles a secret, horrible smile. Or she shakes her fist at them and turns on her heel.

Can witches ever be fat? If so, Grandmother is a witch. Her loathing of cats, which amounts almost to fear (she will not have one in the house; the stray kitten Lucy found on the shore was banished within the hour), would seem to discount this, but there's a tiger on the wall of the main staircase, and a leopard stretched out on the carpet in the hall. And the terrace reeks of catmint, it grows between the paving and in every crevice of the wall. In any case, Grandmother does have a familiar of sorts – a Maltese terrier called Clarence. Clarence is a shivering whingeing piece of fluff, but the worst aspect of him is his smell. He smells, he stinks, of wee. This is because, when he widdles, he balances on both front legs in a handstand, so that his body and back legs go vertically into the air. Naturally the wee runs down his stomach, and as he wees a lot his underside is permanently yellow. Grandmother doesn't seem to notice the stain or the smell, or the dark and damp twist of hair at the end of his thing. She keeps him with her, on her lap in a rocking chair, or nestled beside her in the cushions of the swing seat. She hand-feeds him his dinner, a sickening mess of boiled rabbit and chicken and sodden, baked bread. He is fussy, of course, and shivers and turns his nose away, and she has to coax and beg him. If he dares to escape, she huffs from room to room looking and calling: Clarrie, Clarrie, Clarrie, come to Mother, precious boy.

Grandmother has no taste. She worships the disgusting Clarence and ignores the spaniels who, if anyone leaves a gate open, risk no dinner and a beating to spend the day rabbiting in the pinewoods beyond the golf course.

Grandmother has no taste, but she is always talking about Taste. Taste is to do with shoes and dress stuffs, and also with carpets and curtains and chair covers. Grandmother is houseproud, she likes everything just so, and she has a thing about loose covers. Loose covers? Loose covers may be all right in their way, nothing wrong with loose covers, but not something to get worked up about. Grandmother gets very worked up about them. She leans back in the drawing-room sofa (blue-grey roses, green leaves on a white ground) and strokes its loose-covered arm. Come here, girls, she says, and feel these beeauuutiful loose covers – She does the same thing with curtains – flowered chintz in every room of Grandmother's house. Look, girls, she says, holding them out like skirts from the window, They're lined and interlined, beeauutifully made. You'll go a long way before you see curtains as beautiful as these. Or she bends down (not an easy feat for her) and pats the carpet. Puuure wool Wilton, she says. Come and feel it girls, puure puure wool . . . Grandmother's obsession brings her into the nursery where they are drawing or playing ludo, where Edie is washing their pants in the marble basin beside the window. She huffs and puffs through the door with a roll of something under her arm, and unravels it on to their drawing books or the ludo board. This material is very expensive, she declares, holding a corner of it to her cheek. Look at it, girls, feel it. (She makes them pinch and stroke it). One day – she says with an important pause – You may be lucky enough to own material of this quality . . . After she's gone (very suddenly and huffily, bored perhaps with their lack of enthusiasm), Lucy will lift a corner of the tablecloth and hold it to her cheek. Look at this, girls, she'll says, it's puure, puure gingham. One day you may be lucky enough to own . . . Very naughty, Duck, Edie says, straightening up from the basin, her arms soapy to the elbows. *Very* naughty. But when they shriek and roll around and clutch themselves, Edie laughs too. There's no malice in Edie's laughter. It's the best noise in the world.

Grandmother is unfair. Don't tell tales, she says, should they complain that one of their hero cousins (over for tea) has pinched or punched or hit them on the head with a croquet mallet. But should the hero tell tales on them, they're sent supperless to the spare room. That'll teach you to bully your dear little cousin, Grandmother says. It's not fair, they grumble, but Grandmother has an answer to everything. Life isn't fair, she says. Whoever said it was?

Grandmother breaks all the rules, the rules for living and behaviour that she has laid down. You can't get out of life what you don't put in, she's always telling them, but what does she put in, exactly? Let your meat stop your mouth, she orders when they chatter at lunch, yet she herself talks incessantly, and with her mouth full, a muttered monologue of complaint, addressed to everyone and no one. Sitting in silence while Grandmother mutters on, they may catch Barbara's eye (the maids wait at table and between courses stand either side the fireplace) and if they do, Barbara will wink and pull faces at them. When Grandmother isn't looking, she pulls faces at Grandmother, and sticks her tongue out before resuming a demure posture, eyes cast down, hands folded on her apron.

Grandmother is superstitious. Stop that Cornishman drowning! she barks if anyone accidentally knocks a glass at table; and the culprit hastily touches the rim to silence the ring and save the Cornishman from his fate.

Grandmother is mean. Get me a quarter of pontefract cakes and a quarter of liquorice allsorts, will you, Nurse, she orders as they leave for the village, but she keeps her sweet ration in her bedroom and never shares it.

Once a week Grandmother accompanies them on the shopping trip. She wears a hat (velour, veiled) and sits in the passenger seat of the Hillman with a basket of empty cider bottles on her knee. Stop at Dean's, Nurse, she orders, which is where Edie is going anyway. At Dean's, which is the grocers, Edie gets out and they get out, and Grandmother stays in the car with her basket. Dean's smells of bacon and coffee. Edie stands at the counter reading out her list, and Mrs Dean finds all the items from the shelves and licks her pencil to make it blacker and writes everything down in the invoice book. As soon as Edie enters the shop, Mr Dean peers through the window, and if he sees Grandmother in the car he drops whatever he's doing and abandons whoever he's serving and hurries out to her. Grandmother winds down the window and Mr Dean bows before her, his hands clasped to the chest of his green button-through overall. How are you today, Mrs Moss? he says, and Grandmother's puffy face explodes in smiles. She nods and chats and tosses her head. She laughs in a girlish way. This performance is repeated everywhere they go. Grandmother stays in the car, and Mr Taylor, Mr Cross, Mr Bower and Mr Darbyshire all leave their businesses to pay court to her. And she is charming to them all.

Only at the wine merchants is this pattern broken. Rimmer's is not in the High Street, and does not look like a shop. It's a tall brick house in an ordinary road of tall brick houses. The Hillman jerks to a halt outside the gate, and Edie goes round and opens the passenger door for Grandmother, and then Grandmother, on her own with the basket, huffs and puffs up the path and the steps and vanishes through the front door. They wait in the car for what feels like an hour (Edie taps the steering wheel and looks at her watch), and eventually Grandmother reappears all smiles, with Mr Rimmer beside her carrying the basket which is heavy now because the cider bottles are full.

Shopping is quicker when Grandmother doesn't come, and more enjoyable. They can chew their way from shop to shop because Edie buys them peppermint lumps at Darbyshires, and they are treated like royalty everywhere they go. These are Mrs Moss's little granddaughters from the big house, Mrs Dean or Mrs Darbyshire will announce to the other customers, and the other customers gasp and stare and pass admiring remarks, as though Alice and Lucy were the Princesses Elizabeth and Margaret Rose.

Why is Grandmother so important? Is it because she was married to Grandfather, who was a very rich man? Or because her house is so large? It is enormous, but there are other large houses in that very long road. It does have special features: it is the only one with a hard tennis court and orchards; and it is the nearest to the shore. Outside Grandmother's gate the metalled road gives up and a flatly cobbled, cindered and sandy track takes over. Day-trippers from Liverpool to the sea stop here, and put down their spades and nets and hoist themselves on to the wall or the stone balls of the gateposts to get a view – for Grandmother's garden is the most splendid for miles. If the gate is, unusually, open, the trippers may even venture inside and stand on the white gravel and gaze at the blazing borders and ornamental trees and striped lawns, at the terrace where the lady of the house and her family are (self-consciously, for they feel like a tableau) having tea. Shut the gate now, girls, Grandmother orders when the day-trippers at last back out of the drive, still gazing and exclaiming. (Surprisingly, Grandmother never tells the trippers to go away. She calls out Good afternoon, and waves graciously from the swing seat and beams at them from under her sun hat).

Not many invited visitors come to Grandmother's house. Perhaps it's because she doesn't like women that Grandmother has so few friends. Once in a blue moon a visitor does come (for tea always, never for lunch or dinner), but whatever it is between them, it doesn't seem like friendship. The visitor is always very polite to Grandmother and agrees with everything she says in a way friends generally don't, and calls her Mrs Moss and not Dilys, which is Grandmother's first name.

Is Grandmother lonely? Does she miss the time (the photograph albums in the morning room record) when the terrace steps were ranked with young men waving cricket bats, and girls with tennis racquets and frizzy perms (can that one in the eyeshade be their mother?), when the drive was chock-a-block with Morgans and MGs?

Does she miss her children after all?

Does she, after all, miss Grandfather?

Sometimes when they come across Grandmother rocking and muttering, they find the muttering is weeping. If they can, they creep away before she's seen them – if not, she collars them. Come here darlings, she says – darling a word normally reserved for grandsons and for Clarence. She makes them sit at her knee. She imprisons their hands. She tells them their Grandfather was a great and good man, a wonderful man, a brilliant man. He was the best husband, the best father, the best grandfather who ever lived. Their grandfather was – they must remember this, they must never forget it – a saint. There aren't many saints in this world, but he was one of them. A saint, do they understand? Their grandfather was a SAINT.

What is all this? Grandfather was a kind man, kind to them when they saw him, kind to Grandmother so far as they could tell; and his children had all loved him, so he must have been kind to them. He was hard-working and good at cricket, and he had an interesting way of chomping his bacon and egg and talking while chewing his pipe. But they'd known him to lose his temper, and he sometimes made unsaintly remarks about Jews and Roman Catholics. Does Grandmother believe what she says? Does she believe they will believe it? Can it be she's forgotten how she treated Grandfather after his stroke? After his stroke Grandfather couldn't talk or feed himself or shave. He dribbled and coughed and his nose ran. Long strings of saliva fell unchecked down his shirt or pyjama jacket; if he leaned forward they collected in his lap. It must have been terrible for Grandfather, who'd always taken pride in his appearance, and who not long ago had been bowling to his grandsons and running to the net to smash a volley, but Grandmother mocked and jeered. While he sat slumped in his wheelchair, his eyes sunk and staring, she talked about him as though he wasn't there. Give it a rest, Mummy, Edie would say, very sharply for her. Leave Daddy alone. Let him be. But Grandmother would go on and on. What does it matter? she'd say, he's only a carcass. What does it matter?

Grandfather couldn't speak, or feed himself, or wash or go to the lavatory – but could he hear? What if he could understand? They discuss this possibility in bed at night, in the spare room; they decide that Grandmother is at her most awful when she sanctifies Grandfather. Of all her moods, this one, in which no word of remorse or regret ever interrupts the tearful listing of his virtues, is the worst.

When they can escape her, they run (through the hall, down the passage, past the pantry and the storeroom, through the kitchen) to the maids' sitting-room, a place where Grandmother almost never goes.

The maids' sitting-room smells of smoke and armpits. The smoke of a million Wills' Whiffs and Woodbines has tanned the once-cream walls and ceiling and worked its way into the uncut moquette of the sofa and the stringy rug that lies on the lino in front of the gas fire. To step into this room, to sit on the smoked sofa and lean elbows on the oilclothed table top, is to enter a different house. It is dingily lit (by a cone-shaped enamel light, dangling from a chancy flex); bereft of ornament (two plaster Alsations, merely, and an oak half-moon clock on the shelf above the fire); devoid of comfort (apart from the sofa, two hard kitchen chairs). The room is an odd shape, triangular, and has only one, very small, window, too high up to see out of and always closed.

The room is dangerous. Grandmother may not come here, but when Barbara shuts the door they risk, they are sure, never returning to Edie and safety again. The conversation is dangerous. As Barbara, fag hanging from her mouth, deals the cards – so old and smoked they stick together when she tries to shuffle them – as they pick them up and sort them into suits, she gossips about Grandmother. Mrs M. is a silly old cow, Barbara says, a right bitch, and what she pays her and Mollie is laffable, not mind you that she's laffing. Come here, Clarrie, Barbara says in Grandmother's voice – and she gets up and hunts round the room and under the table for Clarence, walking bow-legged like Grandmother, bending down and patting the inside of her right knee, as Grandmother does: Come to mother, darling, precious boykin . . . . (They don't like Grandmother; they fear her and talk about her in bed in the spare room. So why does Barbara's performance – which is accurate and very funny – make them anxious?)

125

When Barbara has said all she has to say on the subject of Grandmother, they talk Smut. Barbara is the leader, but they all do it, even Mollie, though it makes her more than usually pink-faced. Through round after round of Old Maid (invariably Alice) and Rumblebelly and Strip Jack Naked and Seven of Diamonds and Snap, they talk of bosoms and bottoms, bras and knickers, lavs and chamber pots. Eyes, nose, mouth and chin, Barbara says, touching these features with a small grey hand, all the way down to Uncle Jim (she sticks the hand between her legs); Uncle Jim makes lemonade (Pssssssssss – to indicate wee), round the corner (hand goes round the back, to Barbara's bottom) chocolate's made (plop plop plop plop – to indicate number twos). Red, white and blue, Dirty Kangaroo, went behind the dustbin, and did his number two (fart noises; more plops). My Uncle Billy had a ten foot willy, he showed it to the lady next door – Eee, don't, Barb, Mollie interrupts, you musn't, they're too young.

When Barbara leans across the table to tweak a card from Lucy, her underarm smell fills the room. They know she washes, they've seen her in the maids' bathroom stripped to the waist, bent over the tiny corner basin. She soaps herself with sour yellow soap. Under each arm is a pelt of black fur, like the false moustaches in the dressing-up chest on the landing. Grown-up women don't put soap on their faces, they use Ardena Deep Cleansing Cream, but Barbara works the yellow bar between her hands and lathers her face into bubbles all over, screwing her eyes tight and blowing out her cheeks as though she were inflating a balloon. If invited, they follow her along the passage to the maids' bedroom and watch her change. (The maids wear green dresses and white aprons in day time; black dresses with frillier aprons and cuffs and caps in the evening). The rooms in Grandmother's house are painted cream or pastel shades of blue or grey, but the maids' bedroom is wallpapered with roses, red, yellow and blue, giant blooms, and the door and skirtings are an outdoor green. It's a dark room because the one window looks on to the wash-house wall, and it smells – of smoke and of the contents of the chamber pots, one under each brass bed. (Once, when Alice, for some reason in the maids' bedroom without Lucy, caught sight of Barbara's po and smelt its sickly-sweetish smell, its contents were red – like water beetroot's boiled in, she told Lucy afterwards: Perhaps Barbara had cut her bottom? Lucy suggested.)

The maids wear black stockings in the evening when they change, but in daytime, even in winter, their legs are bare and sore-looking, descending to red ankles and black lace-up shoes. Their legs are bare when they go off on their bikes on Thursday afternoons. In winter they ride away in belted coats and headscarves and high-heeled shoes; in summer they put on shiny rayon dresses which have shoulder pads and ruched sleeves, and they squeeze their feet into tiny sling-backs with peep toes. Grandmother doesn't allow make-up on duty, but on Thursday afternoons when they pedal off, their eyebrows are black and arched, their eyelids mauvey purple, their mouths a hard dark red.

Where do the maids go on Thursday afternoons? MYOB, Barbara says, as she and Mollie wheel their bikes down the path between the tennis court and the holly hedge to the back gate. To see a man about a dog, she says, unlatching the gate, or, Wouldn't you like to know?

But one time when they ask, Mollie says they can come next time, if they like; they'll go shopping in the High Street, and then have tea at home. Our mother's heard a lot about you two, she says. Better ask your Grandma, Barb calls over her shoulder, Better ask Mrs M.

They won't ask Grandmother, they'll ask Edie. I don't see why not, Duck, Edie says, If you behave yourselves.

Grandmother hears about it, of course. What do you want to do that for? she asks, puffing out her cheeks. It isn't suitable. Gentlefolk don't shop in the afternoon.

Later in the week Grandmother comes to the spare room and leans over the end of Alice's bed. Behind her on the wall, muddy clouds gather above a horse-drawn plough. You can't go on your bicycles, anyway, she says, as though adding to a conversation that

127

has just taken place. It's too far and too dangerous, you'll have to walk.

What's all this? They ride their bikes every day, up Larkhill Lane as far as the Army Camp, along College Avenue, down Shireburn Road, all over the place and she never asks questions. Bike riding has never been dangerous before. But Grandmother won't listen to their pleas or change her mind. Don't go, then, she says. Take it or leave it; walk or don't go.

Next Thursday they're dressed in cotton frocks and cardigans, ankle socks and sandals. Let's have a look at you, Barbara says. Well . . . and Mollie squeezes the breath out of them and says, Aren't they lovely, aren't they grand? It's a hot day, and a long walk to the Village, which is not a village like the ones at home are – set among fields with a pub and a shop and a school and a church. The Village is mile upon mile of criss-crossing roads of shiny brick houses, in the middle of which is a High Street of shops. By the time they get there, the maids are wilting in their rayon, and they've got blisters on their heels because their socks have gone to sleep in their sandals.

What happens next, whatever it is, they will try to make sense of in the spare room tonight, and tomorrow night, and weeks of nights to come. What happens, what happened (or did not happen – but it was the same for both of them) was this: They were in the High Street, but it was not the High Street they knew. No, it had to be the High Street they knew, because there at the end of it was the Post Office with its clock and chain railing.

Try again. They were in the High Street they knew, but the shops were not the same shops. The shops they visit daily with Edie were not there; had vanished; did not exist. In their place were other shops that Barbara and Mollie knew well and kept popping into – for knitting wool; for a 'a pound of tripe for our mother, Jack love;' for black stockings; for 'necessaries'; for a tired-looking cabbage.

Everywhere they went, the shopkeepers greeted the maids with: 'Lo Barb love, is yer fellar still at sea, then? or How's my Mollie?

Be a love and take this packet of lard, yer Mam left it behind last Tuesday – while they were ignored. Even when Barb – in answer to a baker they'd never seen before's, You've bin keeping these kids very quiet, I must say – said, They're Mrs M.'s grandchildren from the big house, no one seemed interested. The baker said, Oh yeh, without looking up, and put five buns in a paper bag and swung the bag by the corners and handed it to Barb.

Where were they? Outside, the pavement, the shops, the cherry trees, the parked bicycles and prams, swam in the heat. They looked at each other in panic.

Where were they? Lucy tugged Barbara's arm. Where are we?

We're in the High Street, that's where, don't be daft, Barbara said.

They're hot, poor loves, Mollie said, they'll be wanting an ice.

There is only one place for ices – Darbyshires, where Edie buys their drawing books and peppermint lumps, and the pontefract cakes Grandmother never shares. Mrs Darbyshire will be pleased to see them. They will be safe in Darbyshires.

This way, Barbara said. A blistered door shimmered before them. She pushed it open and a bell jangled. They waited in the dark till a woman in hair curlers came out of the back and leant her bosom on the counter. Two wafers, two cones, Marge, Barbara said. And don't forget me Woodbines –

Out on the pavement the margarine ices turned to sticky rivers that trickled over their wrists. Alice can't eat vanilla I'm afraid, Lucy said to Barb before Alice could stop her. It makes her sick. Oh, my lady can't eat vanilla – Barbara dropped a curtsey – Well, there's some of us as can – and she took the cornet from Alice's hand and finished it off with three sharp bites.

Where are they? Why isn't Edie here? Why doesn't she save them? Where *are* they?

They are in an alleyway between high brick walls.

One minute they were in the High Street, the maids' High Street, and the next they were following Barb through a brick arch, into an alleyway. There is no brick arch, and no alleyway in

Edie's High Street.

Nearly there now loves, Mollie said, as the walls crumbled to iron railings and spiky grass, through which they could see snippets of back gardens and washing-lines and the backs of dark houses. Our mother'll give us a nice cup of tea. Barb's and Mollie's mother will give them a nice cup of tea, and they will be able to go to the lavatory. Lucy was already crossing her legs.

In front of them the alley ended in a bank of pale grasses, dotted with willow trees and rising steeply to the railway line. Just before they reached it, Barbara opened a gate on the right, and they followed her up a brick path.

A witch was sitting on the doorstep, shelling peas into a basin. Her knees were wide apart and the tin basin, full of peas, rested between them on the step. She was bent forward and her long hair fell in front of her face and over her knotted arms. The step, her worn skirt and the path at her feet were littered with pea pods.

'Lo Mum, Barbara shouted above the noise of a train, rattling past on the embankment. How's tricks, our Mother? The witch parted her hair, and when she saw them she thew back her head and cackled. She had no teeth. Her mouth was a black cave. She was a hundred-years old. So these are Mrs M.'s girls, she whispered in a gummy lisp, and she stretched out her arms and pulled them to her as Mollie does, and kissed and squeezed them as Mollie kisses and squeezes them, and her hair went in their mouths and noses. Then she pushed them away and poked their stomachs with a knobby finger. Fat, she said, pinching Lucy's arm above the elbow. Fat, both of them. Fat as butter. And the black cave opened again and she laughed and laughed and laughed.

Never again, Barbara said on the endless walk back to Grandmother's house, Never again, Misses High-and-Mighty. Too grand to say a word to our mother. Not a peep, not a smile, not a please or a thank you out of the pair of you.

But it wasn't their fault they couldn't speak or eat, or drink their tea. The witch had cast a spell on them; she'd turned them to stone. It wasn't their fault. They looked at Mollie, but Mollie, who always defends them, pursed her mouth and said nothing.

On the way back Lucy wet her knickers (and her legs and her socks and her sandals). Having been turned to stone she couldn't, of course, follow Barbara to the wooden hut at the end of the witch's garden.

Grandmother was in the swing seat when they turned in the drive. Clarence yapped and whined, but Grandmother didn't look up as they climbed the terrace steps; she went on puffing and muttering and turning the pages. At the entrance to the porch the maids left them without saying goodbye, and went round the side of the terrace and down the side steps – past the hen run and the first vegetable garden – to the back door.

Did you have a nice time, dears? Edie said when they ran at her. They wanted to tell her, but they couldn't. What could they tell?

Barbara sent them to Coventry for a fortnight. If they met her on the stairs she looked the other way and hummed under her breath. In the dining-room she stared through them or over the tops of their heads. Mollie didn't speak either, but she gazed at them sorrowfully, pink in the face.

It's months before they're invited to the maids' sitting-room to play cards. When they do, Barbara doesn't gossip about Grandmother, and she doesn't pretend to hunt for Clarence, and nobody talks smut. Alice had got the Queen – as per, Barbara says in a bored voice, blowing smoke rings at the ceiling; and she winks – at Mollie, not at them.

They spend less time with the maids now, more time with Edie, more time by themselves.

Most mornings they go shopping with Edie in the Hillman. They go to Taylor's and Cross's and Bower's, they go to Dean's and Darbyshire's. If Grandmother comes, she sits in the passenger seat with a basket of empties on her knee, and all the shopkeepers leave their customers to pay court to her.

As they follow Edie from shop to familiar shop, they fear that at any moment they will find themselves in that other High Street they visited with the maids; the street where there is a greengrocer with tired vegetables, the blistered door of a tobacconist that sells ices and a brick arch that leads to a terraced cottage under the railway line.

# BAD TASTE

'Rinse please,' Mr Payne said. He removed the saliva ejector from Mrs Carter's mouth and gave the instrument tray a little push. It swung smoothly away.

'I shall need to see you again in about a month. Get the appointment book would you, Diane?'

While Mrs Carter rinsed and spat three times with pink mouthwash, Dennis Payne soaped his hands energetically and dried them on a paper towel which he crumpled and dropped into a pedal bin under the basin.

Mrs Carter was still stranded in the chair. He dabbed at the dribble on her chin with a pink tissue from the dispenser, unclipped her plastic bib, and then brought her back to earth with one press of the foot-pump.

Mrs Carter climbed awkwardly off the chair. She'd been coming to him for years and in all that time he'd never hurt her; but she was still a nervous patient, a fact that annoyed him although he never let it show.

'I want you to think about that crown,' he said as he helped her into her coat and as Diane hovered with the appointment book. 'Gold is undeniably expensive, but it should last for ever. And it won't notice, I promise you.'

At the door he shook hands heartily with Mrs Carter and stood smiling, his hand raised in salute, until she was halfway down the stairs and obscured from his view by the landing banisters.

It was his last appointment of the morning. Running late – two extractions, and then the Bronson boy to be fitted in with an abscess – meant only an hour for lunch, whereas he needed an hour and a half. In winter he drove home in the lunch hour, to a house called Heatherdene, a mile from the practice and from the centre of the town, up a steep, conifer-clad hill above the golf course. In summer, and if the weather was fine, he ate his lunch in the park. The notice on the iron gates said Pleasure Gardens, a name he liked for the picture it conjured of pretty women with parasols gliding along well-tended gravel, but could never bring himself to use. When it rained he went to the King's Head in the High Street for a pint of Courage and a Beef Wellington.

Today, the 14th of May, he decided on the park, even though the weather was unsettled and cold. He called in at Blake's to see if the Atco was ready and was told, 'Any day now, Sir': and then walked briskly over the railway-crossing towards the park gates.

The park was almost empty: no one on the paths and benches; no boats on the lake. Only one couple on the tennis courts, a disappointment for he enjoyed watching tennis, a game he'd once enjoyed playing. It cheered him to see healthy young people engaged in healthy activity, particularly when the majority of youth passed their days and nights in stupor on the steps of the Gaumont.

He walked down a pitted asphalt path between the tennis courts and a low privet hedge, beyond which lay the putting green where a boy in jeans and a leather jacket chased a boxless Hayter Senator that expelled a spray of fine green dust. He skirted the empty bandstand – roundabout without horses Donald had called it when he was small – and made for his usual bench. Before sitting, he tested the slats with the palm of his hand, and then covered a section of seat with the fashion pages of the *Telegraph*. For a long time he sat and stared out at the lake, a rectangle of white water and not unlike a giant swimming pool. Its only pretentions to naturalism were the two islands in the middle, but even these were of uniform size, shape and planting, and equi-distant from the two end banks. Later in the summer, the lake and its environs would be intolerable, with ducks having to dodge the fibreglass rowing

136

boats that, despite a large prohibitive notice, behaved little better than bumper cars; but today the boats were imprisoned under the brick arch of the boat house, and the ducks had the water to themselves.

Dennis unwrapped his lunch. Sheila had given him a Scotch egg, home-made and misshapen, the sausagemeat already dissociating itself from a green albumen; two rounds of wholemeal sandwiches that discharged shredded lettuce hearts and salad cream and slabs of shot-silk ham; a can of Export ale and an apple. He rummaged in his lunch box for the tube of mustard that would make the Scotch egg palatable, and then turned his head to check that there was no one about whom he knew. There was always the fear that one of his patients might discover him with cheeks distorted by sponge cake, or with pastry crumbs on his trousers.

He ate half the Scotch egg and all but one of the sandwiches, then threw the leftovers to the rabble of mallard and pintails who shouted at him from the bank.

'Hallo, Mr Payne. I was sure it was you.' He'd got no further than the front page of the *Telegraph* when he was interrupted by a voice that sounded young and female and very close. He lowered his newspaper and saw a blurred vision in white, holding a tennis racket. He removed his reading spectacles, at the same time instinctively putting out a hand to cover his naked lunch box and its display of scrunched tinfoil and tattered greaseproof paper. In focus she became someone familiar, but he did not know who, and he felt at a disadvantage. Sitting down and having to look up was uncongenial to one who spent the greater part of his life standing up and looking down.

'I've been reading a lot about you in the *Gazette* lately,' the vision said. 'I'm sorry you've lost your battle.'

'Thank you.' Dennis knew what she referred to. He'd been fighting for three years to save the park, or a large chunk of it, from being turned into a Leisure and Sports Centre. A brick (this was his one success: they'd tried for concrete), glass and pantile complex was to swallow the putting green, three of the tennis courts – indoor courts would replace these – the Aileen Johnstone Memorial Garden and the Rock Walk. They had promised to move the marble drinking fountain to a new site by the lily pond, but he was sceptical about this. The bulldozers were due in September.

The vision smiled, and Dennis remembered who she was.

'How's the family, Elizabeth?' he could now ask. 'I saw your mother, just before Christmas I think it was.' He recalled the difficulty he'd had in fitting the bridge he'd made for Lady Spenser's upper molars. Elizabeth he hadn't seen for some time. She had large blue eyes and was prettier than he remembered. No, it wasn't prettiness, it was something more –

'I've been meaning to come and see you for ages,' she was saying. 'The trouble is, Mama always made the appointments, and now that I've left home I forget about things like dentists. I expect I've got a mouthful of holes.' He doubted this. Elizabeth had an excellent jaw and had never had any real problems with her teeth. Far fewer cavities than the average.

'As a matter of fact,' she went on, rather pink in the face, 'I've got a sore place under my tongue and a peculiar, well nasty, taste that comes and goes.' He was embarrassed by confidences that ought properly to be confined to the dental surgery. They had no place in the park.

'Telephone my nurse this afternoon,' he said, 'and I'll tell her to try and fit you in on a cancellation.' While they were talking he'd become gradually aware of a young man in shorts, leaning against the black trunk of a prunus and separated from them by a row of wintry flower-beds that lay, neatly dug over, awaiting bedding plants. Every so often the young man swiped at the grass with his tennis racket. Dennis turned his attention to the boathouse. Above a notice which read: 'LAKE PLEASURE GARDENS: Scale of Charges', hung a rusted electric clock whose hands pointed to ten to two. He folded his newspaper and got to his feet.

'Have you still got the Noah's Ark? I was always very keen on it,' Elizabeth said, skipping out of his way as he cleared the bench

138

of debris.

'Yes, of course. You'll see it when you come for your appointment. Excuse me, Elizabeth, I must get back. Remember me to your mother. Don't forget to telephone this afternoon!' he called over his shoulder as he hurried away down a path lined with cherry trees whose pink, double blossoms were beginning to pale and drop. At each tree a rug of petals obliterated the asphalt, silencing his footsteps. As he turned right by the tennis club, he caught sight of Elizabeth. She was sitting on his bench with the young man and throwing bread to the ducks.

'Another potato, dear?' Sheila lifted the lid of the serving dish. She picked up the spoon to serve him.

'No. Thank you.'

'There's only plums for afters.'

'Plums will be very nice.'

They were having supper in the dining-room which, when the double doors were folded back, became an extension of the sitting-room. The room was cold, and the silences in their conversation were drowned by what seemed to Dennis unnaturally loud chewings and scrapings and swallowings. He put his napkin down on the table and got up to clear away. He did what he could to help Sheila with the chores. She'd had polio as a child and was lame as a result. She tired easily and had to rest on her bed for two hours every afternoon.

He put the dirty plates in the hatch and made two journeys to the table with pudding plates, a cut-glass bowl of stewed plums, and a heavy blue jug containing the custard they both preferred to cream.

'There was a letter from Donald today,' Sheila said as she ladled plums on to a plate. Donald was the miracle baby no less than five specialists had decided she couldn't have.

'Oh yes?' Dennis said cautiously. Sheila and Donald were thick as thieves; he felt habitually jealous and left out.

'He wonders whether we'd like to have the children for a fortnight when he and Jenny go to Spain in September.' There was a silence while he took this in and while Sheila attempted to pour tepid custard on to his plums. It was too thick and she had to help it out with a spoon.

'A fortnight sounds a long time.' He took the plate Sheila handed him. A glut of plums last autumn meant kilner jars full of them on all the larder shelves. Meant plum fool, plum crumble, plum jam, plum tart, plums and custard, every day forever and ever. He had recently considered cutting the tree down.

'Even with Mrs D. coming in,' he continued, 'I don't see how you'd manage.' It was not difficult to sound concerned. Donald's children were two and four and a handful. Jenny never said 'Don't' when little Alec jumped up and down on his grandparents' settee in his lace-ups. During their last visit, mercifully for only three days, little Natasha had refused to eat anything except bananas.

Sheila turned her head away to spit a plum stone into her spoon. Then she said: 'With you at home, dear, I'm sure we'll be able to cope.'

It was a direct hit, and below the plimsoll line (but perhaps, to be fair, she had not understood that he'd fleetingly forgotten that at the beginning of August he retired and would be at home all the time. When this happened, Payne, Branksome and Jefferies would become Branksome and Jefferies. And if the cocky young man who joined them six months ago, and who was still on trial – or was it the practice that was on trial? Hopwood made it seem so – proved any use, it would soon be Branksome, Jefferies and Hopwood). He felt something close to hatred for Donald who, at thirty-four, was successful already – two holidays abroad a year, and lots of breaks in-between – and who had an attractive and energetic wife, a physiotherapist. What made them think he'd want the kiddies to stay in the first weeks of his retirement?

'He has a nerve, I must say,' he said, getting up to make the coffee. Sheila would be upset by this remark, he knew; he avoided her eye. As he walked round the back of her chair, he noticed the crown of her head where light from the three-pronged oak candelabra formed a small halo. Her hair did not shine as hair should when light touches it. When she'd first started dyeing – tinting, she called it – her hair, he'd been pleased. But that was a long time ago. Now it seemed out of keeping with his own baldness and made her look hard, like the Duchess of Windsor, and common. Tarty, even. He would never tell her this. Even when she asked him, as she anxiously did from time to time: 'Do you think I should allow myself to go grey now?' he always reassured her: 'Not unless you want to.' He was not sure why he lied to her in these ways – as over the plums – whether it was out of kindness (for it might not be kind) or boredom.

'We needn't make up our minds yet about the children,' Sheila said when he returned with the coffee.

'No, of course we'll have them. Obviously.' He didn't want to talk about it anymore. Instead he said, rolling his napkin into a sausage and pushing it through a silver ring round whose desert a caravan of camels plodded: 'I saw Elizabeth Spenser in the park today. She'd been playing tennis, and came up and spoke to me while I was eating my lunch.'

'Is she the eldest? She must be eighteen or nineteen by now.'

'More like twenty, perhaps.' Still, Sheila, who'd never met Elizabeth and who knew few of his patients socially, wasn't far out. Throughout the years he'd tried to enliven her day by telling her selected gossip about his patients. It was not gossip so much as harmless news of births, marriages and deaths and, increasingly, of divorces and recouplings. Sheila had always appeared interested in this information, even grateful. She looked at him expectantly across the table, but he found he had nothing else he wanted to say about Elizabeth Spenser. Certainly not that, quite unaccountably, he'd thought about her several times in the course of the afternoon. She hadn't telephoned. He knew this because he'd checked the appointment book more than once before leaving the surgery.

She made her appointment the following morning, as he discovered at lunchtime. Tuesday, the twenty-second, at eleven thirty. He stared at this date on the page and at Miss Spencer, written in ballpoint in Diane's neat, backward sloping hand. There was something not quite right. It took him a minute to realize she'd spelt Spenser with a C instead of an S. It was not a mistake he could have made. He was meticulous on all matters concerning his patients, priding himself on his ability to store useful details about their lives and interests so that when some grey-flannelled (though latterly it had been jeans; everyone seemed to wear jeans these days, including the mothers), twelve-year-old came into the surgery, he was able to say, pumping hands vigorously: 'Hello Jeremy/Charles/Nicholas. How are you? And how are the model trains/computer games/stamps? I imagine you must be off to Marlborough/Eton/Radley any minute now?' This sort of thing, especially if the patient had problem teeth or was in any way nervous, was essential, a part of what poor old Neville Thompson – senior partner until his untimely death last October – had, perhaps tautologically, termed 'The Psychology of Confidence'.

It was raining hard. He'd been hoping to go to the park, not, he told himself, because there was any possibility Elizabeth would be on the tennis courts, or that he might find her seated on his bench alone with a book (where did she work? he wondered, if she did work. Where did she live, now that she'd left home? How did she spend her days? Her nights?) but because he needed the exercise.

In the crowded Monarch bar of the King's Head, he saw Joe Hincks having lunch with Mrs Hincks, and looked quickly away. Joe Hincks was a chartered quantity surveyor and his arch enemy on the council. The Leisure Centre was his baby. While Dennis and Brigadier Gough-Naylor had been campaigning to prevent it, Hincks had been organizing fund-raising activities to pay for it. For over a year now, the pavement outside the Town Hall had been taken up by a giant cardboard thermometer with a red needle that showed the target figure and the campaign success to date.

The slogan underneath read: 'It's your Leisure. Your future. Help pay for your Centre'. Inside, a spotlit architect's model of the projected building and the site, complete with miniature bathtub of water – the lake – stood on a rostrum flanked by hessian exhibition screens that displayed working drawings and plans and lists of fund-raising activities.

He had just forked in the last mouthful of chili con carne ('sorry dear, there's been a run on the Beef Wellington today'), and pushed some bruised lettuce and the remains of the pickle to the side of his plate, when Elizabeth walked in through the latticed oak doors, followed by someone who might very well be, indeed probably was, the fellow he'd seen her with in the park. He lowered his head at once, but by craning his neck a little could watch the two of them select a table, walk to it, and Elizabeth, who was wearing some sort of blue pyjamas, slide on to a bench seat with her back to the window. The young man removed a menu from an adjoining table and they conferred; he could see Elizabeth's finger travel up and down the card, hover and then rest at something. He edged round in his seat until they were no longer in sight and until he was fully facing the back of the bar, his eyes on a level with a shelf that supported a brass horse and trap, a laminated photograph of a girl in a track suit with 'I'd Love a Babycham' on her bosom, and rows of stem glasses with gold rims; and immediately Elizabeth's friend was beside him, one check, tweed arm resting on the counter, chubby fingers tapping.

'One glass of dry white, one pint of best, one cheddar ploughman's, one lasagne.' It was an educated voice. Well, it would be. That man knows Elizabeth, he thought. How well does he know Elizabeth?

'That'll be – ' Miriam behind the bar, whose prominent teeth pained Dennis each time he encountered them, was adding up on her note pad: 'Four pounds twenty altogether. Can you pay for the food now, sir, please?' Had Elizabeth chosen bread and cheese or lasagne? He wanted to know, but would not wait to find out.

He stared straight in front of him as he made for the exit and was almost at the door when he heard her, above the din of conversations and scraping plates and sudden hearty laughter, call out: 'Mr Payne!' and he turned his head. She was smiling at him and waving.

'See you next week, worse luck!' In answer, he raised his hand in a stiff little salute. As he headed for the door, he collided with Joe Hincks and Mrs Hincks, also on their way out, and had to apologize.

'Don't mind us, old chap. We can take it!' Hincks was infuriatingly jovial, almost avuncular.

When he opened his surgery door Diane, her back to him, was removing instruments from the sterilizer. Beside her stood Hopwood. His arms were folded across his chest and he half leaned against a glass-fronted cabinet that contained swabs and dressings. Dennis detected an air of easy intimacy between them he did not care for.

'I've been telling your nurse here,' Hopwood began, 'that it's high time you had some proper machinery. That old thing' – he uncrossed his arms and pointed at the sterilizer – 'looks like a toaster.' Diane arranged the steaming instruments on a tray and put her cheatle forceps on the draining board. With a practised tug at the finger ends she peeled off her cellophane gloves, at the same time touching the pedal bin with the toe of one black court shoe. The top flew up like the lid of a jack-in-the-box and snapped shut again, trapping one inflated and accusing finger in the rim.

'And I've told Mr Hopwood our sterilizer is fine, thank you very much.'

Dennis decided to ignore these exchanges. Hopwood had been consistently rude about the 'outmoded equipment' in the practice ever since he'd joined them, even going so far as to suggest, in his interview, that their method of mixing – in a mortar with a pestle – mercury and silver alloy, was potentially lethal. Unfortunately, he'd been by far the best qualified of the applicants they'd interviewed, and he didn't smoke. Once in, Hopwood had taken no time at all to throw out the 'Dickensian' drill he'd inherited from Neville Thompson, and to instal an air rotar unit in its stead. Now each partner had one, a neat little Sirobox with a high-speed drill and a polisher that worked off compressed air. The new equipment had been expensive, and the fees had gone up as a result, which Dennis minded. He refused to admit to anyone that these innovations made life easier and dentistry more efficient, and he'd dug his toes in over the sterilizer which was perfectly adequate and would see him out, at least.

'What can I do for you?' he asked Hopwood, after a long silence during which he'd found himself a clean tunic and put it on.

'My X-Ray machine is on the blink – ' Hopwood's tone was languid ' – and I wondered, if you don't need it for an hour or so, if I might borrow yours?' There was, alas, no good enough reason for refusing. He did not need the X-Ray for his first two patients, and this was something that Diane, who could be relied on to do her homework thus far, knew quite well.

'Give Mr Hopwood a hand, would you, Diane?' He watched them wheel the cumbersome tripod to the door, Hopwood alternately tugging and pushing, Diane struggling with a tail of thick and shiny corkscrew flex that sprang out of her arms at every step. He did not offer to help them.

'Oh, Mr Payne . . . ' Diane, who was outside the door, popped her head round again. 'Mrs Payne phoned ten minutes ago. She said could you get a tin of Whiskas on your way home. She'd forgotten the corner shop shuts now on Tuesday afternoons. Rabbit flavour.' She failed to close the door behind her, and he could hear the Oralix's halting journey across the landing to Hopwood's room, Hopwood's muffled 'whoops' and then giggles. Were they laughing at him? He shut the door. In September, Whiskas, Dreft and Windolene, and whether or not Sheila had sufficient quantities, would be the most exigent problem he could expect to face. He looked round his room. It had been his refuge for thirty-five years, but in August it would be taken over by Mrs Jackson, the hygienist, who came in two days a week and who at present was making do with a cupboard-sized room downstairs. His patients appreciated – he knew this because they said so – the human touches in his surgery. The walls, for instance, were the palest coral pink. There were two Victorian watercolours, one above the fireplace, of a cottage with smoke spiralling from the thatch, a spreading oak tree and a collie dog; and the other, on the right of the door as you entered it, and on the only wall not taken up by cabinets and sinks and machinery, of two small children in straw bonnets gathering cowslips. At either end of the mantle-piece were propped photographs, a studio portrait of Donald aged five, sitting sideways to the camera on a cushion against a background of puffy clouds; and an unframed snapshot of Sheila, taken by himself. She was standing on the curved brick step outside the front door of Heatherdene, laughing and holding up Muffin, a tabby cat long since dead. Between the photographs, a pair of Staffordshire dalmations lay with their heads on their paws and eyed each other round a carriage clock that, despite regular visits to Mr Braine in Station Road, kept only idiosyncratic time. Dennis checked the entirely reliable Rolex – his one extravagance in a life of parsimony – on his wrist: the clock was running fifteen minutes fast.

A large, south-west facing window took up most of the wall opposite to the door. It showed, if you stood directly in front of it, as he now did, a square of mossy lawn edged with laurels and divided by a yellow gravel path, at the end of which a rose pergola, today sagged in the rain. For anyone in the dentist's chair, this vista was reduced to sky, telephone wire and the tops of three ragged Wellingtonias in the garden opposite. What the chair did provide was a panorama of the windowsill, and upon it, of his treasure – the Noah's Ark Elizabeth had mentioned in the park. Thirty-nine animals (fourteen pairs, one elephant missing) walked in perpetual orderly crocodile from right to left, to where the Ark stood with its gangplank down, and Mr and Mrs Noah on deck, to receive them. The Ark, a present to Dennis on his sixth birthday, had once been a bright scarlet and blue, but had darkened through the years so that now, although polished and handsome, it was no recognizable colour.

He got out a duster from a drawer in the wall unit. Since an elephant had gone missing ten years or so ago, and both antelopes had suffered fractures, no one but himself had been allowed to touch the animals except certain children who, he could tell, were the sort to treat them with respect. While he was dusting them – picking up each animal in turn and rubbing it gently and then returning it to its position – he thought about Elizabeth, and while he was thinking about Elizabeth, Diane insinuated herself into the room on tiptoe.

'It's just coming up for two o'clock, Mr Payne. Shall I go and see if the Williamses are in the waiting-room?'

He declined her offer. Her exaggerated and ingratiating steps annoyed him, and in any case she knew that unless he was exceptionally hard pressed he liked to fetch his patients from the waiting room himself. All the partners did, except for Hopwood. It was part of the psychology of confidence, and at the same time it allowed an inconspicuous visit to the staff lavatory, a door marked Private on the half landing.

Oh Elizabeth, thought Dennis as he went down the stairs, where are you now?

The following morning he woke a full hour before the alarm was due to go off at seven. It had been a hot night and was already a hot day; the sheets were damp and his pyjama jacket sodden. He lay very still, his eyes fixed on a triangle of brilliant light at the top of the window where the flowered curtains failed to meet. Elizabeth would still be asleep, he decided. A picture of her sleeping began to take shape. She lay on her back in a pale blue nightdress of satiny material, her golden hair floating out (as though she were under water) on the pillow. He could see her white neck and shoulders quite clearly, but her face refused to come into focus. To get over this difficulty, he turned her on to her side, so that her face was buried in the pillow and so that he could concentrate on her

147

shoulder blades and the delicate and vulnerable little bumps of her backbone –

'Are you awake, dear?'

'Yes,' he said, 'I expect you'd like a cup of tea.' His hand, searching guiltily for Sheila's hand, met with a roll of rucked-up wincyette nightdress and bony hip.

Throughout the morning the temperature continued to rise. It was in the high seventies by the time he opened the waiting-room door for the last appointment.

Three-quarters of an hour later, and sweating heavily, he reached the park gates. He examined the tennis courts with unobtrusive care: they were all occupied, but there was no sign of Elizabeth. He made a hurried tour of the park benches. A golden head drew him, heart thumping, to a bench by the lily pond, but the profile belonging to the hair was not hers. The pain of this disappointment was new and almost pleasurable, and he considered it as he tagged on to a little crowd that had formed round the bandstand, where the St. John's Comprehensive School Band were making an enthusiastic hash of a selection from *My Fair Lady*, a show he and Sheila had enjoyed back in the sixties. He put a pound in the collecting tin a youth in a black and gold blazer held out to him, noticing only after he'd forced the coin through a slit too small for the job, that his money was destined not for Cancer Research or Save the Children, or even Brass Band Funds, but for Your Leisure Centre. Turning his back on the bandstand, he picked his way through sunbathers and discarded ice-cream cartons until he reached the little stream that ran the length of the park and formed its western parameter, and sat down on the bank. With his hands clasped round his knees he stared down at the trickle of water pushing its way round the lily leaves. Snatches of 'I Could Have Danced All Night', Sheila's favourite (sad, really, dancing being something she could never do) wafting from the bandstand, gave way to 'On the Street Where You Live' and then, after a couple of false starts, to 'I've Grown Accustomed to Her Face'.

'I am in love,' he said aloud. 'I am mad.' He took his coat off and then his shoes, and stretched out, eyes closed, in the sun.

'It's too early,' Sheila said again, more irritably this time. 'We could easily have another frost before June.'

It was after lunch on Saturday. Standing on the terrace in glaring sunshine, they were arguing about the pelargoniums, which had sat around the house since last October, sticky with greenfly and dropping sickly spotted leaves on all the sills. He was longing to get them out into the tubs.

'Anyway,' Sheila nodded at the tubs, where dead wallflowers leaned woody stems against each other for support, 'the wallflowers aren't over yet.'

It was too hot to argue. The Atco was back, and he mowed the lawn while Sheila rested on a recliner under a clump of silver birches at the bottom of the garden.

'Don't overdo it, love!' she called out, as for the umpteenth time he grunted past her with the grass box on his way to the compost heap.

'I was thinking of stopping for a bit – blast! I've got oil on my trousers.' He collapsed beside her on the bald sand under the birches. 'I feel a bit queasy as a matter of fact.'

Sheila put down *A Woman of Substance* and her spectacles on a little cushion of dandelions and groped for her stick under the chair.

'You sit here, and I'll go and make a cup of tea.'

He watched her mount the terrace steps. 'That is my wife,' he said aloud, as his eyes followed the bent figure in blue stretch trousers that ballooned round her thighs grotesquely, like a clown's.

He did feel queasy, and his head ached. Heart attack symptoms, he knew. Or stroke. He put a hand under his shirt and held it over his pounding heart. But there was no real pain or tightness in his chest; no pins and needles or numbness in his arms, and after a minute or two he withdrew his hand. Sheila would need help with the tray.

Halfway up the bank he thought: only two and a bit days till I see her; and he stopped and sat down again and plucked a grass stem and chewed it. Where had Elizabeth been all week? (He had searched the park every day for her in vain.) Where was she this weekend? What was she doing and with whom? He selected another stem and crunched along its length: there were three little joints in it that proved particularly satisfying. When he'd flattened it, he chose another and started again. She was sunbathing, in all likelihood, lying on her stomach with her head in her arms. In the hollows at the base of her spine tiny pearls of perspiration twinkled on minute gold hairs . . . . No – he staggered to his feet and mimed a forehand drive into the heathers – she was playing tennis on her parents' court. The Spensers lived in a Queen Anne, or was it Williams and Mary, house, half an hour away, in Hampshire. He had seen the house from the road and coveted it.

He felt worse after tea, and as the evening wore on, not queasy but sick. A band of pain, starting above his eyes, cut through his temples and burst out of the back of his head. At nine, having eaten no supper, he took a mixing bowl from the kitchen cupboard and put himself to bed in Donald's old room next to the bathroom, the bowl beside him on Donald's boy-sized chair. After an hour's uneasy dozing he was suddenly wide awake: someone was stabbing him in the stomach: someone was pulling a rope round his throat. He only just had time to grab the bowl.

When it was over, he felt no relief. Particles of vomit burned his gullet; the agony in his stomach increased. He stumbled to the bathroom and tipped the contents of the bowl down the lavatory. When the flush subsided, the water frothed evilly, its surface decorated with little splinters of tomato skin which, with eyes clouded by tears, he at first took for blood. He sat rocking on the cold edge of the bath. Bright orange fish, swimming busily on the sea-green wallpaper, spewed bubbles at him through rags of yellow seaweed.

'Are you all right in there, Dennis?' There was an anxious tapping on the door. As if to answer her, he was sick again.

'It's gastric flu,' Sheila informed him after he'd vomited bile at ten-minute intervals throughout the night, and after she'd consulted Doctor Benson. 'Half the town's got it.' He felt relieved and disappointed at this news, and turned on to his side, drawing his knees up in an attempt to ease the pain.

'You're to stay there for two days at least, and not get out of bed except to pay a visit. And you can't go back to work till Thursday at the earliest, preferably next week, he says. All right, pet?'

He did not mind this last injunction; he was certain he would not live till Thursday.

'I've spoken to Tom Branksome and to Diane,' Sheila's inexorable voice went on. 'They'll put off all your routine appointments, and split the urgent ones between the partners.'

'Thank you,' he murmured into the top sheet. 'Well done.'

He wished she would go. His tongue was furred and foul. His head, chest, abdomen and buttocks had been punched and kicked. Someone had drilled his joints and filled the cavities with cement. A sizeable chunk of his backbone was missing.

It was not until Monday lunch-time that, propped against the pillows and with an exiguous tray of steamed haddock sliding around on his knees, he realized his week's see-sawing anticipation had been for nothing: he would not be seeing Elizabeth tomorrow after all. The depression that followed this realization was mitigated a little by the certainty that she would not want to be seen by Branksome or Jefferies or Hopwood, and that she would merely postpone her appointment until he was well. This certainty lasted five minutes, after which time doubts began to erode it. Well, at five thirty he'd telephone Diane to see how they were all coping. And find out.

'You haven't managed much of that fish,' Sheila said in disappointed tones when she came to collect his tray. She put the tray on Donald's chest of drawers, then hobbled to the window and opened it as wide as it would go.

'That's better. It was very stuffy in here.'

He agreed that it had been. The little breeze that entered was refreshing. It ruffled the faded curtains, disturbing the orderly guardsmen in their pattern, and at the same time provoked a dusty Airfix Messerschmitt, suspended from the ceiling light on a piece of cotton thread, to fly backwards, then forwards, then back again. It lost height, came back to the centre, and then spun dizzily, its right wing dipping. He drew his legs out of her way as Sheila sat down on the bed.

'You shouldn't come near me,' he said. 'I don't want you to get this bug.' She shrugged at this and smiled. The smile creased her cheeks into a network of criss-cross puckerings, reminding him of a shrunk balloon.

'You look a little better today,' Sheila said, peering at him. She laid her hand on the bump in the bedclothes that was his knee. 'How do you feel?'

He felt, although light-headed and despite blotting paper legs, better after a bath. Back in Donald's room, he found the bed had been made up with clean sheets. Mrs D. was there, flicking a duster over his paperbacks.

'Better today, are we?' she said, as he stood helplessly in his pyjamas, waiting for her to leave.

'Shan't be two ticks – then I'll be out of your way. I don't want the flu, I can tell you.' She stuck the duster in the pocket of her straining overall and unplugged the hoover. When she'd gone, an unpleasant smell – a combination, perhaps, of sweat and Johnson's lavender wax – hung in the air like a threat.

At five-thirty on the dot, in the middle of a thunderstorm, he telephoned the surgery.

'*I* was going to phone *you*,' Diane said, after she'd enquired how he was. 'Everything's fine here, Mr Payne. Mr Branksome and Mr Jefferies have seen three of your patients – Mr Paton and Mrs Grant-Norland. Oh, and James Brooks. I was able to put the others off. Two cancelled with the flu, anyhow. It's an ill wind . . . ' she said, and giggled.

'You're very faint.' He could hardly hear her because of the thunder and the crackling on the line. 'How are you fixed for tomorrow?'

'Pardon?'

He repeated the question, shouting it this time.

'Not too badly. I managed to contact all but two – Miss Barnard and Miss Spenser. I'll try them again after six. Look, we'll cope. You get well and don't worry! I'll phone you again tomorrow evening.'

But how could he not worry? Supposing Diane did not manage to contact Elizabeth? Supposing Elizabeth was seen by Hopwood? He had a sudden picture of Hopwood adjusting the angle of his torch; pressing the corners of Elizabeth's mouth down with his fat brown fingers; saying 'wider please'; running his fingers round her gums; and all this time Hopwood's face was very close to her face, his breath mingling with her breath . . . .

That night he dreamed he gave Elizabeth his Noah's Ark. She smiled her lovely smile at him and kept repeating: 'For me? Really? For me?' and he beamed back and nodded. Awake – and this was not his usual experience with dreams – it still seemed a realistic idea. Something had to happen to the Ark when he retired. He'd long ago dismissed the notion of leaving it to the practice, for without his supervision it was certain to get broken. On the other hand, if he took it home there was the problem of Donald's determination to have it for his children, and he knew what little Alec would do with it. But Elizabeth loved the Ark, she'd said so, and would treasure it. If he gave it to her – how and when was something he looked forward to working out later – it would be a link between them. A more significant, a more mysterious, a more binding link than marriage, or sex.

At eleven-thirty on Tuesday morning, the hour and the day of her appointment, still feeling woolly and wearing an ancient camel-hair dressing gown, he was seated at his desk in the sitting-room, paying bills and answering letters selected from a file marked 'Leisure Centre'. The telephone rang loudly in his ear. He let it ring twice and then put out a hand.

'Hallo, Dad,' said Donald's voice.

'Oh. Hello, Donald.' His heart, which had stopped at the first ring, started up again. 'How are you? I expect you'd like to speak to your mother.' It was tacitly understood by all three of them that Donald only ever rang to talk to Sheila.

'No, I wanted *you*,' Donald said. 'Are you feeling better? Me mam told me you've been proper poorly.' He spoke this in a convincing Liverpool accent. 'Poor old Dad.'

'That's nice of you, Donald.' He was touched. 'Yes, I do feel more myself today, thanks.' Donald chatted on for ten minutes, long distance from Southport at his practice's expense (the call made possible, he explained, because one of his patients hadn't turned up), regaling Dennis with the latest bons mots of his grandchildren. 'And guess what? Alec can actually read!'

While Donald was talking, Dennis stared out disconsolately at his newly-mown lawn, littered, after the storm, with twigs and whole branches and smashed chestnut leaves and candles. Blossoms from the laburnum and lilac bushes at the gate had been blown as far as the terrace and lay limply on the pink paving stones which steamed now in fitful sunshine. When he could get a word in, he described this desolate scene to Donald.

'Rough winds do shake the darling buds of May, you know,' said Donald sagely. 'Take care, Dad. Don't overdo it. No raking, mind.' He rang off. He hadn't even sent love to his mother, Dennis realized afterwards, with astonishment.

Uncomfortable and sweaty in his dressing-gown, he had a bath after lunch and then, dressed in proper clothes, sat in a deck-chair reading, or pretending to read, the paper. As the time for Diane's promised call approached, he became more agitated and anxious. If she hadn't telephoned by five forty-five, he'd ring her. He'd decided this at lunch-time.

The bell that rang at five thirty-eight was the front-door bell. Dennis, hovering by the telephone in the sitting-room, could hear Sheila's dot-and-carry-one progress from the kitchen, across the

Marley-tiled hallway to the front door; could hear her struggle with the catch, and then a man's voice, followed by Sheila's saying: 'Do come in, won't you. Yes, he's up. He's in the lounge, I think, or may be on the patio.'

'Don't move,' Hopwood said as Dennis, having taken the telephone off the hook before the door opened, started to push himself out of the chair he had hastily arranged himself in.

'I promised Alison I'd collect Miranda on my way home. She's at a kids' party somewhere in this neck of the woods, so I thought I'd just pop in for a moment and see how you're doing.'

'Very good of you,' Dennis said. This was the stuff that nightmares were made of. 'I'm fine. Much better.'

'You look washed-out,' Hopwood said. 'I gather it's a very nasty bug – Yes, please, if you're making one ' – he turned to Sheila who was offering a cup of tea. 'I've got to be at somewhere called Ferndale Road by six-fifteen,' he went on as Sheila left the room. 'I'm not exactly sure where it it. These little roads all look alike to me.'

'It's no distance. Have a chair. Please.'

Dennis was nettled by the 'these little roads' remark. Hopwood lived three miles out of town, up a track and in a thatched cottage, with two acres of old-world garden and a paddock that would contain Miranda's pony when she was old enough to ride one. He was always boring the partners with talk of what he called his 'place'. The Paynes had never been invited there.

'You pleased with your Escort? Noticed it in the garage. The 1.6. is quite nippy, I imagine – ' Hopwood, whose scarlet Alfa Romeo had startled the practice when he'd first turned up in it, was flushed and breathy. He had fallen too far back in the sofa cushions, and was struggling to right himself.

'All right so far. Yes, I think so. It goes.' Dennis was uninterested in motor cars. He would not have parted with his old Rover if it had not begun to let him down so badly and so often.

'I hope you're managing at the practice,' he heard himself say, his hands suddenly clammy with sweat. 'Did you see any of my patients today?'

This question was not answered immediately because at that moment Sheila appeared with the trolley and Hopwood, telling Dennis to stay put, struggled out of the sofa to give her a hand and to make a space for a plate of tea-cakes on a table cluttered with knitting and knitting patterns and Sheila's prized collection of china cats. Then there was the business of pouring out the tea, and who took sugar and who wanted a tea-cake. When all this had been resolved, and Hopwood was back on the sofa – perched, this time – with a cup of tea on his knee, Sheila excused herself: 'I've got something on the cooker' – and he was alone again with Hopwood.

'You were asking me – ?' Hopwood stirred his tea. 'Oh yes. I remember. No, I didn't see any of your patients. I was a bit annoyed about that, if you must know. I had a cancellation myself and easily could have done.' He paused for a moment, perhaps expecting Dennis to make some sort of comment. 'I gather Johnny (Johnny! thought Dennis, *Jefferies* to you) had a rather unpleasant experience with one of them. He's going to phone you about it this evening.'

'What do you mean?'

'I'm a bit dodgy on the facts,' Hopwood said, so perhaps you should wait to hear them from the horse's mouth. But I understood that the woman Johnny saw had an epulis on the gum, and he's convinced it's a nasty.'

There was a silence, at the end of which Dennis managed to say: 'They're usually benign, you know.' Perhaps even now, secondaries were forming in Elizabeth's white neck. He wanted to ask Hopwood if he knew the name of the patient; but found that he couldn't.

'Maybe,' said Hopwood, 'but Johnny seemed certain. He's seen nasties before – as I imagine you must have done, in your time.' Dennis had, on at least four occasions. He was not likely to forget the shock of those discoveries; the offensive smell; the having to

156

remain calm and matter-of-fact with the patient. And then passing the buck to some hapless G.P.: 'Look – this is not really a dental problem. You ought to see your doctor about it without delay. If you would kindly give me his name and address, I'd like to write him a little note, if I may . . .' Remaining calm and matter-of-fact was what he now had to do with Hopwood who had launched into an attack on John Jefferies for not calling him in to inspect the mouth in question. It was important, surely, that he, Hopwood, should know what to look for and to recognize, should one of his patients . . . etc.

Dennis was only half listening. His thoughts had raced back to the conversation he'd had with Elizabeth in the park. She'd said something about a sore place in her mouth. Where? Tongue. He was sure she'd said tongue. And Hopwood had mentioned an epulis, a tumour that restricted itself to the bone or gum. What's more, she was too young. Mouth tumours, whatever their nature, seldom appeared before middle age. And she wasn't a smoker, he was certain. She couldn't be. No, the patient had to be Miss Barnard, the English mistress at St Theresa's with whom he sometimes had convivial chat about the Metaphysical Poets. She was about the right age, and she smoked like a chimney. He felt enormously relieved by his deductions, and offered Hopwood a third cup of tea.

Hopwood, declining, got to his feet and put his cup on the trolley.

'Johnny did say there was something unusual – peculiar – about this case, but I'm blowed if I can remember what it was.'

Bastard, Dennis thought. Bastard. He felt, suddenly, very tired and very old. How could life, how could Hopwood, how could *Elizabeth*, do this to him? What had he done to deserve it? Without knowing it, they'd managed to kill off his innocent pastime. He would never now give her the Ark. For he saw at once that even if it wasn't Elizabeth, even if there was nothing seriously wrong with her mouth at all – a minor infection, a touch of uloglossitis, could easily account for the symptoms she'd described

– he would always associate her with this appalling afternoon, and Hopwood's red face against the sofa cushions.

# GRIST

'All my love for you, Sweet*heart*,' he always said. He invariably said. 'All my love for *you*.' So when one night he didn't say it, Babe knew he didn't love her. She waited until next time – the next time his body relaxed on hers – to be sure. But it was only a formality. For by then, the space of two or three days, there were other signs. He stopped touching, fingering, you might say, with one long finger, her shoulder blades and her arms, in the way he did (as though he were drawing pictures on them). He stopped shovelling dog shit from the lawn. He didn't bring surprise whiskies to the ironing board. In their supermarket, he no longer vanished in Cereals so that he could materialize seconds later in the Pet Food aisle: 'Excuse me. You are the Most Beautiful Person in the World, and I claim my Lifetime of Happiness.' A talkative man at home, a mimic, a raconteur, he became silent. His silence grew and grew and filled the house. It was October, and the grass hidden by a weight of wet chestnut leaves, but he, usually the first to attack onerous tasks and the last to abandon them, seemed not to notice. When Babe got out the rake and barrow and started to pull the leaves into heaps, he put on his old garden coat, the garment of his she liked the best, and went for a walk by himself. (He, who'd never allowed her to take so much as a step without him!)

A horrible ten days passed, in which he pretended black was white and white black, in which he played the torturing husband in *Gaslight*, while Babe was stuck with the Ingrid Bergman role (but without Bergman's beauty; without the sure and certain hope of rescue before the credits). At the end of the ten days they had a show down. He turned everything they'd shared on its head. Then he cleared out his darkroom, packed his belongings and left.

When Babe felt able to, she drove over to Aunt's and told her about it. Not all of it, and not all at once. Babe was seeing a lot of Aunt just then. Aunt was dying, or, more accurately, living with Death. Death was giving Aunt a hard time. He followed her up and down stairs, and from sitting-room to kitchen; he had a sweetish, stomach-turning smell. He leant over her shoulder when she was playing patience or doing *The Times* crossword, he kept her awake all night. Aunt had no time for Death, and she didn't want to give him cottage room. Apart from her animals, she'd always lived alone. Depending on the strength of her pain, and on the weather, she fought or ignored him. Or she mocked him. Once, when she'd chucked Babe a cigarette and lit one for herself, she offered the packet over her shoulder. 'Go on,' she said, shaking the pack impatiently, 'take one. Feel free. It'll do you good. He's a humourless bugger,' she said to Babe.

Aunt smoked like a chimney, and the ceiling above the corner table where she did the crossword and played round after round of patience was dark brown, like the ceiling in a pub. Those who loved Aunt found this strange, it seemed out of keeping, because in all other respects Aunt was fastidious. Even with three cats and a dog, there was nothing messy about her tiny sitting room. Except for the overflowing ashtray, of course. Still, as Aunt said, you couldn't worry about getting cancer when you already had it.

Babe convinced herself that telling Aunt her troubles might, if not cheer Aunt up exactly, at least give her something else to think about (although Aunt was always interested in other people; always thinking about them). Aunt was upset by Babe's news. Upset for Babe and upset, in a way, for herself. And surprised. She hadn't seen it coming. Only the month before, Babe had brought his new book of photographs, just published, for her to see. 'That *is* nice,' Aunt had said, looking at the flyleaf on which he'd written 'Your Book, from Your Person' and underneath, his initial, enclosed by a heart. (Babe hadn't told Aunt then her worries about private, lovey-dovey inscriptions, the awful poignancy of them in secondhand bookshops: 'Binkie, Beloved Angel – All My Love for Always, Tiddles. Xmas, 1926.' 'For Clive – as fine a man as any girl could wish for – Denise.' But she had told *him*. And he'd smiled. And drawn a picture on her shoulder blades.) Aunt had sat at her table with the book of photographs, turning the pages slowly, studying each one. There were shots of Babe's grown up sons; views of her house and garden the photographer had called home. There was a whole section devoted to portraits of Babe. 'Is that really you?' Aunt had asked, peering. 'It's not the you I know. I'm not sure I want to see you in bed. Do I?' Aunt had said, of another, 'Though I must say your chins are tactfully lit.'

Aunt was upset by Babe's news. She'd grown fond of the photographer, as she always referred to him. He was interesting; he brought another world into her sitting room; he made her laugh. She was sorry she wouldn't be seeing him anymore. Having admitted that, having got it off her chest ('Look, I've got it off my chest,' she said, cough-laughing into her whisky glass) Aunt did everything she could to make Babe feel better and more positive.

'A nice fellow. Clever, certainly – though not at crosswords. Or was he?' Aunt said, 'A joke, ho ho. Generous? Oh yes. You're still hung about with his baubles, I see. Handsome, I won't deny. But a juvenile lead. Not man enough for you. Not mature enough. No. Let's have another whisky.'

They drank pints of whisky, interspersed, in Aunt's case, with painkillers and minute helpings of the creamed vegetable soup – usually carrot – those who loved Aunt took it in turns to make and bring her. Her fridge, and the box freezer above it, were full of the stuff, in little cling-filmed pots, jostling with the cod fillets Aunt fed to her cats. Every so often Aunt would leave the room, and patter, rice-paper thin, to the kitchen; and return with a fizzing glass of what looked like fruit salts which she'd set down beside her whisky on the table. Morphine every four hours; solpadine (the fizzers) as a supplementary when the pain got unbearable; and all that whisky – why didn't it kill her?

'What did it mean, Aunt? Was none of it true? Was it a game?' Babe asked her. (Babe was still in shock; it had been so sudden.) 'Was it only a game?'

'Could be,' Aunt said. 'How do I know? Yes I do. I'm sure he meant it. I'm sure he thought he meant it, at the time. Anyway, don't you play games? You always beat me at Scrabble, I notice. I think you cheat. Don't expect me to play with you in future. Now, getting back to the crossword,' Aunt said, 'Harpo and Groucho won't do – sorry chaps, no offence – so who were the others? Tell.'

'Chico?' Babe said. She was no good at the crossword (which Aunt regularly solved in ten minutes) but it was nice to be consulted. Aunt always consulted her. 'Then there was Karl, of course,' Babe said.

'*Karl*,' Aunt said, 'Karl. How could we forget him? Quite the funniest of the four.'

A day or so later, a postcard came to Babe's house, written all over in Aunt's famous blue felt tip: 'What say HARPO, GROUCHO, CHICO& ??? ZEPPO ??? So we don't need ~~Lenin~~ Karl (!) Come back SOON. XXX Aunt.'

Aunt's ceiling seemed to grow browner as they sat there, evening after evening, puffing away, swigging away, drunk as life peeresses. Soon snow pressed against the windows. Soon the lanes were full of it. Sometimes Babe had to stay the night, and she lay in the double bed in Aunt's spare room and listened to her cough, and heard her pad to the bathroom time and time again. The light under Aunt's door stayed on until morning.

'We laughed a lot,' Babe told Aunt. 'We were always laughing. Doubled up with it, often. Our cheekbones ached. We did have fun you know. We had a lot of fun.'

'I know you did,' Aunt said, 'I know you did. Laughter's good stuff. I approve of laughter. Tastes better than these fizzers, yuk,' Aunt said. 'A good howl can be therapeutic, too.'

Aunt didn't howl, so far as Babe knew, but she wasn't always able to laugh. Sometimes when Babe telephoned she was sharp. No, she wasn't all right, she was bloody awful. No, Babe couldn't come over. No, no, no. Not today and not tomorrow. Not any day this week.

Christmas cards began to appear on Aunt's chimneypiece. They didn't talk about them. Aunt was dreading Christmas. Not because she'd acknowledged it would be her last (she was making plans for her garden in the Spring: 'Shall I build that wall?' she kept asking, 'What do you think? Give me your views. Should I move the island bed? Should I widen the border?') but because she'd always hated festivals. Festivals were for children. Aunt had had affairs, successful and less successful, happy and not so happy; Aunt loved men and liked them, but she'd never married and she'd never had children. In the past, those who loved Aunt had begged her to spend Christmasses with them and their children (of whom she was varyingly fond) and sometimes she had, providing it didn't mean spending a night away from home. Aunt's old maroon Mini hadn't left its garage now for two weeks. She wouldn't be going anywhere of her own choosing. Her loved ones would be popping in, of course, on Christmas Eve and Christmas Day and Boxing Day; they'd all be bringing presents and booze and fags and carrot soup; Mr Timms from across the road would be coming midday to make up her fire; the doctor and the nurse would call. But there was no getting away from it: some of the time, a great deal of the time, and all of every night, Aunt was going to be – apart from the animals – alone over the Christmas holiday. With him.

Aunt still hadn't accepted her lodger. She was still taking swipes at him, still keeping him at a short arm's length. How, nobody knew. There was nothing of her. The nurse was 'dropping in' every day now, sometimes twice. The morphine was three-hourly. 'One of the advantages of teabags,' Aunt said, peering into the tea she invariably let go cold before drinking – or, increasingly, not drinking – 'is there's no risk of a tall dark stranger lurking in the cup. So there,' she said over her shoulder to him. 'Yah boo to you know who,' she said to Babe.

While Aunt was out of the room getting her fizzers, Babe peeked inside the Christmas cards on Aunt's chimneypiece. She'd thought there might be one from the photographer. He hadn't sent one to Babe, and she was trying not to think of last year, and the fun they'd had, the fun she'd thought they'd had – but Aunt, why no card for Aunt? He hadn't fallen out of love with *her*. Yet he had been fond of her, he'd said so, often. 'Aunt is a major human being,' he'd said, more than once, 'really major,' and Babe had agreed, even though, in her view, major was a word best left to military matters. No card for Aunt, no card for a really major human being, hurt. At a hurtful time, it was one of the things that hurt most. The photographer had had to write to Babe once or twice – brief, typewritten notes on practical subjects, things he'd left behind and so forth, and stamped with a second class stamp – but he'd never mentioned Aunt in these notes, he'd never asked how she was, he'd never sent her his love. Babe kept turning this over in her mind. She stayed awake pondering this. Was nothing good? Was nothing true? Was nothing real? Did nothing mean anything?

Babe couldn't talk to Aunt about this, of course, but there were other things that hurt, and she told Aunt about those.

'This exhibition is painful,' Babe said. 'All those portraits of me. More or less naked. Asleep. In bed. I'm even on the catalogue. And last week in the colour supplement there was one of *her* – his new person. Naked. In bed. We'll be beside each other, you realize, on the ICA walls. Bedfellows, so to speak. How can he do that, Aunt? Why doesn't it bother him? How can he do it so soon?'

'All grist to the photographer's mill,' Aunt said, trying to get a spoonful of carrot soup into her mouth; failing; giving up. 'Anything goes with artists. All must be sacrificed to Art – is photography Art? I'm never quite sure – nothing, no one, is safe. Anyway, they aren't portraits of you or of her, they're portraits of him. He's the subject of all his photographs, even those fuzzy landscapes. That's enough profundities for the time being. I'm not

166

sure I like carrot soup all that much,' Aunt said, 'if I ever did. Could you pass the word round?'

'Do you think he's claimed a Lifetime of Happiness from her yet?' Babe asked Aunt over the telephone. Babe had rung Aunt to tell her Boris had come home. He'd been missing two days, unusual for him, and she'd been frantic. Aunt had been anxious about Boris too, and had rung before breakfast for news – which meant a painful descent of the stairs because she had no telephone by her bed. Those who loved Aunt were working on her to get one connected.

'I once knew a cat who was away eight months, and then just walked in,' Aunt had said before breakfast. 'What a relief,' she'd said a moment ago, when Babe had told her the glad tidings. 'Now we can all relax. Until next time.'

'Do you suppose he's sold her one?' Babe persisted. (She referred to the occasion the photographer had pretended to be a salesman, and had come to her door offering a Lifetime of Happiness on an easy instalment plan.)

'What's a lifetime?' Aunt said. She'd just 'celebrated', the one she loved best had helped her 'celebrate', her sixty-third birthday. 'What's happiness? Anyway, did *you* buy it? Did you say Ta ever so, and sign on the dotted line? I doubt it,' Aunt said. 'Not you. Too dull. Too commonplace. You'd never commit yourself to that.'

'Look, Babe,' Aunt said later, as they sat either side her fire, 'you must try and get a sense of proportion about all this. If Jim and Ted,' she said, referring to Babe's sometime husbands, 'merit a section, say, in Ted's case, and a chapter in Jim's, then the photographer is worth only a page or so in your book. I'm speaking figuratively of course. Only a page or so. Half a dozen, at the most. Remember that.' Aunt, after two stabs at it, swallowed her morphine mix, and a made a face; and then chased the morphine with a swig of whisky. Just recently she'd given up all attempts at soup, no matter what variety, though she toyed with a forkful of scrambled egg, a spoonful of jelly.

'Incidentally,' Aunt said, 'how's your other book coming along? My book, I should say.' (For Babe had asked permission to dedicate the book she was writing – not writing; how could she? – to Aunt. Aunt had said yes. She was flattered, she said, not to say bowled over – though she did rather hope there wouldn't be any filth in it. No explicit bedroom scenes. Nothing a maiden aunt wouldn't be pleased to read. Babe wanted to finish the book in time for Aunt, but she knew she hadn't a hope.) 'Does the photographer appear in your book in some guise or other?' Aunt

said. 'Do I? Are we both a bit of grist to your mill?'

After Aunt died, Babe said to the one Aunt loved best, the one who loved Aunt best, the one who had lost most: 'What shall we do without Aunt? What shall we do without Aunt's voice, and Aunt's laugh, and Aunt's famous blue felt tip and Aunt's postcards? How shall we manage without Aunt to tell things to?'

The one Aunt loved best and who loved Aunt best and who had lost most, the one to whom Aunt wrote not just postcards, but long letters (and had managed to do so from her hospice bed that last harrowing week) said: 'We must go on talking to Aunt. We must keep telling her things. Aunt was always interested. You can tell her about the awful men you meet, and the boring dinner parties you go to. You can tell her when Boris goes missing, and when he comes back. If you feel like cutting your throat, tell Aunt.

Tell Aunt everything. Make Aunt laugh.'

Babe told Aunt. She told her funny things and sad things and boring things; and afterwards she imagined what Aunt's response would be.

For a time it worked. For a time, Babe could hear Aunt's laugh, and Aunt's cough and Aunt's voice. For a time, she could see Aunt. She could see her lighting a cigarette, and padding about with a glass in her hand. She could see Aunt's hand in close-up, turning up the cards, flattening out the crossword page on the table in the corner.

Babe devised all manner of ruses to keep Aunt there, and for a time it worked, but it got harder. It got harder every day. She forgot to tell Aunt, or she couldn't face it, or she put it off. Then when she did, she couldn't always hear Aunt's reply. After two months had gone by, she couldn't see Aunt's face or Aunt's hands in the way she had; she couldn't hear Aunt's voice distinctly, she couldn't see Aunt clearly at all.

Then one day Babe went out to dinner, and when she got home, around midnight, and was having a nightcap, she told Aunt about her evening.

'Aunt,' Babe said, sitting in her easy chair, sipping her whisky, 'here's one for you. I've just been to a dinner party. Not good news, as per. No ashtrays for a start. When I asked for one, my hostess, laughing a v. false laugh, said: "You're not still a slave to that disgusting habit, surely? I thought no one in their right minds was silly enough to smoke these days," etc, etc. Then, would you believe, Bobby Gaskell – who knows the answer perfectly well – asked me why the photographer wasn't there. Had I left him at home, or something? "I got the impression he never left your side," he said. Great. Then we went in to dinner. The first course was soup. "Carrot soup!" the woman opposite me exclaimed. "My favourite! How clever of you, Annabel! Such a fiddle faddle to make, but worth it. One can never have too much carrot soup!" '

The story was supposed to make Aunt laugh, it was supposed to make Babe laugh, they were supposed to laugh together. But perhaps Babe had drunk too much claret before her nightcap; perhaps she hadn't told the story right; because though she waited in the quiet room in the quiet house, she couldn't hear anything. Babe went on sitting there, drawing on her cigarette, draining her whisky glass, listening; and eventually she thought she could hear Aunt, a long way off, saying ho ho *ho*. She thought she could hear Aunt laugh. Babe wanted to join in. She wanted to laugh with Aunt; for a moment she thought she was going to, but she didn't. She howled. She howled up the stairs and into the bathroom and while she was getting undressed and while she was taking her face off. She cried herself to sleep.

# NOBLE ROT

It was on her way back from the hairdresser that Cecily Bressingham saw the picnickers in the lay-by. The lay-by was on the left of the main road, a hundred yards from the crossroads where, in order to get home, Cecily Bressingham turned right. As she waited, indicator ticking, for the traffic to go by, she thought how extraordinary the lower orders were. Who in their right minds, in the middle of the most lovely countryside, and on this boiling hot day, would choose to picnic in a *lay-by,* only inches from this horrendous main road? It was not just extraordinary, it was – she remembered the white head of one, the bald head of the other – pathetic. And pathetically sad. How wonderful it would be to rescue them and transport them to her own garden; to the shade of a willow tree and the peace of the river bank . . . .

Cecily, who since childhood had maintained a partiality for fairy-tale endings, was subject to fantasies of this sort – the sort that allowed her a starring, dragon-slaying role; but commonsense and a busy life usually prevented their being translated into realities. So she sighed, and when there was a gap in the lorries, turned right on to the B road, and then left in to the lane that wound, with passing places only, to the valley where she lived.

Halfway down the lane she stopped; and reversed the car into a field, and drove back the way she'd come.

Arnold had laid the table with the knives and forks Elaine had given them for their silver wedding, and was unscrewing the thermos, when a big grey car pulled on to the lay-by and parked

173

behind his car.

'Blow,' Gladys said, shading her spectacles and squinting, 'Don't look now, but we've got company.'

A woman in jeans and a tee-shirt got out of the car and came over to them.

'Good morning,' the woman said.

'Afternoon,' Arnold said, not looking up. He poured tea into a cup and handed it to Gladys. Gladys put her cup on the table and squinted suspiciously at the stranger, who said – but whatever she said was lost as a juggernaut thundered up the hill. The ground shook, the table jumped; and in the lorry's wake, the black grasses at the roadside rolled inland like waves to a shore. The stranger squatted beside Gladys's chair and rested her hand on the table top.

'Look, forgive me for interfering,' she said, 'but I passed you a moment ago, and I'm very worried about you both. I know this road well,' she continued, speaking the words slowly and clearly. 'It is very, very dangerous, and you are much too near it. Where have you come from?' she asked, looking from one to the other with an expression of interest and concern, 'Where are you going to?'

'Swindon way,' Arnold said, in answer to the first question – though what business it was of hers he couldn't see. 'We're all right, thanks. No need to worry about us,' he said. 'This is a lay-by, for cars to lay-by in. That's what it's for.'

Gladys picked up her cup and took a sip from it. Perhaps their visitor was a plain-clothes policewoman, or a social worker. 'We was sat in this field a while back,' she said pleasantly, 'but then this tractor come up and asks us to move.' As she spoke, a petrol tanker, pursued by a container lorry, pursued in turn by an estate car, chuntered past, and sprayed them with an oily exhaust.

'Look,' the woman shouted, when they'd finished coughing, 'I live just over there, beyond that hill, and I'd love it, I'd be really delighted, if you'd come and eat your picnic in our garden –'

'We couldn't do that.' Arnold was firm. They could've eaten their picnic in their own garden, if they'd wanted.

'– by the river, under the weeping willows' – the woman turned to Gladys – 'in the shade . . .'

A river. Shade. Peace. Quiet. Gladys patted her perm and considered these attractions. She had always liked a river, in fact only the other day –

'You don't know us, and we don't know you,' Arnold said, determined to end the discussion.

'My name is Cecily Bressingham,' the woman said to Gladys, 'How do you do?'

'I'm Gladys Carter,' Gladys said, 'and this is my husband, Arnold.' Arnold nodded, but said nothing. Instead, he took a handkerchief from his trouser pocket and blotted his neck and forehead. The heat was terrible. A man who'd served with the Eighth Army was hardly one to be afraid of an English summer, as he was fond of saying, but – as he was also fond of saying – he was not as young as he used to be; and he winced now as two motor bikes, competing for the summit, raced up the hill.

Cecily Bressingham saw the wince, and decided to play her trump card. This was an Accident Black Spot, she told them, with at least one fatal smash a month. There were plans to widen the road, or to make it a dual carriageway, but until then –

'Oh Arnold,' Gladys said.

Arnold gave in.

'Well, this is an adventure!' Gladys said later as they waited behind the grey car at the crossroads.

'I don't like it,' Arnold said. 'I don't like being pushed round. What d'you think she's playing at?'

She wasn't playing at anything, Gladys told him, she wasn't going to turn them into toadstools, she was just being kind. There wasn't enough kindness in the world these days. It had been dangerous in that lay-by, she reproved him, and smelly, and hot. They should've taken that turning left by the garage where she'd said.

In the lane the grey car braked in a passing place to let a tractor and silage cart go by, and Arnold's car nearly ran into the back of it.

'You two all right?' Cecily Bressingham called cheerfully out of her window. 'Sorry about that! Nearly there now.'

The road meandered downhill between low hedges, over which they could see sheep on one side and young corn on the other. In front of them the downs rolled away, pale grey-green fading to grey-blue, here and there a snippet of yellow, almost treeless.

'In the old days, that would've been mustard,' Arnold lamented.

'Imagine this place in winter, Arn,' Gladys said. 'Think of it in snow.' But when she tried to herself, she couldn't. It was too hot.

At the bottom of the hill they passed a farm with a cluster of barns and a grain silo and cattle standing in a caked yard, and after that a group of cottages with pink roses and purple clematis growing over them. A couple of bends, and then into view came the double row of poplars that, no matter how often she saw them, always reminded Cecily of the Loire valley, their leaves glittering – like tinsel, Gladys decided – in the sunshine.

'Look Arnold – the river!' she said, but it was no more than a stream at this point, and Arnold told her so. He had not yet recovered his humour, and the car, despite all the windows being down, was an oven. 'Some five minutes,' he said, referring to the amount of time Mrs Whateverhernamewas had said it took to get there.'

They passed a pub called 'The Dove' on the left of the road, and a village shop with a PO sign and an ice cream banner on the right. They passed more cottages, grey stone and thatched, and a village hall with an asbestos roof.

'Must be that place, I bet,' Gladys said, as the car in front slowed to a crawl, and the high stone wall appeared on the right. Behind it they could see a square house, painted white, with black window frames. But no. The grey car slid past it and on round a bend between high banks. When they caught up with it again, its left indicator was blinking.

Beyond a stretch of park railing they followed the car sharp left over a cattle grid, through stone pillars surmounted by a fancy ironwork of ribbons and scrolls. The drive was long and full of potholes, and Arnold had to juggle with the steering wheel in order to avoid them.

'I won't have any tyres left,' he grumbled.

How do they manage when they're in a rush to catch a train? Gladys wondered.

On either side, the unfenced route was lined with cows, standing quite still, staring, and one of these lifted its tail as they passed and unconcernedly messed its rump and the ground with black-looking dung.

'It's like being in a safari park,' Gladys said. 'A bit unnerving.' What would be unnerving, Arnold thought, as the drive forked at a clump of trees and the convoy swung right on to a gravel sweep, would be to own a herd as big as this one, dairy products being considered poison these days, and the government subsidy cut by half.

After the splendour of the gates and the length of the drive, Gladys was a little disappointed at the size of the house. It was definitely large. Definitely. But not that large. Not like some of the places they'd visited. Not like Longleat, or Castle Howard, or Knole.

'You didn't tell us you was taking us to a stately home,' Arnold said, struggling with his car door as their abductress approached.

'Well, hardly that!' Cecily Bressingham tugged at Arnold's door (which eventually gave so that he fell, rather than stepped, into the drive) and laughed a merry, embarrased laugh. 'It's just an ordinary, well, manor house, I suppose you'd call it.' As she spoke, she made a squeezing gesture with her finger and thumb that reduced the edifice behind them to tied cottage proportions. 'The front's misleading, it's actually quite small, in fact.'

The Carters stood in the drive and stared up at the quite small manor house shimmering, dream-like, in the heat. They saw, or rather Arnold saw – for Gladys was short-sighted and not much interested in architectural detail – a stone porch with three Doric columns on either side of double front doors; three bay windows capped with pediments; the date 1585 on a central panel above the door. The roof was gabled along its length, and surmounting each gable was a small heraldic beast – lions they might have been, though it was hard to tell when they were so badly chipped. The house reminded Arnold of another house, but what and where he couldn't place. Feeling that some comment was called for, he remarked on the magnificent *magnolia grandiflora* that grew on the left of the porch to the height of the gables. He'd never seen one that size before, he said.

'No? Well, as a matter of fact that's a sore point, it's on its last legs. It *ought* to come down. And we *ought* to plant another, but I can't bring myself to quite yet . . . . Now, before I take you to the river – ' Cecily Bressingham turned to Gladys ' – would either of you like – ' she searched round for the right word, the word that would make them feel at home ' – the toilet? Or a wash?'

Gladys said No thank you, though she meant Yes please. It was a good hour and a half since they'd paid a visit to the convenience in Malmesbury. Her bladder was always playing her up. She didn't need to go yet awhile, but –

'Your picnic must be melting,' Cecily said, 'Let me give you a hand.' While Arnold was fighting with the boot, a man, balding, moustached, in shirt sleeves and corduroy trousers, and followed by two labrador dogs, came round the side of the house calling 'Thistle, Thistle –

'Oh there you are,' he said. 'What's happening about lunch?'

'This is my husband William,' Cecily Bressingham said. 'Mr and Mrs Carter – er, Gladys, is that right? and Albert.'

'Arnold,' Arnold said.

'We met on the main road. They couldn't find anywhere safe and nice for their picnic, and I thought the river garden would be just the place –'

'Quite right, very good, very good,' William said. 'Down, Tess.'

'We're fond of dogs,' Gladys said, and she bent down and

patted the black head of the one that was slobbering over her new sandals, 'aren't we Arnold?' The Bressinghams helped the Carters get their picnic things out of the car, and when everyone had something to carry – a rug, a chair, a table, an orange picnic bag – and was about to move off, a girl, wearing long black flowing garments, drifted towards them over the gravel.

'Lunch,' the girl said. 'Have you seen the boys?'

'This is Mr and Mrs Carter,' Cecily began again, with explanations. 'My daughter Olivia.'

'Oh right', Olivia said, and drifted back to the house.

'I hope your meal won't spoil,' Gladys said, as she and Arnold, fainting with heat and hunger, followed the Bressinghams and the waving tails of the labrador dogs down a stone path edged with lavender that was not yet in flower.

'Not to worry!' Cecily called over her shoulder. 'We always have bread and cheese on Saturdays!'

It really was a delightful garden. On the left a cedar-shaded lawn, planted out with croquet hoops, stretched away to a drystone wall; the giant yew hedge on the right had windows cut into it, and through these squares of brilliant light could be seen pale, flat-petalled roses and sections of herbaceous border. At the end of the path, a lead shepherdess with a dead-looking lamb under her arm gestured her crook towards a pergola, and they bent their heads to avoid ribbons of – Cecily Bressingham informed the Carters with a laugh – Paul's Himalayan Musk. Through this, and the scent of a thousand hot herbs at once rose to them from star-shaped beds, divided and edged with box.

'This is the herb garden,' Cecily said, stopping, bending down to pick a piece of something which she rubbed between her fingers and then held to her nose. 'Far too far from the kitchen, need I say.'

'Where've you come from?' William asked Arnold. They had left the herb garden and were descending a grassy slope where grew gunnera plants, the size of small trees. The ground was soft here, and the heels of Gladys's sandals sank into it, nearly toppling her several times. 'Ah,' William said, when Arnold had told him, 'the train-spotter's mecca.'

At the waterside, by drifts of mimulus and astilbes, under a weeping willow, in Paradise, the Bressinghams put up the Carters' table and chairs and laid out their rug.

'Please make yourselves at home,' Cecily said, straightening the tablecloth. (It was quite hideous, oh dear, dark brown with beige roses all over it.) 'Have a ziz after your picnic. Walk anywhere you like – the lily pond's over there; which might amuse you. We'd be very pleased if you'd join us for tea, at tea time.' Arnold said thank you, but they had to get back to feed the cats – something Gladys never did till eight or nine.

'Well if you can stay, we'd be absolutely thrilled, more than delighted. We'll send one of the children to fetch you up about four.'

'Oh lor, I forgot to offer them anything to drink,' Cecily said at lunch, which they were eating in the garden room, with the french windows wide open.

'They had a thermos, I seem to remember,' William said, stretching a sandy-haired and freckled forearm for the celery.

'No no no, I meant a proper drink. Something cold.'

'Beurre, s'il vous plait,' Mungo said, stabbing Jean-Marie with an elbow.

Frogs were the pits. Jean-Marie never passed anybody anything. Cecily turned to her daughter Sophie. Would she be a darling, and take the poor Carters a bottle of plonk and a couple of cans of beer?

'You have to be joking,' Sophie said. 'I haven't met them, I don't know them.'

'Mungo then? It's about time – '

'Can't. Sorry. Got to to go now.' Mungo looked at his watch. But it was only one twenty, and he was not due on the cricket field until two.

'Who are the Carters?' George wanted to know.

'Your mother's new best friends,' William said, 'I don't like your tone.'

'They're very nice people,' Cecily said.

'Yes they're very nice people,' William said. 'By the way,' he said to his wife, 'your other best friends, the Kiftsgates, can't come tonight. Poll rang when you were out. Harry's malingering. And the Hascombes are bringing an American they've been landed with for the weekend.'

Cecily could have cried. She'd been trying for months to get the Kiftsgates and the Hascombes and the Waddesdons together for dinner, so that they could be nice to the Muckrosses who were new, and until that moment believed she had succeeded. Mungo looked at his watch again, and got up.

'I'm off now,' he said, 'if that's okay with you.'

'No,' William said. (Mungo was being a little pest these holidays, a real little pain.) 'Not until you've taken the Whatsisnames a drink, as your mother asked you.'

'I don't mind going, 'Jamie said, realizing that, lunch being nearly over, washing-up loomed.

'No, Mungo will go.'

'What bottle?' Mungo asked at the door. 'Babycham? Cherry B? A Pony? What's their poison, d'you reckon?'

He could take a Sauvignon, his father told him, and there was some lager in the fridge. 'Bottle opener, glasses, ice. Get on with it. Scram.'


The Carters were finishing off their Danish pastries, when a youth in cricket clothes and with a basket over his arm loped across the lawn, skidded down the bank and landed on the rug at their feet. They were eating their picnic bolt upright on chairs, as was their habit, and this somehow added to their air of surprise on seeing the intruder.

'Liquid refreshment, with my mother's compliments,' said Mungo, against all the odds deciding to play the charmer. 'I'm your barman.' He tipped the contents of his basket on to the rug

181

and held up a corkscrew.

The Carters stared at him, too astonished to speak.

'It's very kind of you, dear,' Gladys said at last, 'but we've just had tea. We never touch a drop in the day time,' she added – an understatement, for, weddings and funerals apart, she and Arnold – not that they had anything against it, mind – were teetotal.

'Go on, it's a picnic. Be a devil.' Mungo hadn't run all this way in the heat to be turned down, no way.

'I'll try a beer, if that's what you've got there,' Arnold said, peering.

'Hooray! I've got a customer!' Mungo threw a can into the air and caught it – just – with one hand. 'Catch,' he said to Arnold. Arnold caught.

'Remember you're driving, Arnold,' Gladys said.

'Change your mind. Go on,' Mungo said, beaming the smile that never failed to win all female hearts, and the hearts of certain senior boys at school.

'Well, 'Gladys was wavering. It was after all, a very warm day. 'Perhaps.'

'Don't worry, this Sauvignon's quite drinkable.' Mungo held the bottle, which seemed to be not the right shape, away from him to read the label, and when he had done so, turned rather pink. Oh well, he consoled himself, nothing but the best for Mum's new best friends. And serve his father right for not fetching the bottle himself.

'You going to have one?' Arnold said, tapping his can of lager. 'Daren't.' Mungo knelt up on the rug, and indicated his cricket clothes. Then he opened the bottle and poured a glass of yellow wine and handed it to Gladys.

'School match, would it be?' Arnold asked.

'Village', Mungo said. 'We broke up last week,' he explained. Arnold was surprised. His grandsons had another three weeks of summer term left to go before the holidays.

'This wine is very pleasant,' Gladys said, sipping. 'Cheers.' It was sweet, and she liked a sweet wine, but if she was honest she'd have to say it was a shade too sweet – and heavy – to be really refreshing on such a warm day.

'What's your name, dear?' she asked, straining out of her chair to put the glass on the table.

'Mungo,' Mungo said.

'How old are you, Mango?'

'Mungo,' Mungo said. 'Fourteen.'

The Carters were very surprised. He looked much older than fourteen, they told him. 'And so tall,' Gladys said, 'and slim.' She looked reprovingly at Arnold who'd got fatter since he stopped work, and who was only five feet six.

'Mungo Park,' Arnold muttered to himself. 'Batsman or bowler?' he asked Mungo.

'Batsman,' said Mungo, whose highest score this season had been ten, whose average, three.

'Our youngest boy, Malcolm, used to play cricket,' Gladys remarked.

'Oh, right?' Mungo said, and he turned to Gladys, but she was silent, having no more to say on the subject.

'Play at school, do you?' Arnold asked. 'In the team?'

Mungo nodded. He did play in a team of sorts.

'Where's that then? Where's your school?'

'Er, Berkshire,' Mungo said, seeing embarrasment somewhere ahead, hoping to avoid it.

'Berkshire's a big place,' Arnold said. 'The Royal County of Berkshire is quite a big place.' He tipped back his head and drained the beer can.

'Slough, then,' Mungo said.

'Slough's Bucks,' Arnold said ruminitavely. 'I know' – he leant forward in his chair and pointed a finger at Mungo – 'you's at Eton College, right?'

'Right,' Mungo said, accused; found guilty.

'Like it there, do you?' Arnold was interested. He'd seen a documentary about Eton boys only recently on the TV.

Mungo considered. He thought of his housemaster whom he

disliked. Of his classical tutor who (he was pretty sure) disliked him. He wasn't good at work. He wasn't good enough at games. Most of the boys in his block were trogs or wankers. The truth was, he'd never liked school, this or any other.

'It's okay,' he said. 'What do you do?' he asked Arnold. 'What's your job?'

'Arnold's retired,' Gladys said. 'He'll be sixty-eight, come September.'

Her tone suggested that sixty-eight was a remarkable age, and one attained by very few; that she was responsible for his having achieved it, and that congratulations would not be out of order.

'I was in waste disposal,' Arnold said. 'My eldest lad runs the business now.'

Waste disposal? Waste disposal? Mungo racked his grey matter. 'Nuclear waste?'

'Sewage,' Arnold said. 'Septic tanks. Evacuation of.'

'Ah we've got one of those,' Mungo said enthusiastically. Putrefaction was one of his favourite words.

'You would have,' Arnold told him, 'out here. There'd be no mains drainage out here. What time's your cricket?'

'Oh lor, I'll be late.' Mungo leapt from the rug.

Arnold wished him luck. Gladys wished him all the best. At the last minute, Mungo remembered his manners and topped up Gladys's glass. While they'd been talking it had become a bathing pool for a wide variety of insect life, and he removed this with a finger and then propped the bottle in the roots of the weeping willow.

'I'll be pickled, you know,' Gladys said untruthfully, not wishing to offend. She could always tip the wine away afterwards.

'Goodbye,' Mungo said. He was quite sorry to swap the Carters for the cricket field, where he felt certain he was going to score a duck. He'd quite liked Arnold. Arnold was okay.

Nice enough lad, Arnold thought when Mungo had gone.

'Nice enough lad,' he said to Gladys.

'Nice manners,' Gladys agreed, 'and lovely hair – wasted on a boy.' But fancy saddling him with a name like that, she thought, a name that sounded like a Latin American dance step, or one of those fruits (she and Arnold hadn't tried, and weren't likely to, at 70p a go) on the Exotic fruits counter at their supermarket.

'I'm going to have a bit of shut-eye now,' she told Arnold; and she removed her spectacles and settled more comfortably into her chair.

Arnold wasn't ready for a rest. Solidly and squarely built, he was too heavy for these flimsy picnic chairs; the metal frame of his cut painfully into the underside of his thighs, and into his back. He got up and stretched and walked about, pushing at the fronds of willow that everywhere assailed him, sniffing the river smell. On his way past Gladys's chair, the toe of his shoe caught the wine bottle lodged in the roots of the tree. It fell over at once, and the wine pumped out and sank into the thirsty soil. The bottle when he recovered it was all but empty, and he propped it back where he'd found it. Then, as he hadn't yet seen the river, obscured from view here by meadow-sweet and willow-herb and clumps of tall yellow irises, he walked along it, looking for a gap; and when he found one he sat down in the rough grass at the water's edge, and took off his shoes and socks, and dabbled his feet. The green water was shockingly cold, and he withdrew his feet quickly and lay back on his elbows, wiggling his toes to dry them. He lay still, with the sun on his face and his eyes shut, and listened contentedly to the watery noises, to a moorhen running along in the reeds, and to a blackbird singing in an alder.

'Better see if they're ready for a cup of tea,' Cecily said to one of her children. And one of her children went ungraciously to do her bidding. Cecily was feeling fraught. She'd spent the afternoon doing the flowers for her dinner party, a task she enjoyed only in theory. Choosing the blooms from the overflow beds in the kitchen garden (the herbaceous border couldn't be raided without upsetting old Goulden, who tended it, and who – because he'd worked there since he was twelve – believed it to be his garden);

snipping at *paeonia lactiflora* and geraniums *pratense* and *sanguineum;* filling her trug with – a weed, really, but pretty – the oh so useful *alchemilla mollis,* she'd been distressed by the shrieks and yells and splashes that came to her from over the high brick wall. They were not her children in the pool (its novelty, only two years after installation, had worn off, so that even on the hottest days none of hers entered it now, unless at midnight, fully clothed or naked), but the vicar's unprepossesing brood. Her invitation – 'Do come and swim whenever you like, *please*' – had been accepted verbatim, whenever they liked turning out to be weekday evenings and Saturday and Sunday afternoons.

If Willie'd been there, he'd have got rid of the little buggers, she was thinking crossly as, muzzy with sleep and hung about with picnic things, Gladys and Arnold came into view behind Sophie on the path.

'Ah, there you are!' she said brightly, and then, having enquired about their afternoon, she led them away to the downstairs cloaks.

At tea, laid out under a cedar on the lawn, the Carters were royally attended. 'Another sandwich for Gladys?' and the plate was proffered. 'Arnold – a drop more tea?' and his cup was filled. King Arnold and Queen Gladys sat on cushionless teak thrones, while their subjects sprawled on the grass at their feet.

They were confused at the number of children, but – as Cecily explained with a laugh as she introduced them – they were not all hers and William's. Jamie and Ned for instance, were her nephews (Jamie and Ned raised their hands in a vague salute, and resumed their conversation); Arabella a friend of Sophie's, and staying the weekend ('Hi there,' Arabella said); Jean-Marie was French, and over from Beynac on a month's exchange visit (Jean-Marie followed his 'allo' with a scowl and a shrug). The conversation was confusing too, most of it seeming to do with the video nasty everyone, with the exception of George ('That's George – the little one with red hair,' Cecily said, pointing) and Olivia, had been watching all afternoon. Mungo, whom Arnold and Gladys consciously missed, and who might not have made things easier for

186

them, was still playing cricket – run out second ball, according to George who'd been watching, 'and now, I presume, dropping catches in the outfield.' William was absent also, having been called away ('On a Saturday! It really is uncivilized!' Cecily had exploded) to an unexpected, and urgent, CLA meeting.

'No, really, thank you. That was very nice,' Gladys said, relieved to be rid of her cup. The milk hadn't been fresh, she decided, or else some fish in the fridge had tainted it – her tea had tasted of kippers.

Olivia, who since lunch had been drawing a view of the stables and the downs behind them, now ambled towards them over the lawn.

'How did it go, darling? Let's have a look,' Cecily called. 'Olivia's at art college,' she explained to the Carters. But Olivia's drawing had not gone well, and she frowned and kept her sketch book under her arm.

'Our grandson's an artist,' Arnold said, 'a student, you might say.'

'Oh right. Where?' Olivia asked, not really interested, only half listening.

'Clerkenwell,' Gladys said.

'Camberwell,' Arnold corrected her. 'Or rather (as Olivia and Cecily opened their mouth to reveal their astonishment) he's just left. He got the top award, degree, I think they call it. They's very pleased with him at the college, his Dad says.'

Cecily was dumbfounded. Her daughter Olivia, nearly at the end of her Foundation Course at Trowbridge, had applied to Camberwell and to Chelsea, had gone for interview at St Martin's and the R.A. Schools, and had been turned down by them all.

'We've never had an artist in the family before,' Arnold went on tactlessly, 'we never had nothing like it. But good luck to the lad, I said to his father, good luck to him. More power to his elbow, is what I say.'

'Quite so,' Cecily said faintly. 'How exciting.'

'He goes to the Royal College next,' Arnold seemed bent on

adding insult to terrible injury, 'on some sort of scholarship.'

Tea was over, but the Carters were still sitting there. They were more than ready to leave – the teak chairs were killers, Gladys's bladder was beginning to fill again, and she was worried about the cats who weren't used to being left – but how did you just get up and go? Wouldn't it look rude? She drummed her fingers lightly on the handbag in her lap and gave Arnold a look. At this moment Cecily got up from the grass. It had been a great success, she thought. But enough was enough. She didn't want to chivvy them, but the trouble was those sort of people – and it was *not* their fault – never knew when to leave, never quite knew when to take a hint.

'Do come and see us again,' she said in the drive, bending her head to Arnold's window, 'anytime you're passing. And bring your artist grandson with you – Olivia would be fascinated to meet him, I know!'

Taking a final look at the house, Arnold suddenly got it, the thing that had been bothering him, on and off, all afternoon. Corsham Court! That's what it reminded him of, Corsham Court! Smaller, mind you, and without the entablatures, but similar, definitely similar.

Goodbyes and thankyous over, the Carters did up their seatbelts, a procedure which took a little time because Gladys could never remember how to work hers. Arnold switched on the engine. Nothing happened.

'. . . and it was two hours before their banger would start!' Cecily told the Waddesdons and the Hascombes and the Muckrosses over the quails' eggs. It had been a nightmare, as they could imagine: she couldn't have a bath or change. She couldn't fetch Mrs Gannett (William interrupted at this point, to explain to the Muckrosses, who weren't in the know, that Mrs Gannett was the wonder who 'did' at dinner parties); William was at some dreary meeting ('Not my fault,' William protested, peeling a fourth egg); Mungo, the only one who knew anything at all about motor cars, was busy hitting sixes; the garage, it being a Saturday, was of course shut ('Typical,' Eddie Muckross groaned, 'of this Godforsaken country'); needless to say, they weren't members of the AA or anything like *that* – 'but to give them their due,' she added, because she didn't want to be unfair – she'd liked the Carters, she really had – 'they were hideously embarrased. They didn't know where to put themselves. I suspect they were longing to get back to Swindon – ' Loud laughter greeted this notion.

'Well I feel real sorry for those poor Carters,' the Hascombes' American said. 'Forgive me for asking – but doesn't it seem a little odd of you, to any of you, even a little patronising, maybe, for a baronet and his lady to spend a whole afternoon entertaining – waiting on – the kind of people you would normally employ to wait on you? Don't you have more relevant ways of relating to people from a different socio-economic background? Of breaking down the barriers? Barriers which surely must – if Great Britain is to survive into the twenty-first century – be broken down?'

A silence followed this extraordinary speech. During it, Cecily felt upset. She hadn't thought of her rescue of the Carters in that light, and she knew, she was certain, they hadn't either.

'What's she on about?' Eddie Muckross eventually hissed in Sally Hascombe's ear. 'What does socio-whatsit mean?'

'Class,' Sally Hascombe hissed back. 'Class to you, dearie, class.'

'Love your flowers, Thistle,' said Boo Waddesdon, who'd only that moment noticed them. 'Very, very pritts.' And she leant forward, and stuck her nose in the arrangement.

William, on the American's left, explained to her that she hadn't got it quite right; that the upper classes and the working classes in England really had a lot going for each other; that it had always been so: that there were good historical reasons for this (he did not elucidate) and that it was the people in-between that one simply couldn't get along with, and had nothing to say to; but that was a fact of life; unfortunately.

'Thank you so much, Mrs Gannett, that was delicious,' Cecily said. Mrs Gannett, coming in to clear, had created a timely diversion.

The Carters were forgotten while the salmon was brought in and borne by Mrs Gannett from left elbow to left elbow.

'Everything's cold, I'm afraid,' Cecily apologized.

'Yum yum yum yum,' Archie Hascombe said.

'Does anyone, offhand, know of anyone who's wanting an adorable – slightly runtish, pr'aps – hunt terrier puppy?' Julia Muckross enquired. But offhand, no one did.

During the eating of the salmon, the Waddesdons and the Muckrosses discovered they had sons at the same school, though not in the same house; and the Muckrosses and the Hascombes discovered they had daughters at the same school, though not in the same year – extremely useful to know, they were all agreed, when it came to exeats and doing the run. Later on, it emerged that Archie Hascombe's nephew worked – on the international investment side – in Eddie Muckross's merchant bank; and then Tiny Waddesdon remembered that as a schoolboy he'd had half a rod on old Lord Muckross's water.

'It all sounds like some kind of exclusive club,' the American complained, and they all agreed that yes, in a way, you could say it was.

The American was non-plussed. She'd envisaged at least some cultural debate – a dialogue on the new play at the Theatre Upstairs, maybe, or on the new movie at the Screen on the Hill. Were the British never serious? Were their concerns only schoolchildren and dogs?

Eddie Muckross, sitting opposite, and suddenly noticing her distress, came gallantly to her aid. 'Tell us about life in Noo Jersey, Ma'am,' he encouraged in an over-the-top southern accent, moving a lifesize silver grouse so that he could see her better. 'Dish us the dirt. Give us the low down.'

The pudding arrived, purple, splendidly conical, bleeding blackly into its dish.

'Summer pud – what spoiling, Mrs Gannett!' Tiny Waddesdon

said, beaming up at her as he helped himself. 'Blackcurrants, redcurrants, raspberries, cherries, mulberries – all *sorts* of goodies in there,' he reassured his American neighbour, whose lot it had been to broach the pudding, and who now prodded the sodden bread on her plate uncertainly with a spoon. 'Rather more palatable than pumpkin pie, I think you'll find,' he added.

The arrival of the pudding, and William's getting up to fetch a bottle of what he always referred to as 'noble rot' ('the fungus they apply to the root of the Sauternes vine' Tiny Waddesdon informed his neighbour) reminded Cecily that the best bit of the Carter saga remained untold.

'Hope you appreciate your pudding wine,' she said, as William ('No, no, no, Willie, I've done frightfully well, I can't possibly drink any more,' Boo Waddesdon said, clamping a hand over her glass) walked round the table with the bottle. Her beloved son Mungo–Cecily told them, waving a hand for quiet – who'd been asked to take some beer and plonk to the river to cheer up the Carters' picnic, had by mistake ('On purpose,' William interrupted her) taken a bottle of Willie's best noble rot, and then when Sophie – who'd been sent to fetch them up for tea – got there, she'd found Mrs C. snoring drunkenly on her chair, Albert comatose on the river bank, and the bottle and beer cans empty under the tree. 'The old biddies had drunk the lot!'

Everyone – except the American, and anyway Americans had no sense of humour – laughed, and even William managed a smile. They were still snorting when Mrs Gannett arrived with the coffee tray, and placed it in front of Cecily on the table. Bathed in candlelight and laughter, Cecily considered her day. Not *quite* a fairy-tale ending for the Carters, perhaps (she'd made them promise to ring and let her know they'd got home safely, she remembered – and they hadn't, of course) but she knew they'd really enjoyed their outing.

I'll be able to dine out on it for years, she realized as she passed the cups down the table, and asked Eddie Muckross to give the sugar a shove.

# SPOILT

TO A.V., WITHOUT WHOM.

# MAEVE GOES TO TOWN

The invitation came from a successful art dealer Maeve knew. Not knew exactly, was acquainted with. Maeve's ex-husband Patrick had bought several paintings and prints from Clarissa Friedlander's gallery, and as a result they got asked to all the exhibition preview parties. They also, from time to time, got asked to dinner in Clarissa's Kensington house. After Maeve and Patrick split up, the invitations, addressed to Mr and Mrs Patrick Mansell, kept coming, and Maeve and her ex took it in turns to go, or neither of them went, depending on what else was happening in their lives. What was happening in Patrick's life was cellular telephone systems, personal communications networks (optical fibres! digital switches!) and cable television franchises. In addition to these was Lara: long-legged, big-bosomed and twenty-nine. What was happening in Maeve's life was teenagers and teenage moods, an up and down marriage to a washing machine, a not-too-secret affair with a Safeway shopping trolley.

Maeve was in two minds about accepting Clarissa's invitation. There were points for, and points against. The points against included Clarissa Friedlander herself, an alarming woman in her mid-thirties whose working clothes, which Maeve had witnessed on a daytime visit to the gallery, comprised skinny bright-white jeans, bulky designer knit with sleeves pushed up to the elbows, and black pumps like ballet shoes. There was a lot of chunky gold, or it might have been platinum, on her ears and wrists and fingers. Enterprise culture, her appearance seemed to say, arts-oriented executive, post-feminist together person. And it was true: Clarissa was highly motivated and go-getting. Private-sector support is where art's largely at these days, and Clarissa spent a lot of her time targeting the business community, researching potential sponsors, focusing on fundraising. She kept detailed files on the companies she approached, and never gave up on the ones who initially failed to show an interest. 'After all, love, you never know!' Another thing Clarissa believed in was taking art to the customer, which meant setting up exhibitions in banks and boardrooms. 'Basically, I see it as my role to establish imaginative links between Fine Art and commerce.' Maeve had read this in a colour-supplement interview, and had found it depressing.

'Why on earth should you find it depressing?' Patrick, in a hurry, on his office telephone, sounded exasperated. 'All Clarissa's trying to do is get work for her artists – to get people like me to buy their bloody pictures. What's wrong with that? It's happened throughout history. Or is it just that you resent people, women, being successful?'

Maeve said she wasn't sure why, and of course she didn't resent success, and she had nothing against Clarissa; it was merely that she'd always felt, for some reason, though it was probably stupid, that Art should, ideally anyway, be for Art's sake and –

'Fucking hell! Look Maeve, I can't discuss this now. I just need your confirmation that the children will be on the ten-fifteen train. And could you please see they've got something decent to wear – we've got friends coming in on Saturday night. Last time they came to us they looked like tramps.' Clunk.

We. We've got. She was never going to get used to this We that embraced Lara and excluded her. It was We this and We that, all of a sudden. It was Us and Ours. When she and Patrick were married it had very often been I and Me and Myself and Mine.

Another reason for refusing Clarissa's invitation was because it was for drinks, not dinner, at Clarissa's house. Drinks parties were bad enough when you had someone, a husband, say, to go with and to leave with. To dissect the event with in the car on the way home, or over supper. In bed. Braving a drinks party on your own, when you were unlikely to know anyone there, that had to be madness, didn't it? Masochism.

The points for accepting – what were they, what did they include? Well, Patrick being away, in New York with Lara (a business trip for both of them, he explained), for a start. Someone had to keep Clarissa's doors, and Maeve's options, open. Also, receiving very few Christmas party invitations this year – only three including this one – had made her feel even more than usually marginal and peripheral. Added to these was family pressure.

'You must go,' Maeve's sister Isobel insisted, disregarding Maeve's prevarications about who would feed the dog and who would stop the children smoking themselves to death or setting the house on fire. 'You can't shut yourself away or people will forget you. You've got to be seen around.'

'Around where? What for?' asked the defeated and negative Maeve.

'Because. Because you never know who you might meet. You never know. One minute there's no one in one's life, the next minute there is. That's how it happens, just' – and Isobel, contentedly married to the same country solicitor for twenty-five years, snapped her fingers to add zip to her argument – 'like that.' There weren't any unattached men in the country anyway, Isobel reminded her sister, spare men were like gold dust, the only ones to be had, the only fun ones, were in London. So if Maeve wanted one of those she had to go.

'You gotta go, natch.' Maeve's son Michael, stretched full length on the floor between the gas fire and the television set, his gold locks resting on a plate that had recently contained fried egg and ketchup, rattled his crisp bag and, finding no joy, exploded it. 'Could be Mr Deeds will be in town.' He jerked an elbow in the direction of the black and white hero on the screen. 'Could be Gary Cooper will be at your rave. Go for it.'

'I'll have you know that film you're watching was made before I was born! Also, Gary Cooper's dead.'

'So?'

Another of Maeve's children, Jessica, informed her that partying was a basic human right and good for people. That you couldn't expect to get anywhere in life unless you were prepared to socialise. Maeve's jaw dropped at this. Jessica never went to parties. She'd been refusing to go to anything that might loosely be termed a party for eight years now. At the age of eleven she had all the makings of a recluse.

The week of Clarissa Friedlander's party, Maeve drove to her nearest town, nearest town, that is, that was any use for clothes shopping, and bought herself an outfit. In a new and deserted shopping mall, in an empty-of-customers boutique called Funfare, in a pre-Christmas sale, she bought a silk jacket in jewel colours and a matching skirt. Maeve was small and short-legged, and the skirt that fitted her in the waist came down to her ankles. She was worried about this, but the assistant said, Why worry? Skirts could be worn any length this season and anyway longer equalled more elegant and made Maeve took taller. The assistant held out the promise of free air miles if Maeve decided to go ahead with this purchase, which she did. Afterwards, in a shoe shop similarly forsaken save for a mother with two weak-looking small boys who were expressing strong views on trainers, she bought a pair of patent leather high heels whose red more or less matched the red swirls in her dress and jacket. Then, cutting through the market on her way back to the car park, her eye was caught by a stall offering Genuine Paris Perfume's At Less Than Half The Recommended Retail Price!!! And she came away with a minuscule bottle of Poison, a scent she'd never tried because too expensive. 'Perhaps the worst thing about not being married any more,' Maeve had once confided to her daughter Maggie, 'is having to buy your own pong.' Maeve had meant this as a joke, the sort of wry remark people make to prove to others and themselves that they haven't gone under yet, that no matter what life throws at them, they're still hanging on in there. She didn't seriously think that no one to buy you scent was the worst thing about being divorced, even though there was, yes there was, something pitiful and poignant about a woman having to buy her own. Maggie hadn't been amused, however. How could her mother say anything quite so vulgar? When half the people in England were on the breadline, having their homes repossessed because they couldn't, through no fault of their own, but because of the interest rate and no job, keep up their mortgage payments? What would all those single-parent mothers struggling to feed handicapped children in bed-and-breakfast accommodation say if they could hear Maeve moaning on about no perfume or scent or whatever? Maggie shook her head, more in anger than in sorrow. (For it's children who are the moral guardians now; it's the younger generation who dictate what their elders should think and how they should behave.) 'I didn't mean it, it was a joke,' Maeve had defended herself wearily. 'I must be allowed to say something silly from time to time without having the social ills of the world thrown at me. And it isn't my fault if this country's in such a mess – I'd remind you I voted Labour last time round. And SDP the time before.' 'Champagne socialist,' Maggie had muttered, not quite under her breath.

Maeve felt no pleasure as she stacked her carrier bags in the boot of her car, she felt guilt. The money she'd spent on her own adornment was part of the money she'd put aside for the children's Christmas presents. And she dreaded what Maggie's reaction would be when she saw the new clothes. I'll burn the bags and tell her the stuff came from the OXFAM shop, Maeve decided. Or I'll say, 'New? What, these old things? Surely you remember these? I've had them for years!'

*

202

The drive to London from Maeve's house took two and three-quarter hours on good days and if you were lucky. On bad days, stormy or foggy or dark or rush-hour-traffic-ridden, it could take a lot longer. So Maeve had to be ready to leave for Clarissa's soon after three-thirty in the afternoon.

In her bedroom, before going down to make her goodbye speech to her children, Maeve concealed her new clothes and old jewellery under an antiquated camel coat, buttoning it to the neck in the hope that her extravagance would not be discovered. On her feet she wore her driving shoes, a pair of scuffed loafers, and she carried the new high heels in a Boots plastic bag. It was just her luck that on the way down the stairs she should meet her daughter Florence on the half-landing.

'Let's see, let's see what you're wearing.' A hand shot out and tweaked the hem of the camel coat. 'Silk. Ace one.' Florence was thirteen and the only one of Maeve's daughters to show what her mother considered to be a natural, and healthy, interest in clothes. She was also, probably (her parents were agreed about this), the kindest and nicest of Maeve's and Patrick's children. She peered into the Boots bag. 'I like your shoes – tart-y! Only problem is – ' Florence held her hands up, palms forward, and waved them from side to side, a gesture to indicate that the following remark was not to be taken too seriously, was in quotes you understand ' – power dressing is out. The Caring Nineties are in. Get real!'

Maeve's self-confidence, which a few minutes earlier had been given a little lift by an encounter with a glamorous and young-for-her-age-looking woman in the bathroom glass, drained away into her loafers.

'Oh dear, am I too dressy, d'you think? I don't know if I've got anything else that would possibly – '

'Of course you're not, you look ace! Some foxy guy'll take you out to dinner, I'm sure. And you smell ace. Didn't know you wore Poison,' said Florence who, scourge of the local cosmetics counters and their testers, had a nose for these things.

' . . . and Johnnie's to be in bed by half past nine at the latest. The last upstairs must remember to let Silas out, and lock up, and turn off the fire and the lights – though it would be a kindness if you could leave the outside light on for me. Please write down any telephone messages. The fish pie's in the bottom oven. I trust you not to smoke . . . '

Anyway, what was the point? None of them was listening. They lay like collapsed dominoes, leaning into and against each other, eyes and minds fixed on the square of jittery light at the far end of the room. They were holed up and dug in as though for a siege. The fruit bowl, the biscuit tin, bags of nuts and low-fat crisps, mugs of tea, cans of Diet Pepsi, had been placed about the floor for easy access.

'Did you hear what I said? I said this room's got to be tidy before you leave it.'

A few arms waved, vaguely, in the air. And Michael, half-turning, called as she reached the door, 'Chill out, Mothereen. Enjoy, enjoy . . . '

Maeve liked being alone in her car. When she'd shut the door and adjusted the seat – for Michael was five foot eleven and learning to drive – when she'd settled herself and her belongings and fastened her seat belt and driven through the gate, she very often felt elated. She very often felt light-hearted and free, even if her journey was only to the supermarket or the cash dispenser. She liked the knowledge that no one could exactly know what she was up to or where she could be found; she relished the possibility that she might, if she suddenly felt inclined to, take off somewhere – to the seaside for the day, to Wales or Scotland or Paris for a night or nights. She had never made these trips, but you never knew, she might. She liked the silence within these walls that allowed her to listen to a radio play, if there was one, or to cassette music of her own choice.

The privacy of the car, the self-containment of it, admitted of other needs and other moods. It was in the car that Maeve went over and over her broken marriage. The form this often took was a letter to Patrick, spoken aloud, in which she expounded the grievances that eluded her when she had a pen in her hand; or else blamed herself alone for her plight and then begged him to come home. In the car she wept and howled, allowed the tears to stream down her face unchecked, rocked backwards and forwards in her seat, gave herself entirely over to grief. Or she would, thumping the steering wheel in rage, conduct fights with Patrick, playing both parts so credibly that afterwards she would be able to convince herself that he had really said those things, those wicked and hurtful things. On the occasions when she was able to banish Patrick altogether, she did so by imagining the man she hadn't met yet who would replace Patrick, and who was waiting for her somewhere – on a train, in the checkout queue, at a drinks party she hadn't planned to go to.

At Clarissa Friedlander's party?

No, looking forward to anything specific, having hopes about it, was dangerous; was enough to court serious disappointment, or worse. Dread was the only safe emotion to feel.

If I dread this party enough – thought Maeve as, ignoring the speed limit at Hammersmith, she obeyed the injunction in the word 'Flyover' – I might just enjoy it. This party is going to be hell, she told herself, braking just too late to abide by a red traffic light in Talgarth Road; it's going to be a complete bummer, it's going to be the worst party I've been to in my entire life.


Clarissa's Kensington house was an opened Advent calendar as Maeve parked her car, each window of its dark face enclosing an alliterative surprise: a candle; a Christmas tree; a cat; a couple under the mistletoe. A chandelier, radiating love and hope from the fanlight above the front door, succeeded so well in its disguise that when the door opened to admit her, Maeve was disappointed to discover not Mary and Joseph, and the Babe lying in a manger, but a pair of quarrelsome early leavers wrestling with their coats. At once she wanted to leave with them, but instead allowed herself to be propelled through the hall and up the stairs to Clarissa's bedroom, a sullenly purple, and fringed and bobbled, chamber of antique aspect and dusty palms. ('I indulge my Gothic side in here,' Clarissa had confided, throwing open the door, on Maeve's first visit. 'It makes for an amusing contrast with the spare elegance of the rest – don't you think?') In the centre of the room a sepulchral fourposter had come into its own tonight as a repository for the remains of wild and not so wild animals, of bear and beaver, leopard and lynx, kid and calf, or for – more probably – synthetic versions of the same. Maeve buried her mangy camel among these. She wanted to check her face for damage and her teeth for lipstick, but the lighting – 30-watt bulbs veiled by grey toadstool hats – was unhelpful, and in any case the several gloomily ornate looking-glasses in the room were obscured by others of her sex who'd had the same idea. 'Vanity, thy name is woman' – Patrick, arms folded, amusedly watching Maeve's dressing-table ritual from the doorway. Maeve had never forgotten this, the injustice of this. Vanity? Frailty, more like. Insecurity, more like. Lack of self-confidence, more like.

Downstairs, the first thing was to get a drink. It had been Patrick's opinion that new arrivals at parties should not have to brave crowds of established merrymakers without the bolster of a full glass of something very good and very strong, but there was no drinks table in Clarissa's sparely elegant hall. In her sitting room ('My double cube,' as she'd explained it to Maeve, 'equalled only in splendour by the one at Wilton'), the merrymakers were all giants, and famous. Laughter, in cannonades, in sudden sharp fusillades, exploded here and there above an unspecific boom as Maeve pursued the flash of white tablecloth that came and went at the far end of the cube. Along the way she apologised to shirt buttons and elbows and bespoke waist-coats and little black crepe bosoms. 'Excuse me. Sorry. So sorry. Excuse me. Excuse – ' And then, just as her goal was almost within reach, she saw that immediately in front of it, and barring her access to it, was an unmistakable back-view, a long creamy neck, a sleek gold club-cut. She touched this goddess on a black, ruched crepe shoulder and Clarissa swung round, and peered, and looked blank, and looked – after a second or two – triumphant.

'Darling, you made it! Wonderful! Maeve is one of my favourite people,' Clarissa said to the famous man she'd been talking to. 'She's come all the way up from the *COUNTRY* – isn't that brave? I'm sure you know every-one,' she said to Maeve. 'Haven't you got a drink yet? The white's the one to go for. Where's your lovely husband? I do hope you've brought him along! Maeve's married to a captain of industry – '

Maeve wanted to say No. No to the lovely husband; No I haven't got a drink; No I don't know anyone at all, introduce me, please – but her hostess had turned her back and was talking to three other people, all men, all famous, and all-attention to Clarissa.

'Red. Thank you.' Maeve recognised the barman. He worked in Clarissa's gallery. He was the one who'd taken Patrick's cheque the last time they'd bought a painting together, a painting for the custody of which Maeve and Patrick had recently fought – and Maeve had lost. She hated the knowledge that Lara was looking at the painting now, living with it. It had nothing to do with Lara.

The barman held up a glass to the light, as though he were looking for something, and lowered it, and poured wine into it. He had a waxy complexion and two ugly moles on his left cheek. His hair, flattened with water or grease and combed straight back from his forehead, had no parting. He handed Maeve the glass.

'How's trade?' Maeve asked, after she'd bestowed on the barman a winning, we-know-each-other-don't-we? smile.

'What?' The young man cupped his ear with a delicate

hand. 'Right, Sir Ian. Two whites, one red, coming up,' he said to the extremely famous Shakespearean actor at Maeve's elbow.

Maeve moved away from the table, keeping her glass at a distance for fear of spilling it down her front — but not too far out for fear of spilling it down someone else's. When she could, when a tiny pocket of space opened up in the crush, she inclined her head to the glass and took a sip. The wine, just a taste of it, triggered, as it always did, a craving for nicotine — but how do you get cigarettes out of a bag, and then light up, with a glass of wine in one hand? Maeve made her way back to the table. She put down her glass and her bag. The bag, which was not the one she'd intended bringing, which was not the carefree piece of nonsense on a string she'd meant to transfer the essential minimum into before leaving home — no, that one was still on the kitchen table beside the tin of cat food she'd been bullied, at the very last minute, into opening — was loaded with the day-to-day clutter of Maeve's life: chequebook and paying-in book and Family Allowance Book; diary and wallet and purse and loose change that had escaped from the purse; car keys and house keys; two Pentel pens, one without its top; a stick of spearmint gum that the last hot summer had irrevocably welded to a sheaf of second-class stamps; a letter whose air mail envelope had doubled as a Christmas shopping list. Her cigarettes were sitting on top of these, but the lighter wasn't. She put her hand into the battered bran tub and let her fingers do the searching for something smooth and round. Ah-ha! But you cannot light a cigarette with a lipstick — a cracked lipstick, as fingers stained and sticky with Hot Cherries proved it to be.

I wish I was married, Maeve said to herself; if I was married I'd go and find my husband now, and creep up behind him and raid his coat pocket for a lighter, and then he'd turn and put his arm round my shoulder and say to whoever he was talking to, 'I don't believe you've met my wife. Maeve darling, this is . . . ' Maeve began removing items from her bag and placing them on the table. While she did this she talked to no one and no one talked to her so she went on talking to herself. I am very unhappy at this party, I am very unhappy indeed. This is a terrible party and I am hating every minute of it. This must be the worst party I've been to in my entire life.

All around her were people jostling to have their glasses filled. All around her people were laughing and shouting and shrieking and hailing each other.

'Is this a white-elephant stall?' It was a man's voice, a familiar voice. Maeve looked up. She saw a face she knew well. She knew the cleft in that chin, the bump on that nose, the quirk of those eyebrows. She knew that widow's peak and that Adam's apple. She did not know how she knew those things, and she could not remember his name.

'I lost my lighter,' Maeve explained, 'but I've found it now.' She held it up proudly, like a small child who expects congratulations. She smiled an enchanting smile. Then she turned to the table and swept the treasures she'd placed there into her bag. I've got someone to talk to, she told herself. I've got a man, a famous and attractive man. She hoisted the bag on to her shoulder. She repossessed herself of the wine glass. 'Do you . . . ?' she began.

To a vanishing backview. To no one.

You've got to get away from this table now, Maeve instructed herself, you've been here too long, you've got to circulate. She tried to make her circuit of the room appear purposeful, not desperate. She tried to make it seem as though she were looking for someone, on her way to speak to that someone. As though that someone were looking for her.

Looking purposeful or desperate, Maeve worked her way through the middle of the room to the door and back again. She made a tour, clockwise, of the room's perimeter, followed by an anti-clockwise one. She crossed the room diagonally, left to right, and when she had accomplished this, right to left. On the way she apologised to Garrick ties and Paul Smith shirts and Giorgio Armani belts and Chantal necklaces: 'Excuse me, I'm just trying to . . . ' Every so often she stopped to sip her drink or to ignite a new cigarette, attaching herself, whenever possible, to a couple or a threesome or a larger knot of chatterers.

'Now that the bottom's fallen out of the Impressionist and the Contemporary Art markets,' a florid man in a navy pinstripe was saying to a pale, and younger, man in a leather blouson, 'and if Sotheby's and Christie's and Phillips, if the big boys, are catching colds, where does that leave the likes of Bonhams and Lawrence's?'

'Prints are still holding up,' Leather Blouson replied. 'Victorian water colours are still doing okay. Small is still beautiful.'

Maeve, several floors below them, inhaled deeply and coughed, and nodded sagely into her glass and smiled a knowing smile.

'Did you say something?' Navy Pinstripe peered down at her. Damp-looking curls, clinging to a bull neck, spilled out over his collar in a little choirboy ruff. 'Do you have a connexion with one of those outfits?'

Time for Maeve to affect a little maybe-I-do, maybe-I-don't shrug. Time for her to drift away. To look a touch superior, or bored.

I'm bored as hell, Maeve told herself as she battled her way to the drinks table for a refill. I'll have one more glass and then I'll go home. She downed her refill in a gulp, set down the empty glass and appropriated an abandoned full one – of white, but what did that matter? Then, having stubbed out her cigarette on a plate of broken cocktail sticks and olive stones and scorned cheesy biscuits, she lit up again, alarmed to discover there were only six cigarettes left in the packet. She picked up her wine glass.

You're driving, you're not supposed to be drinking, a voice in her head reminded her. You could kill yourself or someone else. You could go to prison or lose your licence for a year. You have children at home you love and who need you.

She left the table. Lights from the Christmas tree, a perfect triangle perfectly fitting the frame of a tall window, beckoned and mocked. Only yesterday, she'd looked on critically as her children raided the decorations box, fighting each other to be the first to loop the branches of their lopsided spruce with the battered tinfoil stars and crescent moons of their kindergarten pasts; and when, with whoops of excitement, they'd exhumed those old Blue Peter angels, fusions of yoghurt pots and paper and tinsel and the cardboard insides of lavatory rolls, and Sellotaped them on, she'd said, 'Look, don't you think it's time we threw those out? They really are very bashed, and you're not babies any more. Couldn't we try for something a bit more grown-up and glamorous this – ?' Her words had been lopped by an amazed silence, by stares that contrived to register hurt and pity and reproof and disbelief.

On her way to the grown-up and glamorous tree in the window, Maeve caught sight of a woman she'd met at one of Clarissa's dinners. The woman had been introduced by Clarissa as 'my friend, the old-style feminist art historian'. 'I'm a feminist, of course,' Maeve remembered confiding to the art historian as they sat on the sofa after dinner, 'but I'm not quite sure how much of a feminist I am.' (Maeve had suddenly been aware that she was drunk; a second earlier she'd been okay, and now, without warning, and for no reason, she wasn't.) 'I'm never quite sure what I believe,' Maeve had continued, trying to jerk her head away from Clarissa's Collier Campbell cushions and to manoeuvre herself into a sensible talking position. 'It varies. I'm never exactly sure what I feel or where I stand or what I want or who I am.'

'Then it's time you made up your mind, lovey, isn't it?' The art historian had risen from the sofa and conferred on Maeve the travesty of a smile. 'People who walk in the middle of the road tend to get run over.'

Maeve was in two minds now about accosting this person, whose name she was trying to remember. She had no desire to be run over by her again. On the other hand, any conversation, however brief and uncongenial, had to be better than none. So she hovered on the edge of Janet?

– no, Jackie! – of Jackie's circle, hemmed in on all sides, bracing herself to break in as soon as she caught the historian's eye. While she waited she sipped her wine, rehearsing in her head confident smiles, plus the sort of whacky and upfront greetings that might be likely to disarm.

'Yeah, sure, but wouldn't you agree he's kind of funky and counter-cultural in terms of visual style? I mean that whole visual-grammar bit – ' A man's voice, American, directly behind Maeve, isolated itself in the buzz.

'He's crap.' A new voice, male and English, cut in. 'It's a third-class mind. A colour-supplement mind. End of story.'

Maeve did a little half-turn on her heels so that she could hear, and see, more of this.

'Did you hear him on *Kaleidoscope* last week? I thought they'd at least wheel on some sort of heavyweight who could be expected to land a few punches, but no, it was reverence all the way. And Paul Vaughan treated him as though he was God, for God's sake.'

Maeve did not know who they were talking about, but this did not stop her smiling into her glass and giving a little corroborative snort. If the last speaker were to notice her now, he would turn his head and say, 'Ah. So you heard the programme too. And you agree.' And then Maeve would say, 'Yes. I think he's crap, total crap,' and then . . . But he did not notice Maeve.

I like being me, Maeve told herself as she made her way once more to the drinks table, I like being a country person. Country people are real. They're genuine, they have roots and integrity. Country people are . . . She stopped. A blush, a hot flush of shame, was spreading from her bosom to her neck to her cheeks. She shut her eyes tight, as though by the action she could black out the mental picture she had of herself, only yesterday, at a drinks party in the village. At this, a gathering of selected locals in the house of a retired schoolmaster and his wife, she had been trapped first by a deaf, although not dumb, octogenarian air vice marshal, and second, as soon as she'd managed to escape him, by his wife. She had had to be civil – it was the season of goodwill – to her farmer neighbour who the year before, and despite petitions and protest, had wangled planning permission to convert the stone barns on his side of the wall that separated them into twelve holiday cottages (with garaging for upwards of twenty-four cars). She'd had to dodge the vicar whose workplace she had not entered for six months except to clean it and to show off, to a visiting friend, the rose window and the poignant simplicity of the twelfth-century font. All this while trying to get some mulled wine, the only drink on offer, down, without at the same time ingesting a silt of lemon pips and peel and nutmeg and cinnamon and cloves. She had not been able to smoke at the party because, having asked Barbara, her hostess, if she minded, she'd then been bound by Barbara's reply: 'I most certainly do! Put those cigarettes away, you naughty girl!'

Frustrated and bored, she'd wandered away to the fireplace and was examining a painting of ducks flying in formation against a wintry sky, when she'd been joined by her host, doing the rounds with the punch bowl. 'Here, hold out thine goblet.' A ladleful of citrus pulp had made a cautious descent to her glass. 'Maeve, I don't believe you've met the new owner of Dormers . . . ' The new owner of Dormers had told Maeve about the hazards of moving house in December. He'd told her about the dud heating system and warped kitchen units he and his wife had inherited and what he planned to do about these. Then, perhaps realising he hadn't asked Maeve a question yet, he'd asked her, 'Which of the handsome fellows here is the lucky one who takes you home? Point me out your better half.' 'I'm afraid I haven't got one of those.' (Maeve had meant this to sound jokily defiant, but it hadn't come out that way.) The new owner of Dormers had said, whoops, sorry, he'd got it into his head, from something the Doc had told him, that Maeve was married and had hundreds of children. 'I was married. I do have hundreds of children.' He was sorry if he was being insensitive, the new owner of Dormers said, but she looked too young, and much too glamorous, to be a widow, it was not something that had occur – 'I am *not* a widow!' She'd almost screamed this. The new owner of Dormers had reeled as though from a heavy blow. 'Pardon me,' he'd mumbled, ''scuse I, better get back to the wife, excuse . . . ' On Maeve's way to the door, the vicar's wife, Lesley, had put out a detaining arm. 'Maeve! Just the person I wanted to see. Now about those mince pies for the wassail. I'm not sure yet how many I'll need you to make, but I'll give you a tinkle Saturday lunch time – will you be in? If all the tickets are sold we might require a few extra sausage rolls, and I've been thinking – a cheese fondue would ring the changes and be a pleasant and tasty addition . . . ' And Maeve, looking for her coat in the hall, had thought, What does it matter? What do all these dreary people matter? This time tomorrow I shall be at a proper party, full of amusing people, my peers, where I'll be appreciated and where no one will decide I've got two heads just because I'm divorced.

Refilling her glass at the table – the barman had abandoned his post and was nowhere to be seen – Maeve pitied the naive person of yesterday who had thought these things. Who had believed them. And she tried to shut out Patrick's lecturing voice, as she had heard it once after a similar do: 'Why are you always so critical of everyone, Maeve? Why do you have to be so bloody superior? You like to think you're shy – you're not shy, you're superior. You never give out to people, you're too busy thinking about yourself and your reactions. You never take part. You stand on the sidelines, observing, criticising, sneering. Why? What have you got to be superior about? Tell me that. Go on, tell me.'

This one is for the road, Maeve told herself. 'My children think I'm wonderful, anyway,' she said aloud. 'Clarissa has no children and she's jealous and that's why she has to try and put me down. She has to convince herself that a single life in the fast lane is all a woman needs, but underneath she regrets not having had babies. She's envious, that's all.'

'Why are you telling this to me?' The man who asked this was short, shorter than Maeve in her heels, and balding with ginger tufts above his ears; and he wore a surprising, blue-black beard. It was impossible to tell what colour his eyes were because they were guarded by red and swollen eyelids. 'Got a snout to spare?' he asked, seeing her light up.

Maeve was delighted to give this unappealing person one of her cigarettes, even though it meant she now had only four left. Gratitude dictated that she light it for him.

'Are you a hackette?' He blew a funnel of smoke into her face. 'This bash is stuffed with them.'

'No. Are you?'

'Funny one,' Bluebeard said, 'funny one. I like it.'

'A painter then. You're a painter.'

Bluebeard passed a fat and freckled hand over his eyelids. He shuddered. 'Please. Do me a favour. No no no, I'm a poet.'

'A poet!' Maeve tried to give the exclamation an enthusiastic ring.

'A poet!' she said again. 'Why?'

'Why? I could just as well ask you why you've chosen to dress yourself up as a bad stained-glass window.'

'I didn't mean why,' Maeve said crossly, 'I meant what. I mean what sort of poems do you write?'

'What sort of question is that?' The poet raised his eyelids to the ceiling in an attitude of mock, or it might have been real, despair. 'Would you be any the wiser if I told you?'

'Well, perhaps . . . ' Maeve began, but did not finish. For the floor and walls of Clarissa's double cube were on the move. She put a hand on the table to steady herself. In the distance the Christmas tree was a kaleidoscope, its pattern shifting and breaking up as she tried to fix on it. Shifting and breaking up and re-forming. 'I think I need some fresh air or a drink of – '

The poet snatched up a bottle from the table and leant forward and spilled some wine into Maeve's glass. He sniffed at her neck, noisy excited sniffs, like a terrier. 'What's that poison you're wearing?' He sniffed again. He reeled. 'Jesus!'

\*

Maeve was standing in front of the Christmas tree, examining it with great concentration, fingering a silver bauble.

> 'I think that I shall never see
> A poet lovely as a Christmas tree,'

she sang to the tree, which responded by dissolving into a blur of tears. Maeve's song had without permission transported her to her mother-in-law's bedroom. It was soon after her mother-in-law's death, and Patrick and Maeve were kneeling on the stained mushroom carpet, sorting through old clothes and old letters and old bills and old medicine bottles, stuffing them into boxes and dustbin sacks. It was cold in the bedroom which in its owner's lifetime had been a furnace, but the lack of heating today had not been able to dispel that disturbing, stale but sweetish smell that in Maeve's time the room had always had. They were edgy and bad-tempered, not enjoying their job, guilty at manhandling treasures Patrick's mother had never allowed anyone to touch; rifling through drawers and cupboards they would until this afternoon never have dared (and had had no desire) to open. And then, turning out yet another drawer, this time of his mother's davenport, Patrick came across a theatre programme for an ancient production of *Twelfth Night*. Inside, there was an engraving of Shakespeare's head and large lace collar, and a photograph of 'Mr H. Beerbohm Tree as Malvolio'. 'Poems are made by fools like thee' – Patrick pointed a serious finger at Shakespeare – 'but only God could make Beerbohm Tree.' After that they cheered up. A three-quarters-full bottle of Famous Grouse, uncovered from a commode and drunk out of a smelly bone beaker from the washstand bracket, made conspirators of them. Alcohol speeded their task. It caused letters to fly into the wastepaper basket unread. It sent whole drawersful of support stockings and corsets and hairnets and grey knee bandages and pink face powder into the dustbin sacks. Later, when they'd done their best, or worst, in this room, they went home and straight up the stairs to bed, and made love – the first time for months.

'How could we have let it happen?' Maeve asked the Christmas tree. 'How did we let all that shared experience, that shared life, just go? Patrick's mother was fond of me. I know she was. Lara never even met her. Lara never had to do her shopping or cook her lunch. Lara didn't give birth to Patrick's children, she didn't have to nurse them through measles and mumps and gastroenteritis and chickenpox. Lara hasn't weathered any storms. She hasn't been tested at all. What has Lara got that I haven't got?'

Well, youth for a start. A firm body. A big bosom. Long legs.

But Patrick, when they were married, always insisted he didn't like young women, even pretty ones. He had nothing to say to them, he said. He didn't fancy them. He found them empty and uninteresting. Patrick always swore that the only thing Maeve had to fear was if he should meet a fascinating and worldly older woman – of fifty, say. Fifty-five. If he did meet one, then, yes, Maeve might very well have something to worry about.

One thing, when they were married, Patrick always swore he did like, was Maeve's smallness, her tiny hands and feet, her narrow back, her little breasts. ('Breasts' was the word he used. 'Breasts', which in speech had a tendency to collect some extra s's, so that it came out 'breassstsss', was a word Maeve could not say and, whenever she came across it in print, skated over. It was the plural, it was 'breasts', not 'breast', she had a quarrel with. For whereas a single breast had the capacity to be erotic, or maternal, or metaphorical, or, in middle life, fatally medical, the addition of an 's' reduced the word to the sexual – the crudely and humour-lessly and unsexy sexual.) Patrick liked Maeve's little breasts, and he even liked her short legs. 'I really like your legs,' he used to tell her, 'you may not believe this, but I do. A doll with duck's disease is certain to please.'

'But it's such a cliché!' Maeve had screamed at Patrick in the final mud-slinging before he left. (She couldn't touch him or reach him by this stage. Words which when he loved her would have stung were powerless now that he did not, now that he loved someone else.) 'How can you leave me, how can you leave your children, for that baby?'

'Oh Maeve.' Patrick had been sorrowful and patient. 'If only you knew. Lara may be only twenty-seven, but she's far more mature than you are. She's not self-absorbed and masochistic. She's a grown-up. You've never grown up. You'll never be a grown-up if you live to be a hundred. I need a real woman in my life. I need a partner. I need a *wife*.'

'Everyone needs a wife,' Maeve told the Christmas tree, 'I need a wife, all women need wives.' The tree was decorated, symmetrically, in white and red and silver. A Milky Way of tiny crystal lights, spangling the dark green, struck diamonds off red and silver and frosted-white glass globes which hung, twisting and spinning, from the tip of every branch. At the tip of every branch, a wreath of silver ribbon blossomed into an unlit scarlet candle. It was a designer tree, Maeve suddenly saw, a window display tree, the kind they have in Harrods. It was free from vulgarity, and poignancy and history; it was without magic.

'Are you going to join us at Nico's?' Maeve, swaying on a little cushion of alcohol in front of the tree, thought for a moment the invitation was aimed at her. 'Digby had the nous to book a table for twenty before he left the office, so *ne soyez pas faible – venez!*'

'I'm quite drunk,' Maeve told the designer tree, 'I'm quite sad. I think I'll go home now.' But as soon as she said the words she realised she was not fit to drive; that it was not even open to her to sit in her parked car and wait until she sobered up. A friend of hers had been caught that way. No amount of explaining, to the policeman who'd stuck his head through her window, that she did not intend actually driving the car, had saved this friend from the breathalyser and prosecution and the loss of her licence. A glass of water was what Maeve needed now. Milk. Black coffee. A lie-down in an upstairs room.

'Goodbye,' she said to the tree. 'Too bad nobody told you that power dressing is out. The Caring Nineties are in. Get real!'

Maeve didn't see her children until half past twelve the following day. They never got out of bed before noon in the school holidays. When they did finally get up they'd wander half-dressed into the kitchen and grind coffee beans and squeeze oranges and scatter cereal while she was trying to get lunch together. This morning (this afternoon) Maeve was short of sleep and her head hurt. She slammed a jar of Nescafé and a carton of orange juice in front of them and went straight into the attack.

'Very thoughtful of you, I'm sure, to leave the gas fire full on for me. I appreciated it no end, I can tell you.'

'Did you enjoy the party, Mum?'

'Not putting Silas out was a mistake, a mistake I'm not going to be responsible for. One of you can clear up the mess, the rest can club together and pay the cleaner's bill for the carpet which, I'd remind you, is Turkish and very – '

'Did you enjoy the – ?'

'There are no telephone messages on the pad. I realise you were probably much too busy last night working on your geography projects to write down any messages, but if by some small chance anyone did ring for me, perhaps you'd be good enough to give me the gist of – '

'Daddy rang. From New York.' It was Jessica who said this.

'Oh?' Maeve, about to clamp a saucepan lid on a saucepan, paused, and turned, and caught a row of closed, thoughtful faces and caught Florence's frown, directed at Jessica.

'It's all right, don't worry,' Florence said quickly and comfortingly, 'he didn't want you. He rang to talk to us.'

He didn't want you. He didn't want you. Imagine it. Imagine, only a few years ago, Patrick ringing from anywhere on the planet and not wanting her, and not wanting to talk to her, first and foremost, above all. Imagine it.

'Mum. Did you enjoy the par-ty?'

There were days when Maeve would have given in at this point, when she would have stopped banging cupboard doors and crashing saucepan lids for a while, and sat down, and confided in them: 'If you want to know, the party was hell, I hated every minute of it. Hardly anyone spoke to me at all.' On such a day, she would have embellished the misery of the evening, dubbing Clarissa's bedroom a mausoleum, going to town on the double cube and the Christmas tree and the media folk and the overheard conversations. On such a day she would have sent herself up, also, exaggerating her drunkenness. And there would have been rewards for this sort of confession: laughter, for a start, that embraced all their social failures and made nonsense of them. Comfort, as a follow-up: 'Don't worry about it, Mum. Don't think about it. Those sorts of parties, those sorts of people, are unreal. You're the greatest!' On such a day she could have made allies of her children.

'The party was fine, thank you,' Maeve said briskly, 'it was great fun. Heaps of interesting people – had a long talk with Terry Ross, you know, chat-show host' (she had suddenly remembered who the famous person who'd made the white-elephant-stall remark was), 'had a fascinating discuss – '

'Did you get lucky, Mum? Did some handsome hunk take you out to supper?'

Did some handsome hunk . . . ? Maeve had thrown a dustsheet over the later part of her evening. She couldn't recall much of it anyway. She did have a vague memory of being roused, at some point, from fur-smothered oblivion, by Clarissa's voice: 'Well well well! What have we here? Who's been sleeping in my bed?' She did have a fuzzy picture of herself, hours later probably, trying to turn a key in the frozen lock of her car, hunting for de-icer, hunting for gloves, having to rub frost off the windscreen with the sleeves of her coat . . .

'Ah. That would be telling.' She put on a mysterious face. 'That would be telling.'

'Tell us then. Don't be mean. Tell us about lover-boy.'

'Romance. Is it romance?'

'Wouldn't you like to know? Well, sorry, I'm not going to tell you. You have your secrets, I must be allowed mine. I must be allowed some privacy, some life of my – '

The telephone, drilling from the sitting room, was brilliantly on cue. 'That'll be for me. Don't anyone move. I'll get it.'

Maeve banged the kitchen door behind her and ran to the sitting room. Before picking up the receiver, she shut the sitting-room door, a double precaution, lest an eavesdropper should catch some libidinous chat with Lesley, the vicar's wife, about wassails and mince pies and sausage rolls and cheese fondue.

# THE AMERICAN DREAM

They sing a lot, now they're in America. They sing the songs everyone is singing and whistling this year – 'Cruising Down the River' and 'Put Another Nickel In (Music! Music! Music!)' are two – and they sing the commercial jingles that interrupt wireless programmes over here. *Radio* programmes. They sing about jello and shampoo, soup and soap. One of the jingles they like best, that appeals to them most, because so far-fetched, is a duet. A male voice starts off:

> 'Here comes the Camay Bride –
> Oh! What a lucky groom
> To have a girl with a complexion
> Just like roses in bloom – '

and a female, a girlish, voice intercepts to explain:

> 'It's the Camay mild soap di-et,
> Give up careless care and try et –
> With your vurry vurry first cake of Camay
> Your skin grows softer, smoother, right away-ay.'

They're singing this today as they run down the stairs. They run out of the house and into the street with their ball, and begin kicking it about on the pavement (or on the sidewalk: the words they choose, the words they use, depend on their mood; depend on whether they feel, at a given moment, pro- or anti-America and Americans, loyal or disloyal to home). They are identically dressed in red and white striped T-shirts, cotton dungarees and sandals.

It's a hot day, and after a bit they get fed up with kicking the ball, and head towards Meakin's store for a popsicle. While the boy jogs and dribbles the ball, dodging the shoppers, his twin sister negotiates the tops of low brick walls. She careers like a tightropist, in jerky bursts and sudden stops and headlong dashes, her outstretched arms seesawing for balance. When the street runs out of wall, she jumps down and trots beside him.

A woman in a mauve poplin dress and with a little mauve hat tipped over one eye, and with her arms full of shopping, stops in front of them.

'Say, are you two twins?' this woman asks. 'Aren't you perfectly darling!'

The girl nods vigorously. The boy shakes his head.

'No, no relation at all,' he says.

The woman seems amused. She laughs. She shifts her shopping from one arm to the other. She shades her free eye with her free hand.

'You're British,' she says. 'Why, that's wonderful! I just love your accent. It's the cutest – '

'We're English. We haven't got an accent.' The boy frowns. He bounces his ball twice. 'You're the ones with the accent, not us.'

'Well well well,' the woman says. 'My my.' She does not stop smiling, but her smile now has a stuck-on look about it. If I tug at the corner of that smile, the boy decides, it will rip off in one go, like Elastoplast, and afterwards there'll be a black hole in her face.

The woman stares at them for a moment, still smiling; and then steps backwards and then sideways, and then walks on.

This is not the first time they've been stopped by a stranger. They've been accosted, in one way or another, ever since they arrived in Washington. It even happened on the *Queen Mary* coming over. They might be film stars, the amount of attention they're getting. They might be *movie* stars.

They walk on down the street. The street, Q Street, is empty of school-age children because it's a Tuesday afternoon in term time and school-age children are at school. They're not at school because when their mother went to the nearest suitable one to enrol them, she was told by the principal, yes, sure, it'd be a real pleasure to have Robert and Josephine in school while their father was in Washington; they were nine years old, did she say? – they'd go into the fourth grade. Their mother argued with the principal about this. She'd been round the classrooms, she'd cast an eye over the maps and nature posters on the wall, she'd glanced at the exercise books of people in the fourth grade. People in the fourth grade were just about learning to read and write, their mother deduced. Robert and Josephine had been reading and writing for years, she told the principal, they were extremely articulate, they had an unusually wide vocabulary, they'd been learning French for a whole year at least. Robert was due to start Latin in the autumn. They'd be wasting their time in the fourth grade. The principal, so their mother told them afterwards, shrugged and spread his hands at this, and said he was sorry, you couldn't skip grades. Not in his school. That was how the education system was geared to work in the United States of America, and it worked just fine.

'But we can't have you bimbling about all morning, getting under Carrie's feet,' their mother said. 'We can't have you getting in Celestine's hair.' And so, when there's time, she takes them on sightseeing tours and educational outings, and she sets them work to do at home.

They do this work, which their mother calls their assignments, in a little room at the top of the house that looks over the thin houses, and thin trees, opposite. At a table in the window they sit side by side and write essays on 'My Favourite Painting in the Mellon Gallery' (this, for both of them, is 'The Dead Toreador' by Edouard Manet), 'Our Day in Williamsburg', 'The Visit to Chesapeake Bay', 'A

Walk in Rock Creek Park'. They draw portraits and self-portraits, they paint imaginative compositions and still-lifes. They design posters and book jackets. They learn poems from *The Oxford Book of English Verse* by heart, and write them out in their best writing. When they know the poem, when they're both word perfect – Josephine invariably the first to reach this stage, Josephine 'the literary one, "the chiel amang us",' their mother tells visitors, 'we think, we hope, she's going to be a writer one day' – they take the book to their mother so that she can test them. Their mother will be in the kitchen, showing Celestine how to cook the lunch; or she'll be seated on her dressing-table stool, waving her hands up and down to dry the polish on her nails; or she'll be at her desk, writing letters home. (Or she'll be lying on the sofa with her eyes closed, listening to *The Story of Helen Trent* on the portable.) Wherever she is, whatever she's doing, she'll say, 'Well done, good children, but I haven't time now, I'll hear your poem later.' Their mother, like all mothers probably, leads a busy life. She doesn't always have time to hear their poem later.

No arithmetic, no 'math', is done in the room at the top of the house because their mother is no good at it. It doesn't matter. They're only in America for six months. They aren't missing anything they won't be able to catch up on when they get back to school.

The only thing they might be said to be missing is the company of children their own age, but they have each other. And there is America, new and shiny, loud and colourful, a land of plenty where sweets are not, where candy is not, rationed. It was the 'Land of the Dream', their father told them once, the place where if you bought the product, you got the girl; the country where even a bellhop could, in theory anyway, make it to President. It was the Land of the Free, a term they understood through their being allowed, for the first time in their lives, to roam the streets – of Georgetown – unaccompanied and at will. Not least, it was the land of advertising jingles and peanut butter.

At Meakin's store, they buy double popsicles and tubes of Lifesavers, rum butter and wild cherry. The store is empty except for Mr Meakin and a Negro. The Negro is sitting on an upturned orange box; he holds a bottle of Pepsi in one hand and a bag of salted peanuts in the other. Every so often he shakes a few nuts from the bag into the bottle, and then he tilts back his head and swigs, chewing the nuts and swallowing the Pepsi at one and the same time. How is this done? They drop their popsicle wrappers in the trash can, and stand in the doorway and watch. The Negro is wearing a wide straw hat, tipped back off his face. Sweat, like tears, streams down his cheek and his neck, trickles over a sharp and painful-looking Adam's apple. I will never forget this, Robert tells himself. I will always remember this Negro on this orange box, swallowing and chewing.

Robert discovered this remembering, storing trick two years ago, when he was seven. He was hiding under the grand piano in the Music Room at school, during the hobbies period they have there on wet Saturdays. He was homesick, or perhaps it would be more true to say, mothersick; and while all around him boys and girls (the girls included Josephine: their mother chose a co-educational school so the twins should not be separated) buzzed among the scratched yellow tables and swapped cigarette cards and stamps; or sat at the tables and impressed sheet after sheet of rough drawing paper with pencil Spitfires and Messerschmitts, and bullets and flames and smoke, he stayed under the piano, sniffing his knees and staring at the rain hosing the windows in squally bursts. A climbing rose had broken loose in the wind, and it flailed and whipped the window nearest him. Black rosehips, thrown at the glass one minute, were torn away the next, and the sound they made – a rattle, a sawing scrape, a relentless tapping, like someone desperate to get in – was the most desolate sound he'd heard. I shall remember this afternoon, he told himself then. I shall remember that sound, and the rain, and the way my knees smell. Now, in America, if he chooses to, he can recall every detail.

When the Negro has finished his Pepsi and the nuts, Robert and Josephine leave the store.

> 'Pepsi-Cola hits the spot!
> Two whole glasses, that's a lot!
> Twice more flavour, twice more pep –
> Why take less when Pepsi's best?'

It's Josephine who sings this. 'Shall we go to the drugstore?' she suggests. She's taken the popsicle from her mouth and is examining it. The tip is bleached now, drained of sweetness and of orange juice.

'No point. The new comics won't be in yet.'

And there is no point, for they go to the drugstore for the purpose of reading the comics. Occasionally they may sit at the counter and have a banana split before reading the comics, but mostly they don't bother. The comics are kept on a low rack on the left of the entrance. They'll go in and kneel on the lino tiles and read *Batman* and *Superman* front page to back, and then replace them in the rack. Mike, the drugstore manager, never objects. Perhaps because they're twins, perhaps because they're British, he never suggests they buy a comic.

On the way home Robert dribbles his football through the shoppers and the hurrying businessmen, and Josephine dances beside him, counting her steps in sevens. She starts with the right foot: 'One two three four five six seven,' then shifts to the left: 'One two three four five six seven,' then returns to the right. Everything she does has to be done in sevens. She has to climb stairs this way, she has to brush her teeth twenty-one times – seven goes on the right side of her jaw, seven on the left, etcetera. Robert cannot stop her, although he, and everyone in her orbit, has tried. Josephine has had rituals before. Until the age of three she was a head-banger, unable to get to sleep without first thumping her head against the pillow, at the same time emitting a monotonous moaning hum. She could keep this up for hours. After the head-banging, there was a period of touching things – railings, or lamp posts, or pillar boxes – on walks, of having to go back and touch any she'd left out. And when that blew over, or lost its power? Something to do with neatness, and shoes, and joins in the carpet. Josephine never chooses to explain, or perhaps cannot, what her rituals are about; she won't disclose the terrible consequences she's certain will result from a failure to carry out her 'orders'.

Eight doors from home, the toe of Robert's sandal lifts the ball over a low wall and into a front yard. A fat girl in a frilled cotton dress is staring from the yard. She picks up the ball and holds it against her chest.

'You lost your ball?' She hugs it to her. She looks about the same age as they are, except that she has bosoms already; they can see them wobble through the thin cotton. She has mousey hair, parted in the middle and held at the side with pink plastic bows. The hair is quite short and it sticks straight out from her face, perhaps because the ends are frizzed.

'It's dumb to play ball on the street,' the fat girl says. 'Dumb and dangerous. I'm not permitted to play ball on the street.'

Without consulting each other, they jump on to the wall at the same moment, and jump off it again into the fat girl's yard.

'I saw you two before today. You're twins,' she informs them.

'You don't say,' Josephine says.

'You talk real strange. You foreign or something?'

'Yep yep yep.'

'Why aren't you in school?' Without warning, the fat girl throws the ball at Robert, a dud throw that manages to be both short and wide. He retrieves the ball; then he asks her why she isn't at school anyway? For example?

'I'm sick,' the girl says. 'I've had a fever. I've been sick four days now.'

They stare at her with interest. She doesn't look sick, particularly, merely fat and pale.

'My name's Yvonne,' the sick girl says. 'It's French. My second name's Claybeau. That's French too. My ancestors were French on my daddy's side. My daddy's an admiral. What does your daddy do?'

Their father is a diplomat, and English. Robert tells Yvonne this.

'Uh-huh.' She doesn't seem impressed. 'Uh-huh.' She turns to Josephine. 'What's your name?'

'Josephine,' Josephine says. 'It's a French name, I believe, although I myself am not French.'

There's a silence after this. Robert bounces his ball twice in the admiral's flowerless yard. He turns to go, and so does Josephine.

'Hey! Do you two twins have skates? Come back Saturday. Come lunch time Saturday and meet my mommy and my best friend Bobby Jane. If I'm not sick by then we'll skate the block. Come a quarter after twelve.'

Yvonne Claybeau is a blancmange. It's impossible to envisage her on skates. It's impossible to imagine her wearing anything other than a pink frilly dress.


'Be tactful,' their mother says as they lace their skates on Saturday morning. 'Come home straight away if you're not expected,' says their mother, who like most mothers, probably, does not believe in the validity of invitations issued by nine-year-olds, especially when the parents of the parties concerned are not acquainted.

The Claybeaus are expecting them, however. Admiral and Mrs Claybeau are very old, more like grandparents than parents. Mrs Claybeau's hair is blue-white, and she wears it in a fancy roll down the back of her head. Her large corseted body is draped in a clinging lilac dress. There's a lot of lilac about this year, and mauve. Their mother wears it, and it suits her, but it does not suit Mrs Claybeau, Robert decides. It makes her skin look grey.

231

The admiral is large also, and unfit-looking, and he has a snub nose. He is a tall, old, masculine version of his daughter Yvonne.

Then there is Bobby Jane.

'This is my vurry best friend Roberta Jane Dyson,' says Yvonne, who is wearing Bermudas today, pink ones, so tight across her bottom the line of her underpants shows through.

'Hi,' Roberta Jane says. She shakes hands. She is skinny and tall, taller than Robert, he is displeased to see, skinnier than Josephine, who is not skinny. (Josephine is not fat, either. Not fat. 'Well-covered,' visitors to the house sometimes remark. 'Bonny. What a bonny girl Josephine has become!')

Bobby Jane has an interesting face. She has dark-blue eyes that have a darker ring round the iris. She has dark, straight eyebrows and corn-coloured hair. She is pretty, she may even be beautiful. Josephine's plaits are short pigtails, the texture of horsehair, always escaping their ribbons, but Bobby Jane's plaits hang down her neck in two neat silken cords. She has on old blue pedal pushers that don't fit, they're too big for her, a faded red T-shirt, white gym shoes. White *sneakers*. There's something about her, an air, a look, that isn't young, that's not like a child. She's ten and two months, they'll learn later that day, but she could be twenty. She is the Camay Bride, it comes to Robert. 'Oh what a lucky groom.'

Lunch is peanut butter and jelly and lettuce and mayonnaise sandwiches, and strawberry milk shakes. They eat it in awkward silence in the kitchen, standing up, leaning against the margarine-coloured worktops. When they're finished, Yvonne Claybeau dabs at her mouth with a pink paper napkin.

'You guys wanna come see my boudoir now?' It's more of a command than an invitation, but they're curious, and they follow her through the thick-carpeted hall, up thick-carpeted stairs, along a thick-carpeted landing. Yvonne chooses a door and holds it open.

'No, not you,' she bars Robert, who's waited till last. 'You wait here. Boys can't go into little girls' boudoirs.'

He's seen it, though. Pink walls. A pink, silky bed, smothered with cushions and dolls. Above the bed, a crucifix, its crossbar strangely looped with a string of beads. A downcast plaster Virgin on the windowsill. A picture of Jesus wearing a nightdress and a crown of thorns – wearing an enormous, spiked halo.

> 'Halo everybody, Halo!
> Halo is the shampoo
> That glorifies your hair, so
> Halo everybody, Halo!'

Robert sings this on the landing, kneeling outside Yvonne Claybeau's closed boudoir door.


From now on they meet Bobby Jane and Yvonne after school on weekdays, and in any spare time they have at weekends. The meeting place is always the Claybeaus' house, and arrangements are made by a telephone call to Yvonne. They imagine she must sit by the telephone all day: it's always she who answers it. 'Admiral Claybeau's resi*dence*,' she always says, 'spea*king?*'

At the Claybeaus' house they sit at the kitchen table and test each other on general knowledge, and they swap travellers' tales. The Americans have the advantage when it comes to knowing the population of Arkansas, and they can argue between them about exactly how long it takes to get to Baltimore on the Pullman; but neither of them has the faintest as to what Big Ben might be, and neither of them has been abroad. Neither of them has seen an ocean-going liner. When Robert and Josephine, in order to give some idea of the size of the *Queen Mary*, describe her staterooms and shops, her swimming pools and ballrooms and dining rooms; stopping here to elaborate on the amazing Cabin Class menus and on the decorated menu cards –

a different design for each meal of the five-day crossing; when they enthuse about the mechanical horses they rode every day in the Cabin Class gymnasium, the Americans have nothing to counter with except silence. Silence and raised eyebrows.

At the Claybeaus' house they play Kick the Can in the back yard; they watch *The Lone Ranger* and *The Howdy Doody Show* on TV. Occasionally Mrs Claybeau will take them to the cinema. On these expeditions she chauffeurs the admiral's Lincoln convertible, and they ride in the back on stiffly upholstered, sickly green seats which smell horrible (but she won't allow them to have the window open). Once in the ticket queue, she'll turn suddenly and extend a fat gloved palm, as if offering sugar lumps to a horse, and this is the signal for them to produce their money. The first time this happened, they hadn't any money on them. (It was their mother's fault; they'd asked her for some, and she'd said, 'Mrs Claybeau won't expect you to pay, sillies, you're her guests!' Their mother had laughed at the very idea.) Mrs Claybeau tapped her handbag as they went through their pockets. Josephine eventually came up with a nickel. 'Bring it round tomorrow,' Mrs Claybeau said. 'You two twins had better shape up.'

The Camay Bride never comes on the cinema outings, a blow to Robert because he has fallen in love with her, and thinks about her all the time, and hopes, and fears, to sit next to her in the dark. When the cinema visits are planned she always seems to have something else to do. '*Red River* was wizard,' he told her, 'you really missed something there.' It was the best film he'd seen, he told her, 'better than *Yellow Sky*.' But she hadn't seen that one, either. She listened politely as he recounted the plot. 'Movies are no big deal, I guess,' she said.

'They don't like boys,' is Josephine's explanation when he complains about the huddles the girls get into and the conversations he's excluded from, after tea, in Yvonne's pink boudoir. 'They haven't got brothers,' she reminds him. 'The boys at their school are mean. They call Yvonne a fat pig and they swing on Bobby Jane's plaits. They have no reason to like boys. They put up with you because you're my brother.'

Nevertheless, Josephine's facts do not square with Yvonne's continual boasts: 'We'll be dating boys soon, Bobby Jane and me. We'll be dating boys when we're eleven. I'll be permitted to wear make-up next year, and then I'm gonna date Irving Wentworth. He's the best-looking boy in our class.'

Robert wants Bobby Jane to deny these promises, made on her behalf by Yvonne, but she never does, although she won't confirm them either. When Yvonne goes on and on about boys and dating, she stares down at her hands, spread out on the kitchen table (her nails are oval and clean, and have little white half-moons at the base). Like a sheepdog separating a ewe from the flock, he tries sometimes to nudge her away from the others and get her on her own, but she will not be nudged. His efforts at conversation she blocks, politely evades, slides round.

'Do you like reading?' he asked her once – for despite their mother's lack of faith in the American educational system, it's clear that the two fourth-graders they know can read, and better than haltingly. They were standing in the Claybeaus' kitchen, drinking banana milk shakes that tasted of Kolynos.

'Sure I like to read.' Bobby Jane removed the flattened straw from her tumbler, pinched it to make it cylindrical, blew through it. 'Everybody does, I guess.'

The offhand put-down was a lie – everybody did not like reading – but he plugged on: 'What books then? What d'you like best? Adventure? Murder? Ghost stories?'

'Oh, all kinds.' She smiled, but she didn't look at him. She tipped her glass; with her mouth she guided her straw into the remaining bubbles, where it stuttered like a motor-bike. She turned her face and her attention away from him to Josephine.

'I like your plaits,' he said another time, the words

coming out in a rush of breath as he caught up with her in Pennsylvania Avenue. 'Your plaits are . . . swell.'

She stared at him. She rolled upright, in perfect control, back and forth on her skates. Back and forth. He pointed. He didn't dare touch her plaits.

'Oh. My *braids*. Oh. Thanks.' She flipped one over her shoulder, then locked her hands behind her back and swooped off, neatly zigzagging.

What Robert knows about Bobby Jane he learns from his sister, information imparted voluntarily without his having to probe, but released only slowly, in short bursts – when they are doing their assignments, when they are cleaning their teeth, when Josephine feels like it. When she feels generous. Or is it mischievous?

'Her father's dead, you know,' Josephine remarks as they sit over their Quaker Oats ('Delicious! nutritious! makes you feel ambitious! The giant of the cereals is Quaker Oats!') at supper time, waiting for *The Shadow* to frighten them out of their wits. 'Perhaps I told you? He was a bomber pilot, stationed in Suffolk. He died at the very end of the war. Bobby Jane doesn't remember him, hardly. Hey, it's time.' Josephine stretches a hand to their mother's portable, and fiddles with the knob. 'Who knows what evil lurks in the hearts of men?' Orson Welles enquires menacingly. 'The Shadow knows.'

'Her mother's a cripple,' Josephine announces casually, 'she caught polio when Bobby Jane was six. That's my rubber you've got there, I need it,' Josephine says. (They are not enjoying their assignment which is: 'Give a brief history and, where applicable, explain the functions of the following: a) The White House; b) The Capitol; c) The Lincoln Memorial; d) The Pentagon; e) The Washington Monument. Illustrate in pencil: if you can, from memory.'

'She's a writer,' Josephine says, 'she writes poetry. She's a famous poet, Bobby Jane says. *Quis*?'

'*Ego* decent.'

But it's not decent; it's only Josephine's postcard view of 'The Capitol under snow', which she wants to swap for

Robert's 'The White House in cherry-blossom time'. They got the postcards from the drugstore. They were hoping for an aerial-view shot of the Pentagon – how could you make sense of its five sides otherwise? – but the postcard stand hadn't held any view of the Pentagon at all. 'Well well well,' Mike said when they told him why they needed it, 'that's a kinda serious request. Let's see now what we can do for our friends the twins.' He went through a drawer first, and then a cardboard box of old, black and white, bargain-price postcards, but no luck. He seemed as disappointed as they were, and perhaps because of this wouldn't let them pay for the cards they did find.

'Bobby Jane is a sort of housekeeper,' Josephine confides. They're in the drugstore again, squatting on the lino floor in their dungarees, reading *Batman* and *Superman*, cover to cover. 'She does the shopping and the cooking, and the washing. They haven't got a maid or anything.'

What must it be like not to have a maid or anything? There was always someone in London. In Washington there are two: Celestine, an eighteen-year-old Jamaican who lives in and whom their mother is teaching to cook – 'but it's hopeless,' their mother sighs, 'quite hopeless. She's incapable of retaining the simplest instruction' – and Carrie Hawkins, an American, a Negress, a grandmother, who comes in daily to do the laundry.

Celestine is sad and giggly by turn. She wears a large-brimmed black hat, indoors and out, 'to keep the devils away'. For work she wears a cyclamen-pink cotton dress with white buttons and white collar and cuffs their mother bought her. When not in the kitchen, trying to make sense of their mother's instructions, she shambles about the house with a feather duster. She stares out of windows a lot. They worry about her. They ask her, 'Are you homesick, Celestine?' (They are homesick themselves sometimes, for England, for English newsreaders on the wireless.) She giggles or weeps, but she won't say.

Celestine's bedroom is downstairs, in the basement, and next to it is a shower room – Celestine's own. Once, creeping down the basement stairs, they saw Celestine in the shower. She hadn't bothered to pull the shower curtain round. They sat on the stairs and watched amazed as Celestine's blue-black body – long strong legs, firm stomach, big breasts – dazzling and shiny with water, revolved under the jet like a doll on a musical box.

The basement is where Carrie Hawkins does the laundry. It has a concrete floor, perfect for roller skates, and while Carrie transforms the jumble in the laundry basket into uniform flat parcels on the ironing board, they skate round her. Carrie doesn't mind this. 'You go right ahead, honey,' she says, 'you don't bother me one bit.' While Carrie irons she sings, old sad Negro songs about cabins and cornmeal and cotton fields and deep rivers. About Lindy Lou.

'Lindy, did you hear that mockin' bird singin' las' night?' Carrie will sing, pressing both hands and all her birdlike weight on the iron to remove a stubborn crease, lifting the iron to her cheek as though she's listening to it. 'Honey, it was singin' so sweet in the moonlight.' Every so often she'll place a finger on her tongue and then touch the flat of the iron to test its heat. This produces a hiss and a little puff of steam. It shows off the softness and pinkness of Carrie's tongue in contrast with the dark cracked leather of her lips. 'Lindy, I'd lay me right down and die, and die, if I could sing as that bird sang to you-oo, my little Lindy Lou-oo.'

Robert feels sorry for Bobby Jane that there's no one like Carrie Hawkins at her place. He knows where her place is – a depressing apartment block, a few doors down from Meakin's store. A couple of times after school he's skated there on his own and loitered, but she's never appeared and asked him in. And there've been no invitations to tea there, not even for Josephine.

'She doesn't ask us because of that supper, I bet,' Josephine says. 'I know I wouldn't if I was her.'

By 'that supper' Josephine means the one they invited Bobby Jane and Yvonne Claybeau to, at their house. They asked if they could eat in the kitchen, the way the Claybeaus do; if they could cook it themselves, if they could have a proper American menu.

'You know, Ma, hamburgers, hot dogs, fries, ketchup; ice cream 'n' chocolate sauce. Coke. You know, things they're used to, things they like.'

Their mother was writing letters when they petitioned her. They stood either side of her desk, right up close, as close as they dared, and watched her blue fountain pen etch the blue air mail paper. She wrote in firm bursts, the pen hovering above the page when not pressed to it, her beautiful mouth folded into a concentrating line, the line twitching a little at the corners.

'Okay, Ma?' Robert picked up a heavy glass dome and turned it over and studied the green baize on its bottom.

'Don't say "okay", and don't call me "Ma".' She didn't look up. 'Don't fiddle, there's a good child.'

He put the paperweight down.

'Can we though? Is it all right, Mother darling?'

'Don't be cheeky.'

The pen reached the end of the page. Their mother read through what she'd written, and blotted it, and plucked a new sheet from the tooled-leather paper-holder. He made a face at Josephine. She was sometimes able to succeed where he failed. If he had the advantage of being a boy and the first born – by twenty minutes – she had the bonus of being a girl and the 'baby'.

Josephine shunted sideways to within an inch of their mother's elbow.

'May we, Mummy, please? Please.'

Their mother removed the hornrims she wears for close work and laid them on the empty sheet of paper. She leant back in her chair. Then she picked up the hornrims and put them on again. Then she picked up her pen and continued with her letter.

'We'll see,' she murmured, folding her lips together. The pen gathered speed. 'If you're good children. We'll see.'

On the night they didn't have supper in the kitchen – of course not, it was impossible, they never did – they had it in the hall, which in Washington has to double as dining room. To its formality was added Celestine's gloom as she shambled in and out in her hat with plates and dishes. They sat in silence while she made her sad entrances and exits, just the four of them at the too-large dining table. (The moment their visitors had arrived their parents had gone out, dressed to the nines, to some do at the French Embassy.)

'Hey, what kinda soup is this?' Yvonne peered into her bowl and sniffed.

Robert looked at Josephine; Josephine looked at Robert. They recognised the brew, they knew what it was – their worst, their mother's favourite – a boiling-up of chicken carcass and insides, plus onions and celery and pearl barley, the concoction masked by parsley and a shiny, wrinkling skin of fat. Blistering fat. 'Yum yum chicky broth,' their mother always greets this abomination, taking no notice at all when they gag and moan and slide off their chairs and hide their heads under the tablecloth, 'full of nourishing goodness.'

How could she have done it to them this evening? How could she? How?

'It's chicken,' Josephine said. 'More palatable with a ton of salt, in my experience.'

'You call this chicken?'

Impossible to blame Yvonne, for once. Nothing less like Campbell's Cream of Chicken could be imagined; could have been devised.

They picked up their spoons.

Immediately, at the first sip – in their anxiety they'd failed to warn the Americans to blow on their soup – Bobby Jane burnt her mouth. She cried 'Ow!', she spluttered, her face went red. Robert looked away, to the portrait of their mother in an emerald evening dress above the doorway; but Josephine jumped up and ran to the sideboard and grabbed the water jug (where was the Coke they'd ordered?) and filled Bobby Jane's glass.

'It's okay. I'm okay now.' Bobby Jane put out a fending-off hand. 'No, really, Josephine.' Josephine slunk back to her chair.

They picked up their spoons again in silence. They lifted and sifted the contents of their bowls.

'Uh-oh. Uh-oh.' In Yvonne's spoon, held out for them across the table, lay a grey something with little holes in it, a rubbery something with whiskers sprouting out of it. Yum yum chicky skin. Yum yum yum. *Uh-oh*.

'I can't eat this stuff,' Yvonne said.

'Neither can I, I guess. I'm sorry,' Bobby Jane said.

They put down their spoons.

Hardboiled eggs in cheese sauce, with bullet rice and spinach-in-a-pool, came next – and left again, rearranged on the plates but otherwise untouched, minutes after. The twins had been brought up – 'There's a war on, remember' – to eat everything that was put in front of them no matter how unappetising; even when the war was over there were the 'starving Russians' to 'think of'. To feel guilty about. Robert felt guilty now. Not so much about the Russians, who hadn't been invoked recently, but about Celestine's hurt feelings over her rejected, wasted, cooking. If the visitors weren't prepared to eat it, though, if they weren't even prepared to try it, how could he and Josephine?

When Celestine had taken away the plates, shaking her head sadly as she did so, she set about clearing the rest of the table. She did it very very slowly. Egg dish, rice dish, spinach dish; saltcellar, pepper grinder, serving spoons. Four punishing journeys, made without a tray. She refused to let them help her. Meanwhile nobody spoke. Bobby Jane crumbled a piece of bread and examined the ceiling. Yvonne giggled behind her hand. By this time the twins were in despair at their failure, and their guests ravenous.

'Ice cream, please Celestine! Ice cream! Ice cream! Ice cream!'

Celestine turned at the door. She looked perplexed. She looked bruised.

'Yo mother say nothin' 'bout no ice cream. Dere'm no ice cream.' And she brought them the fruit bowl. In it

were five bright red, tough-skinned, sleepy apples. The one
Robert had rejected at elevenses still had his teethmarks in
it, upper and lower jaw, not a bad print, the flesh dark
brown now where the skin was broken.


It's not surprising there've been no invitations from Bobby
Jane. But if she doesn't ask them soon, it will be too late:
they sail for England, for football and netball and new
brown walking shoes and new grey knee-socks, in three
weeks' time.

She asks them one day when they're taking off their
skates in the doorway of the Claybeaus' kitchen. (Mrs
Claybeau does not permit skates in her kitchen. They make
black marks on the linoleum, she says.)

'You guys wanna come round my place Wednesday?'
Bobby Jane's head is bent over her laces, her face hidden
by her braids. 'It's okay with my mother if you do.'

The question comes as such a surprise, is so out of the
blue, no one answers.

'We can watch *The Howdy Doody Show* and *The Last
of the Mohicans*.' Bobby Jane sounds casual. She doesn't
care one way or the other. 'Let me know Monday. I have
to go now. I have to fetch the groceries from the store.'

'It's too bad I can't go to Bobby Jane's place,' Yvonne
Claybeau says sweetly when Bobby Jane's gone. It's clear
she's longing to be asked why not, and eventually, reluctantly, they allow curiosity to get the better of them.

'Why can't you go?'

'Well. We-ell.' Yvonne stops and puts a small fat finger
to her lips. 'My mommy doesn't like me to.' She simpers
and stops again, then says in a fake whisper, 'Bobby Jane
and her mother aren't Catholics.'

'But we're not Catholics!' Robert is incensed. 'And you
came to our house, I seem to remember.'

'I know, I know' – Yvonne's tone is sweet and pitying –
'but you do go to the Episcopalian church Sundays. You
and your folks are kind of friends of Jesus, I guess.'

Friends of Jesus? Is that what they are? It does not describe their yawning Sunday mornings in the Episcopalian church. The dull sermon, the dreary hymns, their formal, uncomfortable clothes. The only service they've enjoyed in America is the one Carrie Hawkins took them to, at her church. They were the only white people in the congregation. On arrival they were handed cardboard fans, shaped and decorated like palm leaves, and during the sermon and the singing of cheerful and catchy hymns they swayed and fanned themselves as everyone else did. The preacher struck his chest from time to time and cried, 'We're all sinners, Lord!' and from all parts of the church men and women, and even one boy not much older than themselves, leapt up to agree: 'So right! Yes Lord!' Having to give up their fans when it was over was a disappointment, but afterwards they went back with Carrie Hawkins to her place for Sunday dinner: fried chicken and sweetcorn and fried potatoes; apple pie and toffee-nut-crunch ice cream.

'Bobby Jane's mother isn't able to go to church,' Josephine reminds Yvonne. 'She can't walk. She's paralysed. So how could she get to church?'

'She could go in a wheelchair. Or the priest could visit her maybe. If she wanted. The problem is' – Yvonne whispers this – 'Roberta's mother doesn't believe in Jesus. She's taught Roberta that Our Lady was just an ordinary woman, and Our Lord was just an ordinary man. She's raised her that way. Isn't that terrible? Anyways, that's not all. The Dysons aren't our class. They're poor. Real poor. Their home is just a two-room apartment. They have to share a bathroom with three other families across the hall. The bath tub isn't clean, either.' She shudders. 'I saw it once. There's a green stain all over the bottom of the tub. The faucets have gotten mould on them. The living room's real shabby too. They don't have a machine to wash the clothes, they don't have a maid to do the laundry – '

'Seeing is believing!' Robert says. 'See an Oxydol wash! See how Oxydol washes whiter than any other soap product!'

'Bobby Jane's always very clean,' Josephine says, 'and her hair shines. She's much cleaner and tidier than me. She's got white teeth,' Josephine continues, 'as white as Celestine's. And her breath never pongs, except of peppermints.'

'Pep pep Pepsodent toothpaste,' Robert sings,

> 'Beats film on teeth and cleans breath too!
> Pep pep Pepsodent toothpaste
> Beats film on teeth – the old schedule!'

Yvonne Claybeau ignores these interruptions. 'Bobby Jane does the laundry in the sink,' she tells them, 'the same sink where she washes the dishes. They don't have a kitchen, it's just a railed-off corner of the living room. The living room smells bad. It smells of fries and beans. Ugh. It's awful.' She leans back in her chair and puts her hand over her mouth and speaks through her fingers: 'Awful.'

'Gee whizz. Golly gee. Jeepers creepers. Holy smoke.' (But irony is always lost on Yvonne.) 'I thought Bobby Jane was supposed to be your best friend. Your very best friend, you're always telling us.'

'She is too, she is so, Robert Partridge. She can come round my place any time. My mommy's always pleased to see Bobby Jane. It's not Bobby Jane's fault if she doesn't believe in Jesus, my mommy says. It's just that I'm not permitted to visit with her anymore. That's all. But it's okay, I'm never gonna tell her why I can't go to her place. I always think up reasons, so she won't ever know.'

On the way home Josephine has to circle every seventh lamp post seven times, difficult to do on skates. She makes three tours clockwise, three tours anti-clockwise, one tour clockwise.

' "The drapes in the living room aren't clean," ' Josephine lisps. (She's having a breather, between lamp posts.) ' "The whatsits have gotten mould on them. And you should see the tub – ugh" ' – she wrinkles her nose – ' "it's awful, awful dirty." '

'You haven't quite got it, if you don't mind my saying. You don't sound sweet enough. Listen. "Admiral *Clay*beau's resi-*dence*. Spea-*king*?" '

'Anyhow, I can't wait till Wednesday,' Josephine says in her own, nettled, English voice.


But on Tuesday Josephine caught a feverish summer cold, and on Wednesday she's kept in bed, where she wheezes and streams and coughs and blows.

'Poor me, I'm so disappointed.' Little moans from Josephine into a wet handkerchief. 'Poor me, poor Bobby Jane.'

Robert wants to go to Bobby Jane's place. He does not want Josephine's cold. He stands in the doorway, leaning back, trying not to breathe.

'I could go by myself, I suppose,' he says in a bored way, pinching his nose.

'She won't want you without me.' Josephine is authoritative about this.

'She'll have made cookies and cakes though. Someone ought to go. Someone has to eat them.'

'No. Yvonne told me they only had cinnamon toast when she went there. It tasted real bad, she said. But you could go down there and tell her why I can't come.'

Josephine buries her nose in the wet handkerchief. She's having to blow seven times with the right nostril, seven with the left, etcetera. It's very tiring, she tells Robert, and it makes her nose and lip sorer than ever, but what can you do?


On the way to Bobby Jane's place, Robert sees his father's old black Chevrolet parked on the opposite side of the street. The windows are down, and there is his father in the driving seat, one shirtsleeved arm hooked out of the window, fingers tapping the car roof. He's listening to the baseball game, a substitute for the cricket he misses, and something he often does if he comes home early. He chooses the car radio, he tells them, so he can listen in peace without fear of children. (It's true he does fear children and avoids them as much as possible.) Once though, when he saw Robert in the street messing around with his football, he called him over and invited him to listen to the game. Robert enjoyed this occasion – the being singled out for attention, the smell of his father's cigarette smoke, the humbugs his father produced from the glove compartment, his comments on the commentator of the game – but he doesn't want to catch his father's eye today. He puts his head down, and skates on.

Outside Meakin's store he brakes, and goes through his pockets and counts the change he finds there.

'A jar of sourballs please.'

Mr Meakin has his back turned. He's replenishing a shelf with large tins, with large cans, of cling peaches, with smaller ones of fruit cocktail.

'Libby's fruit cocktail, a great selection,
Look to Libby's for perfection!
When you go to the store, look in Libby's direction
Look to Libby's for perfection!'

'You're a crazy boy.' Mr Meakin shakes his head. He has a thin face, all lines and wrinkles, and his grey hair, closely shaved at the sides, grows like a brush on the top of his head. A bristly brush. The brush Celestine uses for the stairs. Mr Meakin wraps the sourballs in striped paper. The skin of his hands is shiny and loose; it resembles the rubber gloves he stocks, Large, Extra Large and Ladies, in a cardboard box on the counter.

'Hot day,' Mr Meakin says. 'How's your mother?' he asks. 'Your mother's a real English lady.' Mr Meakin always says this, or something like it. 'Where's your prettier half?' he says. 'I don't believe I ever saw you two folks apart.'

His mother is well, Robert tells Mr Meakin. She's gone to Garfinkel's for a new dress, or it might be a hat. His

246

sister Josephine's in bed with a cold. 'How much are those, Mr Meakin?' He points to some bunches of red roses gasping in a bucket by the door.

'They're past their best this time of day, I guess. They should be a quarter a bunch, but I could let you have one for fifteen cents. Aw, go on. A dime.'

Outside on the sidewalk, Robert sniffs the roses. They're scentless. A few are still in bud, but the buds look too heavy for their stems and are turning black. It's obvious they will never open. This is the first time he's bought flowers for anyone and he feels foolish, holding them out in front of him as he skates along, while simultaneously trying to keep the sourball jar wedged under his other arm.

'Where are they?' Bobby Jane peers round him. She holds the street door half-open, or half-shut. She's wearing an embroidered blouse with ribbons on the sleeves. She's wearing the blue skirt with red appliqué cherries on the pockets that she often wears and that he particularly admires. He wants to flee. He speaks very fast to get his explanations and embarrassment, her disappointment, over with. When he's finished, Bobby Jane says, 'Oh. I see.' But he can tell she doesn't believe a word of his story about Josephine.

'Even if she had been allowed out of bed, we didn't think you'd want the germs.'

'No,' Bobby Jane says flatly, 'Mother mustn't catch cold. She gets real sick if she catches cold. She had pleurisy and pneumonia once, that way.'

'Josephine sent her love.'

Silence. She's waiting for something. What's she waiting for?

'Oh, and I have a message from Yvonne. She rang just before I left. She said to tell you they've got visitors, so she's got to stay in.'

'Uh-huh. Strange. She was in school today. We talked in recess. How come she never told me then?'

Silence.

'The visitors must have arrived unexpectedly.' But it sounds lame, even to him.

Silence.

'I can go home now, if you like.' Then he remembers the flowers. 'These are for your mother.' He shoves them at her. He pulls the jar of sourballs from under his other arm. 'These are for you.'

Bobby Jane says, 'Thanks.' She says she guesses he'd better come in, her mother is expecting them all. She says her mother hasn't been too well lately, that she doesn't have too many visitors right now.

He takes off his skates. He follows her through a dingy hallway. Behind them, the heavy street door clangs to, shutting out the sweltering afternoon, and locks itself.

The Dysons' living room is shabby and untidy, at first impression much as Yvonne Claybeau described it. Yet within seconds he feels at home in it, and this feeling of recognition and belonging is new: he's never felt really 'at home' at home. (He's wanted to, he's expected to, but each beginning of the school holidays when they've returned to South Kensington, and run from room to room to re-establish themselves, he's met with disappointment, solid as a wall. The ordered flat, the glassy furniture, arouse no response in him except disappointment and a vague unease.) Now, standing in Bobby Jane's living room, taking in the frayed comfort, and the books, he perceives that there will be places he can belong to and feel at ease in, and that this might be achieved without Josephine.

Yvonne Claybeau made no mention of books. They're everywhere: on shelves and tables and chairs, on the floor, on the windowsill, on the divan at the far end of the room where Bobby Jane's mother lies, propped against cushions, under a tartan rug, her back to the wall.

'That's too bad,' Mrs Dyson says when Bobby Jane has explained why Robert is on his own. 'Never mind, honey, we'll get along fine without those girls. Won't we, Robert?'

He nods. Bobby Jane says, 'Mother, Robert brought these flowers for you.' She holds out the roses. They look crushed and sad. They look almost quite dead, he decides.

'Why, aren't I the lucky one! I haven't been bunched by

a young man in years.' She touches the leaves with thin fingers, she sniffs the black buds of his scentless roses. 'Wonderful! You'd best put them in water, honey.'

And he's alone with Bobby Jane's mother.

'Pull up a chair,' she says, 'any old chair. Shove the books on the floor.'

He chooses a chair, he removes the books. Mrs Dyson reaches for a pack of Philip Morris on the table beside her. She shakes a cigarette from the pack. Her hands tremble, the matches rattle in their box, she lights up.

'Camels are milder,' he says by way of conversation. It's what the Camel advertisements are telling everyone this year.

'Which may be why they're no use to me.' Mrs Dyson inhales and then coughs. She stares intently at him. 'Tell me what it's like to be a twin,' she says. 'Tell me the good and bad, all of it. How does it feel to have someone around who looks like you and talks like you, and maybe even thinks like you? I haven't met Josephine, of course, but Roberta tells me you're very alike. I imagine you must get compared all the time. Are you able to have any kind of separate life and identity?'

No one has asked these questions before. The questions he and Josephine do get asked are usually no more than social and incurious and jokey enquiries: 'Are you the Heavenly Twins?' or 'Which twin has the Toni?' – requiring no more than a frown in reply. Mrs Dyson's questions, he senses, are real ones, but he hasn't any answers. Being a twin is just a fact of his life. He's known nothing else, so how can he say? He takes refuge in the medical dictionary he and Josephine looked up once, when they were meant to be doing their assignment.

'We're not identical twins, we're not the same sex. We came from separate eggs. We're fraternal twins. It's only by chance, by coincidence, we look alike.'

'Okay, okay, so you're not identical. But you did spend nine months together, just the two of you, in a confined space before you were born. That must count for something.'

He's thinking about this when Bobby Jane comes back into the room. She walks slowly to the window, bearing his roses in a green glass vase. She places the vase on the windowsill. The neck of the vase is too wide for so few roses, the stems will not stay down in the water, they float to the surface. The dark red flowerheads and the black buds lean almost horizontally over the rim of the vase; they look desperate to get away. They look mean. Why hadn't he bought two bunches?

'Thanks, honey,' Mrs Dyson says, 'that's pretty. How are you doing out there?'

'I'm doing okay.' Bobby Jane crosses the room without looking in Robert's direction, and goes out through the curtain.

'I have the impression you're not too happy to discuss the twin question,' Mrs Dyson says, 'so maybe we should talk about something else. I'd be interested to know,' she says, removing a cigarette from the pack, laying it on the tartan rug, 'what you plan to do or be when you're through college. When you're grown.'

Another poser. He doesn't know; he hasn't thought about it. The future, the very idea of looking forward, frightens him. 'This time last week' is something he says quite often. 'This time next week' is not a phrase he uses often; if he does use it, or something like it, it's with his fingers crossed: 'This time next week the exams will be over.' 'This time tomorrow where shall I be? Not in this academy.' But an answer is expected, and he searches the room for clues, and his eye lights on the terrifying wheelchair – why hasn't he noticed it before? – in the corner, on its canvas and leather straps and chrome. No, not a doctor. What else is there in the room? Books.

'I'm going to be a reader.'

'A reader? An academic, you mean? A publisher's reader? A proofreader?'

'I meant a writer.'

'Oh! Like your sister Josephine! Roberta told me. Two writers in the family – that's really something. Roberta doesn't plan to be a writer, I've put her off, I think. She can't abide poetry. As you know, as she'll have told you, she's figuring on being a gymnast, to teach gymnastics.'

He nods. But she hasn't told him, and Josephine hasn't told him, and he doesn't know.

You get to meet people as a teacher, Mrs Dyson continues, but it's a lonely life being a writer. Did he know that? Also, you have to have something to write about. Ideas, experiences. Does he keep a diary?

He doesn't. Josephine does. He shakes his head.

But he can make himself remember things, he suddenly tells her; and he's reasonably observant and imaginative, his mother has said.

Mrs Dyson blows a long funnel of smoke at the ceiling. He should keep a diary even so, she tells him, it's good discipline. Memory, she'd like to remind him, is only fiction. We invent our own version of the past, of history, to suit ourselves, we improve on it as time goes by. Isn't that true? Doesn't he agree?

No. No, he doesn't, no – and he's about to say so when Mrs Dyson starts off again. She's being unfair on him, she says, he hasn't lived long enough to find out. 'Why don't you go give Roberta a hand,' she says, 'she's baked a cake and some cookies. There are only three of us, so we can have a feast.'

On the other side of the curtain, in the tiny railed-off kitchen, Bobby Jane is putting plates and knives on a trolley.

'Tea's all fixed,' she says, 'I baked a cake.'

'Swansdown cake flour! More women use Swansdown cake flou-err than any other package cake flou-err in Americaarr,' he informs her.

'It's Betty Crocker,' Bobby Jane says flatly.

> 'Just add water, mix and bake
> Betty Crocker angel cake!'

251

'Oh sure. I made devil though. The devil mix tastes better.'

'We haven't got adverts on the wireless at home.' Something in her tone makes him think it wise to explain this.

'Wireless. Adverts. You slay me. Anyway, I know you don't. Josephine already told me, ages back.' Bobby Jane takes two glasses from a shelf and puts them on the trolley. She smiles at him suddenly. 'Milk okay with you?'

Tea is over, *The Howdy Doody Show* is over, episode six of *The Last of the Mohicans* is over. He and Bobby Jane are sitting side by side, tailor-fashion, in front of the television set. Their elbows are almost touching. They're so close he can smell Bobby Jane. It's a fresh, sweet smell, of Halo shampoo perhaps, of the Camay mild soap diet, of pep pep Pepsodent toothpaste. Bobby Jane springs up suddenly and switches off the set.

'I'd better go home now,' he says reluctantly, 'I'd better get back to Josephine.'

'Okay. You can help me do the dishes first.'

They guide the trolley between them, over the bumps and ruckles of the carpet, through the curtain. He does not tell her, of course, that he's never washed or dried a plate in his life; that at home in England, that even in America, he's not welcome in the kitchen and goes there only briefly: to get himself a drink of water, to steal a jam tart, to take a message from his mother to the cook. It would not be tactful to tell Bobby Jane any of this. But the silence now is not the comfortable one they shared minutes ago in front of the television set, sitting cross-legged with only inches between them, cramming their mouths with popcorn, passing the paper bag until it was empty. He must say something.

'I like your place. I like your mother. I'm sorry she can't walk. Perhaps she will one day.'

'No,' Bobby Jane says, 'Mother's paralysed from the waist. She won't ever walk. But you don't have to worry about it. I look after her, and the nurse visits Tuesdays and Fridays.'

Nurse? The matron at his school is called Nurse, it's the name they have to call her by. Nurse wears a flowing white headdress like a nun's, she has a chalky creased face, she wears glinty-rimmed spectacles and she blinks all the time, probably because her eyelids are encrusted with warts. After breakfast Nurse waits outside the bogs with a notebook and a two-leaded pencil, her eyes blinking and watering. You are not allowed to pull the chain until after she's inspected what you have, or haven't, done. A red tick beside your name if you've 'been', a blue cross if you've 'failed to go'. Two consecutive crosses, and she comes at you with the castor oil. All the time they've been in America he hasn't given Nurse a thought, Nurse has ceased to exist. Next time he comes out of the bog and finds her hovering and blinking, he will, he is certain, remember today. He will see Bobby Jane's arms in the sink, the dark water splashes on her skirt, this sunlight on this windowsill. He will see himself standing here beside Bobby Jane, drying blue plates, imagining Nurse.

'Why don't you like boys?' It isn't the question he meant, he has no idea why he asked it. He knows at once that it's dangerous.

'I never said I don't like boys. I don't know too many boys, not that well. Those dishes don't go there, dum dum, they go there.'

'Why do you like Josephine better than me then?'

'What kind of question is that?' Bobby Jane is drying her hands on the roller towel. She examines the palms, then she turns her hands over and inspects the backs. 'How should I know? Maybe Josephine is more my kind of person than you are. Is there a law that says I have to like you both the same? Just because you're *twins*?'

But she says this in a light way, a teasing way, that succeeds in taking some of the unkindness out of the words themselves.

*

'Come again real soon. I enjoyed your visit.'

The cigarette packet on the table beside Mrs Dyson is empty now, the ashtray full. She sounds tired. She's no longer propped up, she's lying flat with one cushion under her head. He looked away while Bobby Jane manoeuvred her mother into this position. Their intimacy was disconcerting; he could not envisage touching his own mother, taking charge of her, in the ways Bobby Jane did and was used to doing.

'I like to meet Roberta's friends,' Mrs Dyson says to the ceiling. 'Did she ever tell you her father's name was Robert? It's a good name. Come back another day, Robert, and bring your sister with you.' (Has she forgotten they sail for England on Monday?) She turns her head towards him and he sees, for the first time, the purple semi-circles, like bruises, under her eyes. She lifts a hand from the tartan rug. The fingers hang limply; he's afraid to take her hand.

'Thank you very much for having me.'

'Thank you for the tea,' he says to Bobby Jane in the hall. 'Thank you for the chocolate cake and *The Howdy Doody Show* and *The Last of the Mohicans*.'

'You're welcome.' Bobby Jane unlocks the street door and holds it open. The evening sunshine, still hot and smelling of pavement, rushes in.

'We had fun, I guess, Robert, even without your sister and Yvonne.'

He's thinking about this accolade, he's down the steps and in the street and putting on his skates, when she says something else, something he can't catch.

'What?'

'I said I can't make Yvonne out. She always accepts Mother's invitations, she always says she'll be glad to come to my place, and then she doesn't show. I don't get it.'

Bobby Jane confiding in him! How extraordinary! How amazing!

'It isn't Yvonne's fault.' For although he can't bear Yvonne, although he and Josephine have never been able to understand how Bobby Jane can be best friends with

254

her, it isn't, strictly, her fault. 'She isn't allowed to go to your place.'

'How come?' She frowns. She seems altogether nonplussed by this.

He hasn't planned to tell her anything. He doesn't think he has. Now, having embarked, he sees that here is a way of getting back at Yvonne. But he's not sure. He wants Bobby Jane to know, and he does not want her to know. He wants both.

'*Well*?'

It's the 'well', the demanding way she says it, the impatient way she puts her hands on her hips, that decides him, that makes him explain how Yvonne isn't allowed to go to her house because they're not Catholics, and because they're poor, and because they're not the same class as the Claybeaus, whatever that might mean. He says he knows all this because Yvonne told him. She told him and Josephine. 'So it isn't Yvonne's fault, exactly.'

After this there's a silence, during which he understands that he's made a devastating and irreparable mistake.

Bobby Jane stands there for a minute, staring at him. Then she tucks her skirt underneath her and sits down on the step. She rests her head on her knees. With the index finger of her right hand she begins drawing slow circles on the step. Big circles and bigger circles, smaller circles, figures of eight.

'You shouldn't have told me that. I didn't want to know that. I never wanted to know any of that.' She doesn't look at him. She's looking at her finger, the one that's making loops and circles on the step. He keeps his eye on the finger.

'What you just told me hurts. I never did anything to hurt you, Robert Partridge.' The finger slows, then stops. 'Yvonne would never tell me what you just did. Josephine would never tell me those things. Josephine may be crazy in some ways, she may be some kind of nut with all that counting stuff, but she'd never say anything to hurt me.'

He keeps his eye on Bobby Jane's finger. The finger's important. It's important to keep his eye on it. It's drawing zigzags now, or mountain ranges. The Alps, the Rockies, the Pennine Chain. Zigzag. Zigzag. Zigzagzig.

'How would you like it if I told you the roses you brought my mother were just dead old roses, ready for the garbage? How would you like it if I told you I don't eat hard candy? You wouldn't. But I wouldn't say those things.'

But she just has. She's just said them.

'It's an odd feeling,' Bobby Jane says slowly. 'Yvonne is my best friend, and I can't see her anymore. Mother'll want to know why I don't go round the Claybeaus' place and I won't be able to tell her. I'll have to fib. I'll have to *lie*.' She pauses. 'I've been friends with Yvonne since we started grade school. We're in the same class. There's no one else in our class lives on this block. There's no one else my age, even. There's no one else at all.'

She gets up from the step. He's aware that she's staring at him – or is it through him? She says, she shouts, 'I want to forget those things you said just now!'

He shakes his head, he can't say anything. What can he say? All of a sudden he wants his twin, he wants Josephine. If Josephine were here . . .

Josephine? Josephine's in bed, sneezing and blowing. Waiting. Waiting for the moment he'll come round the door, so she can pat the bedclothes and say, 'Go on, tell me. Tell me all about it, every single detail.'

'I have to go now,' Bobby Jane says. She takes the street-door key from her pocket. 'I have to get back to Mother. Mother'll need to go to the bathroom.'

And she's gone. She's gone inside without saying good-bye, without saying another word.


They're on the boat going home. The *SS Parthia* is a let-down after the *Queen Mary*, a slow small tub that takes seven days to make the crossing, whose menus and menu cards and gymnasium leave a lot to be desired. On the boat, Robert invents a new ending for his visit to Bobby Jane's place.

In this new ending, Bobby Jane doesn't confide in him about Yvonne. Yvonne isn't mentioned, she simply doesn't come up. He and Bobby Jane say goodbye, in a friendly, reluctant way, on the step. She smiles and thanks him for the sourballs – her favourite candy, she says. At the last minute he bends down (bends down? No, he can't do that, she's taller than he is), he leans forward and kisses her cheek.

Later on, hunched under the grand piano in the Music Room during the hobbies period they have at that school on wet Saturdays, he'll remove the kiss as being unlikely, as being not something he'd have the courage to do. (As being not something Bobby Jane would accept. She would probably have ducked, he'll realise, or pushed him off: 'Hey, what's with all this kissing stuff?' She would have giggled. Or slapped his face.) The kiss is too much at odds with what actually happened, so far from the truth it only manages to point the truth up. So he'll get rid of it. Eventually, for the same reason, he'll reject the bit about sourballs being Bobby Jane's favourite candy.

But the new story won't stick, it refuses to stay down, in the way that a badly gummed label on a used envelope refuses, curling back instead to reveal an earlier, and more authentic, life.

Years later, considering these events, Robert will decide that when Mrs Dyson suggested that people reinvent the past to suit themselves, she must have meant the process, largely unconscious, whereby subtle, gradual shifts and repositionings and blurrings occur deep in the mind. Shifts of perspective, repositionings of events, blurrings of motive, that will be transmuted, in the course of time, into real distortions. That will emerge, eventually, as full-blown fictions. As downright lies. As the truth. Mrs Dyson must have been talking about self-deception.

She could not have meant that facts can be altered at will (or by an act of will), and the mind, the cosmic centre, the conscience, accept them.

Robert's invented version, polished and improved on,

will not be the one that returns to him in dreams. It will remain, at most, an alternative, somewhere alongside, but never supplanting, the truth.

The truth? In middle age, when the twins are reminiscing ('Remember *The Dead Toreador*? Remember the blood on his shirt? Remember when we lay on the floor of the gallery and imagined ourselves dead?') about that time in Washington DC ('Murder capital of the US now!'), Josephine will say that that business at the end with Bobby Jane 'happened, in fact, if you want to know, Rob' to her. That it was he who was stuck in bed with a cold. That he never set foot in the Dysons' flat the whole time they were in Washington. He only remembers it, he only thinks he remembers it, Josephine will say – pacing up and down, stubbing out her umpteenth cigarette, lighting another – because she confessed it at the time. It's her story, Josephine will insist. Her nightmare. It was never his.

# UNCLE VICTOR

We were avid readers of fairy tales when we were small. In fairy tales, the youngest son is the favoured son. Favoured by life, and also by the narrator. Youngest equals beautiful, good, brave, intelligent, true. It is the youngest, when his elder brothers have failed – through stupidity or laziness – their tasks, who will succeed; who will slay the three-headed monster, who will win the princess's hand, who will rule the peaceable kingdom, who will live happily ever after.

Of our Uncle Victor, youngest son of our paternal grandparents and the black sheep of the family, Father once said, 'Should a stranger stop you in the street and say, "I'm your uncle, lend me half a crown" – never fear, he will be.'

We were children at the time, Althea, Amarantha, Lucasta, Chloris, and I, Dianeme (our names allotted to us, as we came along, from Father's passion for the Cavalier Poets whose study he was making his life's work). Gratiana was a baby still, or perhaps not even born.

Years later, when we were all, excluding Gratiana, grown-up, I reminded Father of his stranger-in-the-street remark. I expected him to say, 'Too true,' or to smile a wry smile. He didn't. He said, 'You know, Dianeme, I think I've been a bit rough on Victor. He's not a bad man. He has, after all, had a change of heart.'

A change of heart? Uncle Victor? Maybe Father was joking, his style of humour was so flat and dry it caught us out often. I looked at him. He was propped against the pillows, staring out of the window in an absent, abstracted way. I remember being worried by this, and then almost immediately consoling myself with the thought: Father's not himself because he has a fever; he's light-headed.

Father was feverish, if cold sweats can be called fever. A lassitude, a vague melancholy, which had overtaken him at the end of November, had turned into a cough, which had turned into – what? Somewhere around that point, the point of the question mark, he'd taken to his bed. He certainly didn't look well, but the truth is, he never did. He was one of the those tall, spare, pale men who, essentially robust, never give the impression of health. We were concerned about him, of course, but not really anxious. We were expecting him to be on his feet, and feeling fine, by Christmas Day.

The reason why I reminded Father of his long ago summing-up of our uncle was because of the flowers that had arrived that morning. They'd been sent by Victor. The night before, he'd telephoned, demanding to speak to Father. 'You can't,' Mother had told him, 'he's not well. He's in bed. Out of the question, Victor. Goodbye.' And she'd replaced the receiver before he could argue.

Uncle Victor's flowers stood in a jug on Father's bedside table. Blood-red roses and gladioli, white arum lilies. Crude, stiff, and, apart from the lilies, scentless blooms.

'He must have been to the cemetery and pinched them off a grave' – Mother's conclusion as she stripped the leaves and did her best to tweak some life into the arrangement.

Father, too, would surely have something sharp to say about this dubious tribute, and the message that accompanied it: 'Sorry to hear you're under the weather – chin up, old cove – Victor.' He hadn't. He fingered the roses; he read the message on the card. Then he laid the card gently on the counterpane and held it there, between a graceful finger and thumb.


Uncle Victor, given the name because he was born in 1918, and on Armistice Day, was a petty crook and a con man. We knew this, my five sisters and I, when we were old enough to know it; when we were, in turn, aware enough to be curious about the words 'embezzlement, fraud, counterfeit, bail, bailiff, Old Bailey, Wormwood Scrubs' – words that stood out, as though underlined or ringed round, from half-heard, half-understood conversations, and from behind half-closed doors.

Then there were the discussions that took place at breakfast and which were conducted over the tops of our heads. These had to do with certain letters Father received, written on what appeared to be lavatory paper, and contained in serious envelopes.

'To Althea, from prison.' Father dropped a lavatory paper letter on to my eldest sister's plate. 'Pass it along to your mother.'

Mother put on her spectacles to read the letter, and when she had done so she whipped them off again. She was furious.

'It's your mother's fault,' she told Father. 'She never stood up to him, she never said no to him. She always let him have his own way.'

'Too true,' Father said – and he stroked his nose, a habit of his – 'too true.'

'It's your father's fault,' Mother told Father (this was on another, not dissimilar, occasion). 'If he hadn't run off with all those trollops, if he hadn't abandoned the three of you when Victor was only a baby, Victor might have turned out, well, differently. What he needed, what he lacked, was a firm, father's hand.'

Father, who from the age of eight had not had a father's hand himself, but who had turned out very differently from Uncle Victor, said nothing. He spread his own hands on the table and examined them, as if for clues.

Father's hands were beautiful: long-fingered, oval-nailed, sensitive – yet masculine. Exceptional hands. We could see this for ourselves without Mother's telling us, though she did tell us, often.

'Hands are a giveaway,' Mother used to tell us, 'you can't disguise them. You can tell a lot from hands.'

'I couldn't marry your father for his money,' Mother told us, *ad nauseam*, 'because he hadn't any. I married him for his hands.'

Which surprised us. We'd imagined Mother had married Father for his interesting mind, or blue eyes, or handsome face; or simply because she was dying of love for him.


Our paternal grandfather, begetter of Father and Uncle Victor (and also of Tobias, the second son, who died in infancy when Father was three), was a rake. Not a black sheep. The difference, we were given to understand, being that, although he was a womaniser, a gambler and a profligate, Grandfather's activities were not, in the eyes of the law at any rate, criminal. Added to which, he had charm, Father said.

Didn't Uncle Victor have charm?

Not so you'd notice, according to Father.

What did he have then? We needed to know. He was the one uncle we had, Mother being an only child, and he haunted our home life: a ghost in the machinery of solicitors' letters and unpaid bills and reverse-charge telephone calls; yet we never met him. He did come to what Mother scornfully referred to as 'our sardine tin in Divinity Road' occasionally, but at night time, when we were in bed, or during the day in term time, when we were at school. After his visits, so she told us, Mother would check up on the silver and her two pieces of jewellery and Father's first editions. Having reassured herself on that score, she would run from room to room and throw open all the windows wide. She did this to let the devil out, she said.

The devil? Could it be that Mother, who in our experience feared no one, was in some way afraid of Uncle Victor? Did he, perhaps, have horns and a tail?

There were only old photographs in old albums to go on. In these, so far as we could tell from the bleached sepia, he was dark-haired and curly-haired, white-smocked and frilled, and he had fat knees. Old family snapshots and studio portraits are fascinating, of course, and we were fascinated; but they were no real help in the quest for our diabolical uncle. We consulted Father.

Victor's looks were undistinguished; no, he would rephrase that, they were ordinary, Father told us.

Ordinary?

'Yes, ordinary.' Father sounded bored, not to say irritated. We'd caught him in the boxroom that doubled as his study, trying to work. (Now that I think about it, it's a wonder that anything of an intellectual nature was achieved in that crammed cubbyhole. On the occasions when Father forgot to lock the door, we were in there in a flash, climbing over cots and pram wheels and golf bags and chipped picture frames to rummage through suitcases of old letters; or, in a sudden burst of nostalgia, to seek for some long-discarded plaything we'd decided we couldn't, after all, live without.) Our uncle was, Father said, 'nondescript. If you must have a description, well then, on the small side, on the stout side. Balding.'

How extraordinary. Father six foot five and very thin. With thick, white, straight hair – fine hair, that fell over his eyes when he was working, so that he had continually to push it back with his hand. Uncle Victor short and fat. And hairless.

But perhaps Father was having us on.

We tried again: Uncle Victor must have the family eyes, at least, mustn't he?

The family eyes were blue, a bright electric blue. Our grandfather, The Rake, had had them. We'd all inherited them. Even Mother had blue eyes of a sort. Father's were the bluest and most dazzling of all. 'A sailor's eyes,' Mother insisted, though there'd been no seafarers on Father's side of the family, so far as anyone knew.

'Victor's eyes are brown,' Father said, 'boot-polish brown, if you like. Almost black. Goodbye, and shut the door behind you.'

*

264

'Once upon a time, in the land beyond the mountains, there lived a merchant who had three sons . . . '

While we were curled in our corners, devouring our fairy tales, the youngest son of our grandparents was busy as usual. He broke into the coinboxes of gas meters and public telephones. He rode on underground trains without benefit of ticket. He forged cheques and insurance claims. He opened, but neglected to settle, accounts in high-class London shops, demands for whose payment would eventually find their way to our own front-door mat. And he 'borrowed' from anyone who was fool enough to 'lend' – women mostly: vulnerable widows; barmaids whose brassy exteriors concealed hearts of gold; a succession of dubious, live-in, lady friends. When these and other sources failed, he petitioned Father: 'Dear Hal, Find myself a bit strapped for readies at present and wonder if you could see your way . . . ' The excuses he gave were that he'd fallen on hard times and was behind with the rent; that he'd fallen downstairs and broken his leg; that he'd lost, through no fault of his own, of course, his job; that he'd lost his wallet. Naturally Father was never taken in by any of these. Our uncle had seldom been in honest employ for more than a fortnight without being sacked for 'misappropriation of funds' (fingers in the till, was Father's translation of this); and the one job, as a packer in a firework factory, he'd managed to keep for three months had had explosive consequences. Father, as I say, was never taken in, and his comments were sardonic. Nevertheless, he would get out his chequebook.

Which made Mother furious. 'He'll bleed you dry, Hal. You should let him stew. He'll bleed us all dry.'

We sympathised with Mother. She had come from Nowhere, she was fond of telling us, and was determined to get Somewhere. She had her sights on smart North Oxford, on the leafy filling of the Woodstock and Banbury Roads sandwich, and in anticipation of this move up in the world we were forced to attend Matins at St Margaret's every Sunday. Uncle Victor was to blame, entirely to blame, for the delay in achieving her heart's desire. As for us children, we needed new shoes and winter coats; we wanted bikes. Father had no illusions about Uncle Victor – so why bail him out?

It was more complex than we understood at the time. Father bailed out Uncle Victor and paid his debts in order to protect Grandmother, throughout our childhoods bed-ridden with arthritis in an Abingdon nursing home (the fees, of course, were paid by Father). Uncle Victor's begging letters amounted to blackmail. If Father didn't cough up, Victor would go straight to Grandmother and wheedle out of her what pathetic savings she had left.

Grandmother was deaf to any word against Uncle Victor. Whatever had gone wrong in his life, it was no fault of his. He was her own dear sweet boy, her blue-eyed boy, the generous son who sent her flowers.

'Look, darlings, at the beautiful roses kind Uncle Victor has sent your poor old granny!'

We looked. Grandmother's room was indeed a bower. We looked at Father, who'd brought us on the bus. (Mother never accompanied us on these visits; her blood pressure couldn't stand it, she said.) Father stroked his nose and raised his blue eyes to the ceiling. The roses must have fallen off the back of a florist's van, was his conclusion on the journey home.


'Victor started out on his blackmailing career very early, you know.' Father confided this, matter-of-factly and between mouthfuls of toast and Cooper's Oxford, apropos of a letter from our uncle that had just been delivered. 'From the age of about five he'd corner me and threaten: "If you don't hand over that sixpence" – or penknife, or whatever – "this minute, I'm going to kick Mother." I called his bluff the first time and he did kick your grandmother.'

Althea, Amarantha and Lucasta were approaching their teens when we learned this, and old enough to be shocked. They were shocked. Poor Father! What a terrible story! It was the worst, quite the worst, thing they'd heard about Uncle Victor to date.

The following day they put the volumes of Grimm, Andersen, Lang, Perrault, Dulac, etcetera, into their satchels, and lugged them down to the school library.

The librarian, so they informed us afterwards, seemed pleased, if surprised. She checked through the books, she examined the flyleaves and the title pages, she lifted the tissue veils guarding coloured plates, she pored and lingered. 'These are very nice, Althea. Some of them, I'd say, are valuable. Are you quite sure it's all right to make this donation?' Althea nodded: she was quite sure. She did not explain that the sacrifice – though it has to be said, our three elder sisters had moved on to ghost stories by then – was for Father, and for all hard-done-by eldest sons, everywhere.

When Father was told of these events he was surprised, and not pleased. His daughters had no business to rob their unborn children, his grandchildren, of their inheritance. The Dulac had been a christening present to Lucasta from the Master of Balliol, he reminded them. The Violet and the Green Fairy Books were first editions, the Perrault a collector's piece. Were they cretins, or what?

Later, he relented a little. They hadn't burned the books, which was something. They hadn't made a fast buck out of them. Their criminal careers were not yet assured.


Keeping Uncle Victor out of prison while our grandmother was alive was Father's aim, but as I've indicated, he didn't always succeed. He didn't succeed when our uncle was apprehended in the vicinity of an unattended newspaper stand, his coat and trouser pockets weighted with pennies and halfpennies and farthings and threepenny bits. ('How low can you go?' Mother was beside herself. 'How low can you go?') Then there was the Encyclopaedia Affair.

As usual, we heard about it over breakfast.

'My enterprising brother Victor has been selling encyclo-paedias door to door,' Father began.

Mother had one eye on the clock; she was trying to get us off to school: Amarantha and Lucasta had A-levels looming. All right, so it wasn't an occupation for gentlemen, she said, but Victor wasn't a gentleman, and at least they were encyclopaedias, not brushes.

Father ran an exceptional finger down the length of his nose. That was not the problem, he told Mother. The prob-lem was, there were no encyclopaedias. Victor had merely had order forms and a pamphlet printed, and gone round the houses with those. At the top of the pamphlet was a list of luminaries who unreservedly recommended the encyclopaedia. The luminaries included scholars and aca-demics, one of whom was Father.

Father was wrong, we decided. Uncle Victor must have charm. How else had he persuaded all those housewives to draw out their National Savings, and pay cash in advance – entitling them to a discount of ten per cent – for a thirty-six-volume encyclopaedia that didn't exist?

Father did get up for Christmas Day, but he wasn't better. He was weaker than any kitten. On Boxing Day he went back to bed.

'Rest, and a light, nourishing diet,' the doctor said. 'Aspirin four-hourly; plenty of fluids.' He didn't seem to know exactly what was wrong with Father, what Father had got.

'There are so many bugs flying around this time of year, it's hard to say,' said the doctor, a man prone to hedge his bets.

What was wrong with Father? And why didn't he fight? Did the knowledge that his *œuvre* on the Cavalier Poets was at last completed, and with the printers, give him no satisfaction at all? Why wouldn't he eat?

'I'm not hungry, I'm tired,' Father said, 'thank you all the same.'

Uncle Victor, meanwhile, was telephoning every day, often twice; and eventually Mother took the receiver off its cradle. She couldn't stop the bouquets coming, though, nor the crates of Dom Perignon, nor the Special Christmas Hamper of *foie gras* and beluga caviar and potted shrimps and Parma ham. (The bills for these, from Moyses Stevens of Bruton Street, from Berry Brothers of St James's and Jacksons of Piccadilly, arrived early in January, but by that time Father was dead.)

It would be a partridge in a pear tree next, Mother didn't doubt.

Father was staring out of the window, and seemed miles away. 'How kind of Victor, how extraordinarily kind,' he murmured, lying back on his pillows, sniffing a blood-red, scentless rose.


There was no way of preventing Uncle Victor from attending Father's funeral. He was bound to see the notice in *The Times* or the *Daily Telegraph*.

He was immediately recognisable. On the short side, on the stout side, bald. The one brown coat amongst all the black and grey ones. Fur collar. Fur gloves. Cigarette hanging from his mouth. As we helped Mother from the car, he let the butt drop at his feet, and then ground it slowly with one desert-sand suede toe.

'One good thing, I suppose' – Lucasta turned to me in the porch – 'if our uncle's here, he can hardly be at home, pinching the silver.' There'd been a spate of what the media called 'bereavement thefts' in the Oxford area in recent weeks.

Mother had decided on family and close friends only for the funeral – a memorial service was to be held later in Christ Church cathedral. These old friends of hers and Father's were invited to the wake afterwards, at Divinity Road. We didn't see how we could stop Uncle Victor joining them. (But we did manage to stop him climbing into the hired car with Mother. There hadn't been room enough in it for all of us as it was: Althea, Amarantha, Lucasta and Gratiana had driven to the church with Mother; Chloris and I had followed in Mother's old Ford.)

'Uncle Victor, you had better come with Dianeme and me,' Chloris ordered him with a smile cold as the grave.

I drove; Chloris sat beside me. Uncle Victor, reeking of whisky and never-emptied ashtrays, took up the back seat. Chloris and I were silent; not unnaturally, neither of us felt like talking.

Uncle Victor talked all the way back to Divinity Road.

'This is a sad business,' Uncle Victor said, trumpeting into a red silk handkerchief, 'a sad, sad business . . . '

'Your father was a wonderful brother to me,' Uncle Victor said, and he wound down the window and tossed an empty cigarette packet into a passing hedge, 'I remember when . . . '

'I still recall the day . . . ' Uncle Victor droned on.

We tried not to listen to him. And I tried not to catch his eye – boot-polish brown, as Father said – in the driving mirror, but it was impossible: there were so many round-abouts and crossroads and junctions between St Margaret's and home.

'Constance – your dear mother – will have needs now . . . She will be in need of comfort and support,' Uncle Victor said, pulling off his horrible gloves, fumbling in his pockets for more fags, and for matches. 'You may rest assured I shall do all in my power . . . either of you young ladies care for a smoke?'

Uncle Victor lit up as I changed down for the corner. It was then, in the glass and for the space of a heartbeat, I saw them: Father's hands – his beautiful, his *exceptional* hands! – shielding the flame.

# HABITS

What is it keeps some married couples together long after their Best Before date – you know, when they're no longer compatible, when they don't even like each other any more, and when divorce has lost its stigma and is relatively painless to achieve? You can never guess, can you, which of your married friends will break up and which will stick it out; in fact haven't you noticed that very often it's the most unlikely ones, the obviously miserable ones, who stay the course, whereas the marriages that always seemed to you to have been made in heaven blow apart? And why should that be?

It was a stranger at a party who asked these questions of Nessa (they'd both had a fair amount to drink at the time). He didn't wait for her reply. Instead, he told her his theory, which was that unhappiness is a stronger bond than happiness. That would account, wouldn't it, for all those henpecked husbands and battered wives you read about, who find it impossible to break away?

The stranger leaned towards Nessa and smiled at her with the intimacy only a stranger can afford. He tapped her empty glass and asked her, how would it be if he were to go and get them both a refill?

This encounter took place a few days ago. At the time, Nessa had felt got at. The stranger couldn't have known anything about her marriage – he and Nessa hadn't been introduced and hadn't even bothered to swap names – nevertheless she felt he'd somehow, perhaps with the special, specious intuition of the inebriated, decided she was a battered wife, or Otto a henpecked husband. It was only

272

afterwards that she considered the questions themselves, in particular the first one, the one about what it is keeps people together long after their Best Before date, as the stranger had put it. What was it kept her and Otto together then? Could it be they were bonded by unhappiness merely? What a terrible thought! What a throat-cutting idea!

'Was he right? Is that all we've got going for us?' Nessa asked her best friend Lindsey, via the telephone. (It was Lindsey's call, a Christmas call, ten days early because she and Duncan were off to Spain for the holiday, the first time ever they'd done such a thing.) Nessa and Lindsey talk a lot on the telephone. There was a time when they wrote letters to each other, long ones at regular intervals, but they haven't for years – no one Nessa knows writes letters any more. They do send each other postcards and they talk on the telephone, once every ten days or so, taking it in turns to foot the bill – for their husbands to foot the bill. In these calls they discuss Lindsey's children, the books they're reading, the films they've been to see or want to see, the television programmes they've watched or missed, people they both know. Sometimes, in a frivolous mood, whole conversations will be conducted in French, in school-text-book French:

'Eh bien, mon brave, qu'est-ce tu as fait ce matin?'

'Alors, je suis allée au marché acheter des légumes. J'ai envie de préparer une bonne soupe pour mon mari.'

'De bons légumes? Pour faire cette bonne soupe?'

'Mais bien sûr, de bons légumes!'

'Quelles sortes de légumes as tu achetées, dis donc?'

'J'ai acheté un kilo de carottes, et puis . . . '

'De bonnes carottes?'

'Assurément, de bonnes carottes!'

'You and Lindsey were made for each other. I can't think why you didn't get married' – Otto, jokey but sharp, coming in on the end of one of these exchanges.

Nessa and Lindsey talk seriously about serious things; they discuss their worries and their fears. Cancer, for example. They are both in their forties now, the age when breasts and wombs and cervixes become vulnerable, the time when X-rays and smear tests are advisable. Lindsey believes in preventative medicine and regular check-ups, but Nessa has a theory about cancer which is that if it hasn't been diagnosed it doesn't exist. Should you discover a small hard lump in your armpit, say (Nessa's theory goes), do nothing and it'll turn out the lump was only a boil. See your doctor, spill the beans, and before you know it you'll be under the scanner or being force-fed barium meal. And after that? Operations, radiotherapy, chemotherapy and downhill all the way. – Which was superstitious nonsense, in Lindsey's view. Dangerous nonsense. 'Jonnie would have been dead years ago if my mother'd gone along with your theory.' (Lindsey's younger brother Jonnie developed cancer of the femur when he was twelve. They'd had to amputate the leg, but Jonnie'd been okay. He was still okay, alive and kicking his umpteenth artificial limb, at thirty-four.)

'D'you think unhappiness really is our only bond?' Nessa asked Lindsey, in the course of Lindsey's Christmas call.

Lindsey said no, no she didn't think it was as dire as that. Marriage was complicated. Just as you couldn't tell, from the outside, what kept seemingly incompatible people together, so you probably couldn't tell from the inside, either. Also, habit came into it. It was often habit kept people together when they shouldn't be. Habits were hard to break. 'I mean, look at you and Otto, you've neither of you given up smoking for all your talk. You refer to your "cancer tubes", you make jokes about iron lungs and respirators, but you don't give it up.'

Nessa said she thought that was quite a neat analogy, though not comforting. And she did not tell Lindsey that Otto had cut down recently, from two packets to less than one a day.

Lindsey said that, strangely enough, it was habit, habits rather, she'd missed most when she and Mike split up. (Mike was Lindsey's first husband, and the father of her two children, Angus and Elaine.) She'd never thought about the habits, she'd never imagined she'd miss them, but then when they split up she did.

'What sort of habits?' Nessa wanted to know.

'Well, I can't remember them all now. But I do remember missing Mike saying things like, "I don't believe you've met my wife," to office colleagues and so on, and I missed my being able to say, "I think you'd better consult my husband on that one!" That habit – the habit of belonging, I suppose you could call it.'

Nessa stared at the stoneware jug on the table beside her that Otto's first wife had made and considered this habit, one she was familiar with. She thought: Do I enjoy it? At some level or other? Would I miss it? And decided that yes, she would. Unfortunately, she would. Yes.

Another thing she'd missed, Lindsey remembered, was being a unit, a hyphenated-sounding unit, Mike-and-Lindsey on Christmas cards and invitations, 'a sound and shape our friends all knew, that they recognised as being us'. She'd imagined, she told Nessa, that being just Lindsey again after she and Mike parted would feel like freedom, would restore her premarital sense of identity, but it hadn't. Rather the reverse. And wasn't that odd? Wasn't that an odd thing for a good feminist to feel?

That was the snare of being a woman, Nessa suggested, a woman of their age and class. (Nessa and Lindsey liked to imagine that they, or at least their roots, were working class. Which was crap, according to Otto. No street-corner tobacconist – Nessa's father – and no railway clerk – Lindsey's – was ever working class. Anyway, what about their grammar school education? Lower middle was their roots, middle was what they had become. Sorry, lassies.) 'Working class women of our age were brought up to believe that marriage is the be all and end all.'

'How's your best friend Marion, lovey?' Lindsey asked. 'Seen anything of her lately?'

This question, which anyone listening in would have been likely to consider innocent and genuine, for that is how Lindsey made it sound, was nothing of the sort. It was a tease. The truth was, Nessa did not like Marion, who was a neighbour of hers, and had never considered her a friend, merely as another – irritating and younger – woman, down the road. One thing Nessa didn't like about Marion was the habit she had of calling Nessa 'lovey', and of prefacing remarks with 'If you don't mind my saying'. Nessa usually did mind. 'If you don't mind my saying, lovey, blue is not your colour' – Marion, having watched Nessa lug the dustbin down the steps and on to the pavement, had sidled up and tapped her on the shoulder of her ultramarine sweater, first new garment in months.

'Funny you should ask,' Nessa said, 'I've been seeing a lot of her lately. We've really got a lot going for each other. I'm currently, at this moment in time, into a book she lent me. It's called *Uncoupling*, it's about wanting out and letting go, and it really engages with the issues, believe you me.'

It was true that Marion had lent Nessa a book called *Uncoupling*. Nessa hadn't asked to read it. Marion had got the book out of the library, and told Nessa it was an instructive, in many ways corroborative, read. Nessa ought to read it, Marion said. 'If you don't mind my saying so, lovey, it would concentrate your mind.' (Not long before this, she'd told Nessa that it was high time Nessa stopped playing a walk-on role to Otto's starring one. Nessa should leave Otto, Marion said, so that she could find herself and get to know herself and get to like herself, and use her talents and regain her self-respect and start living. Marion, who often looked careworn; who had mortgage problems and problems with her children – Barney was bedwetting, Natalie had been caught telling lies at school – was not a good advertisement for the manless life she advocated.)

'Is this your call or mine, by the bye?' Lindsey said. 'Ye gods, it's mine! Duncan will murder me. He's threatening to make me pay the whole of the last bill. "You made the calls, you pick up the tab" was how he charmingly put it.'

There was another habit, one that women shared (Nessa thought after Lindsey had rung off) which was to mention their husbands in what sounded like a derogatory way, a putting-down way, when all they were really doing was expressing pride in owning, and being owned by, a man.

Most evenings after supper, if they were alone, Otto and Nessa sat in the sitting room and listened to music – to classical orchestral, Mozart opera, jazz. They listened in silence. Nessa sipped a glass of red wine and stitched away – she'd been making a patchwork quilt for three years now; the 'bitbags' beside her chair had become permanent fixtures. Her eyesight had got weaker since she started out, her magnifiers stronger; even so her fingers were pin-cushions, and she had to work right under the lamp, peering and blinking, crick in the neck, ache in the back, pain in the heart. And Otto?

Otto would lie back in his armchair, black leather and steel, his eyes closed, his hands stuck to the frosted whisky glass in his lap. Every so often he would push himself up and transport his empty glass to the bookcase where the whisky bottle and the water jug and the ice bucket were. Every so often, when an uncompanionable silence fell, he would spur himself to change the tape or the record. When they were first married, and for several years afterwards, Otto's travels within a room had been achieved by little sprints and leaps and pirouettes, the floor beneath him elastic as a trampoline; but for some time now his con-trolled exuberance had for the most part been replaced by a meandering stumble, a preoccupied shamble. Not that age and whisky must have been wholly to blame. In congenial company, Otto could still perform in his old manner, no matter how much whisky he'd sunk; and in his studio – where Nessa was rarely welcome – he would still bound from canvas to paintpot. Once, arriving at his studio with an urgent message, Nessa had surprised Otto conducting the overture to *Figaro*, playing on the tape deck. From the doorway she watched as he brought the violins in and then banished them, nodded his furious head, pointed an accusing finger at the woodwind, flung both arms wide, embraced himself.

Television bored Otto. Any programme Nessa wanted to see she watched by herself in the kitchen, bolt upright on a hard chair, her face within inches of the Sony portable's small face. Come and see this, Otto! It would really interest you! – For years, Nessa, who believed she wanted to share everything, whatever it was, with her husband, had run to the living room with her enthusiasms and offered them up like presents, although for an equal number of years since, she had not.

It's evening, a Tuesday, ten days before Christmas. Otto and Nessa are in the living room of their Hammersmith house. John Coltrane is playing on the Bang & Olufsen. Nessa is seated at a table in the window, writing Christmas cards. On the table is a pile of cards and another one of envelopes, plus the address book Nessa is working from. Working through.

Nessa's writing her cards, getting on with it, but her mind is elsewhere. This morning something momentous and terrible happened. This morning she learned something about Otto that she must tackle him with. She doesn't want to, but she must. She doesn't want to think about any of it. She can't stop thinking about it.

From time to time Nessa looks across to Otto, asleep in his armchair. (No, not asleep; although his eyes are closed, he can't be: his right hand is still gripping the whisky glass in his lap.) She gives him quick, surreptitious glances and long hard stares. In her head she's asking him: Is it true? and Who are you, Otto? WHO ARE YOU?

Out loud she asks him, 'Do you want me to send a card to the Donaldsons?' She feels she has to ask this because eighteen months or so ago Otto and Jim Donaldson fell out, a serious falling-out that hasn't been repaired. Nessa still doesn't know what it was about because Otto's stone-walled her each time she's asked. The Donaldsons are, or were, old friends, perhaps their best 'married couple' friends. Otto and Nessa used to go on holiday with the Donaldsons. Christmases were spent with them, at the weekend cottage they own in Suffolk. Nessa regrets the loss of this friendship, the discussions and arguments and jokes, the horseplay which could sometimes go too far, the freezing walks along Minsmere Cliffs. She regrets the loss of the Donaldsons' two boys, Danny and Sam, in particular Sam, the youngest, with whom she'd always had a rapport. She misses the evenings of Rummy and Oh Hell, and the steady wine-drinking that had accompanied these. Most, she misses Maura, Jim's wife, her accomplice in holiday kitchens and on holiday shopping expeditions, her ally in the ongoing war against the menfolk (this was the term, enclosed by invisible inverted commas, they used for Otto and Jim and Danny and Sam). 'What's up with the menfolk, then?' 'Can it be the menfolk have gone dahn the boozer?' 'Well, that's the menfolk for you!' A lot of giggling accompanied the menfolk talk. A lot of fooling around went on while they were preparing the menfolk's breakfasts and lunches and teas. A lot of drinking was done while they concocted the menfolk's suppers. Oddly, and hurtfully – for it wasn't their quarrel – Maura hasn't been in touch since Otto and Jim's bust-up, although Nessa has written two postcards to her. Sending the Donaldsons a Christmas card this year might (Nessa thought this at breakfast this morning; now she thinks: What does it matter? What the hell does any of this matter?) go some way to healing the rift.

'You can send the Donaldsons anything you like.' Otto takes a swig of whisky that nearly empties the glass. 'So long as you don't put my name to it.'

This Christmas will be the first nobody has asked them over for, not the Donaldsons, of course, not Otto's three married sisters in the home counties, not Nessa's weirdo Cousin Alec, not her mother and younger brother in Arbroath. For the first time in twenty years of marriage, Otto and Nessa will, barring a last-minute reprieve, be spending Christmas in London. Alone.

Neither of them has ever rated Christmas, mind you. Every October, when tinsel and coloured lights take over her local stationers and supermarket, Nessa says she'd abolish Christmas if she could, that Christmas is a farce. She won't be sending cards this year, she says, or presents. Perhaps she doesn't mean this: she always does. She buys presents for her relations and for Otto's, she chooses them for Otto's godchildren as well as her own. When the presents are wrapped, Otto writes his name on the label. He writes 'Otto', or 'Uncle Otto', or 'Your Favourite Brother-in-Law' in the space Nessa points to on the tag. She always tells him what the parcel contains so that he knows, so that he has no excuse for not knowing, so that he won't be caught out. What a waste of time! Otto never remembers, or pretends not to, and he's usually plastered by noon on Christmas Day. When a nephew runs at him with a novelty pen or a radio-controlled police Land Rover and cries, 'Thank you, Uncle Otto, it's just what I wanted!' Otto looks amazed. 'Did I give you that? Don't thank me! Thank your Aunt Nessa – she chose it, she bought it, she wrapped it up – all I did was pay for it!' Why does Otto do this? What makes him want to show himself in such an unendearing light always?

'I am me,' Otto says grandly, 'I am how I am. If you don't like it, too bad.'

Some people don't like it. Too bad for them. Once – this was years ago – at a supper party at friends, Otto (who'd had three double whiskies before leaving home) announced over the vichyssoise: 'What a bourgeois collection! What witless conversation! What dull pointless lives!' In the silence that followed, while shocked eyebrows were being raised and wounded looks exchanged, Otto picked up his spoon and carried on with his soup. The following day Nessa asked him, shouldn't he write to Harry and Joanie and apologise? For all those things he'd said? Why should he, replied Otto, when he hadn't said them? He had no memory of saying them, therefore he hadn't said them, therefore Nessa was making it up. When Nessa told him, exactly, precisely, what he had said, he was very amused. Or he pretended to be. He said he wished he was guilty because the remarks were true. Weren't they, weren't they? Come on now, didn't she agree?

Not surprisingly, Harry and Joanie did not forgive him. Not really. They weren't asked there to supper again. Nessa still saw Joanie – they'd known each other since before they were married – occasionally; she'd call in for a moment on the way to collect her girls from school, but there was a constraint between them, an edgy politeness they neither of them knew what to do with, although Joanie did try, because they were old friends and because Nessa was god-mother to her youngest, Marianne, to make it easier. To find excuses and explanations. Otto, she supposed, was what you might call a larger-than-life character. She supposed all artists were. There was a price to be paid for that, she supposed.

Well yes, there was, Nessa thought, though she did not say so.

But Nessa had a problem, not revealed to Joanie then or later. A part of her could admire Otto for his refusal to compromise, and even for his rudeness which seemed to her an aspect, merely, of his energy and masculinity. Otto was his own man, he didn't curry favour, he didn't care what people thought. When she was not being embarrassed or hurt by his behaviour, when she was not cut to the heart by it, she could, in a way, admire it.

'Stop staring at me!' Otto erupts from the depths of his gloom and his armchair. 'Leave an old man in peace!'

Nessa was not staring at him, as it happens, not this time. She doesn't think she was. She'd merely looked up for a minute and there he was, blocking her view of life, getting in the way of it, no chance of avoiding him.

And what was this nonsense about Otto being an old man? Otto wasn't old, he was young, he'd be fifty-two in

March. He looked forty. He had drive, he was someone who, when not drunk, could get a lot done. He got a lot done in his studio – not unusual for him to complete four large canvases in a fortnight – and he got a lot done at home. The bathroom in their first, rented, flat was plumbed by Otto; the tongue-and-groove panelling of their present kitchen had been sawn and planed and fitted by him. Even now, when they could afford to have someone, a team of professionals, in to do the repairs and improvements that need doing in houses from time to time, Otto was not above putting in a new set of bookshelves or reinventing a cupboard.

Otto was not old, and he did not look old, yet reaching fifty affected him badly. It really got to him. Nessa couldn't understand it. Why should he care? In her view, most men didn't begin to be attractive until they were forty at least. It was the most unfair difference between men and women, that just as a woman was losing her looks and having to work harder and harder with exercise bikes and nourishing night cream to keep a semblance of them, a man was finding his. Without any effort at all. Yet for months before his fiftieth birthday, and for months afterwards, Otto complained about his age. He peered into the shaving mirror, he made faces at himself, he pulled his eyelids down, he tugged the corners of his mouth this way and that, looking for trouble. His eyebrows were going grey – see that, Nessa? – He had old man's whiskers in his nose! In his ears! There was more hair in his hairbrush than on his head!

All nonsense. Otto still had a lot of hair on his head, much of it dark. He had more hair, and shinier hair, than many women of his age. Unfairly, given his drinking and his smoking and his preference for high-fat, high-cholesterol foods – Nessa once tried making her man a Flora man to no avail: the tubs of polyunsaturate in the fridge grew green fur coats unless she ate the stuff herself – Otto seemed in pretty good, trim shape. On the outside, anyway. Who could say what minute changes might be taking place in arteries and organs and blood cells? Changes which one day, perhaps tomorrow, might become significant and serious?

Otto's preoccupation with age and ageing was not just tactless. It was cruel. Reaching forty had far more implication for Nessa than reaching fifty had for him. On her fortieth birthday, after fifteen years of trying, after almost as many years of humiliating tests and consultations, Nessa finally gave up hope of ever having a baby.

'Goodbye, baby' – Nessa, in the dank back garden of the Hammersmith house, said this aloud. 'Goodbye, darling one' – rocking backwards and forwards in a crusty iron chair – 'Goodbye, my sweetheart.' (She'd had a lot to drink by this time, in celebration of her own birth, in recognition of her child's refusal – she saw it as that, a positive decision – to be conceived and born.) It was nine in the evening. Otto, who had forgotten it was her birthday, was late home from his studio. When he did get back, he was sorry for his neglect and took her out to the Tandoori round the corner. She didn't tell him it was the baby that had caused her to drink and then weep. The non-baby. The death of hope.

Nessa's best friend Lindsey, the only person from school Nessa kept up with, once wrote to her apropos of her own indecisive boyfriend Alan, who at that time kept moving in and out of her flat: 'There's always hope – unfortunately.' (This must have been twenty years ago or more; Lindsey's been married twice since then, and neither time to Alan.) Nessa understood this assessment of hope as a destructive force, a poison, a monster. 'Goodbye, baby,' repeated over and over in her dank back garden, killed the monster off. Almost.

There was no biological reason why Nessa and Otto had not managed to have children. No blocked Fallopian tubes, no uterine or ovarian, no penile or testicular, malfunction; no premature ejaculation, no poor sperm count.

'You and your husband are perfectly normal and fertile. Relax. Take a weekend break. Lie in the sun. Get drunk.'

Stress and anxiety were the enemies of conception, the experts agreed.

How many times had she had to listen to that? How many unrelaxed, scorching or sodden, increasingly sexless weekend breaks had they had to take?

Nessa knew Otto long before she married him. Before he married her. They first met when Nessa was at art school and Otto one of the tutors. Being taught by practising painters and sculptors, some of whom, not much older than the students, were beginning to make a name for themselves and to show their work in London galleries, was exciting to Nessa. London was exciting. She'd never been south of Edinburgh until then.

In her second week at the school, during a life class (this was 1965, before the Seventies ban, and when life drawing was still considered a relevant subject of study for art students), Otto came up and stood beside her easel. Nessa had spotted him earlier, talking to a student on the top floor, outside the litho room. She'd thought: What an attractive man! And then, almost immediately: How odd, he's not my type. (As most people seem to, Nessa had made up her mind early about what her type was and thereafter was reluctant to alter her decision, no matter how often events, and men, proved it fallible.) Nessa would have said that her type was thin and tall and fair. Blue- or, at a pinch, green-eyed. Pale and interesting. Haggard and poetic. Whereas Otto was on the small side, five foot six or seven, not much taller than herself. A dark man. His skin was dark, his hair was dark and cut short into a soft, curly brush; he had brown, dark eyes, black eyebrows that met in the middle – 'Murderer's eyebrows,' Nessa's mother said when Nessa told her she was thinking of marrying Otto – thick, dark, curly eyelashes, the sort that are often described as 'sooty'. His chin was dark, but that was because in those days he was economising on razor blades. And he was not thin at all, he was chunky and muscular.

Otto came and stood beside Nessa's easel, hands behind his back, pencil between his teeth. He was wearing a dirty-green corduroy jacket, black corduroys, a black polo neck (a sort of uniform then, anyone in the Arts, anyone who considered himself an intellectual, trying to look like Harold Pinter).

Nessa waited for him to say something rude. She'd heard about his rudeness, had been warned by the second years how rude he could be. She was not sure whether she should carry on with her drawing, or step back out of his way.

'Budge over a minute.' The pencil was still in Otto's mouth. He regarded her drawing, and then the model, and then her drawing. Then he leant forward and scribbled on a corner of her paper.

'See that' – the marks Otto had made were very pale. 'Use a hard pencil like this one. Any old rubbish looks effective if you use charcoal or a 6B.' And that was all.

'Yeah, he's attractive,' Sandra Davis said. They were hanging around the female students' washroom, wasting time before a litho class. 'But you want to watch out. Hard pencil, I'll say. He screws anything that moves. Once. Screw and dump, that's what he does.'

'I thought he was married.' Nessa was shocked by all of this. Shocked and disillusioned. Sorry for Otto's wife and for all betrayed wives. Scandalised. Excited.

Sandra Davis gave her a pitying look. She chased a splinter of black-grooved soap around the basin. She pulled the roller towel out and down, searching for a clean patch; there wasn't one. She shook her hands in the air to dry them, and then wiped them on her jeans. She left the cloakroom.

Nessa was a virgin when this conversation took place. Not a wise thing to be at art school she discovered, where the students' talk, when it was not about work, was about sex. She'd had several near-misses – or were they near-successes? – with boys her own age back home, and thought of her virginity as a technical rather than an actual thing. Now it seemed to her actual, and a problem. The other students knew about it. Not from anything she let slip, but from what she did not; from all the gaps, the omissions, the silences her end of the table in the coffee bars they frequented – the Black Toenail and the Kandinsky. Conversations in these seemed aimed at her, at finding her out.

'Size is important, don' you think, Scottie dog?' Angeline turned to Nessa on a thin grey elbow. 'One fellar I went with had a dick no bigger'n this.' She held up her little finger and jiggled it unpleasantly. 'Honest, no kiddin'. Couldn' feel a *thing*.' And she upturned a bowl of sugar and demonstrated, with a matchstick in the spilt demerara, on the red-mottled formica table top, what dimensions a dick had to have to be of any use to anyone.

Watching this, Nessa's curiosity was mixed with some other, not quite identifiable, emotion. According to Sandra Davis, Angeline had been to bed with Otto. What's more, Sandra Davis said, Otto had broken his once-only rule for Angeline. He'd had her twice.

Angeline's dirt-ingrained hands – it was not just the paint stains they all had – her black-polished yet bitten nails, her waist-length hair (backcombed on top and all the colours of the paintbox), her chalk lips and kohl-rimmed eyes, Nessa would see clearly when other images of art school life had smudged and faded. Angeline personified every resentful taxpayer's understanding of the words 'art' and 'student'. Nessa said as much to Otto in 1989 when they were lamenting the school's proposed closure, but Otto said he had no memory of Angeline at all.

Angeline was a grotesque, an attenuated clown. She reeked of rush-hour tube trains and midnight ashtrays. Why did all the boys fancy her?

Because she was dirty. Because dirt was sexy. Sandra Walters – there were three Sandras in Nessa's year – told her this over coffee in the students' commonroom.

Still, even though she had a bath whenever the hot water in her bed-sit allowed, and rolled Odorono over her armpits before setting off in the mornings, several of the boys at the school found Nessa sufficiently fanciable to try to get her into bed. Or on to the back seats of borrowed cars. Or, on one occasion, on to the sculpture department floor. (This was Roy, who had green teeth.) But Nessa, who wanted to do it, or at least to get it done and over with, couldn't. Confronted by a slobbering mouth, a trespassing finger, an excited trouser front, she froze. (Once to her horror, she laughed out loud.) The boy, whoever it was, would roll off her and sit up. He would say she was a cock-tease, a ball-breaker. Frigid. A lesbian.

'I hear you're a lesbian,' Angeline announced in the Black Toenail. 'What do lesbians do? D'ya fancy me?' She unbuttoned her shirt and revealed her bosom which was small and grey. She wriggled her shoulders provocatively. She put her arms round Roy's neck, leaning into him, and from this vantage point blew Nessa a pouting, noisy kiss.

The following term, her second, Nessa went to bed with Otto.


He had begun to flirt with her when he criticised her work. Not obvious flirting. A light touch on her shoulder, a comment, usually satirical, on her clothes or her red hair or her accent. He would mimic this, as she discovered English people often did, although in his case perhaps 'mimic' was not the right word. 'Adopt' probably came nearer to describing the way he picked up her rhythms and cadences, and then handed them back, recognisable but altered. He would peer at her work, moving in close, then stand back with crossed arms, eventually turning to give her a furrowed, quizzical look. He said little. 'Huh.' 'Uh-huh.' 'Getting there.' 'So-so.' 'So far as it goes.' 'Dishonest.' 'Crap.' 'Work work work, fame fame fame.' (This last chanted in a sort of sing-song.) He would take her pencil or paintbrush from her in such a way that she could feel a slight, only just detectible pressure from his hand.

His hand; his hands: broad palms, small narrow fingers, a ring on the wedding finger. The backs – and his wrists – were hairy. The merest glimpse of his hands, of the black hair on the pale brown skin, triggered a dissolving weakness in her stomach, low down. Another unsettling aspect of him was his smell. No, not smell. Not scent or odour either. This emanation had more to do with temperature than any olfactory sense. It had to do with heat.

One morning he said to her, 'If you're not busy in the lunch break, come and have a jar.'

It was not unheard of for a student to have a drink with a tutor in the lunch hour, but it was not that usual either. Not for a first year. Nessa imagined they'd go to the pub the tutors habitually patronised, the Unicorn it was called. It didn't occur to her they'd be going anywhere in Otto's car. But Otto had to collect some notes and slides from home, 'and then afterwards we'll have a wee bevvy, hen.' Was this true? Or a seducer's fiction? It might be true, it could be: Otto taught art history to the second years.

Otto's car turned out to be a souped-up Morris Traveller. He drove it as though it were a racing car. He pushed it through the gears and through the traffic. Once, when they were stuck behind a delivery van delivering in the Old Brompton Road, he pulled out left on to the kerb, and then drove a few yards along the pavement to overtake the van on the inside. Nessa wasn't frightened – Otto's driving was too confident and authoritative to induce fear – but there were other worries. The glove pocket on the passenger side held a spiral-bound notebook with a shopping list on it in writing that was not Otto's. It held an emery board and a bottle of nail-polish remover. Otto's wife sits in this seat, these objects reminded Nessa, the seat you're sitting on is hers. How do you feel about this? How would Otto's wife feel about your sitting here, in her seat?

In Otto's flat, in the living room, Otto stood behind Nessa and laid his head on her shoulder. He lifted the collar of her jacket and blew softly on the back of her neck. Then he kissed her neck.

'No,' Nessa said, wanting to move; not moving.

'Yes,' Otto said. 'Yes.'

'No.' This second 'no' must have carried more conviction, for he released her.

'Let's have a drink. Wotcha fancy?'

'I don't need a drink.'

'I think you do. I know I do.'

While Otto was getting the drinks, Nessa examined the room, sitting room she supposed it to be. The room where Otto and Janet sat in the evenings and discussed the happenings of their day. Where they had tea, no, supper, on trays in front of the television. Where they made love on that settee. (It was grey wide-ribbed corduroy and large enough, if it did not look comfortable.) Examining the room, making a conscientious study of its colours and furniture and objects, was a way of dealing with a mix of feelings – with lust and resentment, nervousness and guilt. Nessa saw sludge-coloured walls, a curtainless bay window, a square of rust carpet on black painted floorboards. There were only four pictures in the room and these, a series of drawings of a standing female nude, backview, and recognisably Otto's work, were grouped together on the fireplace wall. The mantelpiece, the windowsill, the bookshelves, were supporters of stones or stone-like sculptures, stone-coloured jugs and bowls, and vases with wide bases and thin necks and runny glazes. An earthenware pot, large enough to house forty thieves, stood in the fireplace and contained ornamental grasses, feathery and grey. Otto's wife was a potter. Nessa remembered Sandra Davis telling her this. Not just a wife, not just a mother – as Nessa's own mother had been, as all the women in her childhood were and were expected to be: cooks and floor-scrubbers, fanatical table-polishers and chairback-starchers, nest-builders. These pots and jugs, on the face of it domestic items, described an independence unheard of in the marriages she knew. Their presence on ledges and shelves seemed to Nessa evidence of marital equality, and a real, punchy competitiveness.

The drink Otto brought her was gin and tonic, ice and lemon, only the second time she'd tasted this.

'Sit down, sweetie,' Otto said, 'take your coat off; I'm just going to make a phone call.'

It was hot in the room, but Nessa kept her jacket on. She perched on the corduroy sofa, stiffly upright, her knees together, her hands round the freezing tumbler, while Otto made his call.

'Hallooo there,' an unfamiliar Otto cooed into the receiver, 'hallooo, it's me. No, I'm at home. Can't remember whether you wanted me to do anything else about supper? Yeah, I've got the booze, and the salad stuff. I've made the ice. Yes. Yes, okay. Mischa's going to be very late.' Otto swung round in his chair, and while he was listening to what his wife had to say about this news, he gave Nessa a severe, investigative stare. With his free hand he groped behind him on the architect's desk for his cigarettes, shook a cigarette from the packet, lit up and threw first the packet and then the lighter to Nessa.

'Fine. Okay. No, no one. No, I just came home for some art history slides. Did you say you'd be back about four? Yus. Yus I will. Yus. Promise. Love you.'

How could Otto do this? How was he able to? What shocked Nessa was not so much that he should lie to his wife, by omission, in that cooing, intimate voice, but that he should do it in front of her. How could he bear to show himself up in such a way to someone he hardly knew, to one of his students? What sort of person did he think she was?

'Would your wife mind if she knew I was here?' Nessa pulled hard on her cigarette. Her question was not a real one, because she had no doubts that Janet would mind. She had asked it deliberately, to disconcert Otto.

Otto was not disconcerted. Of course his wife wouldn't mind, he assured Nessa. Of course not! Why should she? Theirs was not that sort of relationship, the sort that cared about such things. They were both creators, creative people had needs, they both understood those needs. Seeing separate friends separately was one. They had no secrets from each other, as it happened, if Nessa really wanted to know.

So she needn't worry about that one! What was worrying him was that Nessa hadn't had anything to eat. He was going to go and concoct a sandwich now. Could she eat cheese and something? Cucumber?

Nessa hadn't remembered Otto taking his shoes off, but in the kitchen he wasn't wearing any. He sprung about the room in thick socks, from fridge to breadbin to table, where he buttered and chopped and sliced and sprinkled. Deft and efficient; lithe – like a cat, or a ballet dancer. He reminded Nessa of all the photographs she'd ever seen of Nijinsky.

'Who are Ben and Dom?' The mugs they were drinking their coffee out of had these names painted on them. Ben on Nessa's mug, Dom on Otto's.

Ben and Dom were his step-children, Otto said, Janet's sons from her first marriage. Janet was eight years older than him, he explained, leaving this information to hang in the air above their heads, where it gathered weight and significance.

Did he like them, Ben and Dom? Nessa wanted to know, did he get on with them?

Well yes of course he did! Why wouldn't he? They were good lads, they were very nice kids.

('Of course'? Why 'of course'? Nessa felt she might have believed him if he hadn't said 'of course'.) She asked him if he wanted children of his own, and Otto said, no, no he didn't, he'd never wanted children, and Janet didn't want any more, so that was all right.

'I do,' Nessa said, 'I want a lot of children. Four or five, mebbe.'

Otto said he'd got it into his head that she wanted to paint.

'I do. I want to paint and have babies.' (Why should this surprise him, when he was married to Janet?) 'I want both. Is there a toilet anywhere round here?'

The toilet was on a little half-landing between the basement and the hall. When she came out, Otto was sitting at the foot of the stairs, his head on one side, his thumb in his mouth. Little boy lost. Wouldn't she like to do a little tour of the house before they left? Little Boy Otto asked engagingly. Wouldn't she like to admire the fruits of his amazing, innovative, masterly, do-it-yourself labours?

No no no no no! But Nessa did not say this, and afterwards she blamed her failure on the gin. Instead she allowed Otto to take her hand and lead her up the stairs, which he did on tiptoe, as if there might be children sleeping on the floor above whom they must be careful not to wake.

Nessa lost her virginity in Ben's room, after she'd inspected shelves and cupboards about the house that Otto said he'd made. He'd even carpentered Ben's bed, he'd cut it down from an old worm-eaten fourposter that came originally from his grandmother's house in Galway.

Nessa hadn't wanted to go into Ben's room. Pinned to the door was a notice in red felt pen: BEN'S ROOM. ADMITENCE TO TICKET HOLDERS ONLY.

'We cannae go in there. We've no got tickets.'

But Otto said not to worry, he had a season ticket, he'd paid over the odds for it, it allowed him entrance any time night or day, she mustn't worry about it at all. He was standing behind her as he said this, and now he put his arms round her in a protective, consoling way, as to one who had suffered a bereavement; and blew on her neck, and murmured into her ear.

'A little lie-down is what we need after that climb,' Otto's voice said inside her ear, 'a little little lie-down. My sleepy Agnes.' His hands, sleepy-seeming themselves yet inexorable, travelled from her waist to her breasts as he spoke, robbing her of protest. (What Otto's hands were doing to her breasts, her nipples, was affecting another part of her body altogether. This was new. No one else's hands had achieved this.)

'You smell delicious.' Otto inched her, slow but very sure, nearer Ben's narrow bed. The bed that he had made.

But the worry over the lack of tickets remained. It inhabited a part of Nessa's mind all the time Otto was undressing her, and while he was undressing himself, and while he lowered himself on to her – the narrowness of the

292

bed did not allow for two adult humans to lie side by side – and while he explored her person, and while he, methodically and devastatingly, occupied her person. The lack of tickets for Ben's room, plus the fact of doing it in Ben's bed, would haunt her with guilt and shame whenever she thought of that first time with Otto, the iniquity of her crime intensifying through the years so that in her forties Nessa would tell Lindsey that she believed, she really believed, it accounted for her failure to conceive a child. Not having babies was a punishment, she told Lindsey. (Lindsey said she'd never heard such nonsense, such dangerous nonsense.)

Afterwards they didn't light cigarettes, or lie still with their arms around each other. On the contrary, things speeded up. Otto looked at his watch and leapt into his clothes and threw Nessa hers. Dazed and sleepy from the gin, Nessa followed the speeding, speeded-up Otto. Down the stairs. To the living room, where he removed the ashtrays and the glasses. To the kitchen, where he washed these and the lunch things up, and dried them and put them away. Back to – taking the stairs three at a time – Ben's room, where he shunted the bed back to the position it had travelled from; and punched the pillows, and sniffed and smoothed the bedclothes, and withdrew the towel he'd thought it wise to fetch when Nessa – rather late in the proceedings – had mentioned it was the first time she'd done this.

The towel went into the twin tub in the kitchen, along with some socks and shirts and a bri-nylon babydoll nightdress Otto extracted from the bathroom on his flight down the stairs.

'Work work work, fame fame fame,' Otto encouraged himself cheerfully as he put on his shoes.

'What about the art history notes?' Nessa felt she had to remind him of these. It seemed strange he should forget them, when he'd remembered everything else.

In the car going back to the college, Otto took his hand from the gear lever and placed it on Nessa's thigh. He ran his forefinger the length of her thigh, pressing down firmly, drawing it along, cutting a groove. A knife through butter. (She would be able to feel that pressure on her thigh for always.)

'Bonnie wee Nessa,' he said, 'bonnie wee Agnes. You were lovely. You are lovely. We must do this again. Soonest.'

They didn't do it again. Not for years. (Not until Janet had left Otto, not until Nessa met him, by chance, one January morning, at the Tate.) Having screwed Nessa, Otto dumped her.

Why did none of the dumped students betray Otto? Why didn't she betray him? Nessa asked herself this then and later. An anonymous telephone call to his wife, or an anonymous letter, would have done it. Or she could have – any of them could have – reported him to the principal. No one reported Otto. At the time, Nessa asked Sandra Davis why not.

'You could have said no, mate,' Sandra Davis said. 'We can all say no, y'know. Anyway, Otto's good at it, and he's useful – if he likes your work. Andrea Watkins was a student of his.' Andrea Watkins was having her first one-man show at the Ariel Gallery just then. Her work had received a lot of critical attention. Nessa had been to see Andrea's show and had decided it was okay, nothing special, but okay.

'Anyway,' Sandra Davis said, 'look on the bright side. No one calls you a lesbian any more, so that's something.'

When men, in the Middle Life Crisis much written about these days, lose interest in their wives, it's invariably to do with sex, with unsatisfactory or boring sex. That's what the women's magazines say, that's what the health pages of national newspapers suggest. Nessa read a great many of these articles, the ones that tell you how to be inventive in bed, the ones with jokey headings like How to Keep Your Man's End Up Through Forty Years of Marriage.

What the message of these usually boils down to is this: that men being men (polygamous; natural philanderers), it is up to women (monogamous; natural homemakers) to keep the sexual interest – and thereby the marriage – going. 'Day after day there are girls at the office, and men will always be men; if you send him off with your hair still in curlers, you may not see him again.' That line of singing and thinking, thrown out in the feminist Seventies, shelved in the Eighties, seems to be being dusted down and polished up for the Nineties. Perhaps AIDS has something to do with it. Nessa thought so. AIDS, spelt out, or euphemised, came into the articles she read more and more.

Nessa and Otto's sex life wasn't satisfactory – well, it couldn't be, it hardly existed. It only ever existed if Otto initiated it, and nowadays he seldom did. Not that Nessa had ever been much of a leader, although for a time she was a keen follower. During those years she followed Otto anywhere his fantasies led him. Take underwear. She wore the black underwear Otto used to insist on when he wanted her to be naughty, and the white underwear he insisted on when he wanted her to be nice – that is, virginal; a school-girl. He would not allow her to wear a coloured bra and pants ever. No flower patterns or psychedelic swirls or day-glo spots – a turn-off, he said. This was a problem in the Seventies, when brilliant flower-power hipster briefs were all you could buy. In those days Nessa bought her white pants in the girls' school outfitters' departments of large stores: knicker linings they were called. In the mid-Eighties, when plain underwear came back in fashion, Nessa didn't have to make a trip to Debenhams, she could buy all the white pants she wanted in her local Marks & Spencer. But Otto didn't mention her nether garments any more. If he had a preference for lacy, strapless bras, if he had sudden and urgent desires to see her in cami-knicks or open-crotch panties, he never said so. Nessa knew this was her fault, that it was she who was to blame for Those Old Bedroom Blues (the expression used in one article she read to describe ordinary, uninventive, infrequent, marital sex) she and Otto were suffering from. Otto was suffering from. For the truth was, once she'd convinced herself there would be no baby, she lost all interest in sex. What could be done about it? None of the pieces she read made the connexion between sex and babies. Sex for pleasure was what they were concerned with. Sex for warmth, sex for comfort, sex for health. Sex as cement for crumbling relationships. Nessa wasn't against any of these, she could see the value of them. If asked, she would have said that most of them had been contained, to some extent, within her and Otto's lovemaking. Desirable in themselves, they had been part of desire, and of its aftermath, of sweat cooling on exhausted bodies, of a shared glass of whisky or of wine.

It was a shock, then, to discover at forty that none of these aspects of sex counted. That all that energy and lust and concentration had had for her one purpose only.


'Have an affair with him if you must, but don't, for God's sake, marry him,' Lindsey said when Nessa was talking about moving in with Otto. 'He'll no be faithful to you for more than five minutes, and he does *not* want children.'

But Otto wasn't interested in screwing around any more, he was only interested in Nessa. He loved her. He needed her, and probably always had (he saw this now). His open marriage to Janet had been – a hard thing to have to admit, but true – a disaster. Commitment was what he was ready for. Also, he'd changed his mind about having children.

'Having babies with you would be delicious,' Otto murmured into Nessa's ear as they were making love.


Nessa was teaching art full-time in a boys' grammar school when she married Otto, a job she saw as a stop-gap, not a career. She was going to be a painter, she was going to be a mother. These were certainties. Teaching had not left her much time or energy to paint, and the school holidays were somehow taken up with other things, with visits home to her mother, with visits to Lindsey, newly married and with a baby on the way; but now Otto's drive and ambition was going to rub off on her. Otto told her it was so, and she believed it. And he took practical steps to encourage her: he whitewashed the back bedroom of their Putney flat, he set her up with lighting and materials. He would do everything he could to help her, he had the contacts, there wouldn't be a problem when it came to showing her work – when she'd done the work. But she'd never get anywhere if she taught full-time.

So Nessa gave up the grammar school and got herself a two-day-a-week job at a comprehensive. Then she waited for inspiration and for babies to arrive.

Throughout Nessa's life with Otto there were mornings when she'd wake and think: Today is the day. Today it will happen. These were the mornings when she believed, from the first moment of consciousness, that she held the key to an enduring energy, a graspable vision, an attainable truth; that as soon as breakfast was over and Otto out of the house, she would climb the stairs to her studio – the room that Otto had whitewashed for that purpose – and paint the paintings, beautiful and true, beautiful because true, it had always been her destiny to paint.

Pie in the sky. Some demon in Nessa had other ideas. This demon kept her busy in the kitchen, washing up, drying up, putting away; wiping surfaces over and over, scrubbing the floor. He sent her into the utility room to wash a bundle of dirt- and polish-clogged dusters by hand, for God's sake (there was a perfectly adequate washing machine under the worktop). He decided it was the ideal day for airing the kelims on the garden line, and once they were there, for mugging them with a broom. (She would have to wash her hair afterwards.) He insisted that the lavatory seats were overdue for disinfecting, and the fridge for defrosting. He pointed out that there were mouse – or were they rat? – droppings in the larder, and water rings on the living room furniture. And how come she hadn't noticed until today how filthy, how stomach-turningly sticky and fluffy, the stair treads and the skirting boards were?

Only when she was exhausted would the demon let her go; only when she was quite safe from any obligation and responsibility to her vision. After that she was free.

There was one consolation Nessa hung on to. The bare walls of her studio, the near-empty sketchbooks and blank canvases that littered its floor, contained, didn't they, a paradox: somewhere in all this vacuity the truth remained intact. White hot. Inviolable.

Whereas Otto. Whereas, who was to say that Otto, in his quest for fame fame fame, on a journey that had taken him from vapid Fifties Figurative, through Kitchen Sink Realism, some Constructivist stuff ('motorway cones' one phase Nessa remembers), a fling with the Minimal and the Conceptual, to the paint-laden Abstract Expressionism of his latest work, had come any nearer to the truth than she had? Who had done nothing? Mightn't he even, with his mania for reinventing and making it new, have profaned the truth, or lost sight of it altogether?

There were times when Nessa could console herself with this hypothesis; moments when she knew her apathy and lack of achievement were not her fault. In one household there can't be room, can there, for two burning ambitions, two artistic temperaments, two super egos?

(What about Otto's encouragement of her, though? She wasn't going to deny that, was she? – It was Lindsey who asked this. He'd always encouraged her, hadn't he?

No. Not really. Not unless you called years of head-patting patronisation encouragement. Not unless you did.)

Other times Nessa told herself that Otto was a gifted, courageous man. That looking after the needs of such a man, or indeed of any man, was a valid mission, and what she was for. What all women were for. That doing it well implied a talent not to be despised.

*

This morning after breakfast, Nessa went round to Marion, next-door neighbour but one, to return the book, *Uncoupling*, that Marion had lent her. Nessa hadn't read it all. *Uncoupling* hadn't concentrated her mind as Marion had predicted, only depressed it. Also, she'd noticed the book was three weeks overdue at the library, a fact which made her feel a criminal. Then there was the embarrassment of having something with so unambiguous a title on the table by her bed, and of reading it in bed while lying alongside Otto. Not that Otto often noticed what she read any more. It was years since they'd discussed the books they were reading, swapped them, read passages out to each other, laughed over or at them. Even so, she'd felt awkward reading *Uncoupling* within an inch of Otto's nose. And he had noticed it. He'd stopped her side of the bed on his way to the bathroom one morning, and picked up the book from her table and scrutinised its jacket.

'Uncoupling presupposes coupling – you have to couple first,' Otto said slowly. 'Or is this a book about trains? What a dark iron horse you are, Nessa, to be sure.'

Marion was doing her washing when Nessa called in with the book. She offered Nessa a cup of coffee. Marion used to be married to a university lecturer, an archaeologist, but divorced him three years ago. She has two children: Natalie who's eleven, Barney who's five. In her kitchen was evidence of this fruitfulness: messily pasted paperchains looped the ceiling; a red-felt-pen message on the pinboard reminded that Natalie's ballet class is on Fridays at six now, not Wednesdays at six-thirty; a magnetic Mickey Mouse clung to the fridge door. And the kitchen itself was an art gallery, a part-retrospective two-man show of Natalie and Barney's work. Most of Nessa's friends' kitchens had looked like this at one time or another. Maura Donaldson's had. Lindsey's had, for years. Alienating years, Nessa had found them.

'Well, apart from anything else, Otto couldn't manage without me,' Nessa said, on the defensive, in Marion's chaotic kitchen. Marion had just quizzed her on *Uncoupling*; she'd just asked if it hadn't helped Nessa make up her mind to leave Otto, once and for all. Nessa had often considered leaving Otto. She was constantly wondering how it was she'd wasted her life on Mr Wrong all these years, but in the same way that she could become a loonie Leftie when in a room full of Fascists, and Hitler when in a room full of loonie Lefties, so she felt a need, in the face of Marion's impertinent certainties, to defend Otto, and herself, and their sad marriage.

'Otto would go to pieces if I left him. His work would suffer. I know.'

Which was balls, according to Marion. Behind her, the washing machine, up to that moment a moaning depressive, turned suddenly manic: screamed hysterically, worked itself up into a complete spin, and went off its rocker.

'No, not balls!' Nessa had to shout above the din.

It was, Marion insisted. Nessa deceived herself; it was a form of conceit to imagine one's spouse couldn't manage without one. Otto had been married before Nessa came along, hadn't he? He'd found himself a new wife then, well, he'd do so again. Anyway, it wasn't Otto she was concerned with, it was Nessa. By turning the argument round to Otto and his needs, Nessa was refusing to engage with the real issue.

'Otto is a difficult man, okay,' Nessa said, 'but he's wrapped up in his work, he's not interested in women any more, not in that way. He can't be bothered. I doubt any woman would take him on. Also' – Nessa added a little, plausible lie – 'he depends on me for critical judgement. There are enough sycophants in his life – '

Marion snorted at his, and wrinkled her nose in an unpleasant way. On her otherwise pale cheeks two round spots of high colour glowed. The cheeks reminded Nessa of a Dutch doll she'd been given one Christmas when she was five, and never liked.

'No man welcomes criticism,' said Marion, whose fund of wise saws was perhaps surprising in one of only thirty-three, 'not from a woman. What men want from women is to have them sitting at their feet, praising them, bringing them sherbert.' She paused here to let a probable literary allusion sink in. 'Otto is no exception.' Marion was silent again while she spooned instant coffee into two mugs, the insides of which were stained a dark rusty brown. 'What beats me is why you've stayed with Otto so long, when there was nothing – no children – to keep you.'

Nessa took the mug Marion handed her. She said it was quite likely that it was not having any children that had kept her and Otto together. That if they had had them, they might well have landed up in the divorce courts years ago.

She was not sure why she said this, but she saw at once that it was true – it was contrary enough to be true.

Marion cleared a space in the leftover breakfast things for her own mug, and sat down opposite Nessa at the table. Then, leaning towards Nessa with a concerned and caring expression on her face, one that somehow managed to involve her eyes and her eyebrows and her mouth and the attitude of her little sharp chin, she said, 'Nessa lovey, if you don't mind my asking, what gives you the idea – what proof have you got – that Otto isn't interested in women any more?'

What an intolerable question! Nessa wasn't going to answer it. She shouldn't have, but she did.

'Well, I'd know, wouldn't I? I don't need proof. I live with the man. I know.'

'I wasn't going to tell you this, lovey. I'd hoped you were going to take some sort of initiative yourself, but now I think you should be warned – ' Marion made breaking off to sip her coffee, and then stretching an arm for the sugar bowl, an excuse for a significant pause. She was wearing a white and dirty crocheted jumper with sleeves pushed up to the elbows. Her forearms displayed the black moles and wiry black hairs that are characteristic of a certain type of white skin, the type that never tans in sunshine, only red-dens and burns. Otto had told Nessa more than once that he disliked that combination very much indeed, and that he found Marion physically repulsive.

' When you went home to see your mother last Easter – remember? – Otto came round here, and tried to get me into bed, tried to get into my bed. He came round twice, he tried twice.' Marion paused again, presumably to allow time for her words to have effect, then she said, 'I had to turn him out because he was drunk. And also because he didn't want me – though he wanted my body, of course. What he really wanted was a confessional, a convenient ear for his troubles. Otto may not be interested in women, lovey, as you say, but he's interested in *a woman*. He's been in love with a woman, a married woman, for years. They have a child. Her husband thinks it's his, but it isn't, it's Otto's.'

Not a quick screw and dump then, or a series of these, but a long-standing affair. A commitment, a loving commitment. With a child.

It wasn't true. Marion was a liar, anyone could see that, she always had been, the truth was not in her.

It was true.

What an extraordinary thing, Nessa thought from a long cold distance, from the uninhabited planet she'd just landed on, that it should be Marion to impart this news. To rain these blows. Blow after blow after blow. What an extraordinary thing.

' . . . Otto told me he's felt for a long time that you aren't really interested in him,' said Marion, who had yet more blows up her sleeve, 'and that you don't really like men. If you don't mind my telling you this, he's convinced you prefer women. "In every way" was how he put it.'

A picture presented itself in Nessa's head, a picture of herself and Maura Donaldson in Maura's cottage kitchen. They were concocting supper for the menfolk. They were giggling; they were adding, between swigs from a bottle of wine on the worktop, increasingly bizarre ingredients to what they'd feared was a dullish stew. And then, somehow – crossing the room? – rummaging for *crème de menthe* or peanut butter or caraway seeds? – they'd collided, collapsed into each other's arms, and stayed there. Hung in, hung on, and stayed there. Relaxed against each other and breathed in the scent of the other's neck, and stayed there. Stayed there too long. 'Well, this won't buy the menfolk a new pair of hiking boots,' Maura had said eventually, releasing herself.

That was all. After that, they'd got on with the supper, as though nothing had happened. Well, nothing had happened. And Otto couldn't know about it because of course Nessa had never told him. No one knew. Lindsey didn't know. No one.

But afterwards, when Nessa was at home in Hammersmith and thought about it, she'd come to the conclusion: 'If Maura and I had been alone in the cottage, and if there'd been a bed in the kitchen, we'd have landed up in it.' She knew this with certainty. What she could never be certain about was whether she was glad or sorry they had not been alone, and that there'd been no convenient bed for them to fall into.

' . . . Otto stays with you because he thinks you're helpless without him, he says he can't leave you . . . ' Marion's parting shots followed Nessa from the kitchen table and out of the house, chased her down the steps. 'He's convinced you aren't capable of earning your own bread. He says . . . '


On Nessa's desk, the pile of dealt-with Christmas cards is taller now than the untouched pile. She's got as far as the Ts in her address book. She's written cards to the Trevillions and Ira Tredgett and Bill Thorpe and the Templetons, and next she's going to do one for the Tuckwells.

Nessa is on her own in the living room. Half an hour or so ago, John Coltrane stopped playing his sax, and when he did Otto put his empty whisky glass on the floor and lay back in his chair and fell asleep.

Is it true? Is it *true*? Nessa, in her head, asked the

unconscious Otto. Is any of it true? When he wakes I'll confront him, she told herself. But when, some minutes later, he did wake, abruptly and noisily as he always did, groping his way to the door (like a blind man, or a sleep-walker, or a *drunk*) as he always did, she said nothing.

'Happy Christmas to John and Suzy,' Nessa writes inside her card to the Tuckwells, 'Love from Otto and Nessa.' John Tuckwell is a sculptor, an old friend, an old sparring partner, of Otto's. Suzy is his second wife. (The Tuckwells used to be John and Alannah, but back in the Seventies Alannah left John and their three children and went off into the sunset with a male model, a boy of twenty.) John and Suzy are in Canada this winter because Suzy, an art historian, has a lectureship in Montreal.

'No news from the frozen North, you so-and-sos,' Nessa writes to the Tuckwells in her version of the italic script she and Lindsey learned at high school in Arbroath. 'How goes it? Otto's retrospective is end of Feb – any chance you'll be back in England by then?'

# LYING DOGGO

I sleep with her. That is to say, I sleep on our bed, above the duvet, under the eiderdown. Only on the coldest nights do I accept her invitation to come in. Usually, a need to preserve a modicum of independence sends me to the end of the bed, where I'll lie crossways on, though sometimes I'll curl into the triangle her bent knees provide (she sleeps in the foetal position as a rule). I have been known to lie with my head resting on her lower legs, and when I do, it is not for reasons of devotion but because of the warmth this posture affords.

She sleeps badly. Very often my dreams will be interrupted by the sudden curtailment of her own, by the bedside light snapping on, by a book thundering to the floor, by plashy gulpings from the bedside tumbler, by pillows being punished and rearranged. Selfish, she will want to make me accessory to her insomnia and her fears. Are you awake? she'll demand, ensuring that I am. Wake up! (hefting me with a foot) Didn't you hear something? Experience should have taught her by now that if there is 'something' in the house, or out there in the dark, to hear, I will hear it, I will sense it instantly and alert her. Experience has taught me, when a warning is called for and acted upon, not to expect gratitude. Oh do shut up, she'll groan, flouncing and thrashing under the duvet, it's only a fox or a badger, it's only the moorhens on the river, lie down for God's sake, stop quivering, we've got three hours left before the alarm goes off, go back to sleep. Her behaviour is histrionic in the extreme.

I am at the mercy of her moods. Prodigal with displays

of affection one minute (she winds her arms round my neck in a stranglehold, she imprisons my head in both hands, she stares searchingly into my eyes, she plants lingering, deliberate kisses on my forehead and cheeks and ears, on my chest and stomach – though never yet, thank heaven, on my lips), she will ignore me the next. Accepting an invitation to join her on the sofa, I'm aware that at any moment I may be turfed off. If I had a say in the matter, I would opt for a mean of kindness and considerateness, for nothing more than consistency in these. As it is, lashed to the pendulum of her emotions, swung from extravagance to parsimony, I suffer and endure.

I try to please her, nevertheless. A hopeless endeavour: she is impossible to please. When visitors arrive, for example. When visitors arrive and I, at the slamming of a car door or voices on the path, gear myself up for a vociferous welcome, run to the front door, greet the visitors individually as they enter – she accuses me of faithlessness. You're not mine, she says, you're anybody's, that's plain to see. If, on the other hand, and taking account of her jealousy, I decide on a low-profile approach, or rather nonapproach, slinking up the stairs as soon as the visitors step into the hall, she calls me down and upbraids me in front of them for lack of manners.

She never asks me to accompany her when she goes out in the evenings. I am her one true friend, she makes a point of telling me, I am her angel, her adored, the love of her life, yet on those evenings when she transforms herself from sloven to prima donna, and glides out of the house, she leaves me behind. So much for love! She knows (I cannot disguise it) how intensely I dislike being left alone, how I fear it. Bolt upright on the bathmat, I sit in the bathroom and watch anxiously as she bathes. Haven't you got anything better to do? she taunts. Why don't you make yourself useful and get me a whisky? Don't go all hangdog on me, please. I follow her to our bedroom and lie on the bed as she dresses and twists heated rollers into her hair. Applying her mascara brush with a shaking hand, she'll catch my eye in the dressing-table glass. Don't stare at me like that! she'll accuse, I shan't be out long. Now look what you've made me do!

She is a tease. My interest in the natural world, the field study, in particular, I have made of the *sciurus vulgaris* that inhabits our garden, is for her the source of unending and mischievous sport. Squirrel, she will murmur softly in my ear as I doze. Squirrel! she will exclaim from the bedroom window, surveying the wilderness below, squirrel on the warpath! The excitement in her voice triggers, not surprisingly, my own, sends me helter skelter down the stairs to the front door, where I scream with impatience until she opens up. And when she does? And when I sprint to the hornbeam and the beech – what do I find? Not a tail, not a whisker. Not a whiff. Recently, fearing perhaps that she has cried squirrel once too often, she has taken to employing the word 'polatouche' instead. Polatouche! (an urgent whisper or a yell) Polatouche, beloved! I am not moved by this chicanery. Is it likely that *sciuropterus volans*, small flying native of Northern Asia, could be caught disporting himself on the patch of balding moss she calls a lawn?

I am giving you my version of our life, of course, but then she is always giving hers, to anyone prepared to listen. Take the delicate/indelicate subject of breaking wind. Should I, after dinner, say, when we are holed up together in front of the television set, inadvertently break wind, all hell will break loose. Thrusting me from the sofa, she'll march about the room fanning the air with her newspaper. She'll make a to-do of throwing wide the casements and the French windows. She'll pronounce me a Fart-Pot, a Stink-Weed, the Gas-Works. Even an outside temperature of ten degrees below will not save me from banishment to the garden for half an hour or more. If, however, she should be the one (all mammals are susceptible) to break wind, then there is a marked absence of hullaballoo. No confession, no dramatics with newspapers, no risk of heart attack or hypothermia from a sudden introduction of freezing air, nothing. The silence I have learned to associate with her gassy emissions, that marks them, would be hypocrisy enough, but that's not the end of her perfidy. It's become her custom, after a characteristically soundless and offensive expulsion, and on those rare occasions when we entertain the neighbours, to accuse *me*. To put the blame for it on *me*. Whew! Cor! (pointing to my rump, making great play with pinching or holding her nose) So sorry about her! (bundling me off the sofa and out of the door) She's getting old and smelly, I'm afraid, not really her fault, poor lamb, there's nowt to be done! Out you go then, Stinky!

She is a lazy cook. I eat out of tins, as a rule. Very occasionally my diet is supplemented by a few leftover vegetables, originally green, dark brown through reheating by the time they reach me, of no nutritional value whatsoever.

She has a drink problem. It could be that her poor culinary performance is the result of her habit; certainly she is well tanked up by dinner time, stumbling round the kitchen in search of the tin opener (invariably under her nose), berating me for getting under her feet. All very well for you, she complains, you don't have to get the supper, you don't have to do anything useful at all. I'm just your slave, I'm just a dogsbody in this place! Teetotal myself, I'm alarmed at the power alcohol has over the human personality, how it alters and distorts. Alcohol can make her aggressive or lachrymose. It can make her garrulous and dumb by turn. It can cause her to put songs of Love Lost or Betrayed in the tape deck. 'Can't go on/Everything I had is gone/Stormy weather!' howls Sinatra as she mooches about the living room, stopping now and then at the drinks cupboard to refill her whisky glass. Alcohol causes her to perch on the edge of a chair and rock and hum, it causes her to slump in the chair and stare at nothing, or at me, lying doggo on the sofa. Why do you have to look like that? she'll demand. Why do you have to look so nervous? Is it surprising if I'm nervous? Is it surprising that I dread her tears and her hysterical elation? Of the two, it's the latter that holds more terror for me. The latter means Elvis, full volume, in the tape deck, itching like a man on a fuzzy tree; it means that sooner or later she will force me off the sofa into her arms, heave me over her shoulder, then bear me, unwilling partner, rocking and rolling round the living room. Round and round, up and down, cheek to cheek, all shook up. (My heart beats so, it scares me to death.) Only when the tape stops do we; only then will she stagger to the sofa. Only then will I be resettled – that is to say, dropped, dumped – on the sofa.

She is a writer. According to her, all writers drink. Drinking, so she would have me believe, is what all writers do. It's the common bond, so she says, perhaps the sole bond.

She writes in the morning. In the afternoon we go for a walk. These walks, up hills, along the ridges of hills, in woods, beside the river, which should be our most companionable times, which can be the times I enjoy most, will be ruined if she decides to play a 'game', or if we should meet a person or persons with a dog or dogs. I am afraid of dogs, even small ones; large dogs terrify me. At first sight of a large dog, an Alsatian, say, I stop in my tracks and holler in alarm. I scream and shout. I tremble and shake. At the very last minute, when the monster is almost upon us, I run to her, and she hides my head against her trousered knees and holds me till the danger passes. Sorry about her! she'll call over her shoulder, she's an awful baby, I'm afraid (stroking my head and ears); she always cries before she's hurt, comes of having been beaten and abandoned in childhood – I rescued her from the Home, you see! The result is, she's afraid of men and dogs, she can't be left alone for two seconds, she won't allow her mummy out of her sight! These unsolicited betrayals and boastings, despite the sickly anthropomorphism of their style, are usually understood by the dog-walker (tut-tutting in sympathy, tightening his or her grip on the 'German shepherd') as evidence of her caring. If he or she could only know what happens, often, on our walks! If he or she could witness what she calls a 'game'! About this 'game' of hers: it cannot be played in open country; I am safe on the downs. It is restricted to woods, to lanes trapped by hedges or bushes, to scrubland areas of bramble and bracken and gorse. We will be footing it in such a place, she, happy wanderer, laughing and singing beneath God's clear blue sky, I, crisscrossing the path, nose to the ground, absorbed in studying the routes frequented by *meles vulgaris* and *lepus cuniculus*, while at the same time keeping a weather eye on her movements – when she vanishes. My back has only to be turned for a second – and she's gone. I stand on the path and look and listen: nothing. I lift my head and sniff the badger-scented air: no one. Panic fills my nostrils and my bones. What if some terrible accident has befallen her? What if she never returns to take me home? (I cannot drive, obviously; the car is invariably parked miles back.) If she has gone for ever, what then? I try to remember her exact position on the path moments ago, when I last saw her; I try to recall whether she was ahead of me or behind. Fear sends me lickety-split in the direction we were headed, on round a bend, on on, but the path is empty as far as the eye can see. I stop still and howl. I turn and tear back the way I came, past the spot where, I believe, she vanished, on on on . . . nothing. I stop again. I howl. I repeat this desperate exercise, again and again and again. Eventually, I force myself into a more measured pace, zigzagging the path and the wayside undergrowth, checking out the sloe bushes and the sweet chestnuts, investigating every flattened grassblade, every snapping twig, every battered fern. And then all at once I'm on to her; a stop, a false start, a stop, a new start, a twist, a turn, and there, at last, she is – spreadeagled in the bracken, crouched in the hollow darkness of a yew. Alive; in one piece; unharmed. You took your time, she'll say, casual, not bothering to look at me, picking burrs and grasses off her sleeve. What happened to you? (unhurriedly dusting herself down) Good thing I hadn't broken my leg! You ain't nothin' but a hound dog, you know, cryin' all the time, You ain't never caught a rabbit and you ain't no friend of mine! Noticing suddenly my lolling tongue and rasping breath; aware, for the first time, of my distress, she'll go through the motions of remorse: I'm sorry, Angel, hey, forgive me (arms round my neck, cheek pressed against my racing heart). It's only a game, sweetheart, Hide and Seek is just a *game*. You ought to have learnt that by now, Mastermind! I didn't mean to frighten you. You know I wouldn't frighten you for all the world!

I fear she may be homosexual. This self-styled mummy of mine continually expresses a desire for us to get married – to each other. Even if there weren't already just cause and impediment why we two should not be joined, there would still be the problem of our both being female. She does not see this as a problem. Marry me, she'll beg, down on one knee in front of the sofa (where I'll be trying to have a kip), be mine, beloved! Embarrassed by her play-acting, defeated by the evilness of her breath, I'll bury my head under a cushion. Had we but world enough and time, she'll whisper, lifting the cushion, stroking my nose, kissing my nose, this coyness, lady, were no crime – Hey (tweaking my whiskers), what are these, O beauteous one? Brides aren't allowed to grow face fungus, you know, we shall have to invest in a Philips Ladyshave, O Bride of Lammermoor, my own! More alarming than this nonsense are the announcements she'll make out of the blue, over the washing-up perhaps: Well! (brisk and business-like, drying her hands, glaring down at me) The banns are read, the church is booked, *the press is squared, the Middle Class is quite prepared* – but what about you? Have you got your trousseau together? Have you had a final fitting for your wedding dress? for your bridal gown?

If she is not a sapphist, then she is mad. She may well be both.

I mentioned she's a writer. She's writing a book – of fictions, she calls them. Yesterday at breakfast she told me she's planning one about me. She took my head in her hands when she confided this and rested it on her knee. She stared into my eyes. What sort of person are you, really? she demanded to know. Tell me. Go on, *speak*. Uneasy, I tried to jerk my head away. Don't then, she said, bored, dismissing me. Anyway, she said, I can do anything I want, you realise, I can make you a brainbox or a cretin, I can reinvent you as I choose. If I like, I can (buttering a piece of toast, breaking off an unbuttered crust to give to me) get *you* to tell the tale – T-A-L-E not T-A-I-L, dum dum – thereby hangs a *tail*, she said, grabbing mine. I can make you an unreliable narrator, a lying doggo, so to speak – hey, come back here at once, and stop that noise! So sorry about her (out of the window to our new postman, retreating down the path), she likes to act the guard dog, but don't worry, her bark is a million times worse than her bite. Believe me, she wouldn't hurt a fly!

# THE WHEELCHAIR TENNIS MATCH

They are picking blackberries. At the end of the garden, beyond the sycamores and the laurels and a dispirited green-stained fence, lay a piece of waste ground. Poll doesn't know who owned it. It was sandwiched between their garden and the next but belonged to neither. To nobody, they thought. To them. It was used as a lavatory by all the children in the road although to the casual passer-by it must have looked impenetrable because of the bramble bushes. These were enormous: tall, wide, dense, circular. White and sweet-smelling in May; dull and green in July; murderous in September when defending their fruit from raiders. In September, the children's legs and arms bore witness to the frenzy of repeated attack: in embedded thorns, in loud weals, in untidy tears and rusty smears, in precise razor cuts beaded with blood.

They were not deterred. They – Poll and her younger sister Annie and their whole gang of six-year-olds (Julie, Nicko, Peter, Jen, Rosemary, Rachel) ate all day. They ate anything, everything. Stealing from garden to garden – their parents' gardens; the gardens of deaf, blind and infirm neighbours – they descended on vegetable patches and orchards and laid waste. The earth-clogged, the worm-holed, the mouth-drying, the throat-burning, the colicky-unripe, the fizzily fermenting, the gone-to-seed and -to-flower, everything.

But on this particular afternoon, the one Poll remembers, their gang is elsewhere. She and Annie are alone, and their visit to the wasteground official. Like the Flopsy Bunnies, they have been sent by their mother to gather blackberries for a pie. To this end they each carry a small wicker basket, and into these go one blackberry in perhaps a dozen. The rest and best they put into their mouths.

From time to time they stop to compare hauls, shaking the baskets to allow the berries to settle; removing the green, the red, the wizened, the mouldy – plus flecks of bramble leaf and grasses that got in there somehow. Quarrelsome children, for once they are not quarrelling. On this dizzy afternoon the heat and silence and their absorption are condensed – so it seems to Poll now. But it cannot quite be silence. Under their feet crackles the dead bracken that is always to be found in this place, and the air around them hums with the annoyance of their competitors: with last-gasp wasps, and senile-demented bluebottles.

'Want a sausage?'

They don't hear him until he speaks. But when they turn, there he is, between them and the gate to the road, a man with a red face and a pale uniform, standing still, breathing fast.

'Want a sausage?'

(Poll thinks now that if they hadn't eaten so many blackberries they would have said, 'Yes,' and gone up to get one. It would have been the natural and logical sequence for children who ate everything, for whom sausage and mash was a favourite food.)

They stare at the man, and suddenly his hands, hanging innocently at his sides, move to the front of his trousers where they fumble, undo, release, pull out – what? Something that springs up, as a Jack from a box, as a genie from a bottle. And at once the hands catch it and close on it and, fast and furiously, polish it.

'Come 'n' get it, come 'n' get your sausage.' The hands fly away, and up it springs again, double the size now, this dark, thick, curving, waving – sausage?

An alive sausage, then! A sausage with a life of its own! A terrifying life. They must have decided this at the same moment, for at the same moment they run – or rather trip, scramble, fall, leap, fight their way – to the fence. Poll's basket is hooked off her arm by a passing bramble, but Annie hangs on to hers, and the blackberries fly after her in a little black cloud as she goes.

The man doesn't attempt to follow them. (Safety in numbers, their mother said later.) It's his stillness that chases them through the fence, into the smelly ditch beneath the fence, up the bank, over the mossed and plantained lawn, where they hear him call: 'Hey! Don't you want your sausage? You never had your sausage!'

He must have been an American GI, their mother said as she stung iodine into their wounds, or possibly a Canadian. She deduced this from the pale uniform they described, from the accent they couldn't place. Now – this was important – had he touched them? Had he done anything to them? Their mother encircled the two of them with her arms, she crushed them against her, she took their breath away.

But – the soft voice of sympathy was exchanged now for the anger of relief – how many times did she have to tell them they mustn't talk to strangers, mustn't take anything from strangers? Ever ever ever. How many times?

But they didn't! But they hadn't!

Hadn't? Didn't? What was this then?

In Annie's basket, nestling in what was left of the puréed blackberries, lay a packet of biscuits, not a make they know. US Army ration biscuits. How did they get there?

Well, into the dustbin with them, horrible, disgusting, sordid, contaminated biscuits! Ugh!

The following day, feeling peckish, they disinterred the packet, shook off its shroud of tea leaves and apple cores and margarine wrappers, tore it open and bit into the first biscuit in the pile. Waste not, want not, as Granny P, their mother's mother, would say.

The biscuit was warm and stale. It collapsed corruptly on their lips as though it had been dunked in tea. It stuck to their teeth and clung to the roofs of their mouths. It refused to be spat out.

*

The child who was murdered was called Kelly. She was six years old. Blue-eyed. Pale-skinned. Fair, wispy and fine-haired. On her chin, a little scar – an indentation you might call it – the result of coming off her scooter in Meadow-sweet Close. (Her mother maintained she was pushed by one of the Boulter boys, Barry probably.) A bright child, if not obviously academic: since starting school in the autumn she had not learnt to read, although she was perfectly cap-able of reading and knew her alphabet, her teacher said. A pretty child, whose smile was spoilt, according to some, by protruding top teeth.

A popular child? Sociable? Friendly-like? Sergeant Mackie flipped a page of his spiral-bound notebook.

Oh definitely. A merry little soul, always in the thick of it, if you get my meaning.

So. So I'd be right in thinking she'd be one to talk to a stranger then? To go off with a bloke she didn't know?

Oh no, never. Joan were always telling her. We all did. We was always telling the children –

Nevertheless, on the evening she disappeared, Kelly had been sighted licking an ice-cream cone on the corner of Shelston Road, and talking to a man. Two people had seen her – Sue Phillips and Jackie Morris. Jackie Morris said the man was red-haired. Neither of them had thought anything of it at the time. The Shelston Road post office and shop, where all the children in the neighbourhood bought their sweets and ice cream, was only a few yards away. It was broad daylight, five-thirty or thereabouts on a July evening; the turning into Meadowsweet Close – where Kelly lived – was less than a two-minute walk; there were no roads to cross; the sun was shining . . .

Jackie Morris told Sergeant Mackie she wasn't worried because she thought the red-haired man was Kelly's uncle, Dave something from Birmingham way. He'd been over visiting once or twice. She thought it must be him, like as not. Kelly hadn't looked upset and she hadn't thought anything of it. She wished she had now! She wished to God she had now! (Jackie M. put her head in her hands.) She was never going to be able to forgive herself, she told Sergeant Mackie.

The last-known person to speak to Kelly was Alan Prentice, shopkeeper of the Shelston Road shop. She'd wanted an ice cream, Mr Prentice told reporters, but she was a penny short. He'd had to count out the change she had on her and explain. In the end she'd bought some loose sweets – cherry bootlaces was one item, if he recalled correctly. He'd given her a paper bag and she'd collected the sweets herself, as was the custom in his shop. Then they'd reckoned up together on the counter. But she was disappointed, he said, she'd wanted an ice cream. Now he regretted he hadn't let her have one, and to hell with the money. If he could put the clock back, this old phoney said on camera, he'd give her all the ice cream she could eat, and she'd never have to pay a penny for it.

Poll didn't know Kelly and her family. She read the reports in the local paper ('Have you seen this little girl?' the headline said, above a smudged, laughing image that already fixed Kelly as a victim); she saw the coverage on the regional TV news. Interviews with Alan Prentice, with neighbours, school teachers, school children. Interview with Kelly's parents, Joan and Harry Taylor, slumped together on their living-room settee, Kelly's dad's arm around his wife's shoulder, Kelly's mum's eyes swollen and closed, her hands twisting in her lap: 'All I can say is – if you've got Kelly – if you're watching – bring her back – please – bring our baby back.'

Poll didn't know Kelly and her family. She and Ned, who'd been married about a year at this time, lived in another part of the town, just off the centre, in a Victorian terrace Poll – though not Ned – liked to pretend was Georgian. Poll was expecting their first baby, and perhaps because of this, perhaps because of all those increased hormones that play havoc in some pregnancies, triggering off food fads and sickness and heightened sensitivity, Kelly and her fate affected Poll more than they would otherwise have done. Watching the TV reports, reading the *Gazette*, Poll frightened herself into believing that Kelly was an omen, that whatever happened to Kelly might, in time, happen to her own unborn child. Another thing she did, only slightly less morbid, was allow her imagination to suppose that had she and Ned been married long enough to have a child Kelly's age, that child would have been at school with Kelly, her best friend even, aware now of Kelly's absence in the playground, her empty desk in the classroom.

Poll allowed herself to imagine this, but it was nonsense. She and Ned and any child they might have had would never have known Kelly. Kelly lived in Meadowsweet Close, part of a network of Closes and Drives and Ways that made up the Shelston council estate of pebble-dashed Fifties semis and bungalows. Her father was a bus driver, her mother a dinner lady at Shelston Road Primary, the school that Kelly herself had been attending. Poll and Ned were professional people. Ned was an architect, newly qualified. He worked for a firm in the High Street, but had plans to set up his own practice. Poll was an assistant librarian in the new public library. The new library, double the size of the Edwardian building it replaced, had been designed to cater for the influx of Londoners that light industry was about to bring, was already bringing, to the town. The surrounding chalk hills, grazing land for centuries, were being carved and crisscrossed, dug up and cemented down, to make way for the housing estates and trading estates the Londoners would need, for schools and shopping complexes, for a church and a crematorium. Ned's firm had been the architects for the library – a concrete and plate-glass construction with a flat roof and blue laminate panelling let in between the ground and first floors – and sometimes Ned would pop in in his lunch hour and lean on the counter and ask cheerful and confident questions, in front of Poll, of the other librarians. How did they find the shelving? The lighting? What was their, what was the public's reaction to the Reference Section? (A circular area, and on a lower level, to the right of the entrance desk.) Oh fine, the other librarians would say, fine. Which was not true. The steps down into the Reference Section put some people off. They put off young mothers with pushchairs and old people with sticks. Wheelchairs couldn't go down those steps. No handrail put some people off. And none of the librarians liked the lighting, overhead fluorescent strip, bright white and dazzling. The nearest thing to daylight, Ned assured them, but it wasn't. Daylight doesn't give you headaches. No one ever had a headache in the old library. Poll thinks now that the other librarians lied because of her, because she was married to Ned; but also because in those days architects were gods you didn't argue with, and not the overpaid environment wreckers they're considered to be today.

Poll didn't tell Ned what the librarians really thought of his library, but she quizzed him about other recent building, stuff his practice was not responsible for. The council houses on the new estates, for example, that appalled and depressed her – he didn't approve of those, did he? I mean, why did they have to have flat roofs? Why couldn't they have had chimneys? No chimneys gave them a concentration-camp look, surely he must agree?

They didn't have chimneys, Ned explained patiently, as to a small child, because they didn't have open fires, or solid-fuel stoves to cook on. They had central heating and electric or gas cookers. Central heating was not only more effective, it was cleaner, it was labour- and time-saving. Who these days wanted to shovel coal and coke? Not the people on those estates, you could be sure of that. And why should they? When their fathers had spent a lifetime digging coal, when their great-great-grandfathers had, in all probability, spent their childhoods climbing chimneys? To stick a chimney on the side of a fully centrally heated house would be a lie, Ned told her, a sentimental lie, a sort of fake *nostalgie de la boue* if you like. Ned should have been a teacher, Poll sometimes thought. He had the power to open up and expand; he had the authority, when he chose to use it, to shut down and stamp out.

Poll and Ned had an open fire, in fact there were fireplaces in nearly every room of their Victorian terrace house, though they didn't use them all. They were living in one room while they decorated. Or rather undecorated. A spare, comfortless elegance of white walls and polished boards was what they were aiming for. In the evenings, as soon as they were home from work, they'd put on dungarees and get out the sander and the Nitromors and the blowtorch. Poll was always the first to flag: being pregnant made her back ache, and the smell of the blowtorch made her throw up. She was too tired, and felt too sick, to cook what her mother-in-law called 'proper' meals. They'd flop on to the lumpy chaise longue Poll bought in a sale, and eat a bacon-and-egg sandwich and watch television.

'The body of a small child, believed to be that of Kelly Taylor, missing since last Tuesday, was today found buried on wasteland near her home. She had been sexually assaulted and repeatedly stabbed.'

Poll had not forgotten about Kelly when she and Ned saw and heard this on the national TV news. It would have been impossible to forget her in a town like theirs, which, for all the expansion and development going on (the new 'trial' one-way traffic system round the centre was exercising tempers, and legs, that summer), was as yet no more than a market town. She had not forgotten about Kelly, but she had pushed her a little to one side, in the way of these things; 'on hold' she would say now, though the expression was meaningless then. What everyone in the town was consciously, or unconsciously, doing was waiting. For the confirmation of fear. No one in the library, no one Poll had spoken to in the street market and at the ante-natal clinic, believed Kelly would be found alive.

'Why?' Poll asked Ned when the news was over; when they'd seen an Identikit impression of the red-haired man police wished to interview (Kelly's uncle had been eliminated from enquiries: he and his family were away from home on a holiday camp holiday; he and his wife had won an Old Tyme Dance competition the night his niece went missing); after the camera had homed in on a small tent set up over the body, to allow for essential forensic tests to be carried out before the removal of the body. 'Why do men do it?'

'Don't look at me,' Ned said. 'It isn't all men.' He had no idea, he said, why some men, some sick, mad, men, did it. Any more than he knew why some women consistently cuffed their children, and slapped their faces.

Ned said this with feeling. His own mother had been a cuffer and an ear-boxer, a whacker and a slapper. 'Habits like those are hard to break in families,' Ned told Poll when they decided to get engaged, 'they reinforce themselves, they continue down from generation to generation. But I'm aware of it, I know the damage violence can do. I shall never hit my children.' (And he had not.) This bruised childhood Ned seldom spoke about moved Poll. It was a cause of her loving him; it was one of the reasons she'd married him.

'Don't look at me,' Ned said again – because Poll was looking at him. She was examining his ordinarily handsome, usually gentle, occasionally tense, face. Because the men who did it, it often came out, were not monsters. Not everyday monsters. For every loner oddball who kept an arsenal of sawn-off shotguns in his living room, and whose crime, when committed, came as no surprise to anyone, there were all these ordinary men. Family men, solicitous husbands, caring fathers, thoughtful neighbours. Men who were liked at work, who were active and respected in the community. Church-goers, team-games players, all-rounders, men of whom neighbours would be prepared to swear: No. Not him. He could never have done it. Not him.

Yet he had. Yet they did.

And women did not. Women did not sexually assault, and torture, and then murder, other women's small children. Whatever they might do to their own, whatever else they were capable of, not this. (After the Moors Murders, Poll had to reconsider her verdict, but came to the conclusion Myra Hindley was a one-off, and that the essential truth of it still held.)

\*

When Poll's children were old enough (Zoë arrived two years after Caro, Nadia five years after Zoë); when they were, in turn, old enough to run outside and play, Poll told them a cut-short and watered-down version of the sausage episode, and she also told them about Kelly. Not to scare them – she managed to contract Kelly's abduction and murder into a sentence – and not to put them off men, though Ned said she was in danger of doing just that, but to make them aware, to make them wary, to protect them, to put them on their guard. Isn't this what all mothers do?

'Kelly lived in this town,' she told Zoë, when Zoë was six or so, 'in this very town.' (This must have been before they moved, five miles out into the country and into the house Ned designed and built, when Nadia was one.)

'Kelly is a rather dreadful name, don't you think?' Zoë enquired innocently. Darkly.


A hundred years later, or so the passage of time since her daughters' babyhood seems to her when it does not seem the mere blink of an eyelid, Poll is waiting for Zoë, her and Ned's second daughter ('middle daughter,' Zoë sometimes says, jokily reproachful, 'middle, unwanted, unloved daughter') who's coming home for the weekend. An unusual occurrence? No. Zoë comes home regularly at weekends. The need to restock her London larder with food from her parents' larder is one reason for returning; a desire to renew her acquaintance with her mother's washing machine and tumble dryer, is another. This weekend is a special occasion, though. Tomorrow, Saturday, is Zoë's twenty-second birthday. She's driving down from Wandsworth to spend her birthday with her father and her mother, and then on Sunday afternoon she'll drive back again to Wandsworth and celebrate with her friends. Scabby, a stained-glass designer and one of the people Zoë shares a flat with, is organising this celebration. Zoë, who often brings friends and, sometimes, enemies with her at weekends – Poll can remember an occasion Zoë brought eight of these, on the train, without warning her mother beforehand; though to be fair this was a long time ago, Zoë wouldn't do that now – isn't bringing anyone with her this weekend. She said so this morning, before breakfast, when she telephoned Poll. She said, Poll thought she said, 'It'll be just me; should be home about eight. But remember it's Friday, and you know what the traffic's like on Fridays. Okay, Old Neurotica?'

And for once Poll stopped herself. For once she did not come out with any or all of the following: Go carefully. Don't speed. No speeding. Don't give a lift to anyone. Keep in the inside lane. Don't fall asleep on the motorway. Don't stop on the motorway. She did not pass on to Zoë the fog warning she'd heard on the early news, and she did not sing out to her, in a zany, cartoon-character voice: Take care-are! Be smarter than the average bear-are!

Poll's children are kind to her on the whole about her anxiety. Even nicknaming her 'Hypercool' or 'Old Neurotica' is not really unkind, is more a joke, Poll knows, a way of defusing the problem, though it does annoy them sometimes. Nadia is the one who gets most annoyed. She is the youngest, seventeen. When Nadia goes to stay with her friend Danielle, and Poll rings to see if she got there safely – Poll doesn't put it that way, naturally; she thinks of an excuse: something Poll meant to ask her before she left; something Nadia asked Poll to do while she was away, and that Poll has forgotten, or is pretending to have forgotten – Nadia is annoyed. And embarrassed. Take last time:

'Why are you ringing me?' Nadia asked, and then, when Poll had trotted out her excuse – the Doc Martens Nadia had left on the stairs that did, or did not, need mending: 'You're not ringing about them. You're just checking up if I got here.' Why d'you do this? You'd soon know if I hadn't.'

'All mothers worry about their little darlings,' Poll said, light and bright as may be, 'it's natural.'

'No they don't. It isn't. Not when they're big.' She was sorry, Nadia said, she couldn't talk now, she was tied up at the moment and had to go – she and Dan and Dan's boyfriend Martin were in the middle of a Bondage Sex session in Dan's bedroom. When they'd had enough of that, they'd be mainlining in the lavatory. They'd be using Martin's needle, but it was okay, she told Poll, there was nothing to worry about – Martin had only had one gay relationship. And she'd be back home on Wednesday, always supposing she wasn't raped and murdered on the train. 'Bye-eee!'

(When Nadia returned home after this visit, she told Poll what had really happened. They'd been eating supper when Poll telephoned, and as soon as the phone started ringing, at the very first ring, Dan's mother had said, with a tight little smile, 'That'll be your mother, Nadia, wanting to know if you got here all right.' Everyone present – Dan, Dan's mother, her Auntie Vi, her two brothers, her boy-friend Martin – had laughed. No way was she prepared to go through that sort of humiliation again, Nadia told Poll.)

Nadia always makes jokes about Poll's fears – jokes that have a sharp edge. A serious person in many ways, she refuses to be serious when Poll needs her to be. She refuses to be serious about AIDS, about the danger of contracting HIV. Well, Poll may be neurotic, but all parents fear AIDS, don't they? All caring parents preach safe sex nowadays, surely? To their teenage children. Take Nadia: she looks sexy, she is sexy; she likes boys. Does she sleep with boys? Poll isn't sure, but according to surveys most seventeen-year-olds do. A lot of fifteen-year-olds do. 'You must get yourself properly kitted up,' Poll has told Nadia, 'just in case.' Nadia should carry condoms, wear a Dutch cap. She should never never have sex without double protection – 'You don't know where that boy's been!' Poll's offered to go with Nadia to the Family Planning Clinic; she's offered to make Nadia a private appointment with her own gynae-cologist. 'Give us a break!' is Nadia's usual response to her mother's care and understanding. 'What d'you think I am? An easy lay or something?'

Zoë is kinder than Nadia about Poll's anxiety, and more tolerant. But she is older. Twenty-two tomorrow. On the table of the dining area is a pile of the gift-wrapped consumer semi-durables Zoë asked for and Poll has bought for Zoë: a wok for the stir-fry Zoë and her friends are into at the moment; a stoneware teapot for the herb teas they brew up night and day; an oil lamp so they can see what it is they're eating and drinking. In the larder is the sad cake with twenty-two candles Poll made yesterday.

'What a sad-looking cake!' Ned said last night when he encountered it on a brief fact-finding tour of the larder shelves. 'Who's going to eat it all? Is Zoë bringing someone down this weekend? Lyn, for example?'

Poll was surprised Ned asked this question. The last time Zoë brought Lyn down Ned had, according to Lyn who complained afterwards to Zoë, as good as made a pass at her. Leered, at any rate. Lyn hadn't liked it. To begin with she'd thought it was a joke, and then when she realised it wasn't she'd hated it.

'What balls,' Ned said when Zoë confronted him with Lyn's accusation at supper one evening. (He'd given her the opening, he'd asked: 'What news of your blonde friend, whatsername – Lyn? We haven't seen much of her lately.') 'What balls,' Ned said at supper. 'I was only doing my hostly duty; I was merely being attentive and hospitable to a pretty girl.'

'That's it, that's exactly it,' Zoë said. 'A pretty girl. If she hadn't been, you wouldn't have taken any notice of her. You didn't take any notice of Evie, who, I'd like to remind you, was also here that weekend. But then she isn't blonde, and she hasn't got legs that start under the armpits.'

'Hey pardner – come to my defence.' Ned appealed to Poll, up the other end of the table.

Poll wasn't sure she could. She hadn't liked Ned's attentions to Lyn either: the quick glances, the protracted stares, the eager, flirtatious teasing, the ready laughter (when nothing funny had been said); and then, on Sunday, his seeking out of Lyn in the garden where she was sunbathing, and squatting down beside her naked back, and showing her his designs for the Business Centre. Poll had watched this from the kitchen window as she cooked lunch. She hadn't liked it. But she'd thought: He's only making a fool of himself, boring her, being ridiculous. Poor old Ned.

Then she'd remembered that of the women she knew whose husbands had left home, three had been thrown over for girls young enough to be their daughters.

Poll didn't support Ned that night at supper. Instead, she gave him a search-me, leave-me-out-of-this, could-just-about-be-seen-as-jokey, shrug.

'Your mother gobbles up all the young men you lot bring to this house,' Ned said. 'Boys, I should say, beardless youths. Now that's disgusting, if you like.'

'Not true,' Nadia said. (Poll wished she hadn't.) 'She talks to them. She asks them about themselves. Some of them may fancy her. That's not the same thing.'

'I'm being got at' – Ned returned to his cheese soufflé and stabbed it with his fork – 'by a coven of witches.'

'Didn't know a coven could be three,' said Nadia, pausing to drain a glass that was already empty of wine. 'Dunno why but I had this sort of idea there had to be thirteen to make a coven. A coven of three is news to me – sounds like poetree, hee hee hee hee,' said Nadia, who never knew when to stop.


When Zoë said, 'Should be home by eight,' Poll thought at once: I won't begin to expect her till eight-thirty. After all, she might be late leaving. There might be roadworks, a contraflow system, somewhere on the motorway. There nearly always is. Also, she might have to stop for petrol on the way. Let's make it a quarter to nine then. Poll told herself this, she prepared and protected herself; but here it is, eight-twenty only, and already she's starting to feel twitchy, to smoke more than she normally would, to drink more than she usually does, to get those fears that, without invitation, will fly into her head at such times, and nest there.

How do you know Zoë's on her way down from London

at all? these nesting fears enquire. How can you be sure she got back to her flat after work in the first place?

Zoë is a painter, her work is painting. She paints portraits to commission. She goes into people's houses and flats and offices with her painting kit, plus the camera she uses as an *aide-mémoire*, and sets up her easel and paints. The number of sittings varies, but it's never many – Zoë's good at getting a likeness. Another thing she paints is murals – muriels she calls them – on bathroom and lavatory walls, on garage doors, and she prefers these commissions because they allow for invention and imagination, they leave room for the exotic and the erotic, the zany and the bizarre. She's going to do a mural for her parents when she can find the time. Poll wants it in the kitchen. Her idea is to take down all that open shelving Ned designed, and have nothing on the wall except Zoë's muriel. Where would she put the saucepans and dishes, etcetera? (It was Nadia who asked this.) Well, she'd chuck most of them. They didn't need half the stuff they had; they only used a fraction of the stuff they owned.

Zoë likes what she does, and she earns enough, most months, to get by. The disadvantage is, you can't get hold of her in the daytime, as you could if she, say, worked in an office or a bank. There's never any knowing where Zoë might be. She could be anywhere in London, or in the country. She could be up a track or down the motorway. In the clutches of a rapist; on the bed of a canal.

When Zoë left art school and, because she did not want to teach or apply her art to industry, came up with the portrait-and-murals combo, Ned and Poll were supportive, although Poll foresaw possible dangers for Zoë in her chosen lifestyle, and certain anxiety for herself.

'You must never go anywhere without leaving your address and telephone number with someone,' Poll warned her, 'and you ought to meet your customers first, preferably in company, before going to their homes or whatever.' (Poll was thinking of that young woman, Suzy Lamplugh, the estate agent from Putney, who – some years ago now –

went to meet a 'Mr Kipper' at a house in Shorrold's Road, and was never seen again.) Zoë should, ideally, keep a book of her appointments by the telephone in her flat. So that if she didn't come home, people would know where to look for her.

'By people, you mean you,' Zoë said.

'Some of your clients will be unknown quantities,' Poll told Zoë, 'who've contacted you through advertisements. They may not all be bona fide. Some of them may have something other than a portrait or mural in mind.'

Most of her customers were women, Zoë told her mother, who wanted portraits of themselves or their children as a present for their husbands. None so far had seemed to want sex with Zoë; none so far had tried to murder her. 'But okay, Hypercool, I'll leave a note of where I'm going.'

Poll doubts that Zoë does this.

Well, did Zoë get back safely from her portrait or mural, or from the studio she shares in Ealing, today? Did she? It's eight-thirty. Poll will phone the flat and find out. No, she'll wait till eight-forty-five. Zoë might ring her before then: sometimes, if she's later than she says she'll be, she rings Poll from the service station on the motorway.

No, Poll will do it now. And put her mind at rest.

Poll lights a new cigarette and goes through to the living area. (She can't make a call without a cigarette; she can't receive a call without one. As soon as the telephone starts ringing, Poll's searching for a pack, a lighter, an ashtray. There've been occasions when the caller has rung off before she's managed to get these items into line.) She pressbuttons Zoë's number. In Zoë's flat the telephone rings twice, then: 'Hi,' says Zoë's voice, 'Jeff, Scabby, Jules and Zoë aren't around at the moment to take your call, but if . . . ' Poll replaces the receiver. She won't leave a message. She doesn't want to hear any more of Zoë's ghost voice.

In the past half-hour the living-area windows have turned navy blue. Late September. Poll dreads the winter. Not the cold, that doesn't bother her, and she prefers naked trees to clothed ones – no, it's the fog and ice she dreads, the invisible roads, the skids, the pile-ups, the Motorway Madness, as the media call it.

But at least today was sunny. It didn't rain. The forecast fog didn't materialise. The roads must be dry. Poll will put the potatoes on now because Zoë could be here at any minute.

On her way to the kitchen Poll stops in the hall and puts her head round her husband Ned's study door. Ned's study has a door, one of the few rooms – areas, as Ned prefers to think of them – in the house, which he wanted to be as open plan as English winters would allow, that has. It's a light and airy – cold, Poll often thinks, beautiful but cold – building, due largely to the vaulted hall and glass roof at its centre. (This glass roof – it's too big to be called a skylight – is a trap for birds' droppings and nesting materials and has proved impossible to clean.) Instead of doors, Ned used archways and varying floor levels to divide his areas. The effect is attractive, but the different floor levels can be hazardous. When Poll's Aunt Lucy comes to stay, Poll has to follow her everywhere with warnings: 'Careful! Two steps down here!' or 'Beware ramp ahead!'

Ned is in his study, not at his drawing board, but at his computer. Playing with it. Feeding it, as though it were a baby in a high chair. The white walls are bluetacked with photographs and drawings. Above the drawing board are photographs of Erno Goldfinger and some of his creations: the Trellick Tower (that Poll hates), Alexander Fleming House and the *Daily Worker* building. Below these is a collage of recent Oxbridge architecture, at the centre of which stands its architect, Richard MacCormac, president of the RIBA and Ned's current hero. (Poll's hero too, as it happens, not so much because she admires his Blue Boar Court at Trinity, Cambridge, and his Sainsbury Building at Worcester, Oxford – although she does admire them – but because she thinks he's a devastatingly attractive man.) Round the walls are Ned's drawings for the proposed Business Centre in their town. He's been invited to submit these, but Poll imagines it's just a courtesy request; she doesn't think he has a hope of getting the job since it was his former practice, after all, that's responsible for the stained and crumbling concrete of the library – the library that the council are, at this very moment, threatening to close and possibly demolish.

Ned doesn't share Poll's pessimism. He's confident. He's a doer and a trier, someone who doesn't give up easily, if at all; someone who goes for it, who – his expression – 'says Yes to life'. (Ned's going to be County Architect when Andrew Pinsett retires – 'just you wait and see'.) Poll respects this attitude when she's not annoyed by it. She wishes she had it herself.

'Hallo there,' Ned says without turning round, 'you've just managed to screw up my jump instruction. Is supper ready?'

'Zoë isn't here yet.' This isn't a moan. This is a bright and breezy statement of fact, the way Poll says it.

'Do we have to wait for her? She probably won't be here till ten. And I want to watch the movie.' There's a Chabrol film on tonight – *La Femme infidèle*, or *Le Boucher* – one of those. They must have seen it at least three times. How on earth can Ned want to sit through it again?

'She said she'd be here by eight. It's twenty to nine now.'

'The traffic's awful on Fridays,' Ned tells his computer, calm and casual. 'Look, if you're going to the kitchen, could you get me another whisky? Just a small one. I'll be through in ten minutes.'

Calm and casual. Calm and comforting. Comforting?

Ned will never discuss Poll's anxiety. He ignores it, he pretends it doesn't exist. Perhaps he thinks it's the best way of helping her, or perhaps he doesn't care. Whichever it is, a part of Poll would like to goad Ned into feeling anxious. To really feel it. To weep with anxiety. To scream with it. She would like him to scream, just once. And isn't it possible that if he were ever anxious, and showed it, she herself would not be?

In the kitchen, Poll scrubs potatoes and puts them on to boil. She places three rainbow trout and some butter and a piece of fennel in a pan. She washes and drains a lettuce, she crushes a clove of garlic, she makes a French dressing. Eight-fifty-five. She takes Ned his whisky. She comes back to the kitchen and pours herself one – her second. She lights a cigarette – her fifth since eight o'clock. She walks through to the living area. Scabby and Jules and Jeff may be home by now and know if Zoë left on time, or at least where she is. In the living area, the telephone rings before Poll can put out her hand.

'Hi there!' Zoë's voice.

'Zoë! Where are you?'

'Zoë? Zo-ie. Thanks a bundle. You're enough to give anyone an identity crisis. I shall tell my analyst about this. It's not Zoë. It's one of your other daughters, your daughter Caro as it happens, calling long distance to talk to her mother who never calls her.'

'Oh Caro! Oh darling!' (Disappointment can sound like relief, can sound like joy, if you try hard enough. Poll believes this.)

Poll's daughter Caro is ringing her from California, which is where Caro lives. She is married to Joel, a Californian and a farmer, whom she met in London when Joel was over on a sightseeing trip. (It was a pick-up, though Poll has never told her friends that. 'They met socially,' Poll tells anyone who wants to know how Caro and Joel got together.) Joel farms grapes and oranges. He and Caro have twin sons, Denzil and Jan, nearly three years old. Poll last saw her grandsons when they were eighteen months. On the table beside the telephone are framed photographs of the boys taken at Christmas; one is laughing, one serious, both are curly- and fair-haired, like Joel. Poll thinks it's Jan who's laughing, she's pretty sure about this. Ned says could be, but what difference does it make?

When the twins were born and Joel telephoned with the news, Ned – who up to then had never hinted that he was anything other than thrilled to have three daughters and no sons – said, with astonishing bitterness, 'Trust Caro to have a son, two sons, first go. She always gets what she wants.

Always.' An eruption which made Poll wonder if there were other things, profound and substantial things, in Ned's life or in their lives together, he might be dissembling about.

Poll talks to Caro over the air waves; Caro talks to Poll. Poll tries not to give Caro any sense of her anxiety, any idea that, just at this moment, she wishes Caro were Zoë. And in any case she's been waiting for Caro's call. The last letter Caro wrote was over a month ago. Six weeks is about as long as Poll can manage without news. After that she begins to feel edgy. To wake at three and not to go to sleep again until six-thirty (twenty minutes before the alarm goes off). To accost or avoid the postman, depending on how the superstition of the day dictates. To jump at the phone, and – why not? Caro might have decided to fly over on a surprise visit – the door bell. Even so, even with all this hyper-anxiety going on, Poll won't ring Caro. Not yet. Not till she's desperate. This is in case there's no one in when Poll telephones. This is because Poll once tried to reach Caro in her faery land forlorn for six days and nights without success. Forlorn! the very word is like an unanswered telephone bell. Where could she, where could they all, be? Out shopping – at midnight? At an all-week disco – with the twins? At the bottom of a lake? (There is no lake where they live, but they do have a pool, a small one, for cooling off rather than swimming in, that Joel dug for his family last spring.) Where were they? Oh where?

Two years before, Ned and Poll had spent their annual holiday on Caro and Joel's farm, in their one-storey, wood and plate-glass, ranch-style farmhouse. As Poll, for the umpteenth time, sat in her living room with her ear pressed to the receiver, listening to the forlorn ringing, she pictured Caro's house and Caro's living room. She made a tour of it. She picked up a painted decoy duck she'd admired; she felt the blade of an old Sioux dagger Joel's grandfather had left him; she stared at the rough stone chimney-breast she and Ned, sleepless on a futon in the back bedroom, had agreed was somehow acceptable in California. She made herself examine the ugly yellow piano Joel plays jazz on, and the bookshelves of unreadable books (on sea-fishing and canoeing, on jazz trumpet and jazz piano) she'd wondered about on their visit. Then she walked through to the kitchen, and out again on to the porch. She leaned over the rail and called them: 'Caro! Joel!'

In front of Caro's porch, a dusty track stretches away to a group of eucalyptus trees. Each evening of her stay, Poll had watched the sun go down behind those trees. She examined the trees now, she watched their leaves shiver and dissolve in the hot wind. She called again. She went back into the house.

What happened next, what she found in the house, she told no one, although she imagined telling Ned. In her imagination she cornered him, and sat him down and told him, 'I won't describe what I found there. I can't. Reread Truman Capote's *In Cold Blood* if you want to know. See the film, if there was a film. I think there was. Watch any TV chiller documentary. Read the report of any horrific, random killing any day in any newspaper, if you want to know what I found in our daughter's ranch-style house.'

Poll got hold of Caro eventually. They'd been away. Of course! She and Joel had taken the boys to Maine for a week, to stay with Joel's sister Ellen – a fishing trip, for Joel. The boys had loved it. And the sharp air, the 'really green' grass, had made Caro homesick for England. Poll didn't mention Truman Capote to Caro, or any of it. All she said was, she and Dad had been a bit worried not knowing where they were.

Caro's exasperation came across in measured, emphatic patience: 'Mum, I'm a grown woman. I'm a marr-ied wo-man. A moth-er. I'm sorr-y I forgot to tell you we were planning this trip. But. But really! I can't tell you everything we do! And don't drag Dad into this. He's not an hysteric, he's cool.'


Poll and Caro have nearly finished their conversation. Caro has just been telling Poll that Denzil, poor old love, has been in bed all day with a bad headache and a high temperature, and Poll has resisted making any mention of meningitis. She is about to pass Caro over to Ned, who has tucked up his computer for the night and is standing by her elbow.

'Just before you go, Mum, is Zoë with you? I believe it's her birthday or something.'

Poll tells Caro, yes, Zoë is expected home for her birthday, but she hasn't arrived yet. She says this in as light and casual a way as she can muster because Ned is standing at her elbow.

'Don't worry about Zoë for heaven's sake,' Caro says. 'She'll be fine. She has the most highly developed sense of self-preservation of anyone I know.'

Poll wasn't worrying about Zoë, not until Caro mentioned her. For the ten minutes or so she was talking to Caro, Poll almost forgot Zoë. Now she has to worry again. It's nine-fifteen.

While Ned is talking to his eldest daughter, Poll goes back to the kitchen, the place dictator Nadia insists ought to be a mini-ecosystem – 'in fact the whole house ought to be,' Nadia told her parents. Poll's kitchen was far from being a mini-ecosystem, according to Nadia. Her fridge and freezer were full of CFCs, her cleaning cupboards bursting with phosphate-ridden detergents and cleaning fluids and aerosols, her larder a poison cabinet of E-numbers and additives. Last Wednesday when Nadia came home from school she gave her mother a lesson in environmental awareness. She scoured the kitchen drawers and cupboards and threw out the worst offenders. She removed the plastic rubbish sack – 'unbiodegradable' – and replaced it with four strong recycled paper carriers which she labelled Bottles, Cans, Paper, Veg. All bottles must go to the bottle bank in the town, Nadia instructed Poll, all cans to the recycling depot, ditto. Poll is not unaware, as it happens, she's been meaning to separate refuse in this way for some time, and she's doing her best now with Nadia's strong paper sacks. But they take up a lot of space and they aren't strong enough. Broken glass pierces them; wet potato peelings rot them. And what time has she got for all these trips to bottle banks and recycling depots? Nadia is unfair, also: Poll's been taking her newspapers to the Save the Children Fund collecting point for years.

In her born-again kitchen, Poll drains the potatoes, what's left of them, and turns the fish. (The heat must have been too high, the trout have jumped out of their skins, their eyes are hard and opaque with surprise.) She takes a clean white tablecloth from the dresser and puts it on the table. She lays the table for three. (Is it tempting fate, when you are expecting someone for supper, to lay the table before that someone has arrived?) She takes candlesticks down from a shelf, she fetches a jug of Michaelmas daisies from the sideboard; she smooths ruckles from the altar cloth. (Altar cloth? No, tablecloth.) She tops up her whisky. She lights a cigarette. Why does anyone have children?

It's quite dark now. And no welcoming outside light on for Zoë! Poll walks to the front door to remedy this, then she opens the door and steps outside.

Poll's and Ned's drive is steep and short. Too short to be called a drive. A driveway, then. She walks down the short steep driveway to the road. When they first came here there was a gate at the entrance, an old farm gate Poll liked, it gave a feeling of rurality, it added a sense of history to the neo-Modernist house that Ned built. But the gate was too old and fell to bits, and now only the gateposts remain.

It's a clear, bright night. Stars, no wind. There could be frost later, Poll realises. She walks into the road. After three whiskies – is it three? – she isn't drunk, just light-headed. Just heavy-hearted. Zoë, where are you?

At the end of Poll's residential road, a farm track when they moved here, is the B-road that cuts through the village, that cuts the village in half. This road is a lot busier than it was when Poll and her family moved here. In those days most of the traffic was agricultural: tractors and ploughs and hedgecutters and silage carts and combines – efficient mud-sprayers that kept your windscreen well greased in winter months; bulky and inexorably slow movers that came between you and any chance of catching the London train. Now the traffic's all sorts of – surprisingly speedy – things: tankers and containers and articulated ten-tonners, cars pulling caravans, cars pulling horse trailers, cars pulling boat trailers (the Water Theme Park at Longmere is only a mile away), and, Fridays-thru-Sundays, the big, high-powered estate cars weekenders drive. When Poll moved here, the villagers would ride their bikes along this road; they walked their children and their dogs along it. Poll had done so. Walkers could stop and chat to neighbours over garden hedges in those days.

Poll stands outside her gateposts and watches headlights on the B-road. They sweep down the hill, black out where the new barn conversions block them from her sight, snap on for the cricket field, off again where the church conversion towers above everything – off on off, like neon signs, like programmed Christmas tree lights. A hundred yards from Poll's turning the road bends sharply, and faint-hearted drivers – women – slow here; drivers bound for Poll's turning have to slow here, they have to slow and change down. Poll follows the Christmas tree lights, she listens to the engine notes. Wait! Even now a car is slowing for the bend, changing down, roaring, slowing right down, turning . . . Headlights swing up and over the hedge, graze it with technicolor, isolate a wheelie dustbin, turn their attention on Poll, dazzle her. Zoë!

The car, sleek and city clean, bound for the Thompsons or the Porters or the Blackwoods or the nameless couple who moved into the Old Pigsty six months ago, and whom Poll has still not asked in for a drink, glides by.

Walking back up the driveway, very slowly, head down, hugging herself, Poll sees more lights. Two tiny penlights this time, under a bush. A cat, the cat, Zoë's cat – that her parents look after now Zoë lives in London. He throws himself at her feet and then rolls on to his back, crying piteously, something he does when he wants his stomach rubbed. (Is the appearance of Zoë's cat, now, at this moment – and crying – significant in any way? In any sinister way?) Poll scoops him up and he clings to her furiously, stabbing her in the neck and the shoulder.

At supper – for Poll has decided it can't wait any longer – Ned says, 'Why aren't you eating?' He bones his fish neatly and delicately, he takes his time squeezing a lemon quarter, twisting the pepper grinder, licking his fingers.

'I am eating.' (Not long ago, Poll is remembering, Zoë, driving back to her flat after an evening out, had to stop at a red traffic light, and a man tried to get into her car. He managed to open the passenger door, but the lights changed and Zoë sped away. Saved by a lucky light and a cool head. 'You must keep your car doors locked,' Poll told her, 'don't go anywhere without locking your car doors first.' 'Okay, Neurotica,' Zoë said, 'but what if I'm in an accident and unconscious and the car's on fire, how's anyone going to get me out in a hurry?')

'This is rather nice wine' – Ned congratulates the bottle, tapping it with a finger. 'Really quite drinkable. Where's Nadia, by the way? Shouldn't she be here? Shouldn't you be worrying about her?'

'She's still in Newcastle,' Poll reminds Ned. Nadia went to Newcastle on Wednesday on a school field-trip. They went by coach, and Poll suffered beforehand envisaging bald tyres and a drunken or sleepy coach driver, an overweight coach driver all set to have a heart attack at the wheel. The party was due back today but Nadia decided to stay on an extra night with a student friend in Jesmond and is coming home tomorrow for Zoë's birthday. (She actually let her mother know this change of plan.) Poll cannot worry about Nadia now because she's worrying about Zoë. She's still thinking about that man at the traffic lights. She's wondering: Is Zoë always lucky? Is her head always cool?

'Where are you off to now?' Ned asks Poll.

Fear, like love, like the state of being in love, turns bowels to water. As a cure for constipation, fear is more efficient than any purgative or enema.

'I don't know how we've managed to bring up our children so badly,' Ned complains when Poll returns from the lavatory, 'so that they don't even have the courtesy to ring when they're going to be late. So that we have to wait two hours for the privilege of eating a piece of desiccated fish. Where did you get it, by the way? Trout farm or supermarket?'

'Trout farm,' Poll says. A lie. At the trout farm you have to stand there accessory while a brides-in-the-bath maniac, wearing protective clothing, does his stuff – that is, nets a swimming, leaping, living creature; electrocutes it in a basin, disembowels it, weighs it and slides it into a mortuary bag. At the supermarket the fish are already in the funeral parlour when you make your identification, decently laid out on parsley pillows in bright white styrofoam coffins. Nadia, who is vegetarian, insists that it's a cop-out to buy fish this way – when they are too dead and too decorated to accuse. If Poll's going to eat them, then she should at least have the guts to witness their execution, Nadia says.

'Zoë usually rings me if she's going to be late. She usually does. And it's her birthday tomorrow,' Poll adds. Irrelevantly, pathetically.

'You're not really worried about her, are you?' Ned pushes his plate away, hacks at a sweating tower block of cheddar, topples it, slaps a wedge of pre-stressed concrete on to a biscuit.

'She said eight – or thereabouts. She said she'd be home for supper. It's now' – Poll looks at the kitchen clock, a schoolroom clock it used to be, which has stopped (did she forget to wind it?) and then looks at her wrist – 'after half past ten.'

(Not long ago, a friend of Poll's, Janet Bowman, had been waiting in just this way for her son Robin to turn up. She'd decided not to worry, she told Poll later, she'd given herself all sorts of plausible reasons for Robin's non-appearance. Then, as the hours passed, she had worried. When a car finally did arrive, it was a police car. Robin had been nineteen.

These things happen; tragedy happens. Fear is no insurance policy, calmness is no protection. Neither Janet's calm nor her fear had protected Robin from the lorry that crossed the central reservation. The line between everything being all right and everything being all wrong, for ever, is just a hairline. A hairline crack. A thought which reminds Poll that Caro and her family live on top of the San Andreas Fault.)

'What do you want me to do?' Ned asks, refilling Poll's glass, refilling his own, 'ring the police? What exactly do you want me to do? Our children, like all children, I daresay, change their plans; they forget to say. I don't know how often they do this, but you never learn from it. You imagine the worst, every time. Why? It's masochism, it's a sort of sickness. I don't know if I can cope with it much longer. I think you need professional help. I think maybe you should give psychotherapy another try.'

This is better. Ned coming out into the open. But Poll doesn't want to go to a therapist, she'd rather talk to Ned about her worries. She did go to a therapist for a time, for post-natal depression after Caro arrived, but it hadn't helped. The therapist had appeared more depressed than Poll, and Poll hadn't enjoyed talking about herself, which was what he'd expected her to do. In the end, she just stopped going.

Poll puts out her hand across the table and touches Ned's hand, which shrivels back up the tablecloth and curls into a ball like a hedgehog.

'All right then,' Ned says, 'let's examine the problem. Let's go through it. What exactly is it you fear? Is it another update of the Kelly syndrome? Tell me.'

Poll tries to examine the problem, she tries to pinpoint her fear. Her conclusion is: I fear everything for those I love. But that will not do for Ned, so she says, 'Well, there's the motorway, and Zoë tired and, you know, not concentrating. Driving too fast, falling asleep. There's that . . . ' Poll nearly tells Ned, but decides not to, her other motorway fear, which is that Zoë's fourth-hand Renault will break down and Zoë have to pull on to the hard shoulder – a death trap at the best of times – and make a call from an emergency phone and then, like that poor tragic Marie Wilkes, wife and mother and expectant mother, be stabbed in the neck from behind while talking to the police from the phone.

'You can't go through the driving bit every time,' Ned tells Poll, 'it makes the children's lives, it makes our lives, a misery. Roads are dangerous! Life is dangerous!'

'Zoë's written off two old bangers already,' Poll reminds him, 'but you didn't let me finish. What I was going to say was, we don't even know if she got back from work all right, do we? The message on the answering machine could have been an old one, they often don't bother to change it.'

'Try the flat again,' Ned says. 'See if one of the others is there.' (Ned has not taken on board the names of Zoë's flatmates. He can never remember that they're Jeff, Scabby and Jules.)

'It's the weekend. They decamp at weekends.'

'Don't be negative,' Ned says. 'Try it,' Ned says, positive and firm.

Poll lights a cigarette, her third in the past half-hour, before leaving the kitchen.

In Zoë's flat the telephone rings four times. Last time Poll tried, the ansaphone cut in after only the second ring, so Poll hangs on, and eventually, 'Yes?' Scabby's voice, breathless from running down all those never-swept stairs to the hall.

'Scabby, it's me, Poll, Zoë's mum. Sorry to bother you. Do you happen to know where Zoë might be?'

Silence. The silence of disappointment? Scabby has an unreliable boyfriend, Zoë once told Poll, someone who plays waiting games, who blows hot and cold and lukewarm.

'Thought she was with you. Thought she said she was goin' home this weekend.'

'When did you last speak to her?'

'Let's see – must a bin yesterday mornin'. She wasn't here last night.'

'What do you mean?'

'Well, this guy whose bathroom she's decoratin' lives miles out, Kent or Sussex or somewhere. She said, I think she said, she'd stay the night if she was tired or somethin'. She musta done.'

'Have you got an address or number for her there?'

'Sorry?' Scabby sounds amazed. 'Look, I'm sure she'll be fine. She probably worked late, wanted to start early this mornin' so she could get done by the weekend. If she turns up here first, I'll get her to phone you, shall I?'

'Yes. Yes if you could. Yes please.'

'But why didn't she tell me she wasn't at the flat when she rang this morning?' Back in the kitchen Poll asks Ned, 'Why didn't she tell me where she was?'

'Why should she? She probably thought you'd panic, which is what you *are* doing. I wouldn't tell you anything if I was her. She's a grown-up woman. She's twenty-two, for Christ's sake!' And Ned hits the table, and pushes it, and gets up, and picks up Poll's nearly empty cigarette packet and chucks it at her. 'Smoking eighteen of these since I got home is dangerous if you like, and for me, too, the poor abused passive smoker.' (Ned and Poll prove all those surveys which say that more women than men are smoking now; that men, even when they're hardened smokers, can give up, whereas women can't.)

'D'you want milk in yours?' Ned is saying from the work top and the electric kettle. Poll nods. She's trying not to notice his jaw, which is working – tightening and contracting – the way it does when he's angry; the way it does when he wants to keep his anger under control. Some lines of a poem have just flown into her head and are nesting there:

> Because I love her
> The sky is dark above her,
> Because I think her fair
> There is menace in the very air,
> A single leaf on the tree
> Is not more frail than she . . .

This poem, or part of a poem, is what Ned quoted to Poll in the first love letter he ever wrote her. The poem – he couldn't remember its author – expressed, he wrote to Poll, exactly what he felt: that merely by loving her he had, in some inexplicable way, put her in danger. Of course reason told him she'd been perfectly all right, was quite capable of looking after herself, before he'd met her, but now the fact of his love, plus the fear he had of losing Poll, put her at risk. Made her vulnerable. 'By loving you I tempt fate,' he wrote. Poll remembers being touched by this letter which she'd kept in her bag and read and reread until it fell apart – and she'd liked the poem. She'd understood the poem.

She also remembers, later on and in another mood, thinking there was something egotistical and paternalistic and patronising about Ned's sentiments – and the poem's. Other poems, to do with love and loss and the fear of loss, had followed it; all had stopped after they were married. After they were married, the poems vanished, to be taken up, presumably, by other young men in love, until dropped by them. (Poll once read an article in *The Library* which said that, in England at least, only the very young and the very old and the so-called in love read poetry from choice.)

'Don't just sit there – say something,' Ned says. 'Drink your wine, drink your coffee, tell me your fears, let them all hang out.'

Is Ned drunk?

'I'm worried that Zoë might have got herself into something, is with someone, she can't handle –' Poll stops. She's just remembered that this morning, while she was talking to Zoë on the telephone, she'd seen a magpie from her bedroom window. A solitary magpie parading its sorrow under the beech tree on the lawn. Throughout her conversation with Zoë she'd kept her sights on this magpie, hoping against hope that its better half would join it; that Sorrow would, as it were, be surprised by Joy. It hadn't been. The magpie was still mooching under the beech tree when Poll

345

replaced her receiver; it was still unvisited ten minutes later, when it flew up into the tree.

'Forget about yourself for a moment,' Ned says, 'forget about your own hangups and think, if you can, about Zoë. I'm going to open another bottle,' Ned says, and does so. 'Think about our daughter. What sort of person is she?'

'Zoë is . . . ' What? Frail. As a single leaf on a tree.

'A creative person, naturally. But not arty-farty. Not wet. She's got her feet on the ground, she's tough in lots of ways. She can be tough with men.' Ned pauses. 'Remember how she got rid of those two wimps? Derrick, was it? And Kit.'

'Nat.' (But they weren't wimps. Nat wasn't a wimp. And Zoë hadn't got rid of him, he'd got rid of her. Another thing Poll knows about Nat: he beat Zoë up once, when he discovered she'd gone out with someone else. Zoë hadn't come home for a month afterwards. She didn't want her father to see the bruises, she'd told Poll; she thought the sight of them might send him bananas, that he'd go after Nat with a shotgun or something.)

'You're not listening,' Ned says, 'you're not thinking.' He refills Poll's glass; he drains his own. 'You don't want to see reason. You don't want to be comforted.'

'I do. I really do.' Poll reaches for her wine glass, and in so doing knocks over her coffee cup, still full. She sits there while Ned mops up round her, the way she used to mop round their children when they knocked their milk beakers over at tea time.

'I'm sorry,' Poll says, 'I can't concentrate because I'm listening for a car. I just want Zoë home. That's all I want,' Poll says.

'You probably shouldn't have had children,' Ned says seriously and thoughtfully. Drunkenly? 'I see that now. Having children — and I don't mean giving birth to them, I know all about that — takes guts. The guts to nurture and protect, and then let go. To withdraw. The guts to keep calm in a crisis.'

How true! How very true!

'And this isn't even a crisis. It's either a misunderstanding

346

on your part, or thoughtlessness on Zoë's. Or a bit of both. The truth is, you don't always listen to what people say, you're too busy worrying about something else, anticipating some new disaster, to listen.'

Ned has the ability to put his finger on aspects of Poll's character, on truths about it, that can make her blush. The truth is, she doesn't always listen. When she gets lost on a car journey, for example; when she winds down the passenger window and leans across the empty seat and hails a passer-by. If by some stroke of fortune the passer-by is not a non-English-speaking stranger to these parts, he or she is usually keen to set Poll on the right track. People like having a sense of importance thrust upon them; they enjoy doing their good deed for the day. 'Go to the end of the road,' the passer-by tells Poll, 'turn left at the second set of traffic lights, take the third, no, fourth turning left, and then at the roundabout . . . ' While the passer-by is talking, Poll will be concentrating hard – on the passer-by's dentures; on a tulip-red front door behind the passer-by; on a tortoiseshell cat washing itself on the step; on a small boy with a football who might be about to chase it into the road. The passer-by comes to the end of the instructions and repeats them. 'All clear then? Got it now?' And Poll will say, 'Yes! Yes, and thank you so much for your help. Yes, I've really got it now.' The passer-by nods and smiles, and Poll will get into gear and pull away – to where? For she won't have taken in a word. It won't even be that she wasn't listening. It will be that she chose not to listen. A positive decision. Why?

'I don't want to be unkind,' Ned says, 'but there's something distasteful about your anxiety, you know. Something unlikeable, and fake. You have three healthy daughters. You have a part-time job you've told me you enjoy. You have, if I may say so, a more than decent roof over your head. You've had no real worries – so far. What do you know about fear? What do you know about pain?'

Ned points to the pinboard on the wall, the wall where Zoë's muriel should be. Will be. On the pinboard is a lot of – mostly out of date – stuff: invitations and bills and memos, a felt-pen speaking likeness of the Queen that Nadia drew when she was five; and also (what Ned's pointing at) an assortment of curling, yellowing cuttings from newspapers and colour supplements. Vietnamese boat people, massacred students in Tiananmen Square, leukaemia victims of Chernobyl, Kurdish refugees burying their dead in mud, a skeletal, flyblown child clutching a hopeless bowl, accuse Poll from this pinboard. Dictator Nadia pinned them there. 'To remind you you're lucky, Neurotica,' Dictator Nadia said as she fixed a new enormity to the board.

What impertinence! What cheek! What intolerable and mistaken cheek! These images have never made Poll feel lucky. Sad is what they make her feel. Appalled. Fearful. Angry. Uncomfortable. Hopeless and helpless. Guilty. Not lucky at all.

'No one can be coerced into feeling lucky,' Poll told Nadia. 'The lucky feeling is one which, like joy, arrives unbidden and then bathes and blinds you in a sort of – '

'Bathes and blinds you, eh? Wow,' Nadia said. 'Is that a poetry quote? Wowee.'

'You shut up and listen to me,' Poll told Nadia. 'I was being serious. I was about to give you an example of what I mean. I was about to tell you something that happened to me.'

'Okay then, I'm listening.' Nadia sat down at the kitchen table. She folded her arms, in a resigned way, on the table.

Poll told Nadia how once, on her way to work at the library – they were still living in the town then – she'd taken the longer route, the one she didn't often take, via the park. It was a hot day and the tennis courts were full. On one of the courts – Poll hadn't noticed until she was right in front of it – a wheelchair doubles match was being played. Four young men (late teens? early twenties?) playing tennis from wheelchairs. 'Not knocking up,' Poll explained to Nadia, 'not playing patball, playing a hard competitive game, a match.' Poll had stayed to watch for a bit. She was amazed that the wheelchairs could cover the court so fast, and that the boys dared to lean so far out of their seats to hit the ball, 'though they were strapped in, of course, and I think the chairs must have been specially designed – they had tiny seats and backs, they were all wheels really, chariots more than chairs' – Poll looked at Nadia to see if she was listening, and she was – 'and then after a while I noticed that they allowed the ball to bounce twice before hitting it – well, they'd have had to, wouldn't they? Even in those fast chairs. Still, I asked them about it. "Do you have a two-bounce rule?" I called to the boy serving my end of the court. "Yeah we do," he said, "yeah we do." The point of this story,' Poll told her captive audience, who had picked up an empty yoghurt pot from the table and was examining it intently, 'is that while they were playing I suddenly felt wonderfully, extraordinarily happy – and lucky. Lucky to be alive. Lucky to be watching this game. You couldn't feel sorry for the wheelchair players, you see, because they weren't sorry for themselves. You couldn't patronise them. They were saying Yes to life, as your father would put it, and in any case they were playing much better tennis than the ordinary people, the fit people, on the next-door court. I went off to the library soon afterwards, but this excitement, an almost revelatory excitement, lasted all day. Even now, when I'm down, I can draw on that tennis match. Are you embarrassed by this?' Poll asked Nadia. 'Do you find it embarrassing?'

'No,' Nadia said, 'no, it's interesting.'

'What I do know,' Poll said, 'is that if anyone had led me to that court and said, "Come and watch a wheelchair tennis match, it'll do you good, it'll make you realise how lucky you are," it wouldn't have worked. It was the chance nature of it all that did it, that and, paradoxically, the sense of fate I had, the feeling that there was a purpose behind my being there.' 'I can see that,' Nadia said, peering at her yoghurt pot, twisting it round, inspecting its outside and then its inside, 'but – if you'll forgive my saying so – it, the match, the fact of the match, didn't really change anything for you, did it? I mean, not permanently? Not, what's the word, fundamentally. It wasn't a turning point. It didn't stop you feeling anxious, did it? It hasn't altered your outlook on life in any way.'

Poll felt deflated. She got up suddenly and left the room. She wished she hadn't told Nadia about the wheelchair tennis match. Telling her was a mistake. Nadia hadn't understood it at all.

'I do feel fear for those I love, I do feel pain,' Poll's head is in her hands, her eyes are on her plate, 'I may not have a right to, but I do.'

'Let's go back to Zoë,' Ned tries again. 'She's cool and competent, sure, but at the same time quite a cautious person, wouldn't you say? Not really a risk-taker, not like Nadia. She's like you in that way. She takes after you in that.' Ned looks pleased with this insight. He drains his glass and refills it. He tops up Poll's glass. 'You don't need that cigarette,' he tells her, but not crossly this time, quite benignly and matter-of-factly.

'I do,' says Poll, who by automatic reflex while Ned was talking had glanced at her watch. Five to midnight, the watch said. Five to midnight. And where is Zoë? Zoë, where are you? Poll's hands are trembling. Her legs are shaking. Had she been alone she'd be pacing up and down by now, prowling; drinking not wine but whisky, swig after swig, glass after glass; smoking fag after fag, pack after pack. Ned's calm is keeping her from this necessary ritual; his presence is holding her prisoner in the kitchen, at the table.

'You're not an easy person, you know,' Ned says. 'It's not easy being married to a woman who's in love with her children. We've been sitting here God knows how many hours and you still haven't asked me – you haven't asked me once – how I got on at the doctor's today.'

'Oh Ned. Oh my God.' Ned's had a problem with his eyes lately, with his eyesight. A focusing problem. Also, and more peculiar, a reading and writing difficulty. It was hard to explain exactly, he told Poll a month ago when he first noticed it. It was just that he'd found himself reading words wrong, in newspaper articles and so on, and having to go back and reread them, to check. He'd been typing things wrong too and at first he'd thought there must be a gremlin in the word processor. Did he have headaches? Poll dreaded to know (the words 'brain' and 'tumour' had flown into her head and nested there), but Ned said not that he'd noticed, no more than usual. 'You must go to the doctor anyway,' Poll told him, 'we must get this sorted out.' He knew what the doctor would do – ban the booze, Ned told her gloomily. Then all of a sudden it had got better, gone away, vanished, just like that. And the same week Poll read a piece in the paper about eye stress and the contribution computer screens and VDUs make to this. She showed the article to Ned. 'That must be it then,' Ned said. He sounded relieved, but disappointed too. 'My job's supposed to be creating fashion, not following it,' he told Poll.

Then last week the problem returned. An intermittent fault, Ned concluded. He didn't sound too worried about it. 'Perhaps I need new specs.' Poll said nothing. She just went to the telephone and rang the surgery and made an appointment.

'Tell me, quick,' Poll says. (How could she have forgotten Ned's appointment, after all those sleepless nights worrying over it? What sort of monster is she? Why didn't Ned remind her at breakfast that he was going to the doctor today?) 'Tell me what he said. Tell me what he did.'

'There's no hurry about that, there's very little to tell you, we'll talk about it in a moment,' Ned says. 'I haven't done with Zoë. I was saying she isn't one to court danger any more than you are. Isn't that true?'

Well.

Well no, as it happens. Not true. Not true of Poll.

Because once, a long time ago, after a day up in London seeing a friend and Christmas shopping, Poll had picked up, or allowed herself to be picked up by, a man, an American, on the train; had got off the train with the man (this was at the stop before her own station), had got into his car and driven with him out of the town; and then, in the entrance to a field, made love to him and let him make love to her in his car.

Done it with him. Gone the whole way. Had sex with a stranger in a remote place in a car.

*Want a sausage? Want an ice-cream cornet?*

*Yes.*

Still, it was a long time ago. Young people do do mad things sometimes, dangerous things, things they later wonder about and regret.

It was not a long time ago – not long enough. Poll had been a woman, not a girl, at the time. A wife, at the time. A mother of three.

Poll has never told Ned about this. If he ever found out, he'd leave. If Ned knew, it would confirm his belief that the victims of rape are seldom entirely innocent; that there is always some measure of provocativeness, albeit unconscious, on the victim's part, and therefore of provocation.

An outrageous belief. Six-year-old Kelly, those teenage girls pulled from bicycles and assaulted in ditches, those octogenarians raped at knife point in their own beds by midnight intruders – provocative?

'I did court danger once.' It's Poll's voice, a drunk version of it, saying this. 'I did, you know.'

'Well, you can tell me about it in a minute,' Ned says, 'because I think I heard the telephone.' (Poll can hear it too, now.) 'Shall I answer it? Or do you want to?'

'You.' Poll hasn't the strength to talk to detective sergeants or brain surgeons at the moment. She can't manage a conversation with a life-support-machine monitor. No. She will sit here and wait. She will sit at the table, numb and dumb and deaf, and wait for Ned to return and tell her the worst. Whatever it is.

But after Ned has left the kitchen, she gets up and glides, a zombie or a sleepwalker, into Ned's vaulted and galleried hall and through the archway to the foot of the iron staircase – from which position it is not difficult to overhear what is being said by a speaker on the living area telephone.

'Thank God for that,' Ned is saying. 'No, of course I

352

wasn't watching the movie. What happened to you? Where are you now?'

Silence from the living area, silence in the hall, while Ned is told the answers to these questions; while Poll releases a long, exhausted, wonderful breath.

'Oh I seeee,' Ned says at last. 'Well, I wish you'd tried again. It wasn't off the hook, it was Caro. What? I can't hear you. Oh I see. I told your mother she must have got it wrong. She'd got it into her head you were coming home for supper, so . . . No, I am not drunk!

'I'm sure you did if you say so,' Ned says.

'Well I was a bit worried, if you want to know. Just a bit – it's catching.

'Oh yeah, of course she was. Oh absolutely, a nightmare evening. Complete panic stations. She had you dead and buried, dead anyway.

'Yes. Yes I did. Thank you for asking . . . I can't go into all that now, we'll talk about it when I see you . . . No – look Zoë not now, it's late. No, no, no, she doesn't. No. Do you want to talk to her? She's in the kitchen. Okay, I'll tell her. Yup. Oh, by the way, happy birthday! What time shall I tell Mum we can expect the birthday girl tomorrow, give or take an hour or six?'

Laughter from Ned. Laughter from Zoë too, probably.

Time, Poll thinks, for her to leave the hall. Time for her to speed back to the kitchen and turn on the hot tap and get stuck into the washing-up. Then, when Ned reappears, the table will be cleared, the plates and glasses stacked, and there she'll be, brisk and sensible in the sink. Getting on with life, saying Yes to it.

'Zoë's all right.' She says this aloud. Not on the motorway embankment with her throat cut, not gagged and tortured in a rapist's lair; alive. Alive, and laughing and joking on the phone to Ned.

Poll stands swaying at the sink, and hot water, a balm, flows over her hands and her wrists. She is free to think lucky thoughts now; she can conjure up a wheelchair tennis match if she wants to; or she can remember Zoë's birth, twenty-two years ago today; she can picture Ned, a constant among the masked and gowned comers and goers in the delivery room, squeezing her hand, giving her gas and air and courage. And she can listen to him, hear him – as Zoë arrived – shouting: 'It's a boy! Oh no, whoops, sorry, it's a girl.' (This is Zoë's favourite story about herself. On the one hand it illustrates her subtlety and ambiguity, on the other it proves her 'poor, unloved, unwanted, middle daughter' theory.)

Poll is free to say 'Thank you' now. She can thank heaven and her lucky stars and God.

Thank you God.

Thank you God – except. No. No, she will not allow herself to dwell on negative things. The fact that Zoë isn't here yet, for instance; the knowledge that Nadia (who also has to get home tomorrow, on dangerous British Rail track, on a dangerous British Rail train) is taking her driving test next Wednesday and with Nadia's luck – and Poll's – will pass it. Nadia's plan to fill her year off between school and university crossing Africa by Land Rover and alone is not a fit subject for contemplation at this lucky minute. And if Caro and her family choose to live on top of the San Andreas Fault, well, good luck to them! So do millions of other intelligent people. There are a lot worse places to live than Southern California, for heaven's sake!

But there's something else, isn't there, not listed in Poll's catalogue of anxieties? Around the edge, below the surface, at the back of the mind, on the tip of the tongue, unfinished, threatening something. She's trying to focus on it at this moment, she's trying to worry it out of its hiding place and into the open, so she can examine it and deal with it.

She's still doing this when Ned comes back to the kitchen and stands in the doorway and leans there, his eyes shut, his arms tightly crossed, hugging himself. Hugging a secret, it occurs to Poll. Hugging a dark secret, biding his time.

# HIGH TEAS

It was over tea that Mrs Peverill had her weekly skirmishes with the vicar. Unsatisfactory skirmishes, where no ground, it seemed to her, was ever gained. The teas, the skirmishes, had come about this way: a year before, at her daughter Imogen's insistence, Mrs Peverill, in her late seventies, long widowed but only recently infirm, had moved from a big old house in the North-East to a little new house in the South-West. The village, five miles from the market town where Imogen and her family lived, had been chosen because it was large enough to support a Church of England church and a High Street of shops that between them purveyed meat, groceries, wine and tapestry wools. There was even a miniature Lloyds Bank.

More than anything else, it was the shortness of the walk to church that appealed to Mrs Peverill. She had been uprooted. She had left behind in Yorkshire all that survived of a lifetime's friends and enemies and acquaintances. She was in need of spiritual solace.

What she could not know was that the church notice-board by the lych gate, whose comforting promises, in black and gold, of Morning Service, Holy Communion and Evensong she could (if she leaned out a little way into the almond tree) see from her bedroom window, was a relic merely. By the time Mrs Peverill arrived in Upton Solmore, the service that prevailed at St Werburgh's was one entitled Family Eucharist.

That first Sunday when, in good faith and in good time and carrying her father's prayer book and *Hymns Ancient & Modern*, Mrs Peverill stepped into the porch, she was handed ('They were forced upon me,' she told Imogen later) a small, red, laminated notebook and a revised *New English Hymnal*.

Mrs Peverill had known, of course, of the existence of the new services, but they had never been a threat to her. At home in Yorkshire, the rector had said he was too old to learn new tricks, and his Parochial Church Council had been determined not to. The trial offers of *Series 2* and *3*, and later, of *Rites A* and *B*, had been speeded back whence they came. (A few years earlier the *New English Bible* had met with a different fate – relegated, within six months of its introduction, to a shelf in the vestry broom-cupboard, where Mrs Peverill had encountered it each time her name came up on the cleaning rota.)

In her pew at the back of the church, Mrs Peverill opened the red notebook and turned its pages in dismay and disbelief. They were printed in alternate blue and black type. The service was to be conducted by someone called the President. The prayers and responses, when not new and unfamiliar, had been chopped and changed almost beyond recognition and appeared to be in the wrong order. God was addressed throughout as 'you'. The Nicene Creed began 'We believe . . . '

When the service was over, Mrs Peverill stumbled out of the porch close to tears, and did not hear the vicar's words of welcome or notice his proffered hand; but later in the week, on Friday, at tea time, he came to call. He followed her into the kitchen and stood jingling his pockets while the kettle boiled, and then he carried the tea tray into the sitting room.

'You've managed to make this room most attractive already, I must say!' the vicar said. 'It was rather sombre when old Jerry Cartwright lived here.'

'Thank you,' Mrs Peverill said. She wasn't at all sure she liked the idea of the vicar having an earlier knowledge of her house and her sitting room.

'This cake is really something!' The vicar beamed. 'Did you make it yourself?'

'In Yorkshire,' Mrs Peverill said, 'which is my home, I was used to making a fruit cake on Fridays, in case I had visitors at the weekend.'

'Old habits die hard!' the vicar said. He munched his cake with enthusiasm. Mrs Peverill sipped her tea.

'Pardon me for intruding' – the vicar put his plate on the tray and brushed crumbs from his trousers – 'but you seemed distressed after the Eucharist last Sunday. And then you rushed away before . . . ' He abandoned this sentence and tried out another: 'Have you some troubles you feel you might like to tell me about? A bereavement perhaps? A loss of some kind?'

'Yes,' Mrs Peverill said. 'Yes, I have.'

The vicar leaned forward, his hands on his knees. They were square hands. He was a stocky young man, whose upper arms bulged in the sleeves of his blouson jacket. A muscular Christian, Mrs Peverill decided. He peered at her expectantly. His eyes were very blue and round.

'I have suffered a loss,' she said, 'the loss of the *Book of Common Prayer*, the King James Bible and *Hymns Ancient & Modern*. This happened to me in church, in your church, last Sunday.'

'Oh dear, oh dear,' the vicar said. 'Oh dear, oh dear, oh dear, oh dear.'

'I had never been to a service of Rite A until then,' Mrs Peverill spoke very slowly, 'and I could not follow it. I did not understand it. Nothing, well, very little, was familiar. They have even altered the Creed, you know, and mucked about with the Lord's Prayer.'

The vicar smiled; he started to say something, but Mrs Peverill put up a hand. 'I felt, I feel – how shall I explain this? – robbed and cheated. Robbed of comfort. Cheated of drama and mystery. Of poetry.'

'Poetry?' the vicar said – as though, Mrs Peverill thought afterwards, she'd said something blasphemous ('as though I'd said something blasphemous,' she told Imogen on the telephone).

'Poetry,' Mrs Peverill said, and after that she was silent.

For the vicar, having got over his shock, was laughing. Not in a scornful way, but in a hearty and appreciative way, as at a good joke. From now on, Mrs Peverill vowed, she would keep her emotions to herself, and fight him on the facts.

'You left out the Comfortable Words on Sunday,' she said, 'though there was some sort of version of them in the notebooks.'

'Optional,' the vicar said. 'Optional.' He tried to drain his cup, but it was already empty. 'I do say them sometimes.'

Mrs Peverill felt obliged to offer him another cup of tea, and more cake. He accepted both.

'I think I understand how you feel,' he said presently. 'Some people, usually senior citizens like yourself, tend to have a bit of difficulty at first. But they get used to it, and when they do, they prefer it. Hopefully, you'll come to see Rite A as a refresher course to your faith, one that adds a new dimension of participation and corporate worship. The laity have far more to do nowadays. No chance of falling asleep while the minister does all the work for you!' He laughed. His teeth were very white, his gums very red. 'Anyway, the 1662 Prayer Book, that you set such store by, is a distortion, a *travesty*, of the 1549 original. The spirit of the new liturgy – one of celebration rather than sacrifice – is far closer, you know, to what Cranmer had in mind.'

Mrs Peverill did not know, and did not believe it.

'In what way, Vicar?'

'Tony, please,' the vicar said. 'We won't go into it now,' he continued heartily, rising to his feet, 'but I'll call again if I may, so that we can continue with our chat and, hopefully, iron out some of your problems. By the way,' he said at the door, 'we won't have to make do with those rather naff little pamphlets much longer. Our ASBs – Alternative Service Books – should be here any day now.'

At home in Yorkshire, Mrs Peverill remembered, watching the vicar jog down the path, the rector had once, over a post-PCC-meeting glass of sherry, asked the members for their interpretation of the initials ASB. '*A Serious Blunder*,

I imagine' – Miss Hawkley, the secretary, had drained her glass and reached for her coat – 'unless *A Synod Botch*.'


Mrs Peverill did not grow to like Rite A, let alone prefer it. A year later, she had, however – and this frightened her – grown used to it, in the same way that she'd become inured to, while not approving of frozen vegetables and decimal coinage. She kept her grief and anger alive by repeating, in church, the true, the only, Lord's Prayer and the Creed; and by responding 'And with Thy Spirit' when the rest of the congregation chanted 'And also with you'. She kept her grief and anger alive by thinking up, during arthritically wakeful nights, questions on doctrine and liturgy to tax the vicar with, and by devising traps for him to fall into. He had got into the habit of calling in, on his way home from weekly visits to the hospice, on Friday afternoons, at tea time.

'Tell me, Vicar,' she said invitingly, having waited until his mouth was full of cake, 'do you believe in the responsibility of the individual?'

The vicar nodded, being unable to speak.

'The new Rite does not seem to,' Mrs Peverill said. 'I refer to the Creed and this "We believe" business.'

The vicar swallowed. ' "We believe" is consistent with the new spirit of unity and sharing,' he said, ' "though we are many, we are one body" – you see.'

'No, not really. No, I can't say I do.' Mrs Peverill took her time and sipped her tea. 'How can I know what anyone else believes? I can only speak for myself. In any case, Creed comes from *credo*, not *credimus*.' In the night, when she'd planned the assault, the vicar had turned pale at this point, and run his fingers distractedly through his hair. In her sitting room, he remained rosy and unruffled and finished his cake without urgency. Afterwards he took a large and not especially clean handkerchief from his trouser pocket and wiped his hands and repocketed it. Then he beamed at her.

'You're a tease, Mrs Peverill. But I don't think this sort of – how shall I put it? – nitpicking, pedantry, over one small word is really helpful, do you?'

It was not pedantry, Mrs Peverill knew, it was passion; and the following Friday she renewed her attack.

'This Gradual nonsense,' she began as, having finished tea, they walked down the garden to inspect the herbaceous border she had recently planted. 'Every Sunday you announce: "The hymn for the Gradual is . . . " You can't have a hymn *for* the Gradual, you know. A Gradual *is*. What it is is an antiphon, sung between the Epistle and the Gospel, from the altar steps. You don't, we don't, sing it from the altar steps. Last week you stuck it in between the Gospel and the sermon. Moreover, there's no mention of it in Rite A – nor in the Prayer Book. It belongs, properly, in the Roman Catholic Mass.'

I've got him now, she thought, I've got him now. Confronted with this evidence, he will have to admit defeat. He will have to –

The vicar continued his progress along the path. 'The new Rite,' he said in equable tones, 'has been designed with a wider and deeper ecumenicism in view, and it allows, at certain stages of the service, for the personal discretion and preferences of the President. There's no room any more for a separatist approach. We live in a secular age. The Church is under siege. We must appeal, we must be seen to appeal, to all our brethren of no matter what denomination, to all who fight under Christ's banner. You're very brave,' he said as they reached the end of the garden, 'to plant perennials – all that splitting and staking. We go for annuals at the vicarage. The minimum of work, I always say, for the maximum of colour.'

Mrs Peverill could not always contain herself until Fridays to bombard the enemy. Sometimes she accosted him in God's house, or rather in His porch.

'No Prayer of Humble Access today, I notice,' she said tartly, shaking out her umbrella and then snapping it open. 'Your version of it, that is. Or is that optional too?'

'We were running a bit late.' The vicar smiled a benign smile. 'But yes, since you ask, it is up to me whether or not I include it. If you look at your service book you'll see that the words "all may say" precede it. "May", not "must". On the credit side, I trust you noticed that the Epistle this morning was taken from the Authorised Version – especially for you! You didn't receive the Eucharist today – I hope the old leg isn't playing you up?'

'I was not in a state of grace.' Mrs Peverill gave him a sharp look from under her umbrella, before braving the rain. 'I did not feel in love and charity with my neighbour.'

'I can never make out whether he's High or Low,' Mrs Peverill said on the telephone to her daughter Imogen. 'He says minister, not priest, but the bell rings before Communion and his vestments are all colours of the rainbow. High, I suppose. And Low. A bit of both.'

'I don't know why you go on with all this, Ma,' Imogen said. 'It isn't getting you anywhere. You won't get the Prayer Book back, or King James. You won't change anything.'

Mrs Peverill said nothing.

'You know I do get a bit bored sometimes with this litany of complaint,' Imogen continued, 'and it's not exactly Christian, is it? Baiting the vicar. He probably means well. No offence meant, Ma.'

Mrs Peverill said nothing.

'If I were a believer,' Imogen said, 'and if it were me, I'd be quizzing your Tony on the issues of the day – his stand on women priests, for example, his views on evangelicalism and homosexual clergy. Things that matter. There isn't a *Mrs* Vicar, by the way, is there?' she added darkly.

'History matters,' Mrs Peverill said coldly, 'language matters. A prayer book is a book of prayer. A service book, on the other hand, is the maintenance bumph one keeps in one's glove compartment –'

' "Kept" in your case,' Imogen said. 'You haven't got a car any more,' she reminded her mother.

'I bet you didn't know they've mucked about with the hymns as well,' Mrs Peverill said. 'You used to be fond of hymns as a child. I bet you didn't know that.'

'Did they have to alter the hymns too?' she asked the vicar over tea.

The vicar put his hands to his head, as if to ward off blows. 'Not substantial alterations, surely?'

'Last week we had "Lead us Heavenly Father", and while I was singing "Lone and dreary, faint and weary, Through the desert Thou didst go", you were all singing about Jesus being self-denying and death-defying and going to Calvary. Odd, isn't it, that we continue to address God and Jesus as "Thou" in hymns? They must get rather confused, I imagine.'

'Perhaps "dreary" is not the right adverb to describe Our Lord?' the vicar suggested, stretching a hand for a third piece of cake.


Mrs Peverill took the last silver-paper angel from the box at her feet and hung it on the lowest branch of the St Werburgh's Christmas tree.

'Angels from the realms of glory,' the vicar sang tunelessly in her ear, 'wing your-or flight o'er all the earth . . .' He was hovering at her elbow, waiting for her to finish her decorating so that he could test the fairy lights. These, a collection of alternate red and yellow bulbs strung along a chewed flex, were more giant than fairy, and too clumsy for the branches. They quite ruined, Mrs Peverill opined, the delicate effect she was wanting to create. She sighed.

'At home in Yorkshire,' she remarked, in the tone of someone determined to extol, to a present, unsatisfactory employer, the virtues of a past one, 'we had real wax candles on the tree. Candle flame sheds a holy light.'

'So you mentioned last year,' the vicar said, 'and I can only repeat: the fire risk is too dodgy.'

'Is it too dodgy to ask, Vicar, if we could have 1662 for Midnight Communion this Christmas? I am, after all, seventy-nine. It could well be my last . . . '

'I doubt that very much, Mrs P.' The vicar laughed. 'But it will certainly be my last Christmas – in Upton Solmore. I couldn't tell you before because I hadn't informed the churchwardens, but the fact is, I'm off to fresh fields and pastures new. I've seen the bishop. Merseyside will present a very different sort of challenge, of course, but hopefully one . . . '

Mrs Peverill did not hear the vicar's next words. She was in a state of shock. It was not his misquoting Milton – hardly a surprise from one who did not know an adjective from an adverb – that upset her, but the implication of his news. What would she do with herself in future on Friday afternoons? How would she endure her wakeful, painful nights? How would she fill her life at all?

'I shall miss your teas, I must say,' the vicar was saying when she'd found herself a pillar and enlisted its support, 'and our chats. But – who knows? – if the PCC deems fit, the new minister may reinstate a form of service that's more up your aisle.'

Mrs Peverill said nothing. The next incumbent would not restore the Prayer Book to St Werburgh's: the ASBs were already in the pews. Far more likely he'd be a rock guitarist *manqué*, and invite his congregation to sing *Lord of the Dance* for the Gradual. The devil she knew was, at least, unmusical.

The devil she knew moved the stepladder away from the Christmas tree.

'That looks great, Mrs P. Now for our Regent Street happening! If you'd like to turn off the overhead lights, I'll switch on the tree.'

Mrs Peverill reached up for her switch; the vicar bent to his. And in the second before the ancient Bakelite plug burst (setting fire to the flex and dispatching Tony to pastures newer, and more challenging, even, than Merseyside), the dark tree bloomed with a thousand candles; while on every branch – Mrs Peverill would later swear – angels from the realms of glory stood poised to wing their flight.

# THE DYING ROOM

I think I left my wireless in the drawing room, his mother said. Could you get it? I'd be grateful.

His mother and he were in the kitchen. He took a big breath. He said, You can't use that word any more, I'm sorry, we've decided.

What word are you talking about? his mother said. She took a tray of cheese tartlets from the oven and put them on the table. His mother is a cook. She cooks for her family when they're at home and she cooks professionally: for other women's freezers and other women's lunch and dinner parties. She also supplies, on a regular basis, her local delicatessen with pâtés and terrines and tarts and quiches. Blast, these look a bit burnt to me, his mother said. Do they look burnt to you? What word can't I use?

'Drawing room', he said. It's an anachronism, it's irrelevant. It's snobbish. It has associations with mindless West End theatre. It's embarrassing.

His mother said nothing for a minute. She looked thoughtful; she looked thoughtfully at her feet. Then she said, Who are 'we'? 'We' who have decided?

My sisters and I, he told her. Your children. All of them.

I see, his mother said. First I've heard of this, I have to say.

The point is, he said, our friends, the ones we bring here, find it offensive – or a joke. And so do we. It is offensive, and ridiculous, to continue to use a word that means nothing to ninety-nine per cent of the population, that ninety-nine per cent of the population does not use.

Hang on a minute, his mother said, I just want to get

this straight. You're at university, and most of the people you bring here, from whatever background, are students too. Are you saying that this doesn't make you an elite of some kind? Are you telling me that the words you use in your essays are the words ninety-nine per cent of the population uses? Don't look at me like that, his mother said. If you want to know, I don't feel that strongly about 'drawing room'; it's what your father called it, it's the habit of a lifetime, but you can break habits. I have wondered about it. The room in question is rather small for a drawing room. What word would you like me to use instead? 'Lounge'?

There were other words, he told his mother.

Are there? his mother said. What's wrong with 'lounge'? I bet 'lounge' is what ninety-nine per cent of the population uses. But if you don't like it, if its airport and hotel connotations bother you, how about 'front room'? Will that do?

The room his mother calls the 'drawing room' is at the back of the house and looks on to the back garden. It looks on to a square of lawn with three apple trees on it, two mixed borders either side and, beyond the lawn and divided from it by a box hedge, the vegetable garden: peasticks and bean poles and a rusty fruit cage and a potting shed. A cottage garden, his mother has always described it as.

I can't call it the 'morning room', his mother murmured, more to herself than to him, because we tend to use it mostly in the evenings. I can't call it the 'music room' because none of us plays an instrument, and because all those gramophones – those CD and tape-deck affairs – are in your bedrooms. To call it the 'smoking room', though when you're at home accurate, would be tantamount to encouraging a health-wrecking practice I deplore.

His mother was mocking him. She was, as usual, refusing to address the issue, a serious and important one. She was declining to engage with the argument. He said so.

Address the issue? Engage with the argument? His mother turned the phrases over and weighed them in invisible scales. Engage with the argument. Is that an expression ninety-nine per cent of the pop . . . ? Well, no matter. Where was I? I know, in the 'parlour'. I like 'parlour', I rather go for 'parlour'. It's an old word. It conjures up monks in monasteries having a chinwag, it conjures up people in ruffs having a tête-à-tête. Then there's the ice-cream side of it, of course – oh, and massage, and nail buffing and leg waxing . . . Which reminds me . . .

Oh for God's sake, he said.

I like 'parlour', his mother said. I think I like 'parlour' best. But on the other hand – *parlare, parlatorium* – a bit too elitist, don't you think? On the whole?

Look, he said, there are other names for rooms, ordinary ones, not jokey or archaic or patronising, that you haven't mentioned yet, that you seem to be deliberately avoiding.

If you mean 'sitting room', his mother said, I did think of it, it did occur to me, and then I thought, No, too safe, a compromise choice, with a whiff of amontillado about it.

It's less offensive than 'drawing room'. And it's more exact – people do tend to sit in rooms.

Probably it is for you, his mother said. You and your siblings and friends are great sitters. Great loungers and withdrawers too, I might say. But I don't have that much time for sitting. In the room that for the moment shall be nameless I tend to stand.

His mother was standing as she said this. She was standing by the stove, lifting the lid from the saucepan, giving the soup a stir. He was sitting on a chair at the table, lounging perhaps. He sat up. He stood up.

You haven't got an ashtray, his mother said, here, use this. By the way, his mother said, did I ever tell you about the misprint your father found in the local paper once? In an estate agent's advertisement? 'Five bed, two bath, kitchen, dining room, shitting room'? Or perhaps it wasn't a misprint, who can say? This soup doesn't taste of anything much, his mother said, come and try it. Come and tell me what you think it needs.

He took the spoon from his mother's hand and tasted her soup. It's okay, he said, it's fine, could do with more salt. The name you're avoiding, he said, the name we use, as you must have noticed, that we want you to use, is 'living room'. A room for living in. The room where people live. Graham Greene wrote a play about it. No, he said (for he could see his mother was about to interrupt him), there are no jokes to be made. I defy you to be satirical about this one. 'Living room' is accurate. And it's classless, it embraces all. The pathetic thing is (and he banged his fist on the table) it'd be impossible to have this argument anywhere else but here! It'd be meaningless anywhere but in Little England. Christ, what a shower!

Nineteen fifty-three, was it? his mother said, or nineteen fifty-four? The year I saw *The Living Room*. Dorothy Tutin was made a star overnight – don't think that sort of thing happens any more, does it? I'd seen her in *Much Ado* at the Phoenix, but . . . Look, it's accuracy I want to quiz you about, his mother said. Pass me that colander, would you. No not that one, the red one. Think for a moment – where are we having this conversation? If we can be said to live anywhere, it's the kitchen – except for your grandfather, poor man, who lives in the lavatory. No, we live in the kitchen and we make occasional forays – withdraw, if you like – into –

You're so clever, he said, you think everything can be reduced to a clever, silly, word game.

No, his mother said, no I don't, I just want to understand your motives, which I suspect are suspect.

Our motives, our motive, is clear, he said. There's nothing eccentric about it. We're egalitarians and we want to live in an egalitarian world. Drawing rooms – withdrawing rooms, as no doubt you'd prefer – have no place in that world. They have nothing to do with the real world as it is now. They have to do with privilege and power. They have to do with tribalism in the worst sense.

His mother took a bunch of parsley from a jam jar on the windowsill. Do come and see what these sparrows are up to! she said. Damn, you're too late, she said. She put the parsley on a chopping board. Then she took five soup bowls off the dresser and put them in the bottom oven. She straightened up.

He said, Look, doesn't it embarrass you when you say 'drawing room' to Mrs Todd, for example? Doesn't it make you feel uncomfortable? Doesn't it? It does us, I can tell you.

His mother looked astonished. She said, You astonish me. Why ever should it? It doesn't embarrass her. I'll tell you how it works. I say to her, Oh Mrs Todd, the children were down at the weekend, and you know what that means, so I think the drawing room could do with some special attention . . . or she'll say to me, Thought I might do the lounge through today, Mrs Symonds – kids home Sunday, were they? Point is, we have our own language, a language we feel comfortable in, and we stick to it. Both of us. Not just me. Don't think it's just me. But we understand each other. We do. And – though you may not believe this – we're fond of each other. We've got a lot in common. We're both working women, we're both widows. We've been seeing each other twice a week now for what? – fifteen years. I know a lot about her life, I know all about our Malcolm and our Cheryl and our Diane and our Diane's baby Gary – who's teething at the moment incidentally – and she knows even more about my life. I remember her birthday, and she – unlike some I could mention – always remembers mine. I went to see her when she was in hospital, and she came to see me when I was. She came on the bus the day after my op, and then later in the week she got Malcolm to drive her over after work. Malcolm's pick-up is very unreliable, you know. He spends all his Sundays working on it, but even so it invariably fails its MOT. If it isn't the gear box it's the brakes, and if it isn't the brakes it's the exhaust . . . I'm very much afraid Malcolm was sold a pup.

If you're such good friends, he said, if you know everything there is to know about Mrs Todd's life, how come you don't call her by her first name? How come she doesn't call you by your first name?

Ah, you can't catch me there, his mother said. The answer

is because she doesn't want it. I asked her once. She'd been here about a year, and I said, Mrs Todd, don't you think we've known each other long enough to call each other by our Christian names? Mine's Elizabeth, as I expect you know. And she said, Think I'd rather leave things the way they are, if it's all the same to you, Mrs Symonds. So we did. I did feel crushed at the time, I did feel a bit snubbed, but I don't think she meant to snub me. I really don't think she did.

About 'living room', he said.

Oh that, his mother said. If that's what you're set on, I'll give it a try. But if you want to bring Mrs Todd into line, I fear you've got problems – she's a 'lounge' person, definitely. 'Definitely' is another of her words. She says 'definitely' very often when I'd say 'yes'. Do you find your microwave has made life easier, Mrs Todd? I'll ask her, and she'll say, Oh definitely, definitely. It definitely do, definitely. Mrs Todd is a very definite person. If you think you can get her to turn her lounge into a living room, well, good luck.

I never said I wanted her to alter anything, he said. You're putting words into my mouth. I never said that. Of course she can keep her lounge. We want you to get rid of your drawing room, which is quite different. He hesitated. He said, We won't bring our friends here unless you do.

Can I have that in writing? his mother said. Joke, she said, when she saw his frown. Could you pass me that baking tray please. Actually, Kit, I don't like your tone. Dictatorship and blackmail seem to be the names of your game. Why? Couldn't you wait for evolution to do the job? You won't have to wait long. 'Nurseries' – in houses large enough to have a nursery – are mostly 'playrooms' now. 'Studies' have turned themselves into 'telly rooms'. 'Drawing rooms' are dying even as we speak. By the time my generation is under the sod, the only 'drawing rooms' left will be in palaces and stately homes. Truly, you won't have to wait long.

If you want to make yourself useful, you could lay the table, his mother said.

What I don't understand, his mother said, is why you have to be so heavy about all this. If your friends don't like the vocabulary I use, couldn't you make a joke of it? Couldn't you just tell them your mother is an eccentric old bat? That sort of confession would improve your street cred no end, I should've thought.

There isn't any point in going on with this, he said. There isn't any point in trying to have a serious discussion with you. You're the personification of the English disease, the English upper class disease, of superciliousness. Everything you've said this morning, and the way you've said it, is offensive, but you can't even see it, you can't even hear it. If you knew the way you sound to ordinary people! 'Our Malcolm' and 'our Joanne' – mocking and superior, that's how you sound.

Diane, his mother said, Diane, not Joanne. I wasn't mocking, I assure you, I was borrowing. I was repeating. And who's calling who ordinary? No one's that ordinary. In my experience most people, when you get to know them, are extraordinary. Look, if you're not going to lay the table, d'you think you could stop hovering and sit down?

I didn't mean 'ordinary', he said, I meant 'other'. Other people. You mentioned palaces and stately homes a minute ago, he said. What you don't seem to understand is that this place is a palace to some of the friends I bring here. In fact that's exactly what Julie said the first time she came down. She walked in the door and said, God, it's a palace! You never told me your mother lived in a fucking palace, Kit.

I don't get this, his mother said. First it's 'drawing room', then it's the way I talk, now it's this house. You keep moving the goal posts. Are you saying people shouldn't be allowed to live in five-bedroomed houses, in five-and-a-half- – if you count the box room – bedroomed houses in case other people, who live in two-bedroomed houses or flats, might think of them as palaces? Is that what you're saying?

I happen to know that Julie liked this house. She came down early one morning that first visit – you were still in bed – and had breakfast with me. She said, I really love this place, Elizabeth – it's magic. I'm going to live in a place like this one day. We went round the garden and she knew the names of everything. Monkshood! she said, my dad won't have monkshood in the garden . . . I was fond of Julie. She was a very nice girl. I was sorry when you gave her the push.

Martin found you frightening, he said. D'you remember Martin?

That's okay, I found Martin frightening, his mother said.

When I say 'frightening' I mean 'posh', he said. I met Martin in the pub the other night and he seemed a bit down and fed up with life – well, with his job really – and I asked him if he'd like to get away to the country this weekend. He wanted to know if you were going to be there. I said probably you would, it was your house. And he said, Well, think I'll give it a miss then. No offence, but your mother and her 'drawing rooms' and 'wirelesses' and 'gramophones' are a bit posh for me. He pronounced it 'poshe'.

Well that hurts certainly. Yes it does, his mother said. Could you come here a minute, I can't read this without my specs, does it say two ounces or four?

Martin spent a lot of his childhood in care, you know, he said. Four ounces, he said. He was shunted from council home to council home. From the age of seven, that is. Before that he lived in a one-room flat with his parents. They ate in it and slept in it and his parents screwed in it. A lot of pain went on in that living room. His father beat his mother up in it – night after night after night. Dreadful, bloody beatings. If Martin tried to stop him he got beaten up too.

That is very dreadful, his mother said. Poor child. Poor Martin. I didn't know that. I am very sorry indeed about that.

So you can probably see why 'drawing rooms' and such would put him off, he said. Piss him off. I mean, what the fuck have they got to do with his life, or with anything he knows about? Like fucking nothing.

Yes I do see, his mother said. I understand now why he's on the defensive. What I don't understand is, why, if you're so fond of him, you didn't warn me about all this before he came down here. It would have saved me asking him all sorts of tactless questions about his life and family, and him having to skate round them – which is what he did do.

How patronising can you be! he said. Martin doesn't need explaining, or explaining away, by me or anyone. He is himself, he is a valuable human being.

His mother took her mixing bowl and egg whisk to the sink and ran the tap over them. She turned the tap off, twisting it hard. Remind me to get something done about this washer, she said. She said, Why do I get the feeling that, for you, only one sort of person, from one sort of background, is a valuable human being? Why do I get the impression that, in your view, a person has to have been brought up in an obviously deprived environment to know anything about pain?

I haven't said that, he said.

So much so that I feel I've failed you, that you'd have preferred to have had Martin's childhood, that kind of misery being the only passport – as you would see it – to full membership of the human race.

You're silent, his mother said. She tapped him on the shoulder. Hey, look at me.

He looked out of the window.

Let me remind you of your father's childhood, his mother said. It was a very comfortable, green-belt childhood. There was a cook, Inez I think, and a maid. Two maids. There was a nanny until your father went away to school. There was a big garden with a shrubbery one end to play in – though he had to play by himself most of the time, of course, being an only child. There was all that. There were also your grandparents who hated each other. They slept at different ends of the house, but in the evenings when your grandfather came home from his office they sat together in

376

the drawing room in their own special chairs and tormented each other. Your grandmother had the edge, she was the cleverer. She was frustrated. Nowadays, I suppose, she'd have been a career woman, and perhaps not married. From all the evidence she despised men. While this ritual was going on, while they goaded and persecuted each other, your father was made to sit in a corner and play with his Meccano or read a book. He was not allowed to interrupt and he was not allowed to leave the room. At six-forty-five on the dot your grandmother would take a key from the bunch on the thin leather belt she always wore and unlock the drinks cupboard, and the serious whisky drinking – and the serious torturing – would begin.

I know about that, he said, you've told me about that.

There was no blood, his mother said, there were no visible bruises, just –

I've got the point, he said, you've made your point.

When your father was dying I thought about the nightmare he'd had to endure while he was growing up. I wondered if it might have been responsible in some way for his illness, if the stress of it had made him vulnerable, damaged his immune system. D'you think that's possible?

Could be, he said. Could be. I don't know.

I wish you'd known him, his mother said. That's the worst of it, your never knowing him, or rather being too young to remember him. That photograph on my dressing table, the one of you aged eighteen months or so with Daddy. You're looking up at him and you're hugging his knees. Now I remember that occasion – I took the photograph. I remember the way you ran, well, staggered up the garden – you were a very late walker, you know, very slow to get yourself off your bottom – and threw yourself at him. You nearly toppled him. And then I pressed the button. I remember that afternoon very well. I remember your father telling me there was no point in taking any photographs, the light was too poor . . . well, I remember it all. I remember how tired your father was. He was already ill but we didn't know. I remember that you had a tantrum about ten minutes before I took the photograph. You lay on the grass and kicked and screamed. But you don't remember. You don't remember him, and you don't remember you – or any of it. It's just a photograph to you.

Cass and Anna remember him, he said, they say they do. They've told me things.

He did his dying in the drawing room – as it was then called – his mother said. He wanted to be downstairs so he could see into the garden – walk into it to begin with. When he was given his death sentence, at Christmas, he set himself some targets. The start of the cricket season – on telly – was one. The peonies and irises out was another. We had wonderful irises in those days, the proper rhizomatous sort, the tall bearded ones, a huge bed of them your father made. He was passionate about his irises, quite boring about them. Irises are tricky things, they like being by themselves, they don't like being moved, they have to have full sun, you're supposed to divide them every three years immediately after flowering – it's quite a performance. It takes patience to grow good irises, and your father was not a patient man. He was a quick-tempered man. I was quite jealous of his irises and all the patient attention they got. Every weekend spent in the garden – or the bloody potting shed. Graham Greene has got a lot to answer for, if you ask me.

He had not known about the irises. He said, Did he see them? Were they out in time?

Some of them were out, the ordinary white flags, and the blue ones. The red peonies were out, the *officinalis*, but the pale ones weren't – you know, the Chinese ones. The ones he liked best weren't.

I don't think I knew he died in the living room, he said. I don't think you ever told me that.

He didn't die in it, his mother said. About three weeks before he died we moved him upstairs. It had become impossible to look after him properly downstairs, and it was too noisy. Small children – you were only two and obstreperous – kept bursting in. When they carried him upstairs, which was difficult because he was in agony, I waited at the top, on the landing; and when he saw me he said, Next time I go down these stairs, folks, it'll be feet first. He said it to make me laugh, to make the doctor and the nurse – who'd made a sort of chair for him out of their hands – laugh. It was brave to make that joke, but it was cruel too, because three weeks later when he did go down the stairs, in his coffin, I kept remembering him coming up, I kept hearing him say, Feet first.

If I don't talk about it much, his mother said, it's because I don't like thinking about it. I prefer to remember your father before he got that bloody disease. He was a different person before he got it. I don't mean just because he looked different – obviously if someone loses six stone in a short time he's going to seem different, he's going to feel unfamiliar – I suppose because we tend to think of a person's shape as being part of their personality, of being them – but that wasn't the real problem. The real problem I discovered was the gap there is between the living and the dying. An enormous, unbridgeable gap.

We're all dying though, aren't we, he said. From the moment we're born you could say we're dying.

Don't give me that, his mother said, don't give me that claptrap. Could you move your elbow please, I'm trying to lay the table. I want to give you a knife and fork.

Sit down, he said, stop working and sit down and talk to me. Just for five minutes. You never sit down and talk. You never tell me anything. You never tell me anything about you.

It's lunch time, his mother said, we can't talk now. Grandpa will be starving. Could you go and tell him it's ready and give him a hand down the stairs. I fear we're going to have to have a lift put in, you know, or –

What is lunch? he said. What are we having? Fish fingers and peas? he said hopefully, beefburgers and beans, sausage and chips?

I wish you hadn't mentioned sausages, his mother said, why did you have to mention sausages? Okay, I'll tell you, his mother said (as though he'd asked her to, which he hadn't, he hadn't said a word), why not? I'll tell you. When your father was dying, before he got to the point of not wanting anything to eat at all, the only thing he wanted was sausages. I'd put my head round the door and ask him, What d'you fancy for lunch today, darling? and he'd say, Bangers and mash. Then I'd go away and cook him something quite other – something I thought would be nourishing and easy to digest, that would slip down. I'd bring in the tray – he'd be sitting with his back to me, shoulders stooped, head supported by a hand, looking out at the garden – and he'd say, without turning his head because turning and twisting were very painful for him, Doesn't smell like bangers. And I'd say, You just wait and see. I'd put the tray down on a chair, and tuck a napkin under his chin and adjust the invalid table and wheel it up over his knees, and put the plate on it and whip the cover off and say, There! Doesn't that look delicious? And he'd stare down at the plate. I asked for bangers, he'd say eventually. I was expecting bangers.

I don't think I let him have bangers more than twice in the whole of that five months, the whole time he was dying, his mother said. I don't know why I didn't give him what he asked for. I've tried to work out why I didn't.

He said nothing for a minute. Then he said, You thought they'd be hard for him to digest, you thought they'd make him uncomfortable.

Did I? his mother said. What would a bit of discomfort have mattered? He was dying, for God's sake! He wanted bangers.

Say something! his mother said. I've shocked you, haven't I? I can tell.

No. No, you haven't, he said. Look, I'd better go and get Grandpa, I'd better go and find the girls.

Could you bring me my wireless at the same time? his mother said, I want to hear the news. I'm not sure where I left it, downstairs I think, in the – in some room or other.

# SPOILT

As soon as Nita and Krystal were strapped in the car, he ran back into the house and dialled Sylvie's number.

'She's gone.'

'You sure? You sure she won't be back for something?'

'Yeh. Sure. She left an hour ago. She's on the train.' He waited a moment. 'I love you. Correction – I fancy you.'

'Yes.'

'You are coming round tonight, aren't you, after the kid's in bed?'

'Well. If it's okay to. If you really think it's safe.'

'What are you wearing?' He always asked this question. Her answer, whatever it happened to be, always excited him. Tortured him.

'I'm not dressed yet.'

'I want you. I want you now.'

'I want you.' But, because she never volunteered any desire, merely repeated back to him, without urgency, his own, he was never convinced that she did want him. Except when they were in bed.

'Sylvie – ?'

'Stew, I got to go. I'm not dressed, I told you, I'll be late for work. See you this evening, 'bout ten, hopefully. You going down the Job Centre later?'

'Might do.' He felt like adding, What the hell business is it of yours? You're not my wife – but stopped himself.

'I only ask because if you are coming into town, pop in and see me.'

\*

This business with Sylvie had started three months ago, not long after Milsom's Motors, where he'd been head salesman for five years, had gone bust. (Expansion just before the recession really bit had been the cause of that: Milsom paying over the odds for the plot next door for additional parking, while not having paid off the bank loan for the new showroom.) He'd been in the Job Centre, casting a hopeless eye over the Miscellaneous board, when she'd materialised beside him: a slight, blunt-nosed girl in a pink shell-suit and pink and green trainers, and with what he thought of – despite evidence everywhere that it was women nowadays who wore it – as a young lad's haircut: quiff in front, razored back and sides. What little there was of her hair was a reddish blonde. She'd taken her eye off the noticeboard for a second and given him a sideways, con-spiratorial look, at the same time sucking her teeth in a way that clearly said 'sod this lot, for starters'; and he'd cheered up suddenly. (Her eyes were grey-green, heavy-lidded, sleepy-looking; and later that morning, sinking his third pint in the regulars' bar at the Crown, he would think about her eyes, the colour of them, the lazy way she opened and shut them.) 'Here's one should fit you to a T,' he'd said, feeling pretty damn sure no offence would be taken, ' "Experienced boner required for local poultry factory, hun'red and twenty pound a week, Mon to Fri, 8 am to 5 pm. Will consider person with butchery experience." ' 'Perfect,' she'd said at once, closing her eyes slowly, opening them half-way, 'just the ticket for a vegetarian. I need look no further then, need I?'

That was as far as it had gone then, but not long after-wards, when he was again in the Centre (Employment Service, they were now calling theirselves), sitting across a table from a bitch who was taking down particulars of his educational qualifications and work experience, who was reassuring him that while it was an undeniable fact that car sales opportunities were, in the current economic climate, on the downturn, she was nonetheless optimistic that a person with his proven work record and selling potential would not be out of the marketplace for long, he'd seen a backview of pink shell-suit over by the Sits Vacant. On his way out she'd accosted him. 'Got one for you – look. "Pollution Control Officer. Degree- or diploma-qualified, with several years' related experience. To develop control procedures and compliance monitoring." Okay?' 'A doddle,' he'd said, 'straight up, Guv, no lie, job's good as mine. Cause for celebration' – he rubbed his hands. 'Care to join us for a coffee at Molly's, over yonder?' To his amazement she'd said yes. (She'd said, 'Yeah, okay then,' and 'Why not?')


When Milsom's Motors collapsed and he had to break the news, Jackie, his wife, who in another role was head stylist at Jason James Hair Studios in the High Street, had been sympathetic. She'd put her arms round him and held him. She'd printed a Max Factor kiss on his forehead. 'It'll be all right, love, you'll see. We can manage for a bit. Listen' (gripping his shoulders), 'you'll be okay. You can sell anything. As I said to Jason only yesterday, "He could sell a cycle to a paraplegic, that one could." So stop fussing. You've got what it takes – unlike some as I could mention,' – 'some' being the layabout first husband she'd traded in for him.

Jackie's sympathy, which after that first evening had manifested itself in practical ways – she'd cut and restyled his letters of job application, she'd given a new look to his CV ('Make that Maths CSE an O-level, Stew, they're never going to check it'), and typed these up – had lasted only a month. When the month was over, leaving no prospect of an interview, let alone a job, she'd turned into someone else, someone who sighed and flounced and found fault, someone who snapped about the place like a dog snapping at flies, the martinet he'd witnessed at Jason James, running a critical finger round the back wash-basins, chivvying the juniors with a broom.

'You're never going to get yourself a job at this rate, not

if you don't buck your ideas up, you won't. You're not even any use as a house husband; couch potato's what you're fast turning into. Look at you' – Jackie, smart as a new paint job, poised for the wonderful world of work, for the great hairdressing salon of life, glared at him from the front door.

'Fine time you've picked to take up cigarettes again. I can't pay off this mortgage on me own, y'know. No way. Turn round, Anita' – brushing some imaginary dust from her small daughter's shoulders, tucking the child's shirt collar inside the collar of her blazer. 'Don't imagine I'm going to fund that filthy habit. Well, we're away now, Stewart. Shopping list's on the worktop, and for Pete's sake, control yourself – I expect to see some change from that twenty pound. Do what you can with the washing machine, it might only be the plug wants looking at. Janet's off, so I'll be working till seven tonight. Can you be sure to fetch Anita from Jean's by four-thirty at the latest, and give her her tea . . . ' The front door slammed behind them, the porch shook, a hanging basket of plastic geraniums, immediately inside the door, dithered for a second before deciding to spin. House husband and couch potato made his way to the kitchen in search of his cigarettes, a can of Hofmeister and the *Express*, transported these consolations to the lounge, settled himself on the settee, lit up, opened his paper, ring-pulled the can of beer – and was caught by Anita, staring and mouthing at him through the patio doors. Small fingers drummed silently on the double glazing. Cursing, he stubbed out his fag, pushed himself out of his Dralon refuge and slid back the doors. 'Well?' 'Stew, can you mend my bike today please? You promised. You said you'd do it last week, you – ' 'Okay, okay. If I have a minute.' (Was it his imagination, or did his step-daughter give him a pitying look?) 'Off you go now, don't keep your mother waiting, you'll be late for school.'

It was later that morning, when, every page of the paper read and double-read, three empty beer cans interred in the dustbin and most of the cigarettes smoked, he'd taken the piece of paper containing Sylvie's phone number out of his trouser pocket and unfolded it. ('I'm stopping up my auntie's at present, Haydn Close – you know, off Hollybush Road,' she'd told him over coffee at Molly's, in answer to a casual enquiry as to what sort of journey she had to get home. 'She's a supervisor at Safeway's. She leaves for work at half-seven. I'm usually in till one. If you want, give us a call. Or don't. I'm not bothered either way.') After picking up the receiver and then ramming it back – he did this twice – he had given Sylvie a call.


No job. No wheels (his car had, naturally, been a company car – well, demo model, Sales for the use of). No dosh. No self-respect. No respect. The butt, increasingly, of jibes from the milkman and the postman, even from Terry, the barman at·the Crown. ('Another pint, was it? What are we using for cash, old son, dare I enquire?') And now Anita, for whom he'd been hero number one, despised him. Around the time he and Jackie were thinking about getting hitched, and talking about it, most of his mates had tried to put him off. 'What d'you want to go and land yourself with another bloke's kid for?' But he had wanted to. He and Anita had hit it off from the word go. So much so that at breakfast on the second morning of his honeymoon, sipping a fermenting pineapple juice – he'd ordered grapefruit – looking out of the hushed dining room at clouds massing above a gun-metal sea, he'd interrupted a silence with 'Wonder how Nita's getting on at Jean's.' 'It's me daughter you're in love with, Stewart Harrison, I've always known it, I've always known you only wanted to marry me because of her.' Jackie had laughed, and then said, 'Many a true word spoken in jest.' And laughed again. An elderly backview at the next table had turned round and glared.

Anita was a great kid, quiet and good-natured, no trouble at all. She was on the skinny side, but pretty in a pale and blue-eyed way. Her hair, which was naturally wavy, was so fair it was almost white. She had a Danish look, he thought, Danish or Swedish, one of those. He discovered early on that he liked it when people who weren't in the know assumed she was his daughter: 'Does your little girl want an ice cream?' 'What pretty hair your little girl has!' He never told them she wasn't his, and though he always feared Anita would betray him with an indignant, 'He's not my dad,' or, worse, 'My daddy's left home, he doesn't love us any more,' with accompanying waterworks, she didn't.

'Nita ought by rights to have a brother or sister,' he'd told Jackie at the start of their year-long engagement. 'Being an only's no good for a kid.'

'I'm an only, I'd remind you, and it's been good for me. Don't call her Nita, there's a love, I didn't give her a pretty name like that for you to go and mangle it.'

The question of another child, his and hers, had come up more than once because he'd always wanted kids, or thought he had. He hadn't been able to budge her. No way was she going to jeopardise her career and the mortgage – and Anita's future, 'my priority, as well you know' – by having another. She'd never said otherwise, she'd been quite straight with him. If he was serious about wanting a kid then that was that, they'd better pack it in now. Pity, wasn't it, he hadn't said all this prior to their engagement, before spending a small fortune – correction, large fortune – on that engagement party?

Not long after, in mellower mood, in bed, she'd brought the subject up herself: 'You don't really want a kid, do you, Stew? Not when we've got so much going for us' (combing a manicured finger lingeringly through his chest hair), 'not when you've already got two girls, not when you've got me and Anita to spoil?'

He did spoil Anita. Correction: he had spoiled Anita. When he'd been in work. Little presents and surprises from time to time, things he knew she hankered after: a matching 'sapphire' necklace and bracelet from Woolies, a watch with a Mickey Mouse face, a Sunday visit to Alton Towers, the latest Cindy Doll outfit. She was always appreciative. She'd make him bend down so she could get her arms round his neck, and then she'd hang there, feet way off the ground, throttling him, refusing to let go. Sometimes, Jean, the neighbour-friend of Jackie's who did the afternoon collecting from school of their two daughters, would drop Anita off at Milsom's on her way home; and Anita would make herself useful in the showroom, dusting his desk and the chrome rims of ashtrays, rinsing coffee cups. (Cona coffee, served in white and gold cups, had been on offer to all his customers.) If, when she arrived, he was busy, arranging finance at his desk with a client, she would stand quietly beside him while he pen-pushed and form-filled and chatted up, a skinny angel in a navy and white uniform. If there was no one in the showroom, he'd walk and talk her through the cars parked on the royal blue, industrial-weight, carpet. He'd give her the whole sales routine. He'd open doors, explain dashboards, demonstrate kiddie-locks and electronic windows and sunroofs, sound off about fuel injection and power-steering, compare the price and advantages of this or that model. 'Which one are you going to go for then?' When, after a bit of female shilly-shallying, she'd made her choice (her decision based more on appearance – she favoured sports models, blue or silver, even red if a metallic finish – than on his info), he'd allow her into the car. Pushing herself forward, sliding on the cellophane protector to the edge of the driving seat, she'd usually just about manage to get her small hands on the steering wheel. Br-r-m br-r-m!

He had spoiled Anita, if you like, but then she was easy to spoil. And spoiling her hadn't spoilt her.

He had wanted to spoil Jackie, but it was impossible. 'Oh Stew, I've had my eye on these for ages' (lifting whatever it was from the tissue paper, holding it against herself). 'Pity it's peach though. Had me heart set on apricot – you won't mind will you if I . . . '

And now, when there was someone else in his life he really wanted, needed, to spoil, he was thwarted.

'I want to give you everything, Sylvie. Anything at all you fancy. I'd like to buy you the whole effing world.'

'Oh yeah – I've noticed. The moment you walked in the joint I could tell you were a man of distinction. A real big spender.' She was always teasing him. Torturing him. Her eyes, challenging, secretive, indifferent, lazily opening and closing, daily destroyed him. He propped himself on an elbow and examined her eyes, the sulky, pale lids, the not quite believable (but they were real) lashes.

'Don't stare at me, Stew. S'only a small pimple, nothing a dab of OXY 10 won't cure. It'll be gone tomorrow. Come here.' Pulling his head down.

Her eyes. Her breath, perfumed with lager and cigarettes. (As must be his own, he suddenly realised.) Her mouth. He kissed it, hard, and then invaded it. Coming up for air, he kissed everything his mouth encountered on that smooth face: eyelids, nose, ears, forehead, spiky hair, a pimple that didn't exist. 'I'm mad for you, Sylvie' – removing a reddish-blonde strand from his tongue – 'it's killing me. I want you all the time. I'm a desperate man.'

'Prove it then.'


She didn't like it when he got serious. She didn't want a heavy scene. 'Keep it light, boy' – as though it was her, not him, had done those eleven extra years on the planet – was her response to his declarations of love. 'Don' spoil it.' Don't spoil it? How could loving a person spoil anything? He'd asked her this and been even more hurt by her reply: 'Listen, I like you very much. You've got a great body. You're a good screw – yeah, you are. You even smell nice – lotsa guys don't. But why should I get involved? What's in it for me? Don' tell me you'd exchange Jackie and that palace of yours for an unemployed twenty-year-old and a flat up Barham.' (Barham was the oldest and roughest of the four council estates in the town, the one people avoided landing up on when they were allowed any choice. Sylvie had lived on it till she was fifteen, till her dad got work in a sausage factory in Trowbridge and moved his family there.) 'Don't tell me you'd be prepared to give up precious little Anita. Be honest. We're havin' a bit of fun, for as long as it suits – till either or both of us gets a job – and let's keep it that way. There's gotta be some compensations for being on the dole.'

No love then. His reward, most weekday lunch times and early afternoons, for his bus and foot slog across town to Sylvie's auntie's place, was sex. Sylvie, when in the mood, was generous and inventive and energetic in bed. (On the bed. Across it. On the bedroom floor. In the bath. In an orange, stretch-covered armchair. Upright, against the vestibule wall.) 'Tell me what you'd like, don't be shy, tell me' – unzipping him like a banana – 'otherwise I shall have to take the matter into me own hands – so to speak – shan't I?' Something that had shocked him at first, that had taken a bit of getting used to, but that once he had got used to it, he couldn't get enough of, was the way Sylvie talked while they were making love – correction, having sex. Jackie, like most of the women he'd ever been with, was pretty much silent on the job. Sylvie talked. What she went in for wasn't chatter. It was encouragement. Encouragement and invitation and suggestion. Rallying and prompting. Very often she'd give him a running commentary on their match – on what she was doing to him and what he was doing to her and what they were about to do to each other.

Drinking a post-coital cup of Safeway's Blend in Sylvie's auntie's kitchen, watching Sylvie – a heartbreaking sixteen in her T-shirt and jeans and trainers – snap off a piece of her gipsy cream and hold it up, giggling, just beyond reach of Tarzan, her auntie's foulmouthed boxer, he found it impossible to connect her with the sorceress on the bed who, minutes earlier, had done those things to him. Who'd done those things, who'd whispered those words. Those dirty, exciting, mindblowing, words.

'I'm at my wits' end, Stewart. You knew perfectly well Anita had to have her blazer back for today. You aren't asked to do much. The little you are asked to do, you don't do. You better get yourself down to Bollom's as soon as they open, and then take the blazer up to school. Give it to Mrs Castle, in the office.'

'Okay. Sorry.' He'd forgotten about the blazer, which Jean had dropped off at the cleaners on her way back from school, to be ready for him to collect at five. All this panic because today was School Photograph day, and Jackie wanted Anita looking her best. It was nonsense anyway because most of the kids didn't even own blazers, which were optional. What the majority had was anoraks – 'any colour, so long as it's navy blue,' as the note from the headmaster, reminding parents of the minimum requirements as regards uniform ('some, who shall be nameless, appear to have forgotten') had – ha ha ha – put it.

'Look, Stew' – Jackie's face and voice softened. She stretched a hand across the breakfast table and touched his hand. 'This situation isn't easy for any of us. But you're not helping us, or yourself, by taking this attitude. Being sorry for yourself's not going to solve anything. It definitely won't pay the mortgage, and let me remind you we're two months in arrears. Finished, pet?' – turning to Anita, who sat, eyes cast down, fiddling with a piece of unwanted toast. 'Go and brush your teeth then.'

When Anita had left the room, Jackie leant towards him. 'Look at me, Stewart.' He had no desire to look at her. The Warm Peach pancake cheeks, the Frosted Turquoise eyelids and Ultramarine Long-Lash lashes, the Wild Tango (Hi-Gloss) lips, all of which had been part of her allure, which at the beginning had made him proud to be seen with her, now disgusted him. A suffocating blast of Estée Lauder knocked him backwards in his chair. 'I said, "Look at me." ' He looked at her. 'Do you have any idea what you're doing to that child upstairs? You're breaking her heart, you know. You are. You never talk to her, you never play with her, she might as well not be in the house for all the notice you take of her. As she sees it, she's lost her daddy, the only one she's got. How you can do this to her, how you can behave like this to a small kiddie, beats me. She's always thought the world of you, you know.'

'I'm sorry.' He was sorry. Somewhere, at some level. He hadn't wanted to hurt Anita. He hadn't known that he had. Or had he?

'She's given over asking you to mend her bicycle. Pathetic, isn't it? Well, I promised her bedtime you'd do it today without fail, so you'd better. We can't go on like this, Stew. I can't. It'd be different if you could make yourself useful at home till you find work. You said you'd do out the bedroom, remember. You have all day, every day, to do it in. The paint and the paper's been sat on the landing over a month now.'

'Okay OKAY OKAY OKAY.' Gordon Bennett.

'I've been wondering whether you shouldn't go down Doctor Taylor's for a check-up. You're always so tired when I get in, and what you've got to be tired about – '

'I said I was sorry, didn't I?'

'Stewart, it's our marriage on the line. That includes the bedroom, and I'm not talking about decorating. It wasn't a brother I was looking for when I married you.'

'Mu-um!' – Anita, mournfully, from the porch.

'Coming, love. Stewart, I need to know that you're going to get your act together – in every department. It's Birmingham next week. I want to feel easy in my mind that while I'm away you'll be coping, and Anita properly looked after. She could stop over at Jean's, but – '

'No.' He suddenly felt very strongly about this. 'She stays here with me.'

'Mum!'


After he'd delivered Anita's blazer to Mrs Castle in the office ('Well, we'll hardly be needing that, I'm glad to say. Proper shirts and blouses weather this is, for a change'), he made his way to Sylvie's place. The residential part of the town had grown up around the sides of a series of steep hills, the northernmost of which had, until the mid-Seventies, been grazing land for sheep. Haydn Close, the last spec-built mini-estate to go up before the building trade went down, had been set in the middle of this, in a cleft between Mozart Crescent – two half-moons of detached, chalet-style homes – and Beethoven Row – a line of reconstituted stone bungalows overlooking the main road. Haydn Close consisted of a series of split-level three-bedroom, maroon brick terraces, four houses to each terrace. Stewart, on his first visit to Sylvie, had sensed something familiar about the layout, and had then remembered delivering a car to the close while it was still being built, to a couple who had just moved in to the one completed terrace. The husband had made him stand in mud and builders' rubble and admire the special features of his home: traditional farmhouse roof in pale orange pantile, curve-topped window frames in natural wood, pantiled porch, solid wood front door (if quick off the mark, the man told Stewart, buyers had been allowed a choice of oak, mahogany, or pine finish) with bottle-glass fanlight. The new Ford XR3i, buffed into hard gloss magnificence by one of Milsom's school-leaver apprentices before departing the showroom, had sat in the road ignored.

Haydn Close, unremembered by him before Sylvie came on the scene, had, since Sylvie, become a magic place, the place he was happy in, the only place he wanted to be. When he wasn't in it, he thought about it, could conjure at whim the landscaped grass frontages, strimmed to within an inch of their lives and planted out with For Sale boards plus the occasional shrub or ornamental tree; the two rows of discreetly sited lock-up, up-and-over garages, facing each other across a pink-paved divide; the tortoiseshell cat which, having taken a liking to him, would often abandon her wheelie-bin look-out to escort him on the last nerve-racking stage of his journey – up the winding, crazily paved path to number 25. Where Sylvie lived. Where Sylvie, and her auntie Shirley she was fond of, and her uncle Raymond she wasn't and seldom made reference to, and Tarzan the foulmouthed boxer, lived. Diamond-paned leaded lights to the windows (some of the houses had plain glass casements). Brass furniture on the front door (some of the doors had iron). Oak finish.

He stood in front of this door now and tugged the fancy brass lever that activated the chimes. 'Ding dong. Ding dong ding dong. Ding.' Music to his ears.

She waited until after they'd tried, successfully, two or three variations of the thing they always did, and were having a fag break, lying on their backs in the not large enough bed, watching the smoke from their cigarettes come together and entwine and eventually disperse along the ceiling, before delivering her blow.

'Stew, I've got a job. Boots.'

'Kinky boots?' Her last job had been sales assistant at Tandem shoe shop in the High Street.

'Boots the Chemists. Dirty pics department – well, photographic counter. I start Monday.'

He'd sat up then, and stared at her. 'You can't!'

'I gotta work, Stew. I gotta pay my way. My uncle put me on final warning last week. "Either you get off your backside and find a job or you go back home to your mother's." No way am I going back to Mother's.'

He said nothing for a minute. Then, furiously: 'You can lie there all calm and tell me that. Knowing it's over, you and me is over, that my life is ov – '

'Stew.' She put a finger on his lips. 'Don't.' He jerked his head away.

'Look, it's not been getting any easier up my end. Remarks have been passed about the "regular visitors – naming no names, mind – certain people entertain". Another thing, I've left the sheets out on the line once too often. My auntie thinks I've got what she likes to call a "cleanliness fetish". At least that's what she's calling it for the minute – but she's not stupid, I might tell you.'

'I've seen your auntie.' He hadn't been going to tell her this.

'Oh yeh? How'd you know it was her?'

'She had her name on her uniform.'

'Sounds possible. Light us another fag, Stew.'

It was possible. (He lit her a fag.) It had been. Like this: Safeway's, 11 am or thereabouts, last Thursday. Him in the checkout queue with a trolley-load of consumer perishables: Bold Ultra all in one, as seen on telly, Typhoo tea bags, ditto, own brand cereal masquerading as Weetabix, own brand jam and coffee and lo-sugar beans . . . and the check-out girl saying to the woman in front of him, 'If you can just hang on a couple of ticks, I'll call a supervisor to attend to your query' . . . He'd been standing there, shifting his feet, boring a hole in the supervisor, willing the old bat to get on with it, p.d.q., when he'd noticed the identity badge on her bosom. Mrs Shirley Jackson. *Mrs Shirley Jackson.* Who's she when she's at home? Sylvie's auntie, that's who! He'd found himself grinning in a daft way. Staring at her (mannish hands, fleshy nose, Princess Di hairdo, late for-ties), he'd told her, silently but quite plainly: I screw your niece. She screws me. We do it every day. We do it in your house. We do it in your orange chair. You've got Spanish dolls in the alcove in your lounge. You've got an avocado bath and basin and toilet. I've pissed in your toilet.

In the car park afterwards, trying to push a trolley, whose wheels were bent on going the opposite way, in the direction of Jackie's Fiesta (she usually lent him her car for the big weekly shop), he'd thought: I'm wicked. I'm a monster. I'm going to hell. And grinned to himself. And done a little dance with his wayward trolley.

'What's this about my auntie, then?'

'Nothing, I just saw her once, that's all.' He buried his face in the paradise that was her neck. If he could just die here. Now.

'Stew, we can still see each other, you know. It's not exactly slave labour at Boots, I do get the odd half-day.' Then, after a pause, she said, 'Didn't you say something about having to fix a bike this afternoon? Without fail?'

Standing inside her front door, trying to leave, not

bearing to, knowing she wanted him to, his hand on the latch, having promised himself he wouldn't mention the subject, he reminded her about Birmingham.

'You haven't forgotten about Birmingham?' Jason James were sending Jackie and Helen, the senior stylists, on a two-day cutting course and competition. (£200 cash prize, plus weekend for two in Minorca, plus a year's free supply of Medusa Hair-Care products to the winning salon.) Jackie was determined to win the competition, which was to be judged by a London big-wig. She and Helen were leaving first thing Thursday, coming back midday Saturday. They had decided to let the train take the strain, which meant Stewart having the use of Jackie's car. Not for joy-riding though. If he thought that (he had, for all of two seconds), he had another think coming. No, he could make himself really useful for once – 'and give Jean the break she deserves' – and do the school runs. Morning and afternoon. All four of them.

(Jackie hadn't mentioned the evenings though, those two long evenings, Thursday and Friday, she wouldn't be home. When Sylvie would be there. 'Well, I s'ppose I could come down and keep you company for a couple of hours while you're babysitting – no harm in that, is there?' – Sylvie's reply, when he'd first put it to her.)

Now she said, 'I haven't forgotten, but – '

'You are going to come?' – as casually as he could manage.

'If you want me to. If you think it's, well, safe to.'

Which was not the right answer.

On the way home he made a detour via Manfreds in Silver Street, and bought a bicycle chain and some nuts and a puncture kit. Afterwards he called in at the Job Centre where he learned he could, if he had a mind, be a part-time bar person, £3.50 an hour, at High Post Hotel; or, if he was fully trained and state-registered and had had experience in caring for the elderly, a general nurse at Sutton Nevey Nursing Home. (29 beds. Wage: to be discussed.)

*

He and Jackie were up with the birds on Thursday morning. He made them both a cup of tea while Jackie ran from airer to ironing board to suitcase, and made lists and fired instructions. 'I'm putting the money for the milkman here. Okay? Anita's to be in bed by half past eight – nine at the very latest – she's not staying up watching TV all hours with you. And you're to keep an eye on her if she goes outside to play; she either stops here in the garden, or she can go down Jean's after tea. Nowhere else, and nowhere on her own.'

An hour later, he and Jackie and Anita stood in the porch, waiting for the taxi that would take Jackie and Helen to the station. He'd offered to drive them, but as Jackie pointed out, it was the wrong direction for school and too early anyway for Anita who 'had to get a proper breakfast inside her and leave time for a visit to the toilet'. The taxi was late and Jackie kept looking at her watch. She was all keyed up and nervous about her appearance, smoothing the skirt of her lime two-piece, inspecting an imaginary ladder, tweaking her shoulder pads into position. 'You look great,' he said, suddenly deciding that heartiness might be the best mode to get them through the waiting, 'doesn't she, Nita? Doesn't your mum look triffick?' Anita nodded. 'Well,' he continued, rubbing his hands, 'Nita and I have certainly got our work cut out while the boss is away! There's the little matter of a certain young lady's bicycle to repair.' (The chain he'd bought yesterday had turned out to be the wrong size, would you credit it.) 'Then there's the master bedroom to decorate, and when we've got that lot sorted m'partner here's going to help us weed the front bed and give the back lawn a trim and brush up – ain't that so?' – winking at the partner, who did not wink back.

The taxi, one of four two-tone (cream'n'green), suspension-free crates belonging to Courtesy Cabs, with Helen on board, jolted to a stop at the gate. 'Good luck, love, you'll win the comp – no prob, it's a cert.' And shutting his eyes tight he braved the Max Factor health hazard zone to press his lips to hers.

Inside the cab, Jackie wound down the window. 'You be good, you two, and behave yourselves. I might try and phone tonight, but there's a reception for candidates somewhen this evening and I may not be able. You've got my number, should anything crop up.' Anita stood on the pavement, quiet and solemn, one hand doing the stiff little sideways wave that royalty give till her mother was out of sight.


'Hop in, then.' Anita and Krystal, Jean's daughter, were standing by the Fiesta, dressed and ready for school. He had made Marmite and lettuce sandwiches for Anita's lunchbox, and put in a strawberry yoghurt with a plastic spoon, and an orange drink in a carton with a drinking straw, as per instructions. As per instructions, he'd checked out the contents of his step-daughter's satchel, and added a clean handkerchief when he found there wasn't one. After he'd settled the two girls in the back seat and done up their seat belts, he said, 'Just remembered something – sit tight, shan't be a minute' – and went back into the house. And phoned Sylvie.


Mid-morning, having stowed the vacuum cleaner in the cleaning cupboard under the stairs, he made himself a mug of instant and took it and his fags out into the sunshine of the back garden, and sat in a white plastic patio chair, special offer from the local filling station, and shut his ears to the accusatory stutter of a senior citizen's lawnmower, and daydreamed until he slept.


It was two o'clock. The kids didn't have to be fetched until three-thirty. But before that there was a bicycle chain to exchange, and a few bits and pieces of grocery shopping to do. He pocketed the twenty-pound note Jackie had put out for him on the worktop, and wrote himself a shopping list. Jogging down the front path, he threw Jackie's car keys in the air and caught them, and as he did so caught sight of Audrey from across the road hurrying to the bus, a toddler in one hand and a cigarette in the other. The longest legs out, he used to think in the days when he'd fancied her. The longest legs out in jeans, the smallest waist, the sexiest bum, the biggest tits.

Sylvie was standing behind the Photographic counter, sideways on, talking to a dark girl on Cosmetics and Fragrance. She was wearing uniform, well of course she would be – white blouse, with short sleeves, navy piping on the cuffs. (Her lower half presumably clad in the pencil skirt, kick pleat, he could see on the assistant with a wire basket wandering the Babyfood aisle.) In her ear-lobes, in place of the tiers of jagged foundry waste, or the shiny chrome hubcaps, that usually weighted them, were demure gold studs; and pinned to her blouse, just above the right breast, was a badge. As he approached the counter he could read BOOTS, the familiar logo-script, in a diagonal across the corner, and alongside it her name: Sylvia Martin. Sylvia, eh? Who's she when she's at home?

'Customer.' Debbie Durnford, Beauty Adviser, gave Sylvie a warning nudge. He was caught in the full green beam of Sylvie's headlights as she turned to face him.

'Can I help you?'

'Sir.' More aggressively than he meant.

'Pardon?'

'Shouldn't you say, "Can I help you, *sir*?" '

'No one's said.' She sounded put out. 'They told me courtesy and efficiency are the keys to customer satisfaction. Nothing about "sir". What would "sir" like then?'

If you're not careful, sir will tell you what sir would bloody well like.

Above her head hung a cardboard oval that had a night sky with a yellow crescent moon and two white stars on it, and the words 'Overnight film processing' underneath.

'I've got this film wants processing.'

She waited courteously with her hand held out while he went through the pretence of searching his pockets.

'Black and white film takes longer. Regrettably, we do not have the facilities on the premises to process black and white film overnight.' She was talking like a recorded message. 'So if your film – '

'Sylvie. For God's sake. Be nice.' He couldn't cope with this, any of it. The hard glass counter that separated them, the unblinking stares of a thousand Canon Sureshots on the display shelf, the cheerful boxes of Kodak Gold 200, the romantic night sky above her head. Her eyes. Her mouth. (She seldom wore make-up and was not wearing it today – unless on her mouth, which bore a faint smear of red, as though she'd been eating strawberries.)

'I am nice. Hey!' – turning to Debbie, who, ears pinned back no doubt, was replenishing a counter showcase with jars of Ultramoist cream make-up – 'I am nice, aren't I? Wouldn't you say I was nice?'

'Very nice.' Smirking and examining her nails.

He was aware of a queue forming behind him, of exasperated sighs and impatient feet. 'Well, I'll be off then.'

'Your film will be ready later, if you'd care to collect it.' A long, steady look. Then, dipping her headlights, engine note a whisper: ''Bout ten o'clock, okay?'


Outside the school he sat in blazing sunshine in a blazing car, and smoked two fags, and felt stupidly happy, and watched the world go by.

They were hardly away from the school gates before a small voice from the back seat said, 'I feel sick.'

Gordon Bennett! 'I expect it's the heat.' He tried to sound sympathetic. 'Put your head out of the window. Take some big big breaths.'

After a minute or two, the small voice said, 'I feel very sick.'

'She felt sick in geography. Mrs Bailey said her head felt

hot. She didn't eat her sandwiches dinner time neither.'
Krystal was evidently enjoying her role of know-all and
doom merchant.

'D'you want me to stop?' – in a bark, braking.

'Yes. No. Yes.'

He pulled in to the kerb; he leapt out of the car; he
pushed the driver's seat forward; he grabbed Anita. Too
late.

Anita lay on the settee, eyes shut, a damp face flannel on
her forehead, a plastic bowl at her elbow. Jean sat beside
her, stroking her hand. Krystal, still in her school clothes,
knelt on the floor and pressbuttoned the TV remote control,
channel-hopping without the sound on. He stood in the
doorway.

'Well, doc, what's the diagnosis?' – with a heart like lead.

'Not sure. She's very hot.' Jean bent her head over
Anita's. 'How are you feeling now, sweetheart?'

'Feel sick. My head hurts.'

'Could be a bug,' Jean said, 'could be something she's
ate. Is there a sickness bug doing the rounds at school,
d'you know, Krystal? Krystal!'

Krystal, momentarily engrossed in the *All-New Popeye
Show*, did not turn round. 'No. Dunno.'

'Bed's the best place for you, my love. Pop your arms
round m'neck, and up we'll go.'

He followed them upstairs with the bowl, scowling,
hating the whole world. And another thing – if it was
anybody's job to carry Anita, it was his.

As she and Krystal were leaving, standing outside on the
path, Jean said, 'Remember, just keep her quiet and see she
has plenty of water to drink. She's had two tablets now, so
providing she manages to keep them down, she could have
another two at' – she looked at her watch – 'half-eight. If
her head still hurts her. With any luck she'll be asleep in a
minute, poor mite.'

Did Jean reckon he ought to phone Jackie and tell her?

'Oh no, Stewart, I don't think that's necessary. No point in worrying Jack, is there? Between you and I, kiddies are always getting these upsets, running high temperatures. Anita'll probably be right as rain in the morning. She hasn't vomited since the car, has she?'

But what if Jackie phoned him? What if she phoned at Nita's bedtime and wanted a word? What then?

'You can tell her Anita was tired and went to bed early. That's hardly a fib, is it?'

He stood on the step and watched them go down the path, Krystal skipping ahead, Jean puffing behind. The back of Jean's turquoise silk-knit was all grooves and hummocks where a too-tight bra fastening, and too-tight bra straps, had dug in.


'You got to try and go to sleep, you know. You'll feel a whole load better if you do.' This was his third visit to the sickroom in half an hour, and he was running out of comforting things to say. At the front of his mind was the question: What do I do if I can't get her to sleep before Sylvie tips up?

'I can't. My head hurts.'

'I know, darlin'.' He picked up the tumbler by her bed. 'How's about another sip of champagne?'

'Yes.'

He sat on a chair and propped her head with one hand while he steered the tumbler with the other. A couple of drops of water made it into her mouth; a gallon ran down her chin and soaked the front of her nightie.

'Sorry, angel.'

Her head fell back on the pillow as soon as he released it. 'Stew, can't I have another Disprol? Pleeease' – in a groan.

He looked at his watch. Two and a half hours to go before Sylvie was due. How was he going to hang on that long? 'Not quite yet. Soon. How's the old tum-tum? You still feeling sick?'

'I don't know. My head hurts.'

He wanted to escape (and tidy the lounge, and get the drinks and the eats together, and think about Sylvie), but she wasn't ready to be left. His eye travelled from the Snoopy poster on the back of the door to Tiny Tears in a bassinet under the window, to the row of books, mostly paperbacks, on a shelf he'd put up last Christmas. There weren't many because Jackie didn't believe in clutter. (All books, and most toys, Jackie considered Nita was too old for found their way to the OXFAM shop, pronto.) 'Would you like me to read you a story?' Once upon a time he'd always read her a story at bedtime. He'd read to her or else he'd got her to read to him. One or t'other. They hadn't shared a reading session for weeks, he realised. Months.

'No. Thank you.'

Before he left the room he turned her pillow over, and planted a kiss on her scorching forehead, and told her he'd pop back soon – 'You better be asleep my girl when I do' – and pretended he couldn't hear the 'I want my mummy', muffled, to the wall.


'You should've told me about this when I phoned,' Sylvie said, 'I'd never have come over if I'd known. I could tell there was something up anyway, you sounded so strange.'

Sylvie had phoned him from a call-box ten minutes ago, 'just to check you haven't got surprise visitors'. When the phone rang, he'd leapt at it, certain it was Jackie. Hoping it was Jackie. (After his last plod up the stairs to Nita, he'd decided that if Jackie rang, he'd tell her. He wouldn't phone her, but if she phoned him, he'd tell her.)

'I wanted you to come.' He took Sylvie's hand across the kitchen table. 'I was lonely. I needed you.'

'It's not right. Not with the kid being so poorly. Being asleep's one thing, being – '

'She is asleep.' (She'd better be. She ought to be. At half past eight, her whole body a radiator, her headache still bad, he'd given her four Junior Disprol, dissolved in water.

He'd consulted the packet first. '6–12 years = 2–4 tablets every 4 hours.' So he'd given her four. Which an hour later hadn't done the trick. Which should have done the trick by now.) 'S'all right, Sylvie, I promise you. She's fast asleep. She's had four aspirin. She'll be okay in the morning.' He beamed at her. 'How's the little wage-earner then?'

'Okay. Not too dusty.' She tossed her head, pleased with herself. 'Stew, this is a gin and a half. You won the pools?' She dipped a finger in her glass and chased among the ice cubes for the slice of lemon he'd been careful to put in. She kept her eyes on him as she sucked it. 'What are you trying to do' – she lowered her eyelids slowly and raised them again – 'seduce me or something?'

'What say you we relocate to the lounge?' His heart was thumping so hard he was sure she could hear it. 'It's more comfortable on the settee.'

They were on the floor, having rolled there from the settee, when Anita started to scream.


'Why didn't you telephone earlier?'

It wasn't Doctor Taylor, it was one of his partners at the Health Centre, a Doctor Kettle (with a big nose and a poncy voice) he didn't know. The medic on duty.

'She slept for a bit, so I thought she was okay. Children are always getting these upsets, running high temperatures, aren't they?' – defending himself, parroting Jean.

'Am I right in thinking you're the child's step-father, not her father?'

'Yes.'

'Where's her mother?'

Where indeed? When Nita had started that terrible screaming, and gone on and on until he'd got his arms round her and held her, he'd known that he had to phone Jackie. Nita was a brave child, never one to make a fuss. German measles, mumps, chickenpox, scarlet fever, she'd weathered all these with scarcely a moan. A little angel, he'd described her to Jackie. And Jackie had said, 'You ought to take a leaf out of your angel's book, Stew. You make more fuss over a common cold than she does with the mumps. Men!' And here was his angel screaming. And then, when she'd stopped screaming, whimpering. Begging: 'Take the pain away, take the pain away.' And wanting no one but 'Mummy, Mummy, Mummy!' – 'I'll get her, I'll get your mummy.' So help me. But when he searched the pinboard in the kitchen, and the notepad by the phone, Jackie's number wasn't there. He'd thought back, he'd tried to remember what she'd said. He'd tried to remember the name of her hotel. And suddenly he'd had a picture of himself leaving the house that afternoon, tearing the top page (which had something written on it?) from the notepad, scribbling a shopping list in a space (or on the back?): 'Bike chain. Oil can. Half bottle gin. Tonic. Lemon. Peanuts. Crisps.' He'd gone through his pockets, desperate. And as he'd done so had had another picture of himself, coming out of Safeway's with his carrier bag, crumpling the defunct shopping list, dropping it in one of those newly erected, black and gold litter bins the council had thought fit to waste his poll tax on . . . Next, he'd phoned Jean – and got her husband Vernon: 'Jean went round her dad's this evening, she's not back.' Clunk. Bloody hell! 'Calm down, Stew. It's the doctor you ought to be phoning, that's who' – Sylvie, pale and serious, her hair still damp from their exercise, zipping up her jacket in the hall.

'Her mother's at a hairdressers' conference in Birmingham. I've been trying to get hold of her.'

Doctor Kettle didn't answer. He was busy with his stethoscope, and then with his fingers, knocking them on Nita's chest and back. Knock knock knock, tap tap. He drew her nightdress down again over her stomach. He lowered her gently on to the pillow. He placed his hands either side of her neck, pressing. 'Does this hurt? Or this? Here? Or here?' Everything hurt. Everything he did, everywhere he pressed, hurt Nita.

'Now I want you, if you can, to lift your head off the

pillow. I'm not going to help you. There's a girl. Take your time.'

Nita couldn't do this. She tried. Tears rolled out of her eyes. 'Take the pain away! Mummy!'

Poor baby. Poor angel. Her looks all spoilt. Black circles under swollen lids; blotched, swollen face; hair dark and matted. Soaked . . .

'I think we should have her in hospital and do some tests. If I could use your telephone?' – rising to his feet. 'Perhaps you could put some night things and wash things into a bag? You've got a car, I take it?'

When Doctor Kettle came back he said, 'They're expecting her. Coulsdon Ward, second floor. Just let the porter know you're there, or tell the reception desk, and they'll send someone with a stretcher.' Before leaving the house, he said, 'Keep trying your wife, won't you? There'll be a payphone on the ward.' And then, as an afterthought, 'I take it you are fit to drive?'


Up on Coulsdon, Anita was put in a side ward. A single room, pink, shiny walls, green curtains. Dazzling overhead lights. 'Next of kin?' – 'Well . . . ' – 'Sign here, please.' He did so. It was after midnight, but in Nita's side ward it might have been midday. A nurse sped past him with a drip, and fixed it up – 'Just hold your hand still a minute, sweetheart. That's it. That's the way. What a pretty bracelet! Did your boyfriend buy you that? Let's have these lights down a bit, shall we?' – whipped the thermometer from Nita's armpit, looked at it, twice, shook it, stuck it in a plastic tumbler, sped out. Sped in again with an electric fan, plugged it in. 'We've got to get her temperature down, okay?' – to him.

And now a male face, and white-coated shoulders, round the door: 'Is this the lumbar puncture patient? Right, Staff, shan't be a minute. – Oh, are you the child's father? Could I have a word?'

Stewart went out into the corridor.

'Look, we're pretty certain that what we've got here is meningitis. What we don't know yet·is what sort. In order to discover that we have to do a lumbar puncture and see what her white cells are up to. When we know more about that we'll know what treatment to give.'

'What – ?' He wasn't sure what question he was asking.

'Well, basically there are two sorts of meningitis – bacterial and viral. If it's viral, it'll largely be a question of bringing her temperature down – tepid sponging, fan, etcetera, and giving her something for the pain – and we'd expect to be beginning to feel better tomorrow. If it's bacterial – well, it's, shall we say, trickier, and we treat it with antibiotics.'

Ridgemont. It had suddenly come to him. The Ridgemont Hotel. 'D'you think I could phone my wife – Anita's mother?'

'Use the one in Sister's office. Third door on the left.'

When he came back from phoning Jackie (who had been asleep, who when she'd understood what he was telling her, had been fearfully awake), Nita was being wheeled out. 'Me and my friend here are just going to take a little ride to the Treatment Room,' the nurse said, hooking up the drip. 'Your daddy will be here waiting for you when we get back – won't you, Daddy?'

'Course I will.' He tried to smile. 'Mummy may be here by then too.' (From Birmingham? In the middle of the night?) 'Mummy's coming.' He touched Nita's burning hand.

'Mummy,' Nita moaned. 'Mummy. Take the pain away. Mummy.'

The nurse called over her shoulder, 'We can probably fix you up some sort of bed in the day room if you like. See if there's a nurse on the desk . . . '


An hour later, pacing the corridor outside the Treatment Room, bowels water, checking his watch every two minutes, he made a bargain with the God he didn't believe in. 'If Nita gets through this, if she's okay, I'll give Sylvie up. I'll never see her again. I'll' – a sudden picture of the broken bicycle in the garage wounded like a punch in the gut – 'I'll be a good husband and father. I'll get a job.' And tried to blot out the memory of Sylvie's look, holding his look, across the kitchen table. And tried not to listen to the voice from somewhere that told him if Nita was okay, if she did get better, he could always adjust the bargain.